Raging Storm

**Center Point
Large Print**

Also by Vannetta Chapman and available from Center Point Large Print:

Deep Shadows
Anna's Healing
Joshua's Mission

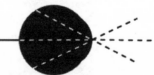

Raging Storm

Vannetta Chapman

CENTER POINT LARGE PRINT
THORNDIKE, MAINE

This Center Point Large Print edition is published in the
year 2017 by arrangement with Harvest House Publishers.

The text of this Large Print edition is unabridged.
In other aspects, this book may vary from the original edition.
Printed in the United States of America on permanent paper.
Set in 16-point Times New Roman type.

ISBN: 978-1-68324-339-7

Library of Congress Cataloging-in-Publication Data

Names: Chapman, Vannetta, author.
Title: Raging storm / Vannetta Chapman.
Description: Center Point Large Print edition. | Thorndike, Maine :
Center Point Large Print, 2017.
Identifiers: LCCN 2016058853 | ISBN 9781683243397
    (hardcover : alk. paper)
Subjects: LCSH: Mother and child—Fiction. | Diabetics—Fiction. |
Survival—Fiction. | Large type books. | GSAFD: Love stories. |
Christian fiction.
Classification: LCC PS3603.H3744 R34 2017b | DDC 813/.6—dc23
LC record available at https://lccn.loc.gov/2016058853

For Barbara Sherrill

Pray for the remnant that still survives.

2 KINGS
CHAPTER 19, VERSE 4

———————————

That will not be the time for choosing:
it will be the time when we discover
which side we really have chosen.

C. S. LEWIS
THE CASE FOR CHRISTIANITY

Acknowledgments

This book is dedicated to Barb Sherrill, who shares a love for all things dystopian. Her perspective and insight have been invaluable, plus she's a fun person to hang out with.

I again want to thank the staff of Harvest House for your support and encouragement during this exciting venture into a different genre—sales, editorial, marketing. The team approach works. I'm grateful to have you backing me up. Reagen Reed provided valuable input as well. And of course, this series wouldn't be possible without my agent, Steve Laube, who was helpful in the negotiation of this contract.

To my pre-readers, Kristy and Janet—I never want to have to write without you. My family has been incredibly patient as I monopolize yet another dinner with dystopian chatter. Thank you to Dorsey Sparks for the use of your name as well as your spunky personality—I believe you will do just fine in the postmodern world. Another thank you to Donna Seals, who has a deep and abiding love for teaching children. Bill Voight, I know you will recognize yourself in these pages. I believe you really can find anything. Also thanks to Jack Clark for contributing to our fund-raising auction at FUMC and allowing me the use of your name.

I have lived in Texas since I was ten years old. Nine years ago my husband and I moved from Dallas to a small central Texas town. It was one of the best decisions we ever made. That move, combined with a good amount of travel throughout our country and overseas, has taught me that wherever you are, whatever your hometown environment, look around and you will find good people. Salt of the earth people. That, combined with our faith, can see us through difficult times.

Last, I would like to thank my readers for embracing this series and sharing your enthusiasm with others. My prayer is that the things that are described in this novel never happen, but as Max has said, "We hope for the best, but plan for the worst."

And finally . . . always giving thanks to God the Father for everything, in the name of our Lord Jesus Christ (Ephesians 5:20).

Excerpts from Shelby's Journal

Abney, Texas
June 10
Approximately 8:20 p.m. EST

While hiking in Colorado Bend State Park, Max, Bianca, Patrick, and I watched as a massive solar flare collided with the earth's atmosphere. The subsequent solar storm affected every aspect of our infrastructure and resulted in a total collapse of the electrical grid. We were later told there were pockets of areas less affected than others, but the event was felt worldwide. Abney and surrounding towns lost all power. From the first moment I saw the aurora, my biggest concern was finding insulin for Carter. I have to find it. Whatever it takes, I will not watch my son die.

June 11
4:00 p.m. EST

In a meeting on the courthouse square, our mayor read a news bulletin she received through the nearby Fort Hood military base.

9

According to Mayor Perkins, the president of the United States declared a national state of emergency and implemented martial law. We are not to expect help from federal or even state government agencies. At this point we're on our own.

June 15
11:34 p.m. EST

The neighboring town of Croghan attacked Abney. The attempt to overrun our town failed, resulting in fourteen casualties. Max wants us to move north, to High Fields, but I need to go south—to Austin, to find insulin.

One

High Fields Ranch
June 28

Shelby made her way slowly, carefully through complete darkness to the small guesthouse. Smoke drifted toward her. Max had assured her the burning structure was on the far side of the state highway. "It won't jump the road."

She couldn't see it from where she stood—couldn't see much of anything. And the silence? It was total.

No jets screaming overhead.

No television blaring in the main house.

No vehicles driving the adjacent country road.

The quiet should have been unnerving, but she took comfort in it.

She walked into the house, catching the screen door so it wouldn't bang, but Carter heard her. He was sitting in the darkened living room.

It was a conversation she'd hoped to avoid, but she sat down across from him and waited. As her eyes adjusted to the darkness, she could make out her son's crossed arms and tense posture.

His voice, when he finally spoke, was ragged. "It's dangerous for you to go alone."

"I won't be."

"So Max is going with you."

"He is."

"And I should too." He practically spat the words, his tone bitter and hard and still mourning.

"You're not going."

"I'm not a child anymore."

"I didn't say—"

"And it's not as if you know everything. Our house? Gone. Kaitlyn? Dead. The town we called home my entire life is hanging on by a thread, so don't pretend you know all the answers."

"Carter—"

He leaned forward, elbows on knees, hands clasped together. Diagnosed with type 1 diabetes when he was four years old, he had always been a thin child, but since the flare he'd lost another ten pounds. Added to that, he was still shooting up and was now a good three inches taller than her. She suspected he would top out somewhere near six feet, the same height as his father. He had her hair—black with a tendency to curl—and her dark brown eyes. It was amazing how much she could see in the darkness, how well she knew her seventeen-year-old son. Anger and regret dripped off him.

"It's for me. You're doing this for me. At least let me go with you."

"You're staying here. This place is safe."

"I can help. I'm a good shot, and I can drive if you get tired or if . . . if Max has another migraine."

She waited until the quietness from outside permeated the room—until the only thing left to hear was the chirp of crickets, a blackbird calling in the night, and the beat of her own heart.

"You make good points, but I won't risk losing you. Max and I will take care of this. We'll find a supply of insulin and bring it back, and I think— I think that Max's parents are going to need you here."

"To fish? You want me to stay here and fish while you risk your life, risk Max's life . . ." He dropped his head into his hands.

Shelby stood, moved over to the couch, and sat beside him. As she'd done so many times over the years, she rubbed his back in slow, gentle circles.

She waited and prayed.

Carter didn't turn toward her, but his voice broke when he said, "I've killed a man. Maybe more than one. And I watched Kaitlyn die in front of my eyes. I don't want to stay here. I want to be doing something."

But he must have known that his words wouldn't change her mind. Shelby understood that he was talking to himself, that he was trying to work through all that had happened and this new world they were trying to survive in.

Without glancing her way, he stood and walked out of the room.

Two

Max waited beside the 1984 Dodge Ramcharger, holding a thermos of coffee.

The two-door SUV was a tough off-road vehicle. More importantly it provided critical storage space which could be accessed from inside. The paint was faded to gray, the cloth upholstery worn thin, and the odometer had turned over more than once. What mattered was that the engine still worked, in spite of the flare. There wasn't a computer chip on the beast, which made Max all the more comfortable about taking it to Austin.

His watch read six o'clock straight up when Shelby stepped out of his grandparents' cottage and walked toward him. She wore cargo pants, which provided plenty of pocket space—they'd also be lighter and dry more quickly than jeans. A long-sleeved shirt covered a cotton tank top. Her backpack was slung over one shoulder, she wore hiking boots on her feet, and her black curls were pulled back and stuffed into a Texas Rangers ball cap. Five foot seven and thin, she was tougher and more resilient than any woman he'd ever known.

The sky had lightened to a robin's egg blue—pale and soft and fragile.

"Carter?" she asked.

Max shook his head and offered her the coffee. "What's in the backpack?"

"Stuff." She sounded defensive and must have realized it. "A change of clothes, a first aid kit— I didn't want to pack it in the back in case we need it quick—and my writing supplies."

"That's a good idea, Shelby. Someone should chronicle this."

"Our grandchildren will want to know how it all fell apart."

"And how we put it back together again."

She didn't answer that. Shelby was once an optimist, but that trait seemed to have disappeared with the power grid.

"Your Ruger 22?"

"Outer pocket. Loaded, and I have one box of extra shells."

"Good."

They both turned to watch Max's parents, Georgia and Roy Berkman, make their way from the main house to where the Dodge was parked. In their late sixties, they were physically fit and accustomed to a life without certain luxuries.

Georgia handed Shelby two paper lunch sacks. "You both need to eat."

She pulled Shelby into a hug. "Don't worry about Carter. We'll watch after him."

Max shook hands with his father, who nodded once and pulled him into a bear hug. Whatever needed to be said had already been tossed around not once but many times. "I called ahead on the CB to check with the night watch. Roads appear to be clear."

"Are you sure you have everything you need?" Georgia clasped her arms around her middle.

"We're fine, Mom. Food, water, items to trade, extra fuel."

"You're taking the rifle?" Pop asked.

"I am, as well as my Sig P232, and Shelby has the Ruger."

The door to the shed banged shut, and Carter emerged—carrying a fishing rod and a bucket. He stared at them for a moment, and then he turned in the opposite direction, toward the creek.

"Six days, seven at the most," Max said, folding his long frame into the driver's seat of the battered Dodge.

"Godspeed, son." His pop stepped closer to his mother, as if together they would find strength for the week ahead.

Shelby glanced after Carter one final time, and then she climbed into the SUV beside him. Max pulled away on the caliche road, headlights off, his parents a shrinking image in his rearview mirror.

"Carter will be all right."

"I know he will." Shelby jerked off the baseball cap and stared out the front window. Dark curls framed her face, masking her expression.

"It's going to take a while."

"For?"

"Him to adjust to life on a farm? Get over Kaitlyn's death? Forgive you for not letting him go? Take your pick."

Shelby sighed and reached for the thermos. "Parenting doesn't get any easier, even with global disaster."

"Did you think it would?"

"I hoped."

They rode in silence, stopping at the roadblock for an update. Farm equipment and diesel trucks stretched across the width of the road—from fence post to fence post. Four men, aged twenty to sixty-five, perched atop the vehicles, each holding a rifle.

"Anything?" Max asked.

"It's been quiet all night." Ray Garrett hopped off the truck and walked over to where they waited. The man was a few years older than Max, six feet tall, with a wiry build and a farmer's tan. He nodded toward Shelby, who was standing next to her open door, and shook hands with Max.

"Fire's still spreading on the east side of the highway. There's only a light wind, but enough to push it south."

"Through Townsen Mills?"

"Probably. The river will stop it to the south of there."

"Any more looting?" Shelby asked.

"Hard to say. No one has attempted to come this way in two, maybe three days. But on the state

17

road? Your best bet is not to stop—for anything."

"We won't," Max assured him.

Garrett wished him a safe trip, and then he signaled for his son, Logan, to back up one of the trucks and allow them through.

When they reached the main road, they began to see signs things had worsened.

The first vehicle they passed was burned out with no sign of its occupants. The second wasn't burned, but the car was riddled with bullet holes and the driver was slumped over the wheel. There was no need for Max to stop. It was plain enough that the man was dead.

"Looks like a war zone." Shelby glanced right, then left—right then left, as if she needed to scan for hijackers. She'd pulled out her notebook and pen and was jotting down a few notes, but she stopped when they reached Townsen Mills. Little more than a crossroads, it had once been a quaint place to stop and fill up the gas tank, grab a sandwich, and shop for antiques. Approaching from the north, they saw a minivan stranded in the middle of their lane. Max slowed to maneuver around it.

"Maybe they broke down."

A string of belongings stretched away from the open door of the van and to the south of the vehicle—blue jeans, a child's shirt, someone's pajamas. Two hundred yards from the vehicle, a suitcase lay abandoned and empty.

"They must have been running . . . running from someone." Shelby leaned out her window.

There was no sign of the van's occupants.

Everything on the east side of the road had burned. Smoke rose from collapsed dwellings, but still there was no sign of people. The few buildings that lined the road to the west had been deserted when they'd driven through the week before. Recently someone had taken a paintbrush and written across the front of the building in bold red strokes.

" 'The end is near'?" Shelby sighed in disgust. "They could at least put something original if they're going to bother with graffiti."

Smoke began to drift across the road. Shelby reached into the backseat, grabbed two T-shirts from the bag she had packed, and handed one to Max. He held it over his nose and mouth. Already his throat was scratchy, and visibility had dropped to less than five feet.

Just when he wondered if they should stop or turn around, they crossed the river and drove out of the haze, the remnants of the fire giving way to a beautiful June morning.

Max resettled the ball cap on his head. "I'm surprised at how quickly we descended into lawlessness."

"You are?"

"What? You didn't realize I was once an idealist?"

"I'm the writer. I'm the one who succumbs to flights of fancy. You are the realist, the pragmatist." She jerked a thumb toward the scene behind them as Max accelerated. "I thought you would have expected this."

But he hadn't. He'd clung to the law, even when there was no way to enforce it. Less than three weeks since the flare, and already the area he'd grown up in looked like a setting for the latest blockbuster apocalyptic movie.

Sunshine spilled across fields green with summer crops—hay and sorghum and corn, precious little corn. Occasionally, Max caught light reflecting off a windshield.

"Lookouts," Shelby murmured.

"Guarding crops—more signs of the time."

They didn't stop or even slow until they approached the north side of Abney.

A billboard sign, riddled with bullet holes, hung haphazardly from a single support. *"Welcome to Abney. Enjoy the Texas Hill Country."*

And just beyond the sign, an even bigger roadblock crossed all five lanes of the road. Max stopped the Dodge, leaving the keys in the ignition.

"Keep the rifle close." But once he began walking toward the trucks, he recognized several of the men on patrol.

"Josh." He shook hands and gestured toward the reinforced roadblock—which now consisted of an eighteen-wheeler, a tractor, four trucks, and a flatbed. "Had trouble?"

"A fair-sized group of men struck two nights ago. Frank Kelton was killed and two others injured."

Max stared toward the downtown area. Finally he shook his head. "Sorry to hear that. Frank was a good man."

Josh scratched at his face where he'd sprouted a full beard. "Perkins upped patrols after that."

"Makes sense." Max glanced back at Shelby. "We're just going through, on our way to Austin."

"Mayor wants to see you both first."

"Are you kidding me?"

Josh shrugged. "She left word. Guess she figured you'd come through eventually, on account of Carter."

"Look, we don't have time to meet with Mayor Perkins. I'll be happy to stop by on our way back—"

"Can't do it." Josh was already signaling to one of the other men standing guard. "Get on the horn to the mayor. Tell her I'll be by with Max in a few minutes. And get someone here to take my place."

"What's this about, Josh?"

"Think she told me?" Josh laughed, but it was a hollow sound. "I'm just a grunt and happy to be one. Anyone who mans a shift receives an extra portion of that week's harvest."

"Harvest?"

"Deer, hogs, dove—you name it." He glanced at Shelby, who had joined them.

"What's this about?"

"Josh was just explaining to me new procedures the mayor has implemented."

"She sends a hunting group out every day, and what they get, well, we can't exactly keep it in the freezer. There's a rotating schedule for folks to receive a portion of that day's take, but if you work a shift your name goes on the schedule twice. My nephews are growing, and they need the meat."

"All right. We'll go see Perkins."

"Why would we go see Perkins?" Shelby had again donned the baseball cap, and now she pulled it down to block out the sun.

"Apparently she's insisting we stop by."

"Wasn't my idea," Josh reminded them. "I'm just the messenger here."

"Got it. But Josh, remember that we are neighbors. I own a house three blocks over and so did Shelby before it was destroyed in the gas line explosion."

"We're not the enemy here," Shelby added. "We belong in Abney."

"Of course you do, which is the only reason I'm going to allow you to keep your weapons." He walked away, leaving Max and Shelby impatiently waiting.

"What can she possibly want with us?"

"I'm not sure, but we don't have time for this."

"Agreed." She tapped her fingers against the thermos she was still holding. "Maybe we can sneak out the south side once he lets us through."

"Not a chance. He's going to escort us."

Josh made a circular motion over his head, and someone manning the barricade jumped down and backed up the flatbed truck, leaving barely enough space for Max to squeeze the Dodge through.

"They're being careful," Shelby muttered.

"If they're being this paranoid with someone they know, imagine how they treat strangers."

Once they were on the other side, Josh jumped into a small sedan and proceeded to lead them toward city hall.

Three

"Do they think we can't find city hall?" Shelby scowled at the scene outside her window. "Or are they worried we'll make a run for it?"

"I know we're in a hurry, but this could be important."

"Important? Finding insulin for Carter is important. This is bureaucracy at its worst."

"Perkins has been a good mayor, in spite of all that has happened. How about we listen to what she has to say? I promise you we'll keep it short."

Everything about their situation grated on

Shelby's nerves. The notion that they'd been detained—that it was possible for the mayor to do so, Josh Hunter's role as escort, and the fact that they were crawling along at twenty miles an hour. And all the while, the burden of Carter's need, of what she and Max would have to do to fill it, pressed in on her heart like an ever-tightening vise.

Then they passed the town's only grocery store.

Max let out a long, low whistle. A fire had taken out the majority of the structure. The roof was caved in, and the glass windows had apparently exploded out, as the parking area was littered with glass.

The gas station, which sat at the far end of the property, appeared untouched, but now there were barricades around it and an officer sitting in a patrol car at the only entrance.

"I barely recognize this place," Shelby said.

"It certainly doesn't look like the town we grew up in."

The Sonic across the street had been looted, and most of the speakers, where you placed your order for a double cheeseburger or tater tots, had been ripped off their poles.

"Why would someone do this? Why destroy our town?"

"People are scared and some are angry. Those two things are never a good combination."

The furniture store where Shelby had bought

her couch, the pharmacy where she'd purchased Carter's insulin, even the bank where she'd made her last withdrawal had all taken a hit—shattered windows, doors busted in, and any contents looted. She thought she could make out bloodstains on the sidewalk in front of the Western store.

Ten minutes after they'd left the barricade, they parked outside the mayor's office. A guard checked them for weapons. Stepping back and raising his rifle, he said, "I'm going to need you to leave your handguns in the vehicle."

Shelby's revolver was still in her backpack. Max's semiautomatic was in a belt holster.

Max glanced at Shelby, shrugged, and placed his Sig inside the center console. She did the same with her .22. After checking once more to confirm they didn't have any type of weapon on their person, the guard nodded them toward the entrance to city hall, where an armed woman walked them to the mayor's office.

Nadine Perkins looked to Shelby as if she'd landed on her feet. She wore jeans and a freshly laundered Western shirt. Her long gray hair was pulled back with a clasp, and her face was devoid of makeup.

"I apologize for interrupting your trip."

"Then why did you?" Shelby asked, not even attempting to hide her irritation.

"Coffee?"

"No." Max begrudgingly sat in the chair she

indicated. "We need to be on our way, Nadine. There's a reason we left before sunrise."

They'd agreed before walking in the building that they would make this as short as possible. They needed to be on the road if they had any chance to be in Austin before the sun set.

"I need your help."

"Any other time, we'd be happy to—"

"No, Max. You're going to hear me out. You're both still technically residents of this town, and right now Abney needs you."

"My son needs me." Shelby perched on the edge of her chair. "That's our first priority at the moment."

"I understand your concern for Carter—"

"Don't do that. Don't placate me. Tell us what you want so we can tell you no, and then we're leaving."

Nadine didn't look surprised or even upset by Shelby's outburst. "These are terrible times, and I understand that you have to put the needs of your family first. But I have to put the needs of this town first, and I'm willing to trade gasoline for your help."

"We have plenty of—"

"Hang on, Shelby. We could always use more fuel." Max turned his attention back to the mayor. "If we could fill up our vehicle and the two gas cans we're carrying on our return, we might agree to help."

"Of course."

"I know how limited your supplies are."

When Max glanced her way, Shelby glowered at him. She didn't want to negotiate with this woman. She wanted to focus on their mission.

Max was once again addressing Perkins. "This isn't just a generous offer."

"No, it's not."

"What do you need?"

"First of all, I'd like to help you both get the insulin you're looking for. Carter can't have more than a month's worth—"

"How do you know my son's diabetic?"

"You gave a presentation to the council when you were petitioning for needle boxes to be placed in public restrooms."

Shelby sank back into her chair. That had been years ago, and the mayor had remembered. *Well, the woman was a politician at heart. Any information she could use, she filed away for a rainy day.* The uncharitable thought pricked her heart. There had been a time when she'd assumed the best of people, but the flare had done more than change their world. It had changed her heart—making her jaded, suspicious. That wasn't who she wanted to be, but she had no idea how to go back.

Nadine cleared her throat, and then she asked, "You left a week ago?"

Max nodded, walked over to the thermos, and

poured them both a cup of coffee. He handed the mug to Shelby and said, "Might as well drink it if we're going to have to be here a while."

"I should start by catching you up. You both know that fourteen were killed in the fight with Croghan."

"We were here when it happened."

"They were all Croghan residents?" Shelby gulped the coffee, grateful for something to do even though it burned her throat.

"Yes. Another eighteen died in the various gas explosions. We haven't been able to determine what caused those."

"And Eugene Stone?" Max asked.

"Still pretending to be the mayor of Croghan, though we haven't heard anything else from him in the last week."

"Perhaps he's come to his senses."

"It's more likely that he's reassessing how best to get his hands on what we have."

"But you don't have that much." Shelby blew on her coffee. It was fresh and strong. The mayor had come prepared. She was surprised there weren't donuts on the desk.

"Unlimited water from the springs, some fuel reserves, and a small cache of supplies that had been stored in the basement of the courthouse. Not to mention Stanley Hamilton's gun store and the stockpile of weapons that Jake Cooper keeps in his survival shelter." She folded her hands on her desk and shifted her glance from Shelby to Max. "We've lost nine more in the last week—four at the nursing home, two at the hospital, two died in their homes, and Frank Kelton on the roadblock."

"Josh told us about Frank," Max said.

Shelby reached down, unzipped her backpack, and pulled out her notepad. She hadn't planned on keeping a casualty list, but perhaps this aspect also needed to be recorded. Would the deceased be forgotten if she didn't write down their names and how they had died? And yet there weren't enough notebooks left to include the names of all who had perished since the flare—something deep inside assured her of that truth. She clicked her pen and began to write as Perkins continued to update them.

"I've reinforced the roadblocks and made sure that someone with military experience is in each rotation."

"What does Danny think of all this?" Shelby had been staring down at her notepad when she asked about the city manager. The mayor's silence cued her in to the fact that something was wrong. "Tell me Danny Vail wasn't killed."

"Actually . . . he's gone."

"Gone? Where?" Max glanced at Shelby and back at the mayor.

"I don't know where. He left after the gas explosion."

"Left?" Shelby's voice rose despite her attempt

to remain calm. "Danny wouldn't just leave. He's the city manager. He's a good man, and he—"

Perkins cleared her throat, shook her head, and finally sat up straighter. "He drove south, through the barricades, two days after the explosion. He never returned."

"Maybe he was hurt," Max said. "Have you looked for him?"

"I sent two officers out to his house, but Danny wasn't there. He'd cleaned out all of his food, guns, and ammo."

Shelby couldn't believe what she was hearing. Danny Vail had stopped by her house after the flare. He had offered to give her and Carter a place to stay. He wouldn't just walk away from Abney. "Anyone could have taken his things. He could have been robbed."

"Which is why we asked the neighbors if they'd seen or heard anything. One noticed Danny loading supplies into the back of his truck."

It didn't add up, didn't make any sense at all. Shelby looked at Max, but he only shrugged—apparently as befuddled as she was.

"The situation at the nursing home has stabilized for the moment," Perkins continued. "But we need antibiotics as well as maintenance drugs. If this town is going to be a safe place, we have to be able to treat people who get sick—"

"Or shot."

"Or injured doing any number of things. If we

don't get more medical supplies, we're going to have a real crisis on our hands."

"Nothing from the state or feds?"

"No."

"I wish we could help. I do." Max leaned forward. "But our plan is to get into Austin, find some insulin, and get out. We don't even know how we're going to do that or where it's going to be."

Shelby added, "We can't exactly take a shopping list and have it filled at a pharmacy."

"I know that. But I might be able to help you. Dr. Bhatti knows where—"

"Absolutely not." Shelby jumped up, nearly spilling the coffee she held. "That man is not going with us."

"It won't work, Nadine. There isn't room."

"Then you're going to make room." The mayor slapped her hand against her desk. "We need this, Max. Your town, the people you grew up with, need this. Bhatti knows what supplies are most critical. He will recognize what drug can be substituted for another, and he might have ideas where you can find it all—including insulin for Carter."

"I don't trust him." Shelby had crossed over to the windows. She stood there now, back to the mayor, arms crossed, staring down at the town square. "I don't trust him, and nothing you are going to say will change that."

"So you don't trust him. Fine. Keep an eye on him, but take him with you. Because if you don't, there are going to be a lot more deaths in Abney."

Four

Shelby walked out of the municipal building wondering how their plan could go so wrong so quickly.

"Nearly nine, Max. We should be well on our way to Austin by now."

"I agree." He pulled her over to a bench that sat under the shade of a crepe myrtle tree. "We need to think long haul though."

"Which is why we're looking for more insulin."

"Exactly. We hope for the best—"

"But plan for the worst."

"Look." He scrubbed a hand across his face. "My folks are going to need more fuel. If there were an emergency at High Fields, if we had to get to Abney in a hurry . . . say if someone got shot or injured . . . there are doctors here."

She closed her eyes against the bright pink of the crepe myrtle flowers. The color hurt her somehow. The idea that nature went on as civilization crumbled.

"One hour." She opened her eyes and leveled her most serious stare at Max. "If Bhatti hasn't shown up in one hour, then you promise me we will find a way through or around the southern roadblock."

"Deal."

She didn't want to see the smile on his face. She didn't want her pulse to jump when he squeezed her hand. She certainly didn't want to admit how close they'd become in the last week at the ranch—how natural it felt to sit side by side, hips touching, his hand on hers. She jerked her hand away and jumped up. Perhaps she'd had too much caffeine and not enough food. Remembering the sack lunch his mother had pressed on them, she strode back toward the Dodge. She'd just opened the door when a 1965 red Ford Mustang pulled up beside them and Patrick Goodnight stepped out.

Shelby threw herself into his arms.

"I knew you'd miss me." Patrick was forty-one, a few years younger than Shelby. Retired military, he had kept the bearing and looks of an enlisted man. His size spoke to his years on the high school football team playing the position of linebacker. And the way he hugged her tight, well that was a real testament to their friendship.

She reached up and ran a hand over his nearly bald head. "Still maintaining your good looks despite . . . everything."

"Good to see you, man." Max slapped Patrick on the back, a grin spreading across his face. "How did you know we were here?"

"Grapevine. It's nearly as fast as texting."

Shelby hadn't realized how much she'd missed their group.

Patrick was the most uncomplicated person she'd ever met. He saw things in black and white, and he rarely hesitated. He was physically intimidating to most people, but to Shelby he was simply one of her closest friends.

Max, on the other hand, could easily have posed for a cover shoot for *Texas Monthly*—tall, gangly, and always wearing a cowboy hat or ball cap. More than once, her mother had said, "Max Berkman is one tall, refreshing glass of water." Add the fact that he was a small town lawyer who had never married, and Max became quite the sought after bachelor.

He'd been in her life for as long as she could remember. They'd grown up next door to each other. He'd been the first to break her heart, and the first to step in and offer help years later when her marriage fell apart. When Carter's father died, he'd become like a surrogate parent to her son.

"How are you?" Shelby asked, pulling a container of shelled pecans out of her lunch sack and offering some to Patrick.

"No, thanks. Had my MRE already."

"Seriously?" Patrick had long been a proponent of field rations, which could be bought at military surplus stores. He had even brought them along on their hiking trips. To Shelby the pork and rice BBQ tasted exactly like the beef stew. And the jambalaya? *Revolting* was the only word that came to mind.

"I told you to buy them in bulk and keep them in your pantry, but you said—"

Shelby interrupted him, not wanting to hear his lecture on the merits of *Meals, Ready-to-Eat.* "How's Bianca?"

Patrick ran a hand over his closely cropped hair and refused to meet her gaze. She knew imme-diately that something was wrong.

"What happened?" Max pulled off his ball cap and slapped it against his pant leg.

"She's fine. Bianca's fine, but her father . . . he died two days after you left."

"How many are we going to lose?" Shelby tried to squelch the panic that threatened to choke her.

"He wasn't healthy even before the lights went out," Patrick said.

"But he had a chance. Before he had a chance. In this world? Not so much."

"Let's go see Bianca and her mother." Max nodded toward Patrick's car.

"Leave the Dodge?"

"No one's going to mess with our vehicle, Shelby. Perkins has guards posted around city hall."

But what if the guards were desperate enough to steal?

She pushed the thought from her mind and focused on what she would say to the Lopez family.

• • •

When Bianca opened the door, Shelby didn't even try to check her tears. She stood there, in the middle of the doorway, her arms wrapped around her best friend.

She tried to absorb some of the misery and mourning.

She tried to give Bianca a little of her strength.

Finally they stepped into the house. As usual, the smell of fresh coffee wafted toward them. Rosa walked into the room, wearing her customary apron and herding them all into the kitchen.

Once they were settled at the table, Max and Shelby offered their condolences. Shelby pulled out her notebook and added Miguel Lopez to her list of casualties, as well as the date he'd died and that it was from complications of a previous medical condition.

"He was a good man, my Miguel. But this life?" Rosa banged a frying pan onto a Coleman stove that had been set up on the cabinet near the open kitchen window. "I miss him, but this life *es una prueba terrible*."

Rosa shrugged her shoulders and began frying eggs.

"The chickens are still laying more than we can eat," Bianca explained. "The flare didn't affect the poultry at all."

"I imagine the eggs are good for trading." Max sipped from his mug of coffee.

Shelby couldn't remember if this was their third or fourth cup. If they didn't mix some food with it soon, they'd both be able to run to Austin.

The back screen door squeaked open, and a middle-aged Hispanic woman stepped inside. "They would be good for trading, if *Mamá* didn't give them all away."

"We've been over this, Camilla." Rosa didn't bother to turn around from the stove. "We help those we can, and they will help us in return."

Camilla didn't seem convinced.

Bianca had apparently heard the argument before. She nodded toward the woman and said, "Max and Shelby, this is *mi hermana*, Camilla."

There was no denying the family resemblance—same long, straight black hair, round brown eyes, and oval-shaped face. Both of the women were short, though Bianca was thinner than her sister. Shelby remembered meeting Camilla once before, but it had been years ago.

"How did you get to Abney? Last I remember you lived west of here."

"I was worried about my parents, so I caught a ride. Fortunately, I arrived just hours before my father passed." Placing both hands on her hips, she turned to Bianca. "Did you finish the laundry already? Because I don't see any sheets on the line."

"Let her visit with her friends, Camilla."

Camilla made a harrumph sound and marched out of the room.

"My oldest daughter copes with her grief by working." Rosa placed fried eggs in front of Max, Shelby, and Patrick. She'd also warmed half a dozen tortillas on the stove and now added those to the middle of the table, placing a jar of home-made salsa beside it. "I wish I had cheese."

"This is more than enough," Max assured her.

"Actually, I already—" Patrick made an effort to nudge his plate in Bianca's direction.

"Do not tell me you already ate an MRE." Bianca frowned at Patrick and pushed the plate back toward him. "Real food. That's what you need. *Mamá* fed me hours ago."

"Where did you find the ingredients to make tortillas?" Shelby asked.

"I never could abide fast food. We had quite a bit of staples in the pantry before the flare changed our lives. Now eat up. You are going on a journey, yes? A mission?"

Shelby nodded, a lump in her throat suddenly making it difficult to swallow. She and Carter had stayed a few nights in the Lopez house after their own home had been demolished in the gas line explosion. She'd forgotten the kindness, love, and hospitality of Rosa Lopez.

Rosa poured herself a cup of coffee and listened as they told of their trip to High Fields, being shot at by the group that called themselves the Bandits, and Max falling unconscious as they bumped over the caliche road toward High Fields.

"You have had the migraines for many years." Rosa sipped her coffee, which must have been cold by now.

"I have," he said simply.

"What were you writing in the notebook?" Bianca asked Shelby.

So she explained about her idea that what they were going through should be written down, that their children or grandchildren might want the details of what had happened as well as the names of those who had died.

"*Es muy bueno*, Shelby." Rosa reached across and patted her hand. "*Gracias.*"

They were quiet for a moment, and then Shelby shared the details of their plan to travel to Austin and the mayor's insistence that they take Dr. Bhatti with them.

"I'm going with you," Patrick said.

"No. You're not." Max pushed away his plate. "I won't be responsible for taking anyone else along."

"It's not your choice. It's mine, and I'm going."

"So am I."

They all turned to stare at Bianca.

"Shelby and Max and Dr. Bhatti in the Dodge. Patrick and I will follow in his Mustang."

Max carried his plate to the sink, and then he turned around to study them. "Patrick's Mustang is hardly a car you can sneak in and out of Austin with."

"You can't do that anyway," Patrick reasoned. "Any car on the roads is noticeable and suspect. At least this way, we'll have each other's backs."

"But Bianca . . ." Shelby glanced at Rosa. "Your mom. I imagine she needs you here."

"I do. So bring her back." Rosa clucked her tongue. "The mayor is right. We must have medicine if we're to survive the next few months. I expect the four of you to get down there, let the doctor find what we need . . . and for heaven's sake get plenty of insulin for Carter. Go and do what you need to do, and when you're done, bring my daughter home."

Five

Max, Shelby, Patrick, and Bianca were waiting outside city hall when their pastor, Tony Ramos, walked up. "Is it true? You're heading to Austin?"

Shelby nodded, and Max gave Tony the condensed version of their mission. The pastor was a big man, and if Max had met him on the street, he never would have guessed his profession to be the ministry. He had a blunt way about him, but always with the hint of a smile and a kind voice—so folks rarely took offense.

As they were talking, a police cruiser drove up and dropped off Dr. Farhan Bhatti. Five foot, ten inches, with light brown skin, dark hair, and a

40

gentle manner, Bhatti had been an ear, nose, and throat specialist before the flare.

Max had first recruited him to help with Abney's medical needs when Bhatti was stranded in town. The man could have found a way out in the intervening nineteen days, but he'd chosen to stay. Whether that was for altruistic reasons, or because there was something he didn't want to return to, Max couldn't say.

"Dr. Bhatti. How are you?"

Bhatti readjusted his backpack and shifted his doctor's bag to his left hand so that he could shake hands. "Call me by my first name, Max. I am living in your house."

"How's that going? I didn't have a chance to drive by and check out the neighborhood."

"We are slowly putting things back together after the explosion. Your house had very little damage—though I had it checked before I spent a night there."

"We don't have time for this." Shelby glowered at the doctor.

Max thought she must have noticed the look that passed between her friends, because she bit down her impatience and tried again.

"You've been a big help here in Abney, and I appreciate that, but this trip—this is about my son, about finding a way for him to survive."

"I understand—"

"You don't. You couldn't possibly. And just so

41

you know, it wasn't our idea to take you with us. The mayor . . . insisted."

Max couldn't tell if Bhatti was offended or amused. He said, "Mayor Perkins can be a very persuasive woman," and left them to say hello to the rest of the group.

They proceeded to transfer some of their supplies to Patrick's car to make room for Bhatti. He'd be sitting behind Max, where Shelby could keep an eye on him. The second seat in the Dodge Ramcharger offered plenty of room, but there were no doors to the area. The only way in was to move the front seat forward and climb in. On the bright side, it would be harder for anyone to carjack them.

As they were shuffling boxes of supplies, Pastor Tony pulled Max and Patrick away from the group.

"I'm sure you realize how dangerous this is."

"We do," they said in unison.

"Is there no other way to get the medications we need?"

Max sighed and looked back toward their motley group. "I'm all ears, if you have suggestions."

"No. No, I don't . . . but there is something I need to tell you."

He turned his back to the group, so Max and Patrick did the same. Max barely had time to register what Tony had told them, was trying to formulate which question to ask first, when the door of city hall banged open, and Mayor Perkins hurried out toward them. She handed both Max and Patrick a radio. "It's only a precaution, but this way you can talk to each other."

She told them the designated frequency to use and then the emergency frequency for Abney. "Which will only work if you're within a mile or so of a roadblock."

"We'll return them on our way back through, when we pick up the fuel."

"Safe travels, and again—thank you." Without another word, the mayor walked away.

Bianca was waiting in the passenger seat of the Mustang, and Bhatti had climbed into the backseat of the Dodge. Shelby stood next to the SUV, tapping her foot and staring pointedly at her watch.

Max turned back to their pastor. "Are you sure? How do you even know? Who was your source?"

"Yes, I'm sure. I know because more than one person from outside Abney has told me, and I can't tell you who my source is."

Patrick rubbed the top of his head. "And you trust these people?"

"Yes." Tony didn't hesitate. "I pray it's not information that you need, but if you find yourself in a tight spot . . ."

"Okay," Max said. "We understand."

"One other thing. Be careful who you share the information with."

"Right." Patrick shook the pastor's hand, Max did the same, and then the two of them walked back to their vehicles. They made a U-turn on the nearly empty street and pulled away from the town square.

Mayor Perkins must have notified the southern roadblock that they were on their way. Max barely had to slow when they reached it—the guards were already backing up a plow to make room for them to snake through.

They'd decided to take State Highway 183, which travelled southeast, allowing them to bypass Croghan completely. The first twenty miles passed without incident, which should have eased the knot of tension taking up permanent residence in Max's neck. It didn't. The apparently abandoned roads seemed more like a storm building on the horizon. It wasn't a matter of if they would run into trouble, only a matter of when.

Shelby checked the radio twice to be sure they could communicate with Patrick and Bianca. As long as they stayed no more than a few car lengths apart, the radios worked fine.

They passed more abandoned cars, but no people.

The radio crackled, and Patrick said, "Could be trouble in Briggs. I suggest we stop this side of it and use the scopes."

Max glanced at Shelby, who nodded once. There had been no time to discuss this, but they'd both seen enough abandoned cars riddled with bullet holes. The more remote the location, the bigger risk of being attacked. Hopefully, once they reached Austin city limits, there would be some semblance of law.

Max moved over onto the shoulder just short of a hilltop, and Patrick pulled in behind him. Shelby held out the radio, but Max waved it away, flashed what he hoped was a confident smile, and grabbed his rifle from the backseat. Patrick was waiting for him by the time he stepped out of the Dodge. Together they jogged to the top of the hill.

After a moment, Max asked, "Can they see us?"

"If we can see them, it's possible for them to see us." Patrick lowered his rifle and swiped at the sweat running down his face.

Not yet noon, but Max guessed the temperature was nearing the ninety mark.

"All I see is a woman hanging out clothes back behind the building."

"I doubt she's alone." Patrick scanned left to right. "Looks like they're living in the convenience store."

"One that fronts a state highway? Seems like a dangerous place to settle down."

"Probably can't tell anyone's there from the road. If we hadn't been looking through a scope, I doubt we would have seen her."

"It could be a trap."

"But I don't think it is."

"Drive through or stop?"

"Information would be helpful." Patrick lowered his rifle. "I say stop."

"Agreed."

Patrick pointed to a clump of trees halfway between their position and the store. "I'll pull over there and wait for your okay."

"If there's trouble—"

"I can make a shot from that distance."

They jogged back to the vehicles and shared their plan. Max expected an argument from Shelby, but she surprised him.

"I want to drive straight through. Our goal is Austin. There's no argument about that." She glanced back at the doctor, who nodded in agreement. "But I'd rather get there alive. If the people in that store can help us, I agree that we should stop."

Max glanced in his rearview mirror and saw Bianca checking the magazine in her Glock. Satisfied, she returned the semiautomatic to her shoulder holster. Shelby removed her Ruger 22 handgun from her backpack and placed it on her lap.

Bhatti was the only one to balk at carrying a weapon. "I'm a doctor, Max. Not a soldier."

"You want to keep doctoring? Better get used to protecting yourself." He pulled a Smith & Wesson revolver out from under his seat and handed it to Bhatti, who confirmed there were bullets in the revolver.

At least the man knew how to use a handgun.

Max spoke into the radio, though his words were meant for the entire group. "We're as ready as we can be. Keep your eyes open for anything out of place, any sign at all that these people are not a family camping in an abandoned convenience store."

He drove at a conservative speed, not wanting to frighten anyone in the building or anyone in their group. He was spooked enough for all of them. He could practically feel a rifle's scope trained on their vehicles. Adrenaline pounded through his bloodstream, rendering him hyperalert.

The sound of their tires against the pavement.

The scent of last night's rain.

The peeling paint on the building.

Every detail accosted his senses, and he was reminded of his granddad's stories of fighting in World War II—the long days of boredom punctuated by moments when every detail was seared into his memory.

Pulling into the service station, Max wasn't surprised when no one came out of the building. Someone had painted CLOSED across ply board that had been placed haphazardly over the windows.

"Bhatti, stay with the car. Shoot anyone who comes near it. Shelby, I want you over by the phone booth. And remember, Patrick has us covered. If we run into trouble, drop to the ground, and let him take care of it."

Max banged on the front door, but there was no answer. Motioning for Bhatti and Shelby to stay in their positions, he walked slowly around the building. He'd reached the back, was looking at the clothes drying on the line, when he heard a click—the cocking of a revolver. Then a voice behind him said, "Drop your weapon, and then get back in your vehicle, mister. Keep driving, and I won't have to kill you."

Six

Carter had caught plenty of catfish in his life, but it had been years since he'd cleaned one.

"Be sure to remove any dirt from your cutting area before you begin." Roy paused to make sure that Carter was watching and following his directions to the letter. He had two five-pound catfish. Carter's single fish was probably closer to three. Roy showed him the correct process for skinning and gutting the fish. "Once you're done with that, you can cut the filets. First you put the fish on its side. Hold the head firmly."

Carter was standing beside Max's dad, following his instructions step-by-step. Roy was a big one for learning by doing, not learning by listening.

"Now insert your knife behind this front fin. It's called the pectoral fin, but don't suppose that matters."

"No quiz?"

"No quiz, but if you fail to take Georgia some nice clean filets, she'll want to know why."

"Got it."

"Cut downward to the backbone. You can feel it. Don't cut through the backbone. It will dull your knife and achieves nothing."

"Yeah, I feel it."

"Now turn the knife, sharp side down, and work your way toward the tail."

Carter watched Roy, and then mimicked the motion. When he was done, he found himself holding a nice-sized filet.

"Think you can do the rest?"

"Sure."

"When you're done, take three of the filets to the house for Georgia to fry up."

"And the other three?"

Roy pointed to a four-wheeler. "Keys are in it. Wrap the extra in some of that old newspaper on the shelf, and then take it down to the Dunns' place. You know where that is?"

Carter shook his head. Was Roy actually giving him the keys to his four-wheeler?

"Take the lane to the road and turn left. You'll go down into a low water crossing. When you come back up, the Dunn place is on your left."

"I've never driven a four-wheeler," Carter admitted.

Roy shrugged. "Not that hard. There's a gas

pedal and a brake. Just don't make any sharp turns. You turn that thing over and Georgia will filet me like you're fileting that fish."

"Yes, sir." Carter felt stupid for saying it, but he pushed ahead. "I could walk. If you're . . . trying to save the charge on the four-wheeler."

"I appreciate the offer, but the generator's holding up pretty well. I have an extra battery that I keep charged." Roy walked over to the water pump and washed his hands. "I've loaded some firewood on the back that I'd like you to take to them as well. Last time I was over, they'd started cooking in an old wood stove that Charles had wrestled up onto the back porch."

"You got it."

Carter thought he would leave then. Roy never seemed to run out of work to do. Even in the short time since they'd arrived, he'd rarely seen the man sit down unless he was eating or it was dark outside. Even then, he'd go out one last time before bed to do an evening check.

But instead of leaving, Roy leaned against the cattle fence. He wasn't watching Carter work, which meant he had something else to say.

"Your mom and Max . . . they care about you."

"I know that."

"When you have a child with you . . ." He held up a hand to stave off Carter's argument. "I know you're not a child, but I still think of Max that way, and he's now forty-five."

Carter shrugged and picked up another fish, inserted the knife, and opened up the stomach to remove the guts.

"The truth is, when you have your own flesh and blood with you, standing there beside you, it makes you hesitate. Makes you second-guess yourself. I suspect that's why they didn't want you along."

"So without me they'll just rush headlong into trouble?"

"I've never known Max to do that. He seemed to have lost any impulsiveness he once had when he was going through law school—they must have lectured it out of him." Roy laughed, pulled a weed growing near the fence, and stuck it in his mouth. "Max is careful. He won't let anything happen to your mom."

"I still don't understand why I couldn't go."

"With you here with us, they'll be able to focus on one thing and one thing only—finding the insulin and getting back. Their love for you . . . it would slow them down."

"And I'm supposed to be happy about that?"

"Doesn't matter how you feel about it one way or the other. Just is."

Carter finished with the fish, placed the filets in a pan for Georgia, and dumped the head and bones into a bucket.

"What are you going to do with this stuff?"

"Set some traps."

"Traps?"

"You'll see. We'll do it later this afternoon. There's always food to be had on a ranch, Carter. But it doesn't always walk up and present itself at your front door."

The old guy walked off, whistling a tune that Carter only vaguely recognized.

All the talk about parents and children and love turned his thoughts to Kaitlyn, to her mom, even to the friends he'd left behind in Abney. Why had he done it? Why had he agreed to leave his entire life behind him? So he could hide out on a farm and learn to clean fish?

Was that his future?

Supposing he didn't die from his diabetes, was this all he had to look forward to?

No college.

No girlfriend.

No friend of any kind.

If there was one thing he'd realized when their house blew up, it was that the changes that had occurred after the flare were permanent. The life he'd lived and the one he'd dreamed of living? Those were both things of the past.

Seven

Patrick's shot embedded itself in the brick of the building, slightly to the left of where Max and his would-be assailant stood.

"That's my partner," Max said, "and it was a warning shot."

Max turned around slowly, careful to keep his own weapon pointed toward the ground. He found himself face-to-face with a man who couldn't have been out of his midtwenties—black, clean shaven, and weighing no more than one fifty.

"Put your revolver on the ground and kick it toward me," Max said.

"Why should I?"

"Because you want me to give the all clear signal. Otherwise, the next bullet will be *in* you instead of *beside* you."

Visibly deflating, the man placed his revolver on the ground and pushed it toward Max with his left foot.

Max picked up the gun and stuck it into the back of his pants.

"What about the all clear signal?"

"That was it. Now tell your wife everything is okay and she can come out."

"Uh-uh. Not happening."

"If we'd wanted to rob you, we would have done

it already. Can we just have a civil conversation?"

The man was shaking his head, refusing to listen to Max, when Shelby suddenly barreled around the corner of the building, clutching her revolver, and skidding to a halt a few feet from them. "What happened? I heard a shot. Are you okay?"

"We're fine. Let's all go to the front—" Max stopped talking when they heard the sound of Patrick's Mustang.

They walked back to the front of the building, Max encouraging the man with his semiautomatic, which he kept out and at the ready. He had no desire to shoot anyone, especially not a young married guy who was desperate enough to live in this dump. But neither was he going to give the man a chance to run. In the back of his mind he realized this still could be a trap. What if there were more people than a man and woman? What if even now they were circling around Max's group?

Patrick and Bianca joined them. Bhatti walked over from the Dodge.

It took another ten minutes to convince the man that they weren't there to pilfer and plunder. The man's hesitancy as well as the fear in his eyes persuaded Max that this was no trap. He was protecting his family, exactly like Max was intent on protecting Shelby, which was why they found themselves at something of a stalemate.

Bianca was the one who stumbled on the magic words that lowered the man's guard. "We don't have time for this. Carter needs that medication, and Dr. Bhatti has patients to treat. Let's go."

"You're a doctor?" He stepped closer to Bhatti, his look of defiance replaced with uncertainty . . . and perhaps hope. "Seriously? Are you?"

"Yes, I am."

"My son . . ." He glanced at Patrick and Max, and then he focused again on the doctor. "He hurt himself a few days back, and now he's running a fever. Could you look at him?"

"Of course."

They pulled their cars around to the back of the store and entered the building through the rear entrance. Soon they were crowded around an old Formica table in the convenience store's work-room.

Max introduced everyone from their group.

"I'm Joel. Joel Allen. My wife is Danielle."

"And your son?" Shelby asked, her voice softening as she glanced toward the area where Bhatti was examining the boy. Bianca had volunteered to assist him.

"Zack. His name is Zack."

There were only four chairs, so Joel pulled up old crates for them to sit on. A single window over a work sink provided a little light. An old blanket was folded and placed on the counter—no doubt for tacking over the window at night. Joel had hung several tarps to divide the large room into a sleeping area and living area.

A few cans of supplies were stacked on the counter, but it was plain they didn't have much. Max could just make out the edge of a sleeping bag in the area where they slept. He heard a young boy start to cry, and the mother—Danielle—say, "It'll be all right, Zack. He's going to help you."

Joel glanced that way. "We were headed to the north," he said. "Hoping that things in the Dallas area would be better than Austin."

"It's probably a good thing you didn't make it that far." Patrick rubbed a hand up and over his head. "Last we heard the area from downtown to the Trinity River was burning. No word at all as to what was going on in the suburbs, but it can't be good."

"Then we'll stay here," Joel said. He sat back, crossed his arms, and studied them.

"Here?" Shelby asked. "In the back of an abandoned convenience store?"

"We're doing all right. There's an old pump out back where we get water. The toilets are still working."

Max stood and began pacing. "It's not safe here, Joel."

"Where we came from was a lot less safe. And your friend Patrick just told me where we were planning to go is a bad idea too. This seems like our best option."

"But we could have easily killed you and—"

All conversation stopped as Bhatti and Danielle

walked into the room. Joel's wife was the woman they'd seen hanging clothes. She was a little on the heavy side, medium height, and there was a hardness in her eyes that Max thought might be strength, or desperation. She was approximately the same age as Joel, with short chopped hair that framed her face.

"Zack is nearly asleep," Danielle said. "Bianca offered to sit with him for a few minutes."

Bhatti stripped off his disposable gloves, walked to the sink, and poured water from a pitcher into a large bowl set in the sink so he could thoroughly wash his hands. He accepted the bottle of drinking water that Max offered him, and then he turned his attention to Joel and Danielle. "I cleaned up the wound and applied antibiotic cream. You're certain that it was a piece of glass he cut himself on?"

"Yes." Danielle sank into one of the chairs. "I had washed some glasses that we found here in the sink. He was helping me, standing on a stool, and he fell. His arm must have hit the glass."

"And he hasn't complained of a headache? Trouble swallowing? Stiffness in his jaw?"

Both Joel and Danielle shook their head to each question.

"If you were near a medical facility, I'd recommend that you get a tetanus shot, just in case." He rubbed his forehead with the tips of his fingers. Max wondered if the man suffered from migraines or was simply worried.

He also noted that Bhatti frowned at Shelby as she took notes in her journal. They were all becoming used to it, though Joel stopped questioning the doctor long enough to ask her what the point was.

"Those pages, they won't change anything—no offense."

"None taken." Shelby looked down at what she'd written, allowed her fingertips to trace over the lines. "But we've lost so much already. Think of all the books, all the knowledge that was on e-readers. Gone—poof, in the blink of an eye."

"But those books were also printed and put in libraries," Danielle said.

"Some were—maybe most. But there are fewer and fewer libraries, fewer print books. For all we know, someone is using them for fuel in their wood-burning stove. And some books? Well, many of them were e-book-only releases. Those are gone. It just seems important that we have some record of this. You might be right, Joel. It might not help a bit, but if it guides the next generation even a little, then it will have been worth the time. Maybe my son's generation, and your son's, can learn from what has happened."

Bhatti cleared his throat. "Speaking of Zack, since we're nowhere near a medical facility and they probably wouldn't have any of the vaccine left even if we were, I want you to keep the wound clean and change the bandage once a day."

He reached into his medical bag, rummaged around, and pulled out a bottle, which he passed to Danielle.

"These will help him?" she asked.

"They're antibiotics and will fight the infection, but this dose . . ." he tapped the label on the side of the bottle. "It was for an adult male. You'll have to cut the tablets in half."

"All right. Thank you."

Max noticed that her hand was shaking as she read the label on the bottle. She set it down, pushed it toward her husband, and said, "I had found some Tylenol, but it wasn't helping the fever."

"It should work now when taken in conjunction with the antibiotics. Continue the Tylenol until his fever breaks."

"I don't know how to thank you." Joel stared at Bhatti and then Max. "I almost shot you, and you saved my boy."

"But you didn't shoot us," Max said. "And you were right to be looking out for your family."

"Now you need to move on." Patrick glanced out the single window. "This place isn't safe. You're too close to the road. Even with the closed signs and boarded windows—"

"There's nothing left in the store or the gas pumps. There's no reason for anyone to stop here."

"Some people don't need a reason." Shelby folded her arms on the table and studied the couple. "You need to go to Abney. It's less than an hour's drive north of here."

"We don't know anyone there," Danielle argued. "No one is going to help us."

"Tony Ramos will." Bianca walked into the room and perched on the edge of one of the crates. "Tony has young boys, one about the same age as Zack. He'll find you a place to stay, and the mayor has started sending out hunting parties. Everyone who works receives a share of the harvest."

"And those who legitimately can't work are taken care of as well," Patrick said. "It's not perfect there —we've had some looting and unrest with the town to the south, but it's better than here. Safer."

"Why aren't you there, then? What's so important that you would leave?"

"My son needs insulin, and I'm going to find it." Shelby met Max's gaze. "My friends wouldn't let me go alone."

Joel glanced at his wife and then back at Patrick. "Abney sounds like a good idea, but our car broke down a few miles south—just my luck. Made it through the flare, but then the engine light came on and the thing just died. We walked to here, and when we saw the place was deserted . . . well, it made sense to stay."

"Then you walk to Abney," Max said. "You could probably do it in a day if you leave at daylight."

"All right. That makes sense. When Zack's well—"

"Don't wait." Patrick warned them. "Leave tomorrow. Carry him if you have to, or find a wagon or something to pull him in. But don't wait. You're sitting ducks here."

Joel looked at Danielle, reached for her hand, and said, "All right. We'll leave tomorrow."

"Good deal." Max stood and walked to the window, peering out.

"How can we ever thank you?" Danielle asked.

Shelby pulled her chair up closer to the table. "Tell us about Austin."

Eight

Joel unfolded a state map onto the table. Shelby wanted to hurry him along. She wanted to tell him to just spit it out! But it was obvious that any discussion of what they'd been through in Austin was still painful. Joel stared at the map, blinking rapidly, and Danielle had walked away to wash dishes.

"Our condo was here, in Jolleyville. Danielle was a fifth grade teacher."

"Who did you work for?" Shelby asked.

"Software engineer." Joel glanced up, stared at her for a moment. "I was a software engineer. We . . . we knew that something like this might happen."

"Something like a flare?" Patrick asked.

61

"Nah. We didn't have a single protocol for that, but we knew the grid was vulnerable. Our biggest fear was cyber attacks. There was a specific process for shutting everything down, quickly, and saving what we could."

"Where exactly did you work?" Max pointed at the map. "Was the company also in Jolleyville?"

"Yeah. A place called IDS. Integrated Distribution Software. We wrote the code for everything from the scanners at your grocery store to how much fuel was shipped to your gas station. If an item isn't scanned, the computer doesn't know to reorder it."

"A person can't do that?"

"Only with an override code. Every aspect of distribution is automated now. When all of the systems went down—when they all went down at once, we knew it wasn't a cyber attack, which has more of a cascade effect."

"And then we saw the aurora." Danielle turned from the sink, wiping her hands on a dish towel.

"We were lucky to be home when it happened. Things were okay for a day or two. But when people realized the lights weren't coming back on, that the shelves at the grocery store weren't going to magically fill up again—then things turned nasty."

"Looting?" Bianca asked.

"Sure, there was some lawlessness. Some of the fires were probably set—out of anger or arrogance or maybe just stupidity. But there was also panic. Folks not knowing how to adjust. More fires broke out because people didn't know how to use a Coleman lantern, or had a lit candle too close to curtains, and when no one came to put the fires out? Then the panic accelerated. Our place—it burned on the third day."

"I'm so sorry." Shelby peered more closely at the map. "Why did you decide to go to Dallas?"

"No reason to stay where we were," Danielle said.

Joel stared at his wife for a moment, and to Shelby it seemed his emotions played across his face like a motion picture on a screen—love, regret, determination.

"We had no place to live, and we have friends and family in the Dallas area. Both of us went to college there."

"Why didn't you go straight up I-35?" Max asked.

"Because we'd heard of the traffic jams. The mayor of Austin supposedly was getting the Texas National Guard in to clear those up. At that point we were living in our car. I drove toward I-35 one afternoon, left Danielle and Zack at a friend's house. Couldn't even make it up the on-ramp. Abandoned cars as far as I could see."

"So you went back, picked up your family, and decided to come up Highway 281." Max traced his route until he landed in Briggs, Texas.

"Right. Our car broke down . . . ." He leaned

forward and pointed to a spot on the map. "Here. But before that we had to come through Cedar Park."

Joel glanced up from the map, looked at each of them until his gaze landed on Shelby. "I understand you need medicine for your boy, and I know I would do anything to get whatever Zack needed. But going through Cedar Park? It's not an option."

"Tell me why." Shelby kept the fear out of her voice. She forced herself to remain calm, to not give in to despair.

"The towns like Cedar Park couldn't patrol the entire area under their jurisdiction, so they pulled back."

"This happened in the first week?" Patrick shook his head in disgust.

"Pretty much." Joel ran his finger along Highway 183 until he reached a spot only a few miles north of Austin. "This area of the highway is lined with shopping centers, but they'd all been looted. When there was nothing left to loot, they were burned. When there was nothing left to burn, they began robbing people who attempted to drive through."

"So how did you get through?"

"Ran over one man." Joel's hand began to shake, and he clenched it into a fist. "I'm not proud of that. He stepped out in front of my car with a shotgun, and I just . . . I ran him over. I suppose I will still hear that sound—the sound of him under my car, until the day I die."

"There's no need to dwell on that," Danielle said. "You did what you had to do."

She turned back to Shelby. "If you insist on going south, take the back roads."

Patrick pushed in between Shelby and Max. Scowling at the map, he said, "It's too slow, and there are too many places where we could get into trouble. It's been almost three weeks since the flare. People have mostly stopped travelling. Thieves have probably turned their focus to secondary roads."

"And the National Guard could have moved some of the vehicles." Max traced Highway 281 to just south of Cedar Park, where SH 45 crossed. "We get up here, maybe we can see what's happening."

Bianca stood, pushing back the crate she had been sitting on. "We can hope that the local governments have had a chance to pull their resources together."

Dr. Bhatti looked as if he might refute that, but instead he shook his head and began repacking his medical bag.

"It's settled then." Shelby's resolve strengthened. They would find a way through. Together—they could do it. "We head south, straight through the center."

Nine

From Briggs to Cedar Park was exactly thirty miles, but it took them another hour and a half. They drove slowly and carefully. Abandoned cars became more frequent.

"Commuters, caught on the way home," Shelby murmured.

"At eight in the evening?" Bhatti's tone was doubtful.

"Maybe. People work late, or they did." Max waved at an abandoned van. "Then there are those leaving on vacation or going into town for a concert. We're a mobile society. At least we were."

The gas stations they passed were deserted. Max had been worried about the section of the road where Highway 29 crossed, but their only problem had been a giant crater in the middle of the intersection. They'd driven over the grassy shoulder to the service road and followed it for a mile before pulling back up on the highway.

"What could have caused that?" Shelby asked.

"A tanker explosion . . . possibly."

"But I didn't see any tankers."

"Could have been an IED," Bhatti suggested. "Wouldn't have been much left."

"What do you know about those?" Shelby turned to frown at him, but Bhatti offered no further comment.

More than once they pulled over to scope out the road before them.

No movement.

No sign of people anywhere.

"Where did everyone go?" Bianca asked as they stood in the hot Texas sun, Max and Patrick leaning against the hood of the Dodge and studying the road before them through the scope of their rifles. To the west, clouds were building. Each day Max realized something else that they'd lost. At the moment, he'd give a week's worth of provisions for an accurate weather forecast.

"Everyone's hunkered down, using the supplies they have." Patrick pulled a bottle of water from his pack and drank half of it. "That will work until they run out."

Max placed his rifle in the car, resting it upright between his seat and Shelby's. "If we find an untouched camping store, remind me to get a good pair of binoculars."

Shelby didn't even smile. She was in full-alert mode. They all were.

Half a mile before the SH 45 interchange, they again pulled to the side of the road.

"Looks blocked," Max said.

"We might be able to push a few out of the way." Patrick nodded toward the line of cars blocking every lane. "There are places near the median where we could squeeze through."

Bianca had put on a sun visor to ward off the sun. She yanked it off and waved it toward the mass of vehicles in front of them. "The question is, how many cars would we have to move? How far does this stretch? A quarter mile, half mile, or ten?"

"I know one way to find out." Max pointed up, to the SH 45 overpass.

"I'm going with you." Shelby was already pulling out her backpack, shrugging it over her shoulder, and covering her black curls with the battered Texas Rangers cap.

"We'll stay here," Patrick said. "Guard the vehicles."

"The range on these radios should stretch from here to the top of there." Max slipped one of the receivers into a side pocket of Shelby's pack. "You see anything, radio us. And if you have to, get out of here."

"We're not leaving you," Bianca said.

Even Bhatti looked alarmed.

"I didn't say leave us." Max turned in a full circle. Like Joel had warned them, the shopping centers to the left and the right were burned-out shells. "If anyone comes after you, take the cars and head back north."

Bianca crossed her arms and scowled at the flyover bridge. "Maybe it's not worth it. We should stay together."

"We could waste an entire day trying to get through on this road. On the other hand, we have no way to know what problems we'll confront on the secondary roads." Max glanced at his watch—three fifty in the afternoon. Four, maybe five more hours of light. The heat was beastly, but the long days might work to their advantage. "If we know what we're dealing with, we can make a better decision."

Shelby nodded.

Max threw one last look north, the direction they had come from. "If we are separated, everyone meet at the barn we passed on the west side of the road, just before Wheatstone Blvd."

"How do we know that's safe?" Bhatti asked.

Max retrieved his rifle as well as a backpack full of ammunition and emergency supplies. "We don't, but I doubt bandits will want to waste their fuel chasing you that far. They'll expect you to freeze, to be intimidated. Drive as fast as you can, lay low, and we'll meet you there."

They'd started to turn away, when Patrick said, "That's five miles, maybe six."

"Wait for us. Wait until daylight, and if we're not back, leave us."

"Not going to happen." Patrick actually grinned. "If you're not there by daybreak, we will find you. Check your radio at fifteen minutes after every hour."

"We're not going to be separated." Bianca

wrapped her arms around Shelby before reaching up and tugging down on the old ball cap. "It's a good look on you."

Shelby rolled her eyes and nodded to Max that she was ready.

The flyover rose eighty feet above them. Max remembered when they'd put it in, when Shelby had been afraid to drive over it.

"Why are you grinning?"

"No reason."

"Out with it, Berkman."

"Remembering the good old days."

That seemed to be explanation enough. They kept to a good pace, though the ramp was steeper than he'd expected.

He stopped her with a hand signal, unzipped her pack, and retrieved her pistol. Handing it to her, he whispered "Be ready," and shifted his rifle to his right hand.

But they needn't have worried. The abandoned cars they passed were deserted. The first few, they checked to see if there were any supplies, but someone had already taken care of that.

Glove compartments were open.

Center consoles ransacked.

Even the trunk areas had been cleaned out. He found an L-shaped lug wrench in one. It felt heavy and solid in his hand. Felt like something he might need if he were to run out of ammunition. Handing it to Shelby, he motioned for her to slip it in his pack.

The heat intensified. The concrete ramp seemed to absorb the sun, or perhaps it was that they were completely in the open now. They were vulnerable, an easy target if anyone were close enough to take a shot.

But they encountered no one as they ascended to the top of the ramp—a bypass that politicians had been quite proud of, claiming it would ease the gridlock of traffic that ensnared their capital. As if by mutual agreement, both had kept their eyes on the ground, the area directly in front of them, the vehicles they skirted.

It wasn't until they reached the apex that they stopped, set their packs on the ground, and turned to study the devastation to the south.

Ten

Shelby wasn't prepared. She'd thought she was, but who could prepare their mind or their heart for the length and width of destruction that lay out before them? Her world tilted, began to spin, and she grasped the side of the bridge.

Max pulled her back—his arms on her shoulders, his voice soft and steady in her ear.

"Not so close, Sparks. Wouldn't want you to blow over."

The wind had picked up, or perhaps it was just that they were standing eight stories up. She glanced west, saw the darkening clouds moving ever closer, and then she turned back toward Austin.

"I'm okay." She shrugged away from him but remained a good three feet from the edge. No sense in surviving the flare, the fires, the gas explosions, and the carjackings, just to fall off a bridge. She'd never forgive herself. The thought struck her as funny, hilarious actually, and she nearly broke out laughing.

Or maybe she was hysterical.

Slapping both hands over her mouth, she continued to stare south.

"Worse than we thought," Max admitted.

"The road is—"

"Impassable, as far as we can see." Cars filled every lane. Some had their hoods up but most were simply abandoned. Had they stopped the moment the flare hit? Even the older model cars, which still worked, had had no way to drive through the gridlock.

Even more disturbing than the massive, desolate traffic jam was the widespread destruction.

"How could there be so many fires? And why didn't we notice it earlier?"

"I suppose we've grown used to the smell. I never would have guessed."

Spirals of smoke rose from every direction—Austin was burning.

Max squinted at something, grabbed his rifle, and stared through the scope. Finally, he handed it to her. "Look to the southeast."

As she stared through the rifle, she at first only saw car after car—burned out or simply abandoned, and every one an impediment to her mission. But then Max turned her slightly, and she felt hope beat like the light, steady motion of a butterfly's wings.

"Who is that?"

"Texas Army National Guard, I suppose."

"So is it state or national? I should know the answer to that question, but I don't."

"Made up of the US Army, the US National Guard, and the Texas Military Forces. Trained and equipped by the army."

"And that's who we're seeing?"

"I suppose. I can see tanks, transports, even all-terrain vehicles. Can't make out any insignia from here, but who else would it be?"

"Foreign invaders? Terrorists who have taken over a military supply depot? Bandits who needed bigger trucks to continue taking over our cities?"

"Hey. Look at me." Max practically snatched the rifle from her hands. "Look at me, Shelby. We are not giving up. I don't know who that is or what they're doing, but it could be someone who will help us. One way or another, we're going to find out."

She closed her eyes, tried to quiet the war

between hope and despair that threatened to push her over the edge, and nodded slightly.

"You're right. I just . . . I didn't expect this." Her hand took in the entire vista, southeast to southwest.

"I know you didn't."

Max turned to look back the way they had come. Shelby followed him to the opposite side of the road. She could just make out their two vehicles below.

"Patrick must have moved them," Max said.

"Across the lanes? Why?"

"In case there's trouble. By putting them across the road, he can go north—"

"Back the way we came."

"Or south."

"Not far though. Thousands of cars blocking the way south."

Patrick waved something at them, and Max pulled the radio out of her pack.

Shelby felt a wave of relief wash over her at the sound of Patrick's voice.

"You two going to have a picnic up there or tell us what's going on?"

"The destruction is widespread." Max hesitated, glancing behind him and then forward again. "There is some military movement to the southeast. If we can reach them—"

Shelby was watching Patrick and listening to Max, and her eyes picked up on what was happening a fraction of a second before her ears did.

Patrick jerked his head to the left, and then she heard the roar of an approaching vehicle, followed by the *tat-a-tat-tat* of a semiautomatic rifle.

Max once again pulled her back from the edge, but then they both realized that whoever was approaching wasn't paying any attention to the top of the bridge. Probably they couldn't see the two of them from the ground, even if they were looking straight up.

She heard the sound of slamming doors, and then Patrick's Mustang followed by Max's Dodge made a hard left and sped north, back the way they had come.

Max snatched up his rifle again, and she thought he would take a shot, attempt to disable the vehicles that were gaining on their friends.

"Too far," he mumbled, continuing to stare through the rifle's scope.

"What happened? Did they get away? Are they all right?"

He shrugged, dropped the rifle, and wiped the sweat from his eyes. Raising it again, he attempted once more to see. Finally he admitted, "I don't know. Patrick and Bianca were driving. They had a good lead. I think they're going to be all right."

Shelby suddenly realized there was no place to hide, no place at all to take cover unless you counted the abandoned cars, and they'd be sitting ducks there.

"We have to get off here," Max said, mirroring her thoughts. "They might come back. They might have seen Patrick looking up at us."

They jogged back to the bottom of the ramp. Fear and uncertainty collided with the physical exertion and heat. Shelby wiped continuously at the sweat pouring into her eyes. Her shirt was drenched, and she hadn't cinched the waist buckle on the backpack, so it swung left and right, left and right, chafing against her back. But she didn't slow, and she didn't lose her grip on the handgun. It would do little good against a maniac intent on running them over, but she'd at least go down shooting.

That was the mantra that ran through her mind.

Go down shooting.

How had her life become this?

How had any sense of normalcy slipped away so quickly and completely?

When they reached the bottom of the ramp, Max pulled her into the shade of one of the support pillars.

"Drink. I don't need you passing out." They both downed half a bottle, then stuck them back in their packs.

"We go that way," he said, indicating the feeder road that passed Lakeline Mall. "We stick to the shadows, move quickly, and stop for nothing. Got it?"

She nodded her understanding, still trying to catch her breath. And then they were again running, her ears filled with the sound of their hiking boots against the concrete and her heart filled with fear.

Eleven

Shelby nearly collapsed against the side of the building—Babies "R" Us. Actually, the R was backwards. Her mind fixated on that, wondering who had come up with the marketing plan, while she pulled in giant gulps of air and held her hand against her side.

"Still get that stitch when you run?"

"I try not to run."

"Yeah." Max slid down the wall beside her until he was sitting on the pavement, groaning as he did.

"Feeling old, Max?"

"Old and out of shape. Wishing I'd made the time to work out more. So many regrets."

He was joking again, but Shelby heard the seriousness behind his last three words.

"Regrets are useless now."

"This has been hard for you, Shelby. Harder even than for the rest of us."

Tears pricked her eyes, but she blinked them away. She felt so raw, so vulnerable all the time, but she wasn't ready to share that. It would only bring the pain to the surface. So instead of admitting he was on target, she changed the subject.

"How far are we walking? To the barn?"

"That's the plan."

"Do you think those guys in the SUV will come back?"

"They probably have a place to hole up—a base, but they approached from the east, so it's not here."

"Then we're safe."

"We might be safe from them. I don't know . . ." He lowered his voice. "We can't know what we have to pass through between here and there. We move quietly, cautiously, and as quickly as we can."

"That's a lot of adverbs."

"Ever the writer. Glad the flare didn't change that."

He helped her to her feet, and when his hand touched hers she fought the urge to throw herself into his arms. She wasn't a damsel in distress. She was a mom on a mission. She pulled back her hand and stepped away.

"You good?"

"Yeah."

The first two sections of the shopping center were deserted. Max stopped before reaching the end of each building, listened, poked his head around the corner, and looked left then right. He would give her the signal to wait, and then he'd cross. Once he was sure it was clear, he'd motion for her. It was a slow, laborious process, and Shelby was beginning to think that his paranoia was uncalled for. Who would be living in these burned-out buildings? The smell alone was atrocious, and then there were the rats that scurried away from the sound of their footsteps.

It was as they'd begun making their way down the third building—a string of shoe stores, dress shops, and children's apparel boutiques—that they first heard people. Max snatched her hand and pulled her into the darkness of a Shoe Warehouse. They stood frozen, their backs against the charred remnants of the inside wall, as a group of people passed.

"I'm telling you, the Guard is widening their perimeter."

A man coughed, stopped, and then Shelby heard the flick of a lighter followed by the smell of cigarette smoke.

"They're pushing out the fences, block by block."

"And clearing the highways."

"Yeah, maybe so."

Shelby realized with a start that the man speaking was standing on the other side of the charred wall—no more than five feet from where she and Max hid.

No one spoke for a minute, then two.

"It's going to be a long time before they get here," he said. "Maybe months."

79

"And then what?" a woman asked.

"We'll be gone by then. But in the meantime, there's still stuff to lift."

"Not much. We've pretty much emptied out this area. And who is going to buy it anyway?"

"We don't sell it. We trade it—for what we need. And if anyone tries to stop us? We do what we did to that security guard. We kill them."

This man, who must have been the leader of the trio, dropped his cigarette to the pavement and ground it out with his boot. It struck Shelby as ironic that he would bother to do so. It seemed to her that everything that could burn had burned.

They continued to talk as they walked away, oblivious to the fact that anyone else was there. Shelby started out, but Max pulled her back. "Not yet," he whispered.

The words were barely out of his mouth when they again heard the sound of steps.

"Better get the lead out."

"I'm hurrying, man."

"Just saying. Spike cut the last guy who was too slow."

When the pair had passed, Shelby didn't move immediately. She waited. Max checked his watch a couple of times, and finally they continued in the opposite direction of the group. They didn't speak of it until the rain had started to fall, drenching everything within the first few moments. Thunder crashed so close that it felt as if the ground shook. She was aware of lightning striking to the west, but she didn't bother to look up. Head down, shoulders hunched, they continued to make their way north.

When they had to lean forward into the wind to make any progress, Max waved toward a small building on the south side of yet another strip mall they were trudging through.

There wasn't a lot left of the front of the building, and absolutely nothing of value inside, but the back of the room still had an intact roof and provided cover from the worst of the storm.

"Sheltering in a coffee hut? Cruel and unusual punishment." She pulled her shirt away from her body, wringing the front.

Max had sat down and removed his shoes. She wasn't too surprised to see him pulling dry socks from his pack.

"Cruel, huh? What would you like? A latte? Maybe a cappuccino?"

"I can smell it, you know. Underneath the top layer of wetness and then the bottom layer of charred lumber—coffee beans." She closed her eyes and inhaled deeply.

"It's the small things," Max agreed. "I repeatedly reach for my phone to check the weather app—even after three weeks."

"Old habits—"

"Die hard."

They grinned at one another, and then Max

cleared his throat and said, "Better put on some dry clothes." He stood, padded toward the opposite side of the room, and waited at the very edge of their shelter, his back politely turned toward her.

She'd given him the all clear, and they were pulling out food when her thoughts drifted back to the first group that had passed them.

"Spike." Shelby unwrapped a granola bar and frowned at it. "What kind of person names their kid Spike? You might as well fill out his prison papers while you're working on his birth certificate."

Max finished a protein bar and washed it down with the last of his water. He stood and walked to where the rain was pouring through the holes in the roof. The place had burned at one point, but it hadn't consumed the entire structure. He set both of his bottles and the one she'd finished under the hole, waited to be sure they wouldn't topple over, and then he moved back beside her. He sat close enough that their shoulders were touching. Normally, Shelby would pull away, but not this afternoon.

"Not his legal name, I'm sure." When she didn't answer, he added, "I saw a lot of that in the courtroom. It was as if people needed to reinvent themselves to justify what they did—Speedy, Arson, Blaze, and the most popular—Harley."

"Blaze? Seriously?"

"Yes, though that was an interesting case. Blaze was afraid of fire, but he had no problem knocking over post offices."

"Post offices?"

"He'd serve time, get out, and go straight to a post office. It was a compulsion of sorts."

Shelby leaned her head back against the wall. "I didn't realize you dealt with such cases."

"It wasn't the majority of my business, but now and then a parent would come to me trying to prevent their child from serving jail time."

"I can't even conceive such a life."

"Yeah. But we couldn't have imagined this one either."

She didn't have an answer for that. It wasn't lost on her that were it not for her, were it not for how much Max and Bianca and Patrick cared for her and Carter, her friends would be in their homes tonight—dry and safe.

"Try to get some rest. We'll leave as soon as the storm passes through."

"What if it doesn't? What if it's one of those rain-for-days monsoons?"

"This thing has turned you into quite the doomsayer." Max nudged her shoulder with his before he stood and picked up his rifle. "We'll give it two hours, and then we go whether the rain has stopped or not."

But she'd seen too much, experienced too wide a range of emotions in the previous twelve hours.

Sleep felt a long way off. So instead, she pulled out her notebook, opened to a new page, and stared at it.

Max turned and stared at her quizzically. "Writer's block?" he asked.

She laughed, but it was a small, bleak sound, and it died quickly. "I have no idea how to describe this."

He walked back over, sat beside her, and pulled the notebook from her hands. Slowly and methodically he began to sketch the scene in front of them—the burned-out building, the storm, the darkness beyond. She had forgotten how much Max had liked to draw. He'd given up all of that when he went away to college, or so she'd thought.

Somehow the sound of the pen whispering quietly across the pages calmed her nerves and lulled her into an exhausted sleep.

Twelve

Max watched Shelby sleep and listened to the storm as it moved off to the east. He didn't want to wake her, couldn't begin to imagine how she was dealing with her fear and anxiety. He understood Carter would not survive if they didn't find the insulin.

But they would find it.

He'd run all of their options through his mind as

he'd waited out the storm. Basically, they didn't have any. They had to move forward, into Austin. They had to find the medication that Carter and the citizens of Abney needed. Surely, God would help them do that. He'd never been one to think of God as a genie—say the right words, invoke the name of Christ, and anything could be yours. That sort of theology had always rankled him.

But neither could he accept that God wanted them all to die. His day to leave behind this| mortal clay would come—as would everyone's, but it wasn't today.

He shook Shelby's shoulders. She jerked awake, wide-eyed and ready to run.

"It's all right." He waited until she nodded and accepted the bottle of rainwater he offered her. After she'd drunk from it, he said, "The storm's moved out. We can go."

She gathered up her supplies and stuffed them in the backpack, including the notebook, but paused to stare at the two sketches he'd drawn. The first was of the coffee shop they sheltered in. The second was of her standing on top of the flyover bridge, shoulders back, gaze steady, determination in her features. It might not have been exactly how she had looked, but it was how he saw her.

"This looks like Joan of Arc," she said, tapping the page.

"It's you!"

"Hardly."

"It is. See the hair flying around her face?"

She glanced up at him. "This person you drew is brave. I jump when someone says boo."

Max shrugged and pulled his own pack onto his shoulders. Shelby Sparks was the bravest woman he knew, but there was no use trying to tell her that. As far as the drawing, he didn't think it was particularly good, but it had been a relief to do something, to create something, to stop, even for a moment, simply reacting. It had actually filled him with energy, which was a little surprising.

They stepped out into a day that was fading to night. Looking west, streaks from the setting sun colored the sky orange, purple, even a deep blue.

Shelby clutched his arm and pointed east. "That has to mean something, right?"

He hoped so. The rainbow hung perfectly arched over the eastern scene of destruction—large apartment complexes built nearly on top of each other. Most looked deserted. Some had been burned and looted. It was obvious from the debris slung across the parking areas that no one was living there any longer.

The rainbow seemed to defy the devastation.

God's blessing? Maybe.

They'd made it to the end of yet another shopping center strip, when he nearly tripped over a man who appeared to be sleeping on the sidewalk, just under the roof's overhang.

"Give a brother a hand? Or maybe you have

86

something to sip that would keep me warm?"

Shelby looked as if she might answer him, but Max shook his head and pulled her along.

The man called after them. "Don't be like that. Uncle Charlie wouldn't hurt you none."

He increased his pace until Shelby was practically running to catch up.

"You worried about that guy?"

"I worry about every guy."

"How much farther do we have to go?"

"Maybe four miles."

"I need to use the bathroom."

He stopped, glanced around them, and finally pointed toward a Dumpster.

"Behind there?"

"See anyplace better?"

"No. Unfortunately, I don't."

She scuttled off to the far side of the Dumpster. Max stood waiting, trying to be patient, when he heard the sound of voices. They weren't close, but the fact that they weren't bothering to whisper worried him. More of Spike's goons, if he had to guess.

He hurried toward Shelby, deciding it would be better to embarrass her than for them to get caught by hoodlums, and pulled up short when he heard a voice on the other side of the Dumpster.

"What's a little thing like you doing out here all alone?" The voice was male, gravelly, and to Max's ears the person sounded strung out.

"Why do you think I'm alone?"

"Because no one's with you. Now how about you toss that backpack over here and let me see what's in it."

Max soundlessly set his backpack on the ground and pulled out his semiautomatic. Then he heard the voices from the far side of the block, not any closer, but not going away. He let go of the gun and reached for the lug wrench.

Closing his eyes, he tried to picture where the man would be positioned in relation to Shelby. There was no way to know.

He could hear that the man had unzipped the backpack and was rifling through her things.

"Nice little gun, missy. Too bad you weren't carrying it in your pocket. Might have saved your life."

Max stepped around the Dumpster. Shelby was facing him. The man standing in front of her, with his back to Max, was raising the gun. Shelby's mouth formed an *O,* but she didn't say a word, and Max didn't hesitate. He swung the wrench as if he were holding a bat and hoping for a home run. The man collapsed in a heap.

"Are you okay?"

But Shelby was already on the ground, throwing everything back into her pack. Her hands were shaking, but that didn't slow her down. Max retrieved his pack and stuffed the lug wrench into it.

Shelby glanced back toward the voices and then nodded in the direction they'd been headed. They jogged for the next fifteen minutes, putting space and time and destruction between the hoodlums and themselves.

The sky grew dark with no moon at all, but their eyes adjusted. Stars shimmered in the west. The storm continued to rumble to their east. At first they kept to the grassy shoulder of the service road, being as inconspicuous as possible. But as they put more distance between them and the SH 45 interchange, Max led the way up onto the shoulder of Highway 183.

"Should be able to make better time now."

"Did you kill that man?"

"I don't know."

He thought that would be the end of it, but she reached out a hand, squeezed his arm, and said, "Thank you."

And how did he answer that? How did he admit to Shelby that he would sacrifice his life for her?

The next hour passed without encountering anyone else, unless you counted the two times they heard cars in the distance. Both of those times, Shelby had frozen in the middle of the road.

"Long way off," he'd assured her. "We're about halfway. Maybe one more hour."

During the day he'd done a good job of keeping his doubts at bay. But as the clock ticked toward midnight, those doubts pressed in, nearly pushing him to the ground.

Had it been foolish to split up their group?

Did Patrick and Bianca and Bhatti get away unharmed?

Would they encounter Spike again?

How many other groups like his were in the city?

The questions circled round and round, and try as he might he couldn't find a single answer.

Soon Shelby was pulling him to a stop and pointing to a barely discernible shadow to their northwest.

"That it?"

"Yeah."

"Should we call first? So they don't, you know, shoot us?"

"Good idea." He pulled out a flashlight, and Shelby checked her watch.

"We wait here until quarter past the hour."

Thirty minutes later, he turned on the radio.

"Patrick, you there?"

Nothing but silence. Shelby was standing close enough that he could hear her breathing, practically feel her pulse. "Try again," she said.

"Patrick, come in. Are you there?"

"We're here." He must have been standing guard because he sounded wide awake.

"Just knocking on the door, buddy. Shelby didn't want you to shoot us."

"I always said she was the brains of the group."

"Okay. We're coming in."

"West side."

They hurried across the field, their steps lighter, anticipating the reunion.

Bianca and Bhatti were sleeping, but they both struggled to a sitting position as Max and Shelby and Patrick greeted one another. Patrick slapped Max on the back and pulled Shelby into a hug, sweeping her off her feet.

Bianca hopped up and practically threw herself at the two of them. Bhatti shook Max's hand and nodded toward Shelby.

"Tell us what happened," Max said.

So they sat near an upturned flashlight—Bianca and Shelby next to one another, Patrick and Max on either side of the girls, and Bhatti completing their circle.

"Not much to tell." Patrick placed his rifle on the ground next to him. "They managed to shoot out one of your side view mirrors."

"That's all?"

"Yeah. We got lucky."

"We saw you and Bianca peel away, but then nothing else."

"Bianca's driving is as good as mine, but it was Bhatti who saved us."

All eyes turned to the doctor, who shrugged his shoulders and offered no opinion.

"What happened?" Shelby asked.

"They never would have caught my Mustang.

That old jalopy of yours, though—well, they were gaining on us." There was no mistaking the laughter in Patrick's voice, but then he grew more serious. "The SUV was bearing down on Bianca."

"And what? You shot out the tires?"

"I shot the driver," Bhatti said.

"You killed him?" Shelby's voice rose in alarm.

Patrick came to Bhatti's defense. "Kill or be killed, Shelby. We didn't have a choice. We're fortunate that Bhatti knows his way around a rifle."

Max was watching the doctor, trying to put together several things at once.

On the first night he'd met him, Bhatti had admitted that he "needed some distance from a situation in Austin."

Shelby claiming she'd seen him bury something under a tree in Max's backyard.

Bhatti's comment about the IED.

And now this—his proficiency with a rifle.

Patrick was describing how they'd found the barn, confirmed it was empty, and then moved inside. He'd been checking the perimeter every thirty minutes but hadn't seen any sign of other people.

Max was listening to Patrick and thinking about Bhatti, when suddenly the quietness of the evening was broken by the sound of a truck.

They stood and grabbed their weapons. Max

climbed up the stairs into the loft. When he looked out the window, he knew they were in trouble. More than a dozen men were quietly exiting the truck, moving into position to surround the barn. He could see them because the guy in charge—an older guy with a completely white beard and mustache, had turned on a spotlight which would blind anyone coming out the front of the barn.

And then the man picked up a bullhorn. "Leave your weapons inside and come out with your hands up."

Thirteen

Carter couldn't sleep.

He'd put in a full day of work. In fact, his muscles were screaming at him to stay in bed, which his mother had set up on the back porch of the cottage.

Max's parents had suggested that he move back into the main house, but Carter resisted and they didn't push. He wanted to be here when his mother came back. He wanted to believe that she was coming back. And besides—if he wasn't safe here, he wasn't safe anywhere.

He couldn't blame his insomnia on hunger. Georgia had fried the catfish to perfection.

His blood sugar level was fine. He'd checked it before climbing into bed.

But something had woken him up. What?

The storm had long since passed through, and everything smelled fresh—clean, even. Seeing the dark clouds approach, they'd gathered up every pot and bottle they could find and set them out in the yard.

"But we have the springs, and you have a hand pump on your well." He'd been surprised when he first arrived at High Fields to learn there was water when you turned on the tap. Roy had explained that there was a generator in the pump house. When the electricity went out, the generator kicked in. In the first week he'd switched back over to the old windmill built next to the pump house in order to conserve generator power. It ran on gas, and there was a limited supply of that.

As he'd set out the pots to catch rain water, Carter wondered if Roy was looking for work to keep him busy. But Max's father wasn't like that. Carter was quickly learning that there was plenty of work on a ranch. No one had to think up extra things to do.

"The springs can go low," Roy explained. "Down to a trickle in July or August. I've seen it happen before."

"What about the well?"

"It's never gone dry, but twice the water level has dropped so low that we had sand running into the kitchen sink. Not something that made Georgia happy."

So they'd put containers everywhere and waited. In his mind, Carter began designing a new water reclamation system. With the surface area of the barn's roof, they should be able to catch quite a bit. They could store it in barrels or tanks and use it to water the vegetable garden. He'd even sketched out some ideas and shown them to Roy, who had nodded and said, "Good to have you around, son. I never would have come up with that. Max said you were a bright one."

Max had said that about him?

The rain hadn't disappointed them, but the storm had passed through hours ago.

Why was he awake?

Then he heard it again, the sound of wheels on gravel. He'd fallen asleep fully dressed, so all he had to do was put on his shoes and grab his rifle. He made it outside the same time that Roy did.

"Georgia needs you to go with her."

"Where?"

"There's been an accident. Tate Markham was hurt."

"What about the vet? Wouldn't he be better able to—"

"Jerry Lambert left yesterday for Hamilton looking for more livestock vaccine. I want you to go and help however you can."

Georgia hurried out the front door, paused to squeeze her husband's arm and nod at Carter,

95

and then she was practically running toward the idling truck.

"Should I leave my rifle?"

"Always keep that rifle with you, son. Now hurry. Don't want to keep them waiting."

Carter didn't have time to ask why he was going and why Roy was staying at High Fields, but he didn't have to wonder for long.

"Roy is passing the word on for the guards on roadblock duty to be on the lookout." Georgia cleared her throat. "Andy, how did it happen?"

"Ambushed down near the low water crossing an hour ago."

"Any idea who did it?"

"No, but if I find out, the person will regret the moment he pulled the trigger."

Georgia didn't respond to that. She waited, and then she asked, "Why was he out so late?"

The man—he must have been Tate's father—rubbed a hand over his face. He'd never once glanced back at Carter or over at Georgia. His eyes were completely focused on slinging the truck around corners and crossing cattle guards at a speed that rattled the fillings in Carter's teeth.

"A girl. He snuck out to go and see a girl."

"And the injury?"

"Shoulder."

Carter still couldn't fathom why Georgia had wanted him to ride along. How could he help?

For that matter, how could she? They slammed to a stop in front of a double-wide trailer with a rather large deck built across the front. Tate's father jumped out of the truck and took the steps two at a time, Georgia close on his heels.

Carter glanced around before entering the home. A small Chevy S-10 truck was parked in the middle of the yard. Carter walked over, reached out, and touched the bullet hole in the front windshield. The driver's door remained open. Peering inside, he was able to make out dark, wet spots on the upholstery. He shut the door, shifted his rifle to his left hand, and hurried toward the house—skirting around a basketball, a bicycle, and a box of cans that someone had been using for target practice.

There was a single light on in the living room. A boy of about ten years old sat on the couch, his legs pulled up and his arms circled around them. He nodded toward the left, and Carter made his way down a darkened hall.

He stepped into a small bedroom, probably the size of his room back in Abney. There were two beds and one dresser. A lantern on the dresser bathed the teenager lying on the bed in a bright light. Black curtains had been pulled across the window.

"I'm going out to keep watch." The father turned to Carter. "You come and get me if anything . . ."

For a split second the hardened expression on Andy Markham's face cracked. It was like watching a curtain be pulled back to reveal the man underneath. The naked pain and fear there reminded Carter of Kaitlyn's mom the day of her funeral. It reminded him of the hurt and bitterness that he was still fighting to overcome. Bile rose in his throat, and he feared he might lose last night's dinner, right there in Tate Markham's room as the boy bled to death from a gunshot wound.

"Come get me if anything changes."

And then Andy Markham was gone.

Georgia pulled Carter to the far side of the room. "I'm going to need your help. I need you to hand me things. Follow my instructions closely. We have to work quickly, and we have to do it right. We won't get a second chance at this."

"But I don't know anything about gunshot wounds."

"Just follow my directions."

He wanted to run. Right that moment, he wanted to rush back through the living room, out into the night, and run until he found himself back in his old life. Only that life didn't exist anymore, and Georgia needed his help. Tate needed his help. The younger brother on the couch and the father outside were depending on their help.

So instead of running, Carter said, "All right. Tell me what to do."

Fourteen

Max confirmed what he was seeing from all four windows of the barn's loft, one situated on each side. Then he slung his rifle over his shoulder and hurried back down the ladder.

Patrick and Bianca were at the west side of the main room, positioned on either side of the large doors. Shelby stood near a window on the north side, and Bhatti was covering the south. Max motioned them to the middle of the room.

"There's at least a dozen men, all armed, and they've surrounded the barn."

"What do they want?" Shelby hissed.

"Doesn't matter." Patrick's expression was inscrutable, his voice hard. "We're not walking out of here without a fight."

"First thing we need to do is knock out the rack of spotlights on top of their vehicle, which can't be done from here. The driver positioned the vehicle where we don't have a shot."

"They've done this before."

"Yeah. Looks like we walked right into somebody's territory."

Max nodded toward the ladder. "I think it could be done from upstairs, but it won't be an easy shot."

"I've got it," Patrick said.

Max took his position near the doors.

Patrick's first shot missed, but the second found its mark, plunging them back into darkness. Max flipped his rifle's thermal night scope to the on position. Standing to the side of a window, he rested the barrel of his rifle on the ledge and scoped left to right. At first he saw nothing, but then someone stepped out from the left. Max would have hit his mark, but the man fired at the same time he did. The window he was looking out of exploded.

The bullet didn't hit him, but shards of glass did.

Shelby screamed.

Max jumped away from the window.

Bianca let loose a barrage of fire.

"Save your ammo," Max called out just as the barn doors burst open and the entire group rushed into the room.

Eleven weapons trained on five.

No one flinched. No one lowered their firearm. Then they were bathed in the headlights of the truck, and a twelfth man walked in—leaving no doubt in Max's mind that he was the group's leader. He scanned his people quickly to make sure no one was hurt and assessed what they were up against, his gaze pausing as he noted the blood running down Max's face.

With the precision and execution of the attack, Max would have expected a military guy to be in charge. The man who stopped in the center of the room didn't look like a member of the armed forces. His stomach strained the buttons of a denim shirt. He sported a thick white beard and mustache, but his head was bald.

Max couldn't actually feel the cuts on his face—maybe because of the adrenaline coursing through his veins, or possibly the cuts weren't deep. He forced himself to ignore the blood dripping down his forehead, cheeks, even into his eyes. Blinking, he gripped his rifle more tightly, careful to keep the leader in his sight.

They might be outnumbered. They might die in the next few minutes, but if they did, this man would die with them.

"Maybe we should all put down our weapons," the older man said.

"Why would we do that?" Patrick was perched halfway down the ladder, also training his rifle on the leader, and he looked completely at ease.

"Because you're on my property? Because you're outnumbered? Because we'd rather talk than shoot? Take your pick."

"You have a funny way of starting a conversation," Max said.

"Didn't know what we were going to find in here. Do yourself a favor and lower your weapons."

"Put yours down first."

"Not going to happen." This from a man who had the shape of a professional athlete and was carrying an M-16.

"It seems we have quite the standoff." Instead of looking worried, the leader chuckled. He turned to a small, thin guy. "Micah. These folks seem to require a show of faith. You and your five men lower your weapons."

Max's head jerked up at the man's words. He finally took his eyes off the leader, glancing toward Patrick, who also looked startled.

Could it be that simple?

Could they trust what Pastor Tony had told them? Or was it a coincidence? The leader was studying them, waiting.

If they fought, they had no chance of surviving. But if what he'd heard was the signal . . .

He glanced again at Patrick, who nodded once. Pulling in a steadying breath, Max said, "I'm putting mine down, and so will the rest of our group."

Bianca and Shelby both began to protest, but Max had already set his rifle on the ground. "Trust me. Put them on the ground and take two steps back."

Fifteen

Carter was pretty sure he was going to be sick.

The boy lying on the bed looked to be fifteen or sixteen. The stench of blood filled the room, and he wished that he could open the window, turn on a fan, anything. But fans were a thing of the past, and opening the window would make them a target if anyone was out there.

He watched as Georgia opened what looked like a makeup bag and began pulling out bandages and creams. "Can you sit up, Tate? I need to see if the bullet came out the other side."

The boy's face was whiter than his sheets. His dark hair flopped into his eyes, and he looked left and right as if he couldn't focus on one thing for longer than a split second.

"Pa said it went through."

"Let me see for myself." She slipped on a pair of disposable gloves and motioned for Carter to do the same. "Help me sit him up."

Pulling scissors from her bag, she cut away the blood-soaked shirt. "All right. That's good. Carter, hand me the bottle of water."

He didn't notice it had a squirt top until she began cleaning the wound, squirting the water on it in short rhythmic bursts. Tate didn't holler, though it must have hurt. Instead, he began to shiver, his teeth actually knocking together. Sweat broke out across his forehead, and his breathing became faster.

"He's going into shock," Georgia explained. "Try to keep the blankets tight around him. Can you do that and help me?"

Carter nodded and yanked up on the blankets with his right hand. With his left he held a clean towel below where she was working, to catch the water as it ran off the wound—stained with blood and containing bits of cloth.

When she'd finished, he handed her several of the gauze pads. She squirted antibiotic ointment onto the first and pressed it to the wound, then covered that with another pad and yet another.

"Help me lay him back." She repeated the procedure on the front of the wound.

"Will I . . . will I . . . lose my arm?"

"No. I don't think so, Tate. Must have been a small caliber bullet—clean entry, clean exit, and I don't see a lot of damage. Can you wiggle your fingers?"

When he did so, a wide smile replaced Georgia's concerned expression.

"You boys, you're living in a different time now. A time when sneaking off to see a girl could get you killed." She shook her head and motioned for Carter to help Tate sit up as she wound a bandage around his shoulder—under the arm, up and over, back and around. "Isn't fair, but it's something you're going to have to accept."

Carter thought again of Kaitlyn, thought of what he would have done to see her, and felt a sudden empathy with Tate.

"Yes, Mrs. Berkman." Tate refused to meet her gaze. He continued to shake, but already his color was better. "Same thing my pa said."

"Well, your pa is right, and he needs you around

104

here. So does your brother. So no more stupid stunts."

As Carter bagged all of their soiled towels, Georgia asked Tate if he felt well enough to drink some water. He'd stopped shaking, which Carter thought must be a good sign. Georgia helped him to drink from the water bottle, and then she pulled the covers up and turned down the lantern. "We'll send your brother in, and I'll come back around lunchtime tomorrow to check on you again."

Tate's father drove them home in silence. It wasn't until he'd stopped in front of Georgia and Roy's house that he turned to her and said, "Thank you."

"Of course, Andy."

"I'm indebted to you. If you ever need anything, please just let me know."

Instead of answering, she patted his hand. Together Georgia and Carter walked into the house. Roy must have seen them coming, because he already had hot water heating on the stove. He placed a cup, saucer, and bag of tea in front of Georgia as soon as they sat down. "Water will be ready in a minute."

He kissed her on top of the head, and Carter looked away, suddenly embarrassed by the affection that passed between the two of them.

"Hot chocolate?" Roy asked Carter, which made Carter smile. His mother would never have offered that.

"I'll just have some water." But he was suddenly ravenous and gladly accepted a cold biscuit and the jar of peanut butter.

"Is the boy going to be okay?" Roy asked.

"I think so, though I wish I had antibiotics to give him."

"Maybe Shelby and Max will bring some back."

"We could go house to house and round up old prescriptions." Carter popped half the biscuit into his mouth, surprised that he could be hungry after treating someone with a gunshot wound.

"Not a bad idea," Georgia admitted.

"It's what we did in Abney. Mom, she collected all of ours in this bin—I think she was hoping to trade it in Austin. But Mayor Perkins, asked everyone to bring what they had to the hospital, so it could be dispensed to folks who need it."

"Sounds like your mayor has a good head on her shoulders." Roy poured the hot water over the tea bag and sat down next to Georgia.

"I guess. Some people refused, saying they had to look out for their own families. Others, though, realized they might need something they didn't have, so they gladly donated."

Georgia dunked the tea bag up and down, and then she wrapped it around a spoon and pressed it against the side of her cup. "I imagine someone around here has some leftover penicillin. Even a few days' worth would be a big help in Tate's recovery."

"Maybe Carter can start going house to house tomorrow." Roy grinned at him as he sat next to his wife, folding his hands around an old coffee mug. "Now tell me about Tate."

Georgia sighed as she rubbed at a muscle on the back of her neck. "God was watching over that boy tonight. He'd snuck out after his father thought he was in bed—wanted to go and see a girl. On his way back, someone ambushed him at the low water crossing."

"So he went outside our perimeter?"

"Not on the road—he drove across a few pastures and then down into a spot in the river where the cattle cross. Stupid thing for a boy to do." Georgia sighed. "What was he thinking?"

"He wasn't." Carter finished another biscuit and gulped down the cup of water. "When Kaitlyn was alive, I would have done something like that. I didn't . . . I didn't understand how much things had changed."

Roy and Georgia waited. He loved that about Max's parents. Somewhere along the way, they'd learned to wait, to listen, to allow a person to work through things in their own time.

"After she died?" Carter shook his head. "Well, then I understood that this was our life for good. That things weren't changing back—even though a part of my mind already knew that. But inside, I guess I was still hoping."

"Hope is an important thing," Georgia said.

"Maybe. But it can also get you shot." Carter stood and walked to the door, stopped, and turned back. "Where did you learn that? To patch up gunshot wounds?"

Georgia smiled, and though it held a good bit of sadness in it, the expression lightened something in Carter's heart. "Max wasn't always the careful person he is now. That boy had more stitches by the time he was twelve—"

"Was he ever shot, though?"

"No. We were spared that. Same principle applies—clean the wound, swab on some sort of salve, and bind or stitch it up."

Carter said good night and walked back over to his cottage. Georgia and Roy were something else. They took whatever came their way with such calmness and faith. He wasn't sure he could ever be like that. He wasn't sure he had any faith left. But maybe that, as well as staying calm, was something he could learn. Setting his rifle next to his bed, he didn't bother taking off his shoes, and as soon as his head touched the pillow, he sank into a deep sleep.

Sixteen

Shelby decided that Max had lost his mind. She shook her head, unwilling to concede defeat, but their group quickly folded. First Patrick and then Bianca put their weapons down. She noticed that Bhatti waited, his eyes on hers.

"Put it down, Shelby." Max's voice was calm, and the look in his eyes assured her that what he was doing made sense. But it didn't make sense.

The numbers were now eleven to two—correction, five to two. Micah and five of the other men had dropped their weapons. Why would they do that unless they were trustworthy? Except the odds were still in their favor. Perhaps Max had a plan. She set her .22 on the ground, and Bhatti immediately did the same with the Glock Max had given him.

The group around them didn't hesitate. Each person holstered their gun or set their rifle against the wall.

"Good. It's good to see that we can all be reasonable." The leader ran his fingers through his beard, and seemed to come to a conclusion. "We can discuss our next step here or go back to my place."

"Here," Max said.

"All right." The man held up his hands in a

surrender gesture. "But we can't do it like this—watching to see who will reach for their weapon first."

"If you meant what you said, you don't have to worry about that."

"He didn't say anything." Shelby wanted to grab Max and shake him. The cuts on his face looked superficial, though blood continued to drip from his wounds. Had he lost too much blood? Maybe he'd hit his head. He was not acting sensibly.

"My name is Clay Gilbert," the old guy said. "Would you feel more comfortable if I instructed some of my men to move outside? They could keep an eye on the perimeter. Wouldn't want any surprises while we're having our powwow."

"We'd appreciate it," Max said.

As if they'd done this before, six of the group picked up their weapons and trooped outside.

Clay nodded toward their circle of crates. Two of his men headed that way, pulling up bales of hay to sit on. Max and Patrick followed without hesitation. Bianca shrugged and followed Patrick. Only Bhatti and Shelby held back.

"Best come hear what he has to say," Max called back to her.

She hurried over to his side and whispered, "You don't even know this man. Why are you trusting him?"

"Because he's part of the Remnant." Max sat down with a groan, pulled his backpack closer, and fetched a clean washcloth. He blotted the blood from his face, but didn't expound on what he'd said.

Bianca snatched the cloth from his hand, shone her flashlight on the largest cut to be sure there was no glass still in it, and applied pressure to the wound. "The Remnant? What is that?"

"A group of folks who are still trying to do the right thing," Clay said.

"You fired on us." Shelby practically spat the words. "Just look at Max's face."

"I'm fine."

"You could have killed us."

"My men would not have shot you unless I gave the order." Clay was sitting on a crate, but he leaned forward to study Max. "Are you okay? We have some first aid supplies."

"The cuts sting, but they're not fatal."

"Don't want to risk infection. Best clean it up first, and then we'll talk."

Max didn't resist when Bhatti brought over his doctor's bag, slipped on a pair of gloves, and began examining the wounds. After ten minutes, he'd cleaned each one, applied a topical ointment and bandages. Only one required a butterfly strip.

"Don't guess this will help my chances with the ladies." Max was speaking to Bhatti, but looking directly at Shelby.

"I have heard that women are actually attracted to a man with a scar or two."

Patrick laughed at that, and Shelby wondered if they'd all lost their minds. Maybe the pressure had become too much. They were making jokes, treating wounds, and having a powwow with strangers who moments ago threatened to shoot them.

Once Bhatti had repacked his supplies into his small medical bag, Clay cleared his throat.

"We have a lot of folks who shelter here in this barn. Most never see us coming. They're just looking for a place to rest for the night. When that's the case, we let them be. Usually the next morning they move on."

His gaze drifted around the circle. "Your group is obviously different. We saw you—" He looked directly at Patrick. "You were doing regular perimeter sweeps."

"So you have night vision goggles." Patrick was studying the man closely.

"And scopes." Clay nodded toward their weapons, which one of his men had gathered up and set in the middle of the circle. "As do you, I see. That's good. You came prepared."

"I don't understand," Shelby said. "You normally allow people to stay in your barn, but when you saw that we were as well supplied as you, that was when you decided to move in?"

"We couldn't know what side you're on."

"And if we'd been on the other side?" For the first time, Bhatti spoke directly to the man.

"We'd escort you back out to the highway and watch until you were out of sight."

"That's risky." Max stuffed the bloody washcloth into a plastic bag and pushed it down into his pack. "Someone could circle back."

Shelby found her attention split between Max and Clay. Max was obviously fine, so she pushed away the panic that had clawed at her throat since seeing the glass in front of him explode. She turned her attention to Clay, still unsure whether she trusted him. The two men who flanked him looked like guys she would see at the local diner. One had a farmer's tan, and the other had dark black skin. Both wore soiled ball caps and sported wiry builds. Neither spoke, letting Clay tell their story in his own way. Obviously, they'd done this on more than one occasion.

"It's happened before that someone has circled back," Clay admitted. "When it does, then we have to take more drastic measures."

Bianca shifted on her crate. "You kill them."

"Yeah, and don't think that's an easy thing. It keeps me awake some nights, sends me back into God's Word. Taking another man's life—even in self-defense—is a weighty thing."

"God's Word?" Shelby felt as if her head were going to explode. Who were these people?

"She doesn't know," Patrick explained. He shifted his gaze to Bianca and Shelby. "Pastor Tony took us aside before we left and told us

113

there was a group—the Remnant—who might be able to help us."

"But it wasn't like they'd be wearing T-shirts that proclaimed what side they were on." Max actually grinned at her. "Instead they have code words. *Micah five.*"

"Micah, that's your name . . ." She turned toward the man on Clay's right, the man that Clay had told to put down his gun along with five of his men.

The man grinned. "Actually, my name's Jamie. Pleased to meet you, ma'am."

"And you didn't think that maybe you should share this with us?" Shelby turned on Max. "You didn't think we should know?"

"Hey. We've had a busy twenty-four hours. There hasn't exactly been time. And I think . . . well, the thing is that we weren't sure such a group actually existed. Seemed like a reach to believe anyone could have formed up so quickly."

"Desperate times," Clay said.

"Why *Micah five?*" Bianca sat forward, staring at Clay. "Why that reference? And what does it mean? What do you all do?"

The other man flanking Clay answered. "Name's Kenny, and I can answer that, or part of it."

Shelby thought he was probably in his early thirties, the youngest of the group as far as she could tell. His skin was a dark black and his hair trimmed short. "In the Old Testament of the Bible,

Micah chapter five, verse seven, says, 'The remnant of Jacob will be in the midst of many peoples like dew from the Lord, like showers on the grass, which do not wait for anyone or depend on man.' "

Shelby stood and began pacing between her crate and Max's. "You're some extreme religious group?"

"Depends what you call extreme," Clay said.

Kenny continued as if she hadn't interrupted. "When things went bad, which happened within hours of the flare, some of us understood that the government wasn't going to step in and fix things . . . at least not for a long while. We would need to defend ourselves, but we also wanted to be able to help others. The problem is that once you declare yourself to be on a certain side, then you become a target for people who would oppose you."

"So we came up with a code," Jamie said. "Almost immediately after the grid went down, preachers were proclaiming that we are in the last days. Now, I don't know if I believe that, but I do know that what we're facing is unprecedented, and that many people . . . well, many good people have already lost their lives."

"Declaring ourselves the remnant of God didn't seem like such a far-fetched idea." Clay shifted on his crate, moving his right leg out in front of him and massaging his knee. "I pretend that

Jamie's name is Micah, and we throw out the number five. I could tell that you two recognized those words immediately."

"Thought I was hearing things," Max admitted.

"If there's no reaction, then we follow plan A—move people out of our area."

"But if they recognize the words, then we try to help." Kenny leaned forward now. "So tell us. How can we help you?"

Perhaps too much had happened too quickly. Shelby prided herself in being resilient, in handling whatever was thrown at them. The remnant of Jacob? Operating out of a barn? She couldn't take it all in. Instead, she leaned forward, propped her elbows on her knees, and covered her eyes with her hands. The others continued to talk, but what they said was garbled, distant.

She only raised her head when Max said, "It's a lot of information in a few minutes." Max glanced at her, and she straightened as he continued. "I realize we have decisions to make, but perhaps we could take a fifteen-minute break. There are things my group needs to discuss, and I know you won't mind that we need to do so privately."

Seventeen

Everyone agreed to disperse for thirty minutes and then reconvene. Max laid a hand on Shelby's shoulder, glad to see she seemed to have recovered somewhat. As the shell-shocked look faded, though, it was replaced by an intense scrutiny aimed in his direction. Max tried to convince her he was fine, but she continued to stare at him as if he might sprout a bullet hole in his forehead at any moment.

"You're lucky it wasn't much worse," Bhatti muttered. "And do you actually think you can trust these people?"

"We have to trust someone," Max said.

"Do we?"

"What options do we have? We weren't making a lot of progress on our own. We can't go south into town, and it's not safe on the secondary roads." He told the rest of their group about the people he and Shelby had hid from while making their way to the rendezvous point, as well as the man he'd hit with the lug wrench.

"Did you kill him?" Bianca asked.

"Maybe." Max swallowed and shook his head. "I'm not sure. All I knew was that he was threatening Shelby, and we could hear others closing in. So we grabbed our stuff and ran. We didn't stop to check for a pulse."

"Probably ragtag groups like that are all over town," Patrick said. "It's what we expected."

"Expecting it is one thing," Bhatti pointed out. "Actually encountering it can be completely different."

Shelby turned to look at Bhatti. His usually placid face was creased in a worried frown.

"So we're going to tell these people what we're doing?" Bianca asked.

Max studied each of them before he said, "I don't see how it can hurt."

"It does make sense," Bhatti agreed. "They might have ideas for how to get into the city."

Shelby didn't attempt to hide her agitation. "I thought you didn't trust them."

"I'm not saying I do, but we obviously are going to need help to get into the heart of Austin."

Everyone in the group nodded in agreement, though Max noticed Shelby did so quite reluctantly. The others made their way back to the circle, but she held back, glaring at him, standing with her arms crossed. A sixth sense that told him she now questioned his judgment. That and the accusatory look on her face hurt him in ways that shattered glass never could.

"Anything else you need to tell me?"

"Shelby, I'm sorry."

"That's not going to cut it. I need to know the

things you know, all the things you know. What if we were separated?"

"I'm not going to let that happen."

"You might not be able to prevent it. We were separated from the others. It could happen to you and me just as easily." She stared past him for a moment. When she turned her gaze back toward him, the look of despair—of naked fear in her eyes nearly broke his heart.

"I'm glad you're here, Max. I'm glad you all came along, and I even . . . I even want Bhatti to find the medicine Abney needs. I won't say I completely trust him. I can see he's a good doctor, though. And I'm starting to think he has good instincts for this kind of thing."

"I was going to tell you about the Remnant."

"You didn't, though, and that information you withheld could have made all the difference. We can't afford those types of mistakes. We can't afford any mistakes. The stakes are too high. What we're doing could mean whether Carter lives or dies."

Now there was a steely resolve in her eyes, and somehow that eased the ache in Max's heart. This was the Shelby that Max knew—tough as nails. One way or another she would patch, hammer, or hold her world together.

"I'm not going home until I find his insulin, with or without the help of *the Remnant*." She put virtual quotations marks around the last two words.

"That's why we're here," he assured her. "And it's what we're going to do. Now let's go see if Clay can help."

He turned back, stepped closer, and lowered his voice. "That journal of yours? I think it's a good idea. I want you to get it out and take notes as we talk. We're witnesses, Shelby. Witnesses to something monumental—both the destruction and hopefully the rebirth of our society."

"Okay. Yeah, I agree."

"But do not specifically name the Remnant or put the code words in your journal in case it falls into the wrong hands."

"You don't think that someone would target them for simply trying to help folks?"

Max glanced around the barn before settling his gaze on her again. "People are attempting to fill a power void—good people and evil people. If your pack or that journal ends up on the wrong side, I have no doubt that they would try to dismantle what little exists of this group. I don't want to be responsible for that, and I know you don't either."

They walked over to the circle of people waiting. Clay had placed a battery-operated lantern in the middle. Shelby took a seat near the lantern, pulled out her notebook and pen, and waited for the meeting to begin.

Jamie and Kenny had gone out to replace two of the men on perimeter patrol. Those two came into the barn, but they didn't join the circle—opting instead to collapse against hay bales set in the far corner of the room and doze.

Shelby didn't waste any time getting to the point. "I'm here to find insulin for my son."

Clay nodded his head once, but he didn't interrupt her with questions.

"Dr. Bhatti is looking for medications the people in our town will need. We have items to trade if you have anything at all."

"We don't. It's a problem in every community, and we've had other folks coming through looking for food, fuel, and medical supplies."

"Did they find any?" Bianca asked.

"If they did, they didn't come back this way."

"So you can't help us?" Shelby's voice wobbled, but she bit down on her bottom lip and made a valiant attempt of putting on an expression that said *I'm fine*.

"He didn't say that, Shelby." Max met her gaze and held it for a long moment, willing her to wait this out. Over the past three weeks he'd seen the violence and betrayals and tragedies they'd experienced scrape away at her optimism, leaving her soul raw. What he didn't want was for her to become jaded. There were still good people to be found, God continued to provide for their needs, and it was possible that the Remnant could in fact help them.

Clay glanced between them before addressing his next comment directly to Shelby. "We don't have what you need if that's what you're asking. Where were you planning to look?"

"Our thought was to head to downtown—to the capitol building," Max said. "Surely the government has supplies. We tried going south on 183, but the road was blocked at the SH 45 interchange."

"We saw some military vehicles to the south." Shelby tapped her pen against the notebook. "It looked like they were trying to carve a path through the cars."

"Not yet. What you saw was almost certainly a patrol. They're not able to do much as far as eliminating illegal activity, but from what we've heard, they want to maintain a presence."

"You're telling me the National Guard can't control some two-bit vandals?" Patrick shook his head. "I have trouble believing that."

"They're spread pretty thin. We haven't been downtown to see things firsthand, but from what we've heard, the governor's plan is to solidify the area immediately around the capitol square and then slowly push out . . . block by block."

"It's been twenty days." Shelby sat straighter, crossing her arms. "How long is this plan going to take? And what are people supposed to do in the meantime?"

"No one knows how long it will take. Until then people are going to have to depend on their own resources. More than one source has told us that the state government and the feds are at odds. What that's about, I can't tell you. But because of it, much of the Texas National Guard was sent to cover our state borders."

"That would explain the troops we saw going through Abney." Patrick reached for a water bottle and uncapped it. "There were rumors about defections at Fort Hood."

"We heard the same thing, and that it's happening at all of the military bases. Our military personnel are not cowards, but if their orders aren't clear or if they feel it's contradictory to the Constitution, there is a fair probability that they're not going to follow through."

Patrick guzzled the contents of his water bottle and stuffed it into the side pocket of his pack. "Most of the enlisted men I served with had never read the Constitution, or if they did, it was in a high school government class that they probably slept through."

"Yeah. But if their CO tells them to seize the resources in a local town, and if they have any connection to the people in that town, then many of them aren't going to do it. Instead, they disappear in the night, go home, and take care of their families. It's not . . . it's not the same as being in Fallujah or Kabul. Many of our soldiers are not clear on who the enemy is."

"Everything has unwound so quickly." Bianca pressed her fingertips to her forehead. "This is

America. What you're describing isn't supposed to happen here."

"Agreed, but we've never faced a catastrophe of this proportion. Sure, we've had plenty of natural disasters—floods and fires and tornadoes. We've even had the occasional civil unrest, but we've never had a situation where the majority of Americans don't know where their next meal is coming from."

"The Great Depression," Max muttered.

"Maybe. Which was what—two, maybe three generations ago? In my opinion, we've become somewhat soft since then, and many people have never even imagined the scenarios we're facing today."

"All right." Shelby held up a hand to stop him. "But there is a central government in the capital. We need to try there first."

Max noticed Clay waited until each person in their group had nodded in agreement.

"We can get you close—within five blocks," Clay said. "Word is they have a heavily guarded perimeter fence, and they're not letting civilians through."

"We'll worry about that when we get there." Patrick pulled out a map and set it on the empty crate between him and Clay.

They discussed routes and obstacles. Clay began to outline a plan. As Max listened, he glanced up, expecting to see signs of sunrise. After all, they now had a plan. There was at least hope that they could find Carter's insulin and the medical supplies that Abney needed. Such progress should be accompanied by morning light splashing across the fields.

Instead, he was surprised that the sky outside remained blanketed in darkness.

Eighteen

Carter saw the man raise his rifle, take aim, and shoot, but he was powerless to move. The bullet pierced his stomach. He felt nothing. He looked down, surprised to see his hands and clothes soaked in blood. He held one hand to his stomach and attempted to grip his rifle with the other. His hand was too slick. The rifle slipped from his grasp as the man walked closer. Carter fell to the ground.

Mom was worried I'd die from my diabetes. She never imagined I'd go this way.

Then the man was standing in front of him, crouching down, and grasping his shoulders. Shaking him and repeating something that made no sense to Carter. He tossed his head and tried to pull free, but the man was too strong.

"Son, wake up. You're having a nightmare. Wake up, now."

He opened his eyes to see Roy's wrinkled face

only inches from his own. "It's only a dream. Here, drink this." Roy pushed a bottle of water into his hands.

Carter stared at his fingers, surprised to find no blood there. He tried to slow his hammering heart, sipped from the water bottle, and finally pushed the covers off. "Sorry. I . . ."

"Bad dream?"

"Yeah."

"Take a minute."

"Yeah, okay." He took another swig from the bottle, but then he realized that Roy was in his room. "Is everything all right?"

He set the bottle on a crate he was using as a nightstand and reached for his rifle.

"Everything's fine. You missed breakfast, and Georgia was worried."

Carter wiped the sweat from his eyes. Glancing out the screened wall of the porch, he saw that it was much later than he'd guessed. "I'm sorry. I didn't mean to sleep in."

"You two were out late last night." Roy stood and walked to the screen door. "Sure you're okay?"

"Yeah. I'll meet you in the barn."

"Take your time and get some breakfast first. I don't need you passing out from hunger." He paused before walking out the door and added, "We have a lot to do today."

For some reason, those last seven words made

Carter smile. Somehow the memory of Kaitlyn hurt less when he was busy. Those first few days after her death, lying on Bianca's couch, he'd thought that there was no point in even trying to survive. If you could die walking down the sidewalk, then why even make an effort?

But Georgia and Roy needed him. He'd noticed the day before how Max's dad paused to massage his hands.

"Arthritis," he'd muttered when he caught Carter staring. "Enjoy your youth while you're pain-free."

Carter's pain was inside, but he understood what Roy was saying. It didn't hurt when he grasped a bale of hay or cleaned a fish or weeded the garden. Still fully dressed, he scrambled out of bed and checked his blood sugar levels. A few years earlier, he'd switched to using an insulin pen. Each pen held 300 units, which generally lasted him three to four days. Once opened, it didn't require refrigeration. It was the boxes of unopened pens that his mom had freaked out about. They were supposed to be kept cold.

The pens he used contained premixed insulin which combined rapid acting, what he needed before meals, with intermediate acting, what he needed to get through the day. He primed the pen, dialed in the correct dose, and injected it into his stomach. After storing his supplies on the crate next to his bed, he glanced around the small cottage, grabbed his ball cap, and jogged over to the main house.

"Hungry?" Georgia asked.

"Yeah, but I have to wait a few more minutes for my insulin to kick in."

"Then we can talk about the day." Georgia sat down across from him, cradling a cup of coffee. He'd seen that same posture so many times from his mom that it almost made him laugh.

But then he remembered how things had been between them when she'd left.

"Penny for your thoughts."

"I should have said goodbye."

"You were upset."

"Yeah, but that's not much of an excuse."

"Your mother knows that you care about her, Carter."

"Still, she's risking her life for me . . . both my mom and Max are, and instead of thanking them, I acted like a brat."

Georgia sipped from her coffee, studying him for a minute.

Carter waited.

Finally, she tapped the table and said, "They'll be back here soon, eating at this very table. When they are, you say you're sorry. A simple apology goes a long way toward soothing hurt feelings."

Carter nodded, reassured by the thought of them all eating again around Georgia's table.

"Now about today. Roy needs your help in

the fields, and I have to go and check on Tate."

"Do you need me to go with you?"

"Not this time, but if he's progressing as well as I hope he is, then I'd like you to go tomorrow."

"All right, but what do I do when I get there?"

"You'll need to check his wound for infection, clean it, and rebandage it. Do you think you can do that?"

Carter shifted uncomfortably in his seat. He didn't want to do it. Open wounds made him queasy. But if Georgia needed him to, which she obviously did or she wouldn't have asked, then he would. "Yeah. You showed me how last night."

"Good. Hopefully that will be the last bullet wound we'll have to attend to."

"No idea who shot him?"

Georgia stood and bustled around the kitchen, pulling out food for his breakfast. "Oh, we have some ideas. Later this afternoon there will be a meeting in our barn to talk about that."

"Even if you know who did it, what would you do? It's not like you can call the local sheriff, and you can't just take the law into your own hands. Can you?"

"I honestly don't know. It's something Roy and I have been praying about. Something that each person will have to wrestle with in their own heart." She made a clucking sound with her tongue. "Everything isn't perfect at High Fields, so don't fall into the trap of thinking that it is."

"But you all work together. You share your food, man the roadblocks—and there's even that old lady who moved in with the other family because she didn't feel safe."

"All those things are true, but not everyone has bought into the concept of a regional watch group. Some families are insisting that they're better off on their own. They don't want to share, and they don't want to spend time on the roadblocks when they could be hunting or fishing."

"Sounds kind of shortsighted."

"Maybe they'll come around. Until they do, it's best you go directly where we tell you and nowhere else." Georgia set a plate of food in front of him. It held a warmed biscuit, a slice of cheese, and something that looked like wet rice.

"What is that?"

"Grits. They're healthy. Eat them." She placed butter and salt and pepper on the table. "But doctor them up first."

Carter remembered eating some pretty strange meals at his house before it blew up. He'd even had tuna for breakfast. Grits? Couldn't be any worse than that.

Nineteen

Shelby was restless, eager to be on their way, but Clay insisted that they wait until the sun was well up before leaving. "Other people will be out by then. If we have any hope of blending in, it will be in the middle of the day."

Patrick cleaned their weapons, though they hadn't been fired and each of them knew how to maintain their firearm. "I like being busy," he'd said when Shelby had pointed that out to him. He had given her a wolfish grin, making her laugh in spite of their circumstances.

Bianca found a corner of the barn where a weak shaft of light was slanting through, curled up with her backpack under her head, and promptly fell asleep.

"I'm envious," Shelby confessed to Max. "I couldn't sleep in a barn full of strangers if I tried."

"That would be because you can't sleep in public."

"You remember that, huh?"

"Sure. That time when I was sixteen and you were—"

"Fifteen."

"And our families went on vacation together."

"To Florida."

"Something about free airline tickets that our parents had earned on their credit cards."

Shelby sighed. "Planes, credit cards, and loyalty points—all things of the past."

"I imagine so. That trip our flights were delayed due to weather or something."

"Lightning strikes. They'd had lightning strikes around the airport, so all flights in and out were delayed."

Max slid down onto the ground and patted the spot beside him. Shelby started to resist, but what was the point? They weren't leaving anytime soon, and she wasn't going to sleep. Why stand on her feet until Clay gave the go-ahead?

"We were in that airport, delayed, for six or seven hours." Max leaned his head back against the barn's wall and allowed his eyes to drift shut.

"Seemed like an eternity."

"You didn't sleep there, and you didn't sleep on the plane."

"It was still public."

He opened his eyes and squinted at her. "We finally made it to the condo on the beach. I can still hear my mom saying that like it was emblazoned on tour vouchers . . . *Condo on the Beach*."

"And I crashed for fourteen hours. My mom thought I had mono."

"Everyone else had napped, so we were outside swimming, building sand castles, doing things tourists do . . . and little Shelby was up in her room sound asleep."

He reached over to squeeze her neck, and she batted his hand away.

"I don't like this. We're just sitting around. We need to get in, get what we need, and get out."

"And we will." All teasing had left his voice. "We will, Shelby."

She pulled her backpack beside her. The note-book rested on her lap, and she thought of opening it to check her notes, confirming she hadn't forgotten anything. She didn't, though. She was too tired to string three words together. Instead of reading what she'd written, she held it, laid her palm flat against the cover, and allowed her eyes to drift shut. She heard Max's breathing deepen, but she didn't sleep.

Instead, her mind replayed images from the last forty-eight hours.

The contents of a suitcase scattered across the road outside of Townsen Mills.

Nadine Perkins wearing a determined expression.

Bianca and Bhatti bending over young Zack Allen.

Burned-out buildings.

Max swinging the lug wrench.

All of those details were recorded in the journal. The need to keep a record of everything they were seeing was becoming more urgent every day. She didn't know why. Honestly, she couldn't imagine anyone important ever reading it, but perhaps that wasn't the point. Maybe the important people now were the common folks. Maybe that was who she should have been writing for all along—not publishers or editors or sales departments.

The morning grew even darker and wind began to buffet the rafters. At 10:00 a.m. sharp, Clay called them all together.

"The weather's worse, as you can tell, but it might work to our advantage—maybe the bad guys will stay inside." That drew a few grunts of agreement. Clay ran his hand over the top of his bald head and continued. "Kenny is going to ride in the Dodge with Max and Shelby."

The black man shouldered his rifle and walked over to stand beside them.

"Jamie is going to ride in the hot rod with Patrick and Bianca." Jamie pumped his fist in victory, and everyone laughed.

"I'll be in the lead vehicle. I'd like Dr. Bhatti to ride with me. I want each vehicle to maintain a three-car-length distance between one another. We don't want to bunch up and make for a big, plump target. We also don't want to spread out where we could get separated, so watch your distance."

Max and Patrick gave him a thumbs-up.

"The rest of my crew will wait back here."

"What good are they here?" Max asked. "No offense, guys."

"None taken," a tall, gangly man assured him. "It's a good question."

"The truth is they're our fallback plan." Clay scanned the room, his gaze settling on Shelby and Max. "If you get in trouble, if we get separated, if someone is injured . . . we come back here. Clear?"

Everyone nodded, followed by a flurry of activity.

"I feel like I've been in this barn for months," Shelby admitted. And then they were dodging raindrops, what looked like the beginning of a Texas-sized storm, and climbing into the Dodge. Max started up the engine, and Kenny slipped into the backseat, taking Bhatti's spot.

Humidity was high, and temperatures were holding steady at too hot. A heavy gray mist draped the hills and fields. The landscape was dreary and tired. Or maybe it was that she knew what lay to the south. Maybe that was coloring her perceptions.

"Clay didn't talk much about what we're likely to encounter," Kenny said. "You might want to prepare yourself."

Shelby angled herself in the corner of the front seat. She could see out the front window and still easily look at Kenny as they spoke. His tone was earnest and his expression more than a little worried.

"What are we likely to see that we haven't seen

already? Max and I walked from the interchange —burned-out buildings and thugs. It was a mess."

"I'm sure it was, but that's sort of the fringe. The real trouble is in the more crowded areas."

"Can you be a little more specific?" Max asked. "Like you said, it's better that we're prepared."

Kenny glanced left, out the window, and then returned his gaze to Shelby's. "Bodies—a lot of them."

"Bodies?"

"The stench is something terrible. Folks have nowhere to bury their dead and no means to do so. Most people living in an apartment don't own a shovel."

"So no one is in charge?"

"Some people think they are, and some neighborhoods are better than others. Trash is a problem. When the food that was in the freezers went bad, people just tossed it beside Dumpsters as if someone was going to show up and fetch it for them. Sanitation is a problem. Toilets don't work. Hospitals . . . well, most of them had to close their doors because no one came to cover their shift."

The rain began to patter on the roof, growing increasingly louder as the sky continued to darken. Peering through the windshield, Shelby had a hard time believing it was midmorning.

"Rats, wild dogs, children . . . that's probably the worst for me, seeing the children."

Farmland gave way to urban sprawl. Apartment buildings crowded up against one another, vacant stores offered nothing to buy, and cars were abandoned everywhere. They followed the thoroughfare another mile before Clay turned to the north, away from downtown.

"Most of the roads to the south are blocked," Kenny explained. "But don't worry, there's a way through if you know how to zigzag. At least there was last week."

Twenty

Max wanted to speed up. Groups of people were milling around, even in the rain. They seemed impervious to it. Some were on bicycles, others simply stood near the side of the road—waiting, watching. A few sheltered in abandoned cars.

"Are they living there?" Shelby asked.

"On the streets or in the cars?" Kenny leaned forward to see what Shelby was staring at.

"Both."

"Could be. At first the local authorities tried to offer assistance. They opened up public buildings like the library, the high school gym, that sort of thing."

"I'm going to guess that didn't go very well." Max maneuvered over a railroad track. He glanced to the left, saw a railcar overturned and empty cartons spilled out on the ground. It wasn't until he was past it, looking in his rearview mirror, that he saw what must have been the conductor—his body hanging half out of one of the cars, half obscured by vultures.

"That's for sure. The first assault, the first rape, the first murder . . . the people in charge decided to close it down, or they tried. When that didn't work, when the people staying there turned on the workers who weren't getting paid anyway, the authorities abandoned ship."

"Every man for himself?" Shelby's voice sounded far away. Her gaze was locked out her side window. Max slowed even further, peered around her, and saw three children, hand in hand, walking down the middle of a side road.

"Should we go back?" His gaze flicked up to the rearview mirror.

Kenny's gaze met his. One quick shake of the head.

"Explain that to me," Shelby said. "You're supposed to be the Remnant. You're supposed to help people. If you can't do that, what's the point in existing?"

"We're helping you," Kenny reminded her.

Max noticed that he didn't sound defensive as much as tired.

Shelby pulled in a sharp breath. "And we appreciate it, but what about all of these people?"

"We help where we can, and we did stop in the

beginning—whenever we saw kids or old people —we stopped to see what we could do." Now it was Kenny's turn to stare out the window. "We lost three men that way before we decided the risk was too high. Some people pay the kids to do that, to walk around and look lost and alone, which they probably are. But if you pull over, the adults lurking in the background rob you . . . or worse."

"You said they pay the kids. With what?" Shelby's voice was indignant.

Max knew that tone. She'd never been one to stand for social injustice, and this was so much worse than anything they'd faced before. He was surprised she wasn't trying to hop out of the moving car.

"Food. They pay them with food. Not much I imagine, but it's something, and before you ask, there is still some food to be had, and more to be stolen."

Max wanted to speed past the desolation outside their window, but Clay had slowed for the storm, and he was trying to maintain the distance of three cars. He tapped the brakes, and a crowd of people standing at the corner surged toward their vehicle.

He pulled away as one person reached for Shelby's door handle and another bumped up against his window.

Shelby jumped toward him.

"They're locked," he assured her. The windows

were rolled up to keep out the rain and the people. The heat created a sauna-like effect. He had to reach forward every few minutes to wipe the condensation from the windows. And he constantly glanced in his rearview mirror. Max knew there was no reason to worry about Patrick, but what they were driving through was off the charts. It was beyond anything he could have imagined.

They could smell the stench of the area even through the closed windows of the Dodge. A pack of dogs pawed through a mountain of trash next to a Dumpster. As they watched, a man joined the dogs, and then another person joined him, and then a kid who couldn't have been more than ten. Max couldn't imagine what they expected to find.

"Less fires in this area," Shelby noted.

"That's true here, but three blocks that way"—Kenny nodded to the left—"fire took out an entire neighborhood. The only thing that stopped it was a creek on one side and a six-lane road on the other."

Lightning flashed, the rain increased, and the sky darkened to something resembling twilight. Max didn't dare reduce his speed any further. He approached a yield sign, checked both ways, though he could see very little, and pulled forward at the exact moment a giraffe stepped in front of the Dodge.

Slamming on his brakes, his right hand shot out across Shelby, who gasped and leaned forward, her nose practically touching the front windshield.

They all three watched in silence as the giraffe ignored them, reached up to pull leaves off an overhanging tree, and then plodded forward down the street.

Max glanced in the rearview mirror. Kenny's gaze darted toward him and then away. His voice melted into the drumbeat of the rain against their roof and the crash of distant thunder. "Like I said, prepare yourself. The people are hungry, the neighborhoods are a disaster, and the animals? They're not in the zoo anymore."

"How did they get out?"

"The prevailing theory is that one of the keepers let them out because he or she didn't want to see them starve and thought they would be better off fending for themselves."

"And the other theory?"

"Folks went in thinking they could . . . harvest them."

"You mean eat them," Shelby said.

"It might have worked with the birds or the smaller mammals. The guy I heard it from said that three bodies—or what was left of three bodies —were found outside the lions' cage."

"Who would try to eat a lion?" Max asked.

Kenny shrugged. "Story goes that the guy took a handgun with him, but the gun was on the ground outside the cage, and all the bullets were still in the chamber."

"Sounds like the stuff of urban legends." Shelby leaned forward to better see out the window.

"Yeah, I would agree, except for that giraffe. The last time we were through, we encountered a hippo. Thing was much faster than you'd expect and bigger. Giant teeth that can cut a person in half faster than . . . well, you don't want to know about that."

They'd driven through a park which was dotted with tents and lean-to shelters. Past that, they abruptly moved into a better neighborhood. A sign at the entrance proclaimed that you could *Live at Your Perfect Pace*. The houses were farther apart, none of the dwellings were burned, and the owners were doing something with their trash. It certainly wasn't piling up at the curb.

"These folks look like they're doing all right."

"Maybe. Maybe not. It's hard to know. Most of the homes you see here are occupied. The people inside are locked up tight, and they can afford good locks. Plus they have cameras that weren't fried because they're shielded, and backup monitors for what was fried. They have solar panels and generators, and they usually have a handgun that they kept in a safe beside the bed for home protection. Never thought they'd need to use it. Never expected this to happen."

"So they were better prepared."

"Some were and some weren't."

"How do you know these things?" Shelby asked.

"So far we've talked to a maid, a grounds-keeper, and a butler."

"Seriously?"

"Yeah. Sounds like people who would be working for British aristocracy, not rich Austin families."

"What else did they tell you?"

"Some of these houses have a lot of food inside. Some . . . well, they were waiting for the maid to do the shopping, but the maid never came back."

"How do they keep out the folks we saw back there?"

"They shoot the first one who tries to break in. The hoodlums we saw a few blocks back have easier prey who aren't so well armed. Why risk it?"

"Until people stop coming through. Until there's no one left to prey on."

Clay tapped his brakes twice and turned on his signal as if he were afraid that Max wouldn't see him. He turned right into what looked like a golf course. No golf carts on the greens. No lights on at the clubhouse. They continued down a winding road and came out at an elementary school.

GT Elementary.

"GT?" Shelby asked.

"Green Tech."

Clay parked on the side of the school, in front

of a fence and a barricade. Max parked behind him, and they waited for Patrick.

"What you saw back there? It's nothing compared to what this city will look like in six weeks, or six months." Kenny's voice was low, solemn. "We're trying to get as many folks out as possible, before that happens. Before this whole situation breaks down."

Max glanced up at his rearview mirror and saw Patrick pull in behind them.

"So we're headed opposite the flow," Shelby said.

"Pretty much. We haven't had too many people trying to get inside, and like Clay said . . . those who have? They were never seen again."

Twenty-one

Shelby stared out the Dodge window. The rain had not eased at all. If anything, it was pouring harder than before, but they couldn't exactly wait in their cars for it to stop. And what difference did it really make? Wet, cold, hungry, and tired were all irrelevant. They had to keep going. The other stuff would work itself out.

The group paired up as they walked toward the barricade positioned to the side of the school.

Clay and Bhatti in the front.

Kenny and Jamie next.

Shelby and Bianca in the middle.

Max and Patrick bringing up the rear.

The school did not have cameras, at least not that Shelby could see, and even if it did, they probably were not functioning ones. She had trouble believing that any cameras could survive something that knocked out the entire electrical grid, regardless of what Kenny said about rich people and their resources.

No cameras—but the school did have guards. Shelby didn't see them, not at first, but she did see two rifle barrels poke up and over a barricade that had been built on the other side of a fence.

Clay barked out, "Micah. Five. Remnant. Clear."

A ball cap appeared over the top of the barricade, followed by a smiling face. "Figured we might see you today. Only the fish and the crazies are out." The woman disappeared and almost immediately the barricade opened up.

She popped through the opening and enfolded Clay in a hug. Stepping back, she said, "Pull your cars inside. Donna doesn't want any indication that we're here in case someone happens to pass by."

So they all walked back to their cars, their clothes now thoroughly soaked, and drove into what looked like a teachers' parking lot. Only it was surrounded by a fence and blockade and guards.

The barricade closed behind them, and the

woman—she was probably in her early thirties, Hispanic, and wearing a raincoat—walked them to a back door.

She did some complicated knock, and Shelby could hear a chain being unlocked and pulled through the handles of the door. Then they stepped into the school.

There must have been summer school classes going on there before the flare. Or maybe, given the high-priced neighborhood, an enrichment program for kids during the summer.

Family trees had been drawn on construction paper, small hands traced on the trees, names crayoned across the hands. Some of the hands were from Manila paper, others from a light tan, and others still from a dark brown. An integrated community—apparently.

They followed the woman in the raincoat down the hall. She took them deeper into the building, which Shelby expected to be dark, dark as a tomb with no light and no windows. It wasn't though. Soft lighting lined the walkway, like an aisle at a movie theater. They stepped into a large open area, and light filtered down through huge skylights. It must have been something on a sunny day. Today? It lessened the darkness, and that was all.

The large room had sunken areas, like indoor amphitheaters. It had a snack bar, where kids had probably been served popcorn or fruit drinks. It had bathrooms to the left and the right, and it had an open library area on one side with large over-stuffed chairs.

Shelby had never taught, but she'd spoken to many groups of schoolchildren about fiction and writing and the importance of doing well in school. She'd probably been to several hundred schools in the last ten years—poor schools and rich schools and everything in between. Her jaw dropped, and she stood staring, frozen in her tracks, until Bianca said, "This doesn't look anything like the schools in Abney."

"It's amazing. It's like something out of a wonderland tale. It's what school should be."

Max and Patrick had moved around them when they'd walked into the large open room. They stood talking to Clay and the woman in the raincoat. Max caught Shelby's attention and motioned with his head, so she and Bianca hurried to catch up.

A large wall was positioned in the middle of the room, a kind of divider. It didn't reach to the ceiling, not even close. But it did separate one half from the other. Maybe they projected movies on it, or it might have been designed that way to cut down on noise. A couple hundred kids could get pretty loud.

When they walked around the wall, Shelby stopped in her tracks. This half of the room was filled with children, all ages and colors and shapes and sizes. They were all lying down, as if they'd been told it was nap time, and maybe they had. Some of the older ones were reading to the younger ones in soft voices. Some of the younger ones were curled up with a light blanket, thumbs in their mouth, gentle snores proving they were asleep.

Shelby scanned the room left to right, and then worked her way back left again. "Looks like groups of ten with an adult in each group."

The woman in the raincoat had come back to where they were standing. "Exactly. We have an adult with every pod at all times."

"Pod?"

"That's what we call the groups."

"Pods."

"By the way, I'm Maria."

"My name is Shelby, and this is—"

"Bianca Lopez." Bianca shook Maria's hand, and Shelby did the same.

"Where did they all come from? What are they doing here? What's your plan to reunite them with their families? And how much food do you have?"

Maria grinned, removed her ball cap, and combed her wet hair out of her eyes. "Let's go see Donna. She can answer your questions better than I can."

Donna was a smallish woman, probably five foot four, with short, spiky brown hair and a serious expression. She glanced up and saw them and held up a finger for them to wait. When she squatted down to talk to a small boy, her scowl brightened into a smile. Her voice was soft. Her eyes filled with compassion.

She handed the little boy off to Maria. "If you could help Justin find his mat . . ."

"Of course."

Justin's face was wet from crying, and his shoulders shuddered when he pulled in a deep breath, but he put his hand in Maria's and allowed himself to be led away.

"Clay. Good to see you. Why don't we go into my office?"

Her office was a kindergarten classroom off the large open area. No one had bothered to take the artwork off the bulletin boards, but the desks had been pushed back against the walls, and chairs for adults had been brought in and set in a semi-circular fashion.

"Have a seat." She sat behind her desk. "We hold our meetings here, which is the reason for so many chairs. Would you like to take a few minutes to dry yourselves off?"

"Actually, we're in a bit of a hurry." Shelby stepped forward. "My name is Shelby Sparks. We're from a small town to the northwest of here—Abney. I'm here for medical supplies. I'm looking for insulin for my son."

Donna was already shaking her head, but Shelby pushed on. "We have things to trade—

food, other medicine, a few items of jewelry that are gold, even some fuel. We'll give you whatever we have, whatever you need, but I have to find some insulin."

Donna exchanged a quick look with Clay, a look that confirmed Shelby's fears even before she spoke. "We have very little medicine here and no insulin."

"Then this was a pointless side trip for us. I'm sorry we've wasted your time."

"I didn't say your trip was pointless. I don't have what you need, but one of our crew—Bill—he can find just about anything. Which doesn't mean he can get it for you, but he can probably tell you where to look."

"Can we talk to him?" Max asked.

"Sure you can. He's out on a supply run, but I expect him back soon."

Shelby felt her frustration rising to the point it might boil over. How many detours would they take? She'd known that it wouldn't be easy to find what Carter needed, but she felt blind, as if she were fumbling around, following sounds that might lead to the one thing that could save her.

Bianca was the first to step forward and reason with her. "If this guy knows, it's a lot better than us driving around aimlessly."

"She's right," Patrick said. "Given what we've just driven through, I'd rather have a clear destination in mind."

Max nodded in agreement. Bhatti stared up at the skylight, as if his fate weren't tied to theirs.

So it was decided. Shelby knew waiting was the right thing to do, but that didn't mean she had to like it.

Donna stood, effectively dismissing them. "Excellent. Any friend of Clay's is a friend of ours. Have a look around. I'll be happy to answer any questions you might have when we meet later. In the meantime, Maria will be happy to take you where you can hang up your wet things. We also have hot tea or coffee."

"Coffee?" Shelby almost laughed and wondered if her desperation was causing her to hear things.

Maria had appeared at the classroom door.

"If Bill still isn't back once you've cleaned up, you're welcome to take a tour of our facility."

They walked back out into the main room, and Maria closed Donna's door behind them.

"A tour of their facility?" Patrick asked. "Is she for real?"

"Oh, she's for real," Maria said, smiling to show she wasn't offended by their skepticism. "She's proud of what we've done here. Follow me and you'll see why."

Twenty-two

Shelby wanted the coffee. She did not want to dry her clothes, tour the facility, or wait for Bill.

Unfortunately, the group vote went against her.

"When did this become a democracy?" she grumbled.

"Stop complaining. You need coffee, something to eat, and to get out of those wet clothes." Max held both hands up when she gave him a pointed, don't-mess-with-me look. "Just saying."

In some way, the teasing helped to ease the knot in her stomach. What they'd driven through was more devastating than anything she'd seen, anything she'd imagined, and exponentially worse than what they'd experienced in Abney.

They walked down a hall that bordered the large room with sleeping children. At the end of the room was a kitchen. The aroma of coffee drifted toward them, and she felt her pace quicken. Ten minutes later they were sitting around a table, clutching mugs of coffee and eating bowls of oatmeal flavored with raisins and nuts.

"This place. It's like something out of the past." Shelby cleaned her bowl and then walked toward the sink.

"We'll do that," Maria said. "Donna has set

certain protocols in place to maximize our water usage."

"Including how you wash a bowl?"

"Including everything. She's a take-charge kind of person."

"That's an understatement." Clay walked into the room, poured himself a cup of coffee, and sank into a chair at the table.

"Where are Jamie and Kenny?" Max asked. "I imagine they could use a cup of this coffee."

"They're taking care of a shipment."

"Shipment?"

Clay waved away his question and changed the subject.

"You all look good in the new clothes."

Shelby stared down at her scrubs—scrubs! Where had they come from?

"Our clothes are drying in the laundry room," Max explained. Then he leaned forward, his gaze split between Clay and Maria. "Where did these scrubs come from? Why does a school have a laundry room? How do your lights and fans work if there's no electricity? I certainly don't hear a generator."

He jerked a thumb back toward the main room. "And whose kids are those?"

Maria glanced at Clay and shrugged. "She said to give them a tour. I suppose that means explaining what we're doing here."

Shelby noticed that everyone in their group

153

leaned forward a little—interested to hear this story. Everyone except Dr. Bhatti. He seemed lost in another world as he stared at the opposite wall.

Shelby still hadn't figured the man out, and she still didn't trust him. That thought was interrupted by Patrick.

"Donna is part of the Remnant." When everyone turned to stare at him, he chuckled. "Not that hard to figure out. Your code words? When we first drove up to the school? 'Micah. Five. Remnant. Clear.' "

"Yeah, she is. But her passion has always been children—before the flare and after." Clay sat back, his hands cradling a mug of coffee, and he and Maria told the story of the school, the story of Donna and the children.

Bianca leaned toward Shelby and whispered, "Better write this down."

"Donna worked here as a language arts coordinator for the school. Some of the adults you'll see were employed here as well. I was a first grade teacher." Maria shrugged. "I was living in an apartment on the east side. Rode my bike to school every day. It was the healthy, urban renewal thing to do. The city had even put in bicycle lanes to encourage people to ride more, drive less. The Saturday after the flare, I thought I would come over to check on my classroom. There's plenty of lighting with the skylights, so I figured I could change my bulletin boards, maybe grade a few papers."

"You have papers to grade? In first grade?"

Maria smiled, as if she'd heard that question before. "It was a good thing I decided to come when I did. I don't think I'd have made it through the mobs on my side of town if I'd waited until Monday."

Clay nodded in agreement. "Donna had planned to come in on Saturday to catch up on some paperwork."

"Something she did far too often."

"She drives an old Subaru—no electronics on it to speak of. When she realized the extent of the outage, she decided to stay here."

"This school was built as a living lesson in sustainability." Maria's entire countenance changed as she warmed to her subject. "As you can tell from the neighborhood, our students—our families —were upper class. They could afford the very best, and that's what the school board built. GT Elementary was designed to run on solar and wind energy. We have a greenhouse and animals. We have the latest in sustainable technology."

"An oxymoron if there ever was one," Shelby said.

"True. But Donna understood that this would be a perfect place to use as a retreat until the madness out there calmed down. When we first came, that first weekend, we thought it might be for a week or so. Now we know how wrong we were."

"So you plan to stay here? Indefinitely?"

"No. That won't be possible. Those people you drove through? They'll find their way here eventually. At that point we need to be gone. All of these children, they need to be gone."

"Where can they go?" Max asked. "And whose kids are they? Because the people who live in the mansions we drove through . . . I imagine their kids are home and bedded down in a safe room."

"Donna and I showed up on Saturday. By Monday, we had twenty-four adults. Some were workers here, some were maids and caretakers for the houses in the area. They all found themselves locked out of their place of employment. That was our first crew of workers—maids, gardeners, janitors, teachers, a security guard . . ."

"Bill set up the perimeter blockade and found weapons to distribute." Clay let his gaze drift toward the other room, where the children were. "Without him—they wouldn't have made it past the first week."

"A few of the homeowners tried to continue as normal. They answered the doorbell when it rang, went out in the neighborhood, attempted to find additional supplies at the local stores." Maria stared at her coffee, and when she glanced up, her eyes had taken on a pained expression, as if even the memory of those first days had the ability to hurt her. "They were killed. We began to do neighborhood sweeps—always in groups of three, always armed, and we were very careful to not lead anyone back to the school."

"You found the children." Shelby leaned forward, completely enthralled by the story.

"Many of them were in the neighboring homes, though the parents were dead or missing. We brought them back here. Some were children of the employees who had shown up the first few days. The others . . ." Maria glanced at Clay.

"We were bringing a family into town. They were looking for their daughter at the university. We guided them as far as this neighborhood. Never did hear if they got the girl out. But that trip was the first time we stopped in the apartment areas and rescued a group of children. They were hungry, scared, and filthy. We were headed back to our base when we came across Maria and two of her friends."

No one spoke for a moment, digesting all that had transpired over the past few weeks. Finally Bianca asked, "How did you know their parents weren't coming back for them?"

"In most cases, their parents were dead—right there beside them." Maria pulled in a deep breath. "Someone had robbed them, shot them, left them. The kids they didn't bother with."

"But Kenny said the children we saw were decoys," Shelby said.

Clay nodded. "More so now than then. And even those children—even the decoys—need to be saved. We just haven't figured out how yet."

"Sounds dangerous." Patrick crossed his arms on the table and leaned forward.

"It is. We move slowly. We're careful, but it's something we're committed to doing. Every life is precious. Right? Every soul is loved by God."

"But you can't save them all," Max said.

"No, and as Maria said, we soon realized that while this seems to be an ideal place, it will eventually be overrun."

"You take the children back out." Patrick's tone was definitive. It wasn't a question.

"We do."

"Where do you take them?" Shelby asked.

"The modern world may have ended, but there are still good people out there. People who are willing to love and care for a child."

"Host families?"

"You could call them that, though each family realizes that the situation is probably permanent."

"So you bring in supplies and take back children."

"Or sometimes we bring in people—like you all—and take back children."

"What kind of supplies?" Max asked.

"Whatever we can find. It's true they have fresh vegetables and a sustainable facility." Clay put a heavy emphasis on the last two words.

"There are some things they don't have, some things they're beginning to run low on. And when we find children who are truly abandoned, we bring them here until they are ready to travel."

"How can you tell if they're truly abandoned?" Bhatti asked.

He'd been typically silent during the conversation. Shelby was learning that the doctor didn't speak much, didn't interject his opinion, but he took in everything. He was like a biological recording device. He could probably spit the entire conversation back out at them.

"I don't know how to explain it. Experience, I guess. Not saying we always get it right. We're more careful now than we were at the beginning."

"Some of the children got sick," Maria said. "We've quarantined them in a separate area. The school was well stocked with ibuprofen, that sort of thing, but no antibiotics. Clay brought us some, and Bill managed to find what Clay didn't."

"How are they doing?" Bhatti asked. "Are they still sick?"

"Some are." It was the first look of uncertainty Shelby had seen pass across Maria's features.

Bhatti stood and glanced at Patrick, who said, "I'll fetch your medical bag."

"Medical bag?" Maria stood too.

"I'm a doctor," Bhatti said. "Take me to the children."

"I'll help," Bianca said.

Which left Clay and Max and Shelby staring at one another.

"Looks like I'm in charge of the tour," Clay said. "Unless you want to attempt to catch some winks."

Shelby shook her head, trying to ignore Max's knowing smile. "Show us the school."

Clay slapped the table. "All right. Hold on to your scrubs. This place is going to knock your socks off."

Twenty-three

Clay wasn't exaggerating. As they walked from the greenhouse to the chicken coop, he filled them in on the "green school" concept.

"Their goal was to integrate sustainability principles throughout all aspects of the school."

The cloudy skies had lingered, but the rain had stopped completely. The concrete was wet, the air muggy, and the temperature rising as they approached an animal pen.

"Goats?" Shelby sounded as surprised as Max felt. Her pen hovered over her notebook, temporarily unsure how to spell *goats*. She was more tired than she thought.

"Tennessee fainting goats."

"A Texas goat isn't good enough?" Max laughed, but he peered closer into the fenced area.

"I hear you. These are a multipurpose breed, known for being good pets in some cases. Other folks raise them to provide meat, milk, and fiber. The school used the milk to make cheese."

"But not now," Shelby said.

"No. Now every drop of milk is going to the children."

They visited the chicken coop, which was large, elaborate, and filled with a good number of chickens pecking at the ground. Next they stopped by a composting pile, walked around a recycling center, and stopped at the water-harvesting facility.

"Could you sketch this for me, Max? It might be something we could re-create back at High Fields."

So they waited while Max drew the water tanks, the pipes fitted to them, and the unique design of the rain gutters attached to the adjacent barn.

"Are we really in an elementary school?" Max handed the notebook back to Shelby, moved to stick his hands in his back pockets, and then remembered he was wearing scrubs.

Shelby caught the motion and bumped her shoulder against his. "You can take the cowboy out of the blue jeans, but . . ."

"You have to admit it's pretty amazing," Clay said.

"True, but what you're calling a green program, we call 4-H."

"Max is right." Shelby peered closer into the full barrel of water. "Students in rural communities have been raising goats, harvesting water, and working with crops for generations."

"I'm a rural boy myself. Do you think you're telling me something new? Remember, we live to the west of Highway 183. Not much between us and west Texas except a bunch of farms." Clay shook his head. "My grandson has had a different life, though. He was raised in Austin."

Clay caught their look of concern and held up a hand. "No worries. His family was visiting for my wife's birthday when the flare happened. They're all fine, but David knew nothing about country living. Sure, they've visited before, but he's always been too busy to spend much time— what with select soccer camps, engineering camps, and summer SAT prep classes. David wasn't ready for a change of this magnitude, and so it's been harder on him. If he'd participated in a program like this? Maybe what he's facing now wouldn't seem so daunting."

"It is a pretty amazing setup," Shelby agreed. "A school like this, in the middle of the city, must have cost a fortune to design, build, and then operate."

"Sure, but these people can afford the enriched programs, and there were grants too. Much of what you see was funded by the major green groups, and you can imagine their agenda."

"Carbon footprints, global warming, that sort of thing?" When Clay nodded, Max asked, "And you buy into that?"

162

"I don't know, and when you think about it, those old arguments don't much matter anymore. In one evening, everything was reset. What I keep thinking about . . . while I'm picking up kids and driving through an urban jungle . . . is whether this could be a prototype for the next generation. Whether we could maybe do it right this time."

They made their way back inside, Max chewing on what Clay was suggesting. He hadn't thought that far into the future. Initially, he'd been worried about convincing Shelby and Carter to move to the ranch. And the last few days it had been all he could do, all any of them could do, to deal with the present. The future? Well, it had shrunk to the next forty-eight hours, to finding Carter's insulin and getting home.

It was hard to wrap his mind around the technology he was seeing—applied to rural concerns like raising goats and harvesting water. They'd always done things simply at High Fields, but that had been for a single family. If society as a whole was going to fall back on a rural lifestyle, perhaps green technology could soften that fall.

He glanced at the student-made posters as they walked down the hall past classrooms for older kids, maybe fourth or fifth grade. The posters touted things like hydroponic agriculture, energy conservation, and the buzzword of the last few years—sustainability.

Sure, he'd read about environmental concerns and advances in green technology. He tried to stay up to date with the daily news, but mostly he had stuck to law reviews. Maybe he should have paid closer attention. Maybe what they were seeing, in spite of the flare, was the future.

They stepped back into the main area of the school and continued down the hall to rejoin the rest of the group. Max pulled Clay back as Shelby moved on ahead. "This is amazing, and what you're doing? Saving the kids? It's commendable."

"But . . ."

"You're risking your life every time you bring someone in and every time you take someone out."

"You sound like my wife."

"I'm just reminding you to be careful and be realistic. You're no good to anyone if you're dead."

Clay studied him a moment before he asked, "What did you do before the flare?"

"Lawyer."

Slapping him on the back, Clay grinned. "Now why doesn't that surprise me?"

They met again in Donna's office, but this time there was an additional person sitting next to her desk. Maria was gone—no doubt helping with the children in the next room. In her place was a giant of a man, and he didn't look very happy.

Twenty-four

Bill Wilson was at least six foot six and two hundred and fifty pounds. His white beard resembled Santa Claus's in the Macy's Thanksgiving Day parade. He had the crinkly blue eyes to match, but there any holiday resemblance stopped.

His mouth was drawn down in a frown, and sweat glistened on his bald head. From what Max was seeing, he had not had a good day.

"I've asked Bill to join us," Donna said. "First, I'd like him to tell you what he saw this morning, and then we can talk about the items you're looking for."

Max glanced at Shelby. He could tell by the set of her shoulders that she was bracing herself for bad news—more bad news.

"The situation is deteriorating, as we suspected it would. People are becoming more desperate and more violent. Two weeks ago, no one challenged me if I drove down their street or walked around a block." He studied each of them in turn, and then he continued. "I'm a big guy. There are easier victims than me."

"You haven't been challenged by people who are carrying a gun?" Max asked.

"Guns are noisy. They draw a crowd. No one wants that right now—even the bad guys. At night? Maybe. Then they could slip away. But not during the day, and I only go on supply runs during the day."

"Alone?" Patrick asked.

"Usually. I want to get in and out. I don't need anybody slowing me down." Bill didn't shy away from Patrick's glare. "Military, right? You partner up in the military. Your CO would never send you out alone, but this isn't the military. Things work different now. In and out. Just me. Works fine, or it has in the past."

"But today was different." Shelby sat back, sank into her chair, and began to chew on her thumbnail.

"More roadblocks, which sometimes is just a large group of people who refuse to budge. I see those ahead of time, back up, go around. No big deal. But now they're planning, they're working together. And the way I would go around? It's blocked too."

"So what did you do?" Max asked.

"I went through. Didn't slow down. In fact, I accelerated."

"Did you run over someone?" Shelby's frown intensified. "Did you kill someone?"

"No. I didn't. Not this time. This time they scrambled like buzzards from a corpse. But if I had to run over one of those punks in order to get back here and bring these kids what they need, I would."

"Where's the police presence?" Clay asked. He was sitting forward, hands clasped between his knees.

Max could practically hear the gears of his mind whirring. How many trips would it take to get all of the kids out? How many days? Should they accelerate their exit strategy?

"The police are gone."

"Completely?"

"Yes, completely."

"We've come across roaming patrols on our previous trips," Clay said. "They don't actually stop and help anyone, but their presence calms things down a little."

"I'm telling you, they've pulled out. On the north side of Austin, a person's on his own."

Shelby sat up straighter. "Has Donna told you why we're here? What we're looking for?"

Bill nodded and stretched his long legs out in front of him, crossed at the ankles. "Insulin. I'm sorry about your son. It's a terrible thing seeing people who had treatable diseases suffer."

He didn't add *and die,* but the words were there, hanging in the air.

"My son is not suffering. He's fine, and I will find him more insulin. There has to be some left in this city."

"You're not listening to me, lady. I barely made it back here today. You wouldn't stand a chance."

Shelby stood and began pacing behind her chair.

"There has to be a path to what we need. If you can tell us where to look, we'll find a way."

Max could hear the mama-bear rumbling. He needed to intervene before Shelby spiraled out of control.

"I assume all of the pharmacies are empty."

"Yes, they are. Shelves are bare. Drugs are gone."

"Do you know of any pharmaceutical ware-houses nearby?"

"A couple."

Shelby whirled toward him. "Where?"

"You can't get in there."

"Show us. I'll pay you. I have money, a little gold, some extra fuel . . ."

"I don't want your stuff."

"Or if you're afraid, just tell us where. Draw us a map."

"I'm not afraid, but I'm not stupid either. You can't get there."

"So you've been?" Bhatti asked.

"Sure. Plenty of times. Got what I could—basic stuff like cough syrup, Tylenol, Advil. Last time I tried? The inner-city gangs had taken over the distribution centers—both of them. And these people are armed with AK-47s. You're not getting in there, and even if you did? They're not interested in what you have to trade."

Bianca rubbed her fingers against her fore-head. Finally, she looked up and asked, "What about the hospitals?"

"Deserted," Donna assured her.

"She's right," Bill said. "What the gangs didn't take, the military did."

"The military?" Patrick shook his head in disbelief. "You're telling me the military went into the hospitals and took all of the drugs?"

"*Requisitioned* was the word they used."

"What about the people that were in the hospital?" Bianca asked.

"I don't know. They were gone by the second week. Moved or taken home or maybe they died. There are bodies everywhere, and that's another concern—disease. You want to be careful what you touch and even more careful about any food or water that might be contaminated."

"You're telling us it's hopeless." Shelby sank back into her chair. "I don't accept that. I won't accept it."

Bill stood and stretched, his hands nearly touching the ceiling. He rolled his shoulders, cracked his neck, and rubbed a hand across his jaw.

Max wondered when he'd last slept.

Finally he walked over to where Shelby was sitting and squatted in front of her chair. He was so big that they were nose to nose, with him squatting and her sitting.

"Nothing's hopeless, but you need to ask yourself if it's worth the risk. Ask yourself if you're willing to die, and if you're willing to see your friends die. Because that could happen."

Bianca said, "I'm in," followed by Patrick and Max and even Bhatti.

Shelby's voice was stronger now, calmer. "We're doing this. With or without your help, but we don't know where to go. We don't know where to look."

"You go to the capitol."

"We're in—"

"You go to the capitol building, where the governor is, where the supplies are being logged and stored. It's your only chance, and getting there won't be easy."

Shelby raised her eyes to Max. He felt himself nod, saw the relief flood through her body as she deflated. All the nervous energy—gone. "All right. We'll do that. We'll go to see the governor."

"Then we leave in four hours."

"Four hours?" Shelby half rose out of her chair, but Bill wasn't paying her any attention. He was already walking toward the door. He disappeared down the hall without another word.

"Bill needs sleep," Donna explained. "And from the looks of it, you five could use the same. Maria will show you a place to bed down. We'll wake you thirty minutes before you're supposed to leave."

Max didn't think there was any chance that Shelby would sleep, though his own eyes were stinging, and he felt as if his head were stuffed with cotton. Had they really only left High Fields the day before?

They were led to a room with only a small sky-light in the center. Mats had been set up around the perimeter. Each had a pillow and blanket.

Where had all these supplies come from? Bill?

Where had Bill come from?

Bhatti, Bianca, and Shelby each grabbed a corner mat. Max chose one in the middle, thinking he could keep his eyes on things. As he watched, Shelby lay down, pulled the blanket over her, and turned to face the wall.

She didn't speak. Didn't ask any questions. Didn't raise any objections. She was re-fueling, assimilating all that they had learned, coming up with a new plan. He knew her well enough to know with complete certainty that she might be down for a few hours, but she was not out.

There were two sounds he heard before allowing his eyes to close.

The soft, rhythmic breathing of Shelby, already fast asleep.

And Patrick, who had chosen a spot up against the wall across the room, where he was once again cleaning their guns.

Twenty-five

Carter stood at the door and stared in surprise at the large group of people who had assembled in Roy's barn. He hadn't realized there were so many people in the area. He rarely saw anyone. Each person lived on a place that was well over a hundred acres, or so Georgia had told him, which translated into a lot of space between you and your neighbor.

He certainly didn't recognize anyone from the roadblock they'd originally passed through. He'd still been deep in his grief at that point, not to mention scared for his life since they were being pursued by bandits. No one looked familiar at all, except for Tate's dad.

There were some teenagers who looked close to his age, but Carter wasn't much interested in making new friends. What was the point? Something would happen—they'd be killed or have to move or maybe just decide life on the farm was too hard. The future was too uncertain for any kind of relationship anymore—friends or otherwise.

He avoided any eye contact and shuffled over to where Georgia was sitting.

"Just in time," she whispered, and then Roy was standing up, addressing the group.

"Many of you know that Tate was shot last night."

"How did it happen?"

"What time was it?"

"Tell us who did it, and we'll take care of them."

Roy held up a hand and waited until the crowd had quieted. "I'll let his father explain how it happened, but we don't have a clue as to who did it. Tate didn't see them. He didn't stop to catch a good look, which was smart. He just kept driving even after he was shot, and that probably saved his life."

Roy nodded to Andy Markham, who looked as if he hadn't slept at all since Carter last saw him. Dark rings circled his eyes, and his hand shook slightly as he reached for his ball cap and tipped it up to better see everyone.

"You all know my boy. Tate snuck out of the house after I thought he was already asleep and went to see a girl. Now, that's on him. There's no excuse for it, and I don't believe he'll be doing it again." Andy paused, brushed at his eyes, and then he pushed on with his story. "Nothing worse than you or I did when we were his age, but times have changed. Worst I would have got for sneaking out was some quality time with the switch my daddy liked to use."

This brought a little laughter and eased the tension a bit. Carter noticed everyone had their eyes glued on Andy. There wasn't any sound at all except for the last of the rain dripping off the roof, the distant call of a cow, and Andy Markham, baring his soul to his neighbors.

"It was when he was coming back, when he was in the center of the low water crossing, that they ambushed him. Shot three times through the windshield. One hit him in the shoulder. If it hadn't been . . . if it hadn't been for Georgia, my boy might be dead right now."

He swiped at his eyes again, cleared his throat, and stood up a little straighter. "I don't know who did it. Tate doesn't remember anything other than hearing the gunshots and feeling the one that hit him. I'd like to meet the man who did it. Ask him what he hoped to gain by shooting a sixteen-year-old kid."

He shuffled his feet, stared out over the crowd, and said, "Could be someone who is here today, but I have trouble imagining that."

A few heads nodded in agreement.

"Could be someone who didn't belong here. Someone who snuck by our roadblock and hoped to get a truck or whatever was in it. In that case, I suspect the person's already long gone."

Andy pulled back his shoulders, and it seemed to Carter that his gaze hardened. "Or it could be some of our neighbors who have decided to go it alone. Someone who thinks they don't need anyone else, thinks they're better without the rest of us."

He waited, but there were no comments.

"I don't know which of those three groups the person is from. If you have any suspicions, I'd appreciate hearing from you. Thank you."

He sat down on an overturned crate, and Roy moved back to the front and center of the room.

"It would be easy to believe we're safe here, as if we've created a little sanctuary where the world can't touch us. I'm afraid that's not true, though, and we need to be alert to problems."

A man in the back stood up. "My boys are already serving shifts on the blockade when I could really use them at home. What else do you want?"

"I want you to check your fence line. Confirm there are no places that have been recently breeched. Check for evidence of someone trespassing. Repair any gaps and reinforce any area that needs it. Make absolutely sure that the only way a car or truck can drive through to our properties is through the two roadblocks."

"That makes sense." A middle-aged woman with long hair—brown turning to gray—didn't bother to stand, but her voice was loud enough to reach where Carter sat. "Sounds like the smart thing to do. Only I'm working from sunup to sundown just trying to keep my crops alive, knowing . . . knowing they are all that stand between my family and starvation."

"You're not going to starve, Millie. We're going

to help each other, and we're going to make it through this. I'm only asking you to spend a little more effort on security to keep out the people we can't trust. If they get in, they can take what we have, and they can kill those we love. We have to make sure the perimeter is strong and that we're on our guard."

The room was silent, defeat weighing heavily in the air.

An older man in bib overalls stood up. "These times are hard."

He was leaning on a cane, but he shifted his weight to a bale of hay stacked to his left side and thumped the cane against the ground with his right hand. "Maybe we all got a little soft, eh? Tractors with GPS. Machines to milk your cows. My wife even had one of those fancy little robot vacuums that whirred around the house and picked up the dirt and dust."

Everyone laughed, even the white-haired woman who had been sitting next to him.

"But now times are hard again. They've come before. We survived them. They're here now, and we will survive them. They will come again. The Good Book tells us not to fear. It tells us to stand strong. It tells us to believe."

No one spoke. No one contradicted him.

"The lights will come on again, folks. I might not live to see it. Some of you will. When they do, you'll be surprised at how tough you have become. How you don't need, or even want, that luxury. How you've learned to depend on the sweat of your own labor."

He leaned the cane against the hay, stared down at his hand, rubbed his thumb against his palm, glanced up, and smiled.

"You'll be surprised how you've learned to depend on God's goodness because that isn't gone. Only hard to see at times. Like the sun . . ."

He pointed toward the roof of the barn, where as far as Carter could tell the sun was still hidden behind heavy clouds.

The old guy sat down, and another farmer took over the meeting—talking about hunting parties, how they needed to limit the number of deer they harvested, and what other wildlife was available.

Georgia stood up and asked again for medicine so they could pool their resources and catalog what they had.

Carter pretty much tuned out. His thoughts had turned to his mom and Max, wondering if they were on their way home.

Twenty-six

Carter waited around after the meeting broke up, thinking that Roy would tell him what work he needed to do next. But Roy was surrounded by men, and Georgia was talking to the few women who had attended. Carter figured he could find something that needed doing, so he walked out of the barn, surprised to see the barest hint of sunshine peeking through the clouds.

Usually in Texas farmers worried about drought. But since the flare? It seemed as if nature was determined to drown their crops. Maybe it was another El Niño. Hard to say without the weather channel. He was thinking of that—weather apps and floods and work that needed to be done—when he practically walked into a group of teenagers.

"New kid, right?" The spokesman for the group looked to be about seventeen. He had a bandana wrapped around his head holding back his hair, which was shoulder length and greasy. In his right hand, he flipped an unlit cigarette between his fingers, back and forth—over and again. No doubt it was a trick he'd practiced in front of the mirror.

"I guess."

"Heard you went to the Markhams' last night."

Carter shrugged.

"What did it look like? The wound?"

"I heard it was messed up," a shorter, rounder boy said. "Heard he might lose his arm."

"Is that true?" the first asked. "Because I'm thinking a one-armed farmer doesn't stand much of a chance."

The two of them found this terribly funny. The

rest of the group—another five or six girls and guys—smiled, or shuffled their feet, or stared at the ground.

Carter probably should have kept his mouth shut and kept walking, but somehow that quiet, stay-low, and don't cause trouble kid that he'd always been had vanished. Perhaps it had been burned away by the flare. Instead of walking off, he stepped closer and said, "I'm thinking that a one-armed farmer would stand a better chance than a dumb—"

A girl stepped forward, effectively between him and the apparent leader of their group. "I heard you had a plan to improve Roy's water reclamation system. Can you show me what you're going to do?"

Carter's gaze flicked to her. "I guess."

The leader of their group was still attempting a stare-down, which made him look pathetically like a character from a bad western. Carter wasn't sure he wanted to let this go. A confrontation up front was better than watching behind your back, but the girl was now tugging on his arm, pulling him away from the group.

"Great! Which way is it?"

At first Carter didn't know what she was talking about, and then he remembered her question. "Uh —over here."

As they walked away from the group, he heard snippets of conversation—the words *weed* and *midnight meeting* and *moonshine*. He almost turned back, almost warned them about the dangers of ignoring curfew, but the girl tugged on his arm and pulled him in the opposite direction.

"You don't really want to mess with them. Brandon, he's kind of an idiot."

"The one with the cigarette?"

"Yeah. He's a big smoker. 'Course, everyone's kind of run out of cigarettes, so he mostly plays with them instead of smoking them."

They were walking toward Georgia's vegetable garden on the opposite side of the barn. Carter stopped next to the three metal tanks.

"My name's Monica."

She held out her hand. Carter shook it because he didn't really know what else to do. Monica was probably his age, weighed a good bit more than he did, and had long, wavy brown hair. Her eyes were crinkled in amusement, and a smile tugged at her lips. What was she in such a good mood about?

"I'm Carter."

"Yeah. Everyone knows that. You're from Abney."

Carter nodded, wondering why everyone would know about him. He didn't have to wonder long.

"We heard about what happened on your way here, when you were traveling with your mom and Max. Pretty scary, huh?"

"Yeah, it was."

"Do you want to talk about it?"

"Not really."

"Fair enough. So explain all these tanks to me. Why do you need more than one? Why the trellis with the metal thing on top? How does this even work?"

"Do you always ask three questions at once?"

"Sort of. Yeah. I guess I do."

Carter laughed. The sound surprised him. It had been a while since he had found anything worth laughing about, but Monica's enthusiasm took some of the worry out of the air.

"All right. Well, this isn't finished. I had a few hours to work on it this afternoon, but there's still a lot left to do. As you can see, this barn roof is huge."

"Most barn roofs are."

"Correct. Lots of surface area. Roy had positioned tanks to catch the water at all four corners, but he still wasn't reclaiming even half of what he could have."

"Because of what drops down the sides."

"Exactly."

"But it's not like anyone has enough rain gutter to put across the entire thing."

"True." He put his hands on her shoulders and turned her toward the barn. "Tell me what you see when you look at that roof. Describe the angles."

"Like in geometry?"

"Exactly."

"Well, there's a pitch at the top."

"Uh-huh."

"And coming down from there about . . ."

"Forty-five inches."

"You measured it?" She looked over her shoulder at him.

"Not exactly, but I can tell from looking."

"Okay. Forty-five inches down, the roof angles out wider."

"That first slant, the area before that angle, is thirty degrees."

"The second slant looks about double that."

"Exactly. It's more than seventy inches long, and the angle is sixty degrees. Most barns are built this way because it distributes the weight of the roof."

"Which is a big roof."

"Very big."

"Barns are always bigger than houses around here." Monica pulled her hair back with both hands, as if she were about to gather it up into a ponytail, but then she let it fall down her back. "So what's your plan?"

"Add two sections of gutter, in the middle of the sides."

"How long?"

"Only a couple of feet, but you'll be surprised at what we're able to harvest. That sixty degree angle? It helps slow the water, only a little, but enough for it to increase what we catch."

"I don't get it."

Carter turned back to the tanks, picked up a metal cup, and filled it from the smallest tank.

"Hold out your hand, and see how much you can catch."

He dumped half of the water on her hand.

Monica shook her head. "Too fast. I only got about three drops."

"Exactly. When water is coming straight down, you catch some, but not a lot. Now try it again."

This time he tilted the cup at an angle. The water still splashed over her hand, but she was left with a palm full.

"Angles slow it down," she said.

"Just a little."

He went through the rest, how they planned to use a pipe set on top of a trellis to divert the water to the large, medium, and small tanks. He'd found a black hose which he hoped to use to connect the tallest tank to the medium, and the medium to the small. "Use gravity, don't fight it," he explained.

"All right. I'm with you so far. With the tanks full you can fill up pitchers and water the garden."

"It's rained so much, we've barely needed it," Carter admitted. "But Roy says the weather will be much drier next month."

"It always is."

"That last pipe we'll fit into a garden hose, which I'll punch small holes in, make a sort of soaker hose. Then we'll run it through the rows of

Georgia's garden. She can come out, turn on the flow—not much, just maybe a quarter turn. It will water the plants directly—much more efficient than the sprinklers we used on our lawn back in Abney."

"I want to do this at home." Monica placed her palm flat against one of the tanks. "I think I can even find the supplies."

"Just be careful if you decide to walk up on the roof. It's scarier than it looks."

Monica tilted her head, a smile forming on her lips. "City boy."

"I wouldn't call Abney a city."

They were walking back toward the group of adults leaving the barn when Carter reached for Monica's arm.

"Whatever those guys were planning for tonight, tell me you're not going."

"Like I said, Brandon's an idiot."

"Yeah, but sometimes . . ." He glanced left and right, and finally he looked directly at Monica. He didn't know her. She seemed like a nice person, though, and the world was going to need more of those. "Sometimes you do something just because you're bored, or you don't want to feel . . . I don't know, on the outside."

"I'm not bored, and that group? I don't mind being on the outside."

"Good."

He thought they were done, but she turned back

184

toward him and asked the very thing he'd been wondering, "Why do you care?"

He didn't know how to answer. Couldn't really explain that she was the first person—outside Georgia and Roy—to pierce the bubble he'd been living inside since Kaitlyn's death. He wasn't even interested in her. But it would be nice to have a friend. In that moment he realized how much he missed his friends back in Abney.

Instead of attempting to explain all of that, he said, "I don't want the next gunshot wound Georgia gets called to fix to be yours."

Twenty-seven

Shelby had thought they would all be leaving together, but of course Clay and his group didn't need supplies from deep in the heart of Austin. They didn't need to put themselves or their cargo in jeopardy. Their car was now full of children. They were headed home.

The boys and girls must have been prepared for the separation. Maybe they'd seen other kids go. Or maybe they were so shocked from all that had happened that another change couldn't pierce their exhaustion. Four girls and two boys were in the backseat—six kids sharing three seat belts. They looked as if they ranged in age from four to preteen. Two were white, two Hispanic, one black, and one Asian. And none of that mattered. What did matter is that, according to Clay, there were families willing to shelter them, to give them a home permanently if need be.

She started to ask if traveling with six children in the backseat was wise, if he shouldn't take fewer kids and be safer. What if they were in an accident? But then she remembered what they'd driven through, the wave of desperate people that was slowly rolling toward the school. Clay was right to move the kids, to get them out of harm's way. He and Kenny and Jamie were crammed into the front seat.

"Having second thoughts?" Max asked.

"No." She glanced at him and was certain he knew what she'd been thinking. Instead of forcing a confession from her, he winked.

Max Berkman, winking at her as they headed off into unknown danger. Yeah, that was what her life had become.

"Do you think . . ." She glanced toward Clay's full car. He'd started the engine. Donna was standing next to the car. They were about to move away.

Max was watching her, but she couldn't wait for his approval or opinion or whatever it was she wanted. Instead, she jogged over to the idling vehicle.

"I wanted to thank you again." She glanced from Bill to Donna to Clay. "And I wanted to say that we'll try and come by after we find the insulin. We'll come by, and if any of your kids needs a ride out to Clay's—"

She'd turned her gaze to the kids in the backseat. She stopped midsentence because her throat was tightening and tears were stinging her eyes, and she didn't know how to say what she needed to say.

"That's good," Clay said. "Welcome to the Remnant."

And then he was gone.

Shelby walked back over to Max and Bianca and Patrick and Bhatti.

Bill and Donna joined their group.

"We keep the cars nice and tight." Bill waited for each person to nod in agreement. "No one gets between us. If I stop, you stop. If I don't stop, you keep going. No matter what."

It was the opposite strategy from what Clay had used, but, then, they were going to a more dangerous area. To Shelby, it made sense to keep as tight a group as possible.

The rain had stopped, but water stood in puddles everywhere, even dripping from their cars. Bill wiped the water off the hood of the Dodge with the palm of his hand, pulled out a laminated map, unfolded it, and slapped it down.

"We're here, still a couple miles northwest of the center of Austin. The governor has cordoned off the roads from 15th to Mesquite." He ran a finger from the northeast side of the capitol area across to the southwest. "And from Colorado to San Jacinto." He traced from the eastern to western sides.

"Not that big an area," Patrick said.

"Not really, but from what I've heard, they're planning to push out."

"So we have a straight shot if we take this road," Patrick leaned forward and traced a line southwest.

"Which we are not going to do. It's gangster land from corner to corner that way."

"So how do we get in?" Bhatti asked. He'd been staring at the map intently.

Shelby realized that he was from Austin. Wasn't he? When Max had first asked him to help with their patients in Abney, Bhatti had said he was from Austin, and that he'd left to get away from something. He'd never said what, and that had been the beginning of her distrust of the man.

Now he was completely focused on Bill, as if his answer about their route mattered more to him than it did to Shelby.

"We're going to follow North Lamar down."

"Beside the park?" Bianca had to wiggle in between Shelby and Max to get a good look at the map. "Isn't that dangerous? Won't there be people living there?"

"Yes. But it's families for the most part. The gangs have taken over what apartments they can find. They aren't too interested in sleeping out in the rain." He stood back and began refolding the map. "We take Lamar south, past the capitol buildings, then turn east and approach from Congress Avenue."

Twenty-eight

They were back in their original seats. Max driving, Shelby riding shotgun, Bhatti sitting behind Max. When Max looked in his rearview mirror, he could see Patrick driving, Bianca by his side. And when he looked ahead, he saw Bill, driving a very old, very beat-up sedan.

Bill's plan was to drive at a steady 20 mph—no faster because they didn't really want to run over anyone, and no slower because they didn't want to become a target.

The school quickly became a dot in their rearview mirror. They drove out in the opposite direction they had come, through streets with more large houses that quickly transitioned into a typical downtown Austin neighborhood, albeit an upscale one—townhouses and remodeled historic homes. The dwellings weren't burned down here, but the scene was no less catastrophic.

"What happened to the people who lived in these houses?" Shelby asked. "Were they forced out, or did they just leave?"

"Probably a combination of both."

It was plain that those now living in the homes were not the homeowners.

Most of the balconies were filled with people to the point that Max was afraid they would collapse. They leaned out, watching, sometimes shouting down to someone below. In places, people had sheets hung around the balcony, as if it had been blocked off to form another room.

People slept in the yards, in tents, on benches, and on the porches. They carried trash sacks of goods, pushed shopping carts, held on to children. The scene was a giant, thrumming mass of displaced humanity. Displaced and increasingly desperate.

Max gripped the wheel tighter.

"Where did they all come from?" Shelby asked.

"Bill mentioned apartments that had burned closer to downtown." Bhatti spoke without looking at her, as if he couldn't pull his gaze away from the tragedy outside the window. "Apparently they migrated out to a better neighborhood."

"Migrated? Is that what you call it?" Shelby's question was accusatory, but her tone was simply tired.

Max glanced in the rearview mirror. Bhatti looked back at him and shrugged.

The guy was a doctor, a scientist basically. He spoke in scientific terms. He wasn't being disrespectful, only blunt.

Max sucked in a quick breath, and Shelby clutched her seat belt as if it might protect her. Ahead of them, across the width of the street and at least as deep, a throng of people moved their way. Some held rifles and handguns. Some carried cases of beer. Others held children. A few pushed wheelchairs holding the elderly.

Were they actually going to drive through that many people?

Bill had warned them that they might have to, had assured him that the people always parted, though sometimes at the last second.

Fortunately, they didn't have to test that theory. When they were still a hundred yards away from the throng, Bill made a right. Max was practically on his bumper, and Patrick was just as close.

He understood now why Bill had wanted them to stay so close together. Space in between the vehicles would equal an opening, and an opening could be taken advantage of.

The street they turned on was in no better shape, but the people looked to be less of a threat.

One family sat in the back of a mail truck, staring at them as they passed.

Another walked slowly down the sidewalk, pushing a shopping cart filled with children.

The next block was entirely burned out. Sitting in front of the charred remains of an apartment building was a dog. It looked to Max like a chocolate Labrador. Was he waiting for his family to return? How long would the dog stay? He'd heard stories of dogs waiting weeks, even longer, for a family to come home. But whoever had left this place wasn't coming back. What was there to come back to?

Max was looking at that, at the dog, when Bill suddenly applied his brakes.

"Don't hit him!" Shelby's foot stomped the floor, where the brake would be if she were in the driver's seat.

Bhatti reached forward and grabbed the back of the front seat.

Brakes squealed, and then they were stopped, inches from Bill's back bumper.

Patrick, who had been watching more closely, stopped several feet from the Dodge.

Everyone piled out of the vehicles at once.

Bill was already talking to a thin man wearing a T-shirt with the sleeves cut out, his cap turned backwards, and tattoos snaking down his arms.

"Why are we stopping?" Max asked, as he approached the two men.

"Because we need to know what the situation is, and Raven probably knows."

"Raven?" Max realized with a start that the man was a woman. He would never have guessed, which was perhaps her intent.

"It's not safe to talk here," she said. "Keep going another block, turn right into the alley. I'll meet you there in five minutes."

She walked on in the opposite direction.

"You trust her?" Patrick asked.

"I do. She's given me good information in the past."

Before they could ask any additional questions, Bill was back in his car, pulling away. The others hurried to their vehicles to catch up.

"I can't believe we're doing this." Shelby slammed her door shut.

"You want the insulin?" Max asked.

"Of course I do," she snapped.

"Then we have to trust somebody. We're not going to find it lying on the ground."

"So we're just going to follow this guy. Follow Bill into what could very well be a trap. Why? We can find the capitol without him."

"Donna and Clay recommended him. That's good enough for me."

Shelby crossed her arms and stared at him. "How far do you think we are from where we need to be, Max? Three or four miles? Miles. We could cover that in five to ten minutes."

"A month ago—maybe, but not today." He jerked down on his ball cap. "Shelby, I understand you have trust issues. I do, and I respect that, but you have to give me a little slack here."

"We're going in the wrong direction."

"Let's just follow him. Okay? Let's see what Raven has to say, and then we can re-assess."

They pulled into an alley, which fortunately was open at the other end. The last thing Max wanted was to get trapped between two half-burned-out buildings.

They once again all spilled out of their cars, and then they waited.

"She's helped you before?" Max asked.

"Yeah."

"What do you think she can tell us?"

"I don't know. That's why I'm waiting."

"This is a waste of time." Shelby began pacing between the cars.

Bhatti stood halfway between Shelby and the Dodge. Patrick had his back to them. He was watching the west end of the alley, and Bianca was watching the east end. They both had their weapons out. If this was a trap, they'd go down fighting.

Raven walked in alone, straight up to Bill. She slapped his hand, shook, and then smiled.

"Long time, man."

"Yeah, two or three days."

"That's a long time in the new world."

"Is that what you call this? The new world? Because it looks pretty old and wrecked to me." Shelby's tone was aggressive. She'd been sitting around too long, and perhaps her patience had reached its limit. Too late Max realized she'd moved even closer, right up into the girl's space. Max stepped forward to pull her back, to try and keep their situation from spiraling out of control, but he was too late, and he knew it even before his eyes and ears told him so.

Twenty-nine

Shelby couldn't have said what made her do it.

Fear?

Desperation?

Stupidity?

Maybe the girl's clothes were too purposely ragged or her attitude too condescending. Possibly the gun that she was wearing boldly on her hip irritated Shelby, or maybe it was the casual way Raven and Bill greeted one another—as if this were another day in paradise, as if her son's life weren't hanging on whether or not they were successful.

She stepped forward and challenged the girl, but instead of backing down, Raven stepped closer and began shouting back.

In the back of her mind, Shelby registered the fact that Patrick was shouting for them all to get down, and Bianca had raised her rifle, and Bill was hollering for everyone to put down their weapons.

"Tell that to your sniper on the roof!" Patrick snarled.

Shelby turned, saw the direction that Patrick had his own rifle aimed, and spied the rifle barrel and the top of someone's head.

"He's with me!" Raven shouted. "Zane is with me, so everyone just chill."

No one moved. No one lowered their weapon. Raven marched over to Patrick, pulled her weapon, thumbed off the safety, and pointed it directly at him. "The dude on the roof is with me, so if you're thinking about shooting him, you'd better have someone shoot me at the exact second you pull the trigger."

"Better not hesitate," Patrick said.

"I never do."

Bill pushed in between them. "We are wasting time."

But Patrick was still talking to Raven. "Why do you need a sniper on the roof?"

"Because without him I'd already be dead several times over."

"Is that why he was following you out on the main drag?"

"Yeah, and it's why he's here now."

"So you don't trust anyone?"

"Bill I trust. You, not so much."

If Patrick was bothered by the girl's audacity, he didn't show it. He grinned and said, "Looks like we have ourselves a Wild West standoff then. Tell Zane to lower his weapon, and I'll lower mine."

Shelby thought that Raven would walk away at

that point, taking whatever information she had with her. Instead she whistled, and made a circle motion around the top of her head. The guy on the roof disappeared. Patrick lowered his weapon. "If you don't mind, I'll just wait here to make sure he doesn't come back."

"Suit yourself." Raven nodded toward Bill's vehicle, and the two of them moved away.

Bianca stayed at her end of the alley, still on alert.

Patrick remained where he was, rifle down, but at the ready.

Max, Shelby, and Bhatti followed Bill.

"This your idea? Bringing crazy people into my hood as if I don't have enough to deal with?"

Bill shrugged.

It was Bhatti who asked, "What makes the neighborhood yours?"

"Because I'm taking care of it." She turned back to Bill. "What did you bring me today?"

He opened the trunk of his vehicle, pulled out a box of MREs and a case of water.

Raven whistled again—this time two short notes and one long.

There was the sound of someone, her sniper Shelby supposed, running across the roof and then down a ladder near the end. When he stepped closer, Shelby saw that he looked to be Carter's age, had a buzz haircut, and wore a shirt with the sleeves cut out. Maybe it was a type of uniform. Without a word to any of them, he slung his rifle over his shoulder, picked up the supplies and hurried out of the alley.

Bill closed the trunk of the sedan. "Can he get those back to your people okay?"

"Zane? Zane's like a cat. He can get in and out before anyone knows he's there."

"Who are the supplies going to?" Bhatti asked.

Shelby turned to stare at him. He'd shown more interest in the last hour than he had since they left Abney. What was with this guy? The closer they got to the city center, the more intense his gaze became, and his questions had taken on an urgent tone.

"Old folks, mostly." Raven looked him up and down. "You want to join us in the fight? Something tells me you'd fit in better with us than with this group."

"What fight?" Shelby asked.

"What fight?" Raven's voice went lower, harder. "The fight to survive, maybe? Or how about the fight to just outlive the hundreds of cowards who'd rather take from old people than figure out how to make it on their own? There's about a dozen fights—so choose whichever you'd like, pick up a weapon, and jump in." Now she stepped closer to Shelby. "Or get out of my way."

Shelby didn't need anyone to come to her rescue, but Max made an attempt anyway. "Shelby's in a fight of her own. We're looking for insulin. Do you know where we can get any?"

"No, man. All the meds around here—they're gone. The few people I know who have them, you don't want to deal with. Plus, the only thing they will trade for is cocaine, heroin, or weed. Unless you have one of those, you're not getting what they have."

"I'm taking them to the capitol buildings," Bill said. "Or as close as we can get."

"They won't let you in. The government people aren't letting anyone in."

"Let us worry about that," Shelby said. "It's not your fight."

It had been a long time since Shelby had been in an actual physical altercation—in fact, she'd only been in one, her sophomore year in high school when a girl had been talking trash about her and Max. The memory came over her like a wave, and she felt sixteen again—young and strong, full of anger, and ready to take on the world.

Her adrenaline had just surged, and she'd stepped forward to confront Raven, maybe push her or force her back, when Raven punched her in the mouth.

She stumbled backwards. Bhatti and Max stepped in between them, and Bill backed Raven away from the group.

"You need to watch your mouth." Raven jerked her arm out of Bill's grasp. "Let me go. I'm not going to hit her again."

"Shelby, are you okay?" Max's back was to

her, effectively blocking Raven from moving any closer. "Are you okay?"

Shelby almost gasped at the pain that radiated through her jaw. She tasted copper, put her hand to her mouth, pulled it away and stared at her red fingers. Her lip was swelling already, but a quick check with her tongue assured her no teeth were loose. Bianca started toward her, but Shelby waved her away and marched back over to where Raven stood. She pushed her way through Bill and Max. She didn't stop until she was standing toe-to-toe with her newly sworn enemy.

"You hit me again, and I'm going to scratch your eyes out."

"We don't have time for this." Bill sounded disgusted, but Shelby ignored him.

"What is your problem?"

"My problem?" Raven's mouth twisted in a snarl. "You want to know what my problem is? I watched two more babies die this morning, that's one of my problems. And the old people? Well, they sit silently in their wheelchairs and soiled clothing waiting for help to come—but it ain't coming. It's me, and you, and the hoodlums who are trying to take what we have. We're all that's left."

A tiny bit of Shelby's anger slipped away, but her tone remained hostile. "You're struggling. I get that. We're all struggling."

"Yeah, you look like you're starving—driving

around in your cars like nothing's happened."

"We are looking for insulin. You don't know where we can find it? Fine. Tell Bill you've got no information for him. We'll keep going without your help."

She'd turned away and was stomping back toward the Dodge when Raven called out, "Stay off North Lamar."

"That route was open two days ago," Bill said.

"Yeah, well, that was two days ago. Now it's Diego's territory, and you won't get through even with G.I. Joe and G.I. Jane tagging along."

"How do you suggest we get through to the capitol square then?" Bhatti asked.

"I don't. I suggest you go back wherever you came from."

"That's not going to happen," Max said.

"It's your life. Do what you want with it."

"Suggested route?" Bill asked.

Raven shrugged. "Stay on the west side of the park area. Diego's in what's left of the apartments and businesses on the east side. He hasn't crossed the park yet. I'm not sure why."

"Thank you," Bill said.

"Sure, and next time you come into my neighborhood? Do yourself a favor. Come alone."

Raven walked to the end side of the alley, past Bianca, and disappeared out onto the main road. Shelby stared after the girl, wondering what had just happened, suddenly imagining the kind of life she had been forced to live. Remorse tugged at her, but she shoved it away.

"Are you sure you're okay?"

Max tried to touch her lip, but Shelby squirmed out of his reach. "I'm fine. You got any ice?"

"No."

Max stepped away from her, shook his head, and then strode right back up to her, stopping only inches away. "You put us all in danger here."

"I did not."

"Yes. You did. Why? Because a girl you'd just met failed to offer the hand of friendship to you?"

"She was arrogant."

"Grow up, Shelby. We have to learn to work with people we don't like."

She didn't know how to answer that, so she jerked open the car door and collapsed into the passenger seat.

They drove out of the alley, parallel to the street they had been on, and turned back in the direction they had come. Shelby stared out the window, Max's words pricking her heart like thistles. Had she put them in danger? What had happened to the sweet Christian woman who sat at her computer and pounded out clean romances? How long had it been since she'd even prayed about their situation? Praying had come easily enough when her biggest concern was an approaching deadline.

She wanted to cry out in frustration. She wanted a do-over for the last twenty minutes.

But there were no do-overs. Maybe there never had been.

It seemed to Shelby that for every step forward, she took three steps back. Soon she'd find herself in Abney and then at High Fields with only an empty cargo area and a fat lip to show for it.

Thirty

They drove north, tried three different times to cross Shoal Creek, which was full to overflowing from the recent rains. Once Shelby would have sworn she saw a kangaroo drinking from the stream. Another time they swerved to miss a crocodile that was lying in the middle of the street. The city park brimmed over with tents, RVs, even trucks with tarps propped up and thrown over the bed. Each time they tried to cross into the park, cross over the creek, their way was barred by semipermanent piles of debris, which had no doubt been stacked there for that very purpose—to keep people out. To keep Diego and his thugs from using the park as a thoroughfare.

Finally they came to a stop in a vacant lot across from the park. They'd left at four thirty, and it was now close to six. They were farther from their destination than when they started. Shelby didn't want to think about what they'd do if they were stuck outside after dark.

Everyone piled out of the cars. Bill looked unhappy, but then again Shelby had yet to see him smile. That wasn't quite true, though. One of the children had come up to him at the school, and he'd squatted down and handed her something from his pocket. It had been a doll—some kind of Polly Pocket thing. The memory stuck in Shelby's throat, blocked any words she might have said.

Bhatti wandered toward the street, as if he needed to study it, to remember it.

Max, Shelby, Patrick, and Bianca walked up to where Bill was waiting by the door of his huge, decrepit sedan. The thing was like a tank, which was exactly what he needed in this situation.

"I was hoping I could get you closer." Bill ran a hand up and over the top of his bald head. "As we were warned, the situation is deteriorating."

"It's a good thing you were with us," Patrick said. "Otherwise we would have driven right into Diego's area."

"Any suggestions as to where we should go now?" Max asked.

"Another block north of here is a major thoroughfare. I'm fairly sure you can get over the river, turn, and make your way south."

"Then why did we stop?" Bianca asked.

"Because I have to go to an abandoned warehouse on the east side. There's a guy meeting me there in thirty minutes. I can't afford to miss him. Supposedly he has baby formula, diapers, that sort of thing. Donna needs those supplies, and I promised her I'd bring them back."

"Where does he find the diapers?" Shelby asked. Her words came out thick and misshapen. She ran a finger over her top lip, which had swollen considerably. "And where did you get the MREs that you gave to Raven?"

She thought he might not answer, but he did. He walked next to her, rested his back against the Dodge, and she did the same.

"There are supplies to be had, Shelby. It's a matter of knowing where they are. Think of everything that was in transit before the flare. It's a lot of goods."

"But who has them now?" Tears pricked her eyes, and she blinked them away. "How do you know the people . . ."

"How do I know the people who know the people who have the supplies? How can you know? You ask, you listen, you follow your instincts. That's what it's about now—listening to your instincts."

Patrick nodded. "In the military, my CO said surviving was fifty percent training and fifty percent following your instincts."

"In this situation, I'd weigh slightly more heavily on the instinct side. The point is that the people who recognized this quickly got a jump on the rest of us." He scratched the side of his face, stuck his hand in his pocket, jiggled his car keys, and glanced in the direction of the sun. Then he looked directly at Shelby.

"I understand your desperation. I understand you would do anything for your son. But turning the only people who can help you into your enemies? That's foolish."

"Raven."

What had she read in her devotional mere weeks ago? Ecclesiastes 3. It had reminded her of the hit song *Turn! Turn! Turn!* by the 1960s group the Byrds. She'd even laughed and showed it to Max. Everything had changed since that day three weeks ago. Except Scripture. God's Word was timeless. What had she read? She squeezed her eyes shut, pictured it on the page. *A time to kill and a time to heal. A time to tear down and a time to build.*

She'd confused the two.

"Yeah. Raven is one of the good guys . . . or gals. Her ways may be a little unorthodox, but she's actually helping people. In this world . . . the new world . . . some of the people who look like you can trust them, you can't. And some of the people that you would have passed by before, they're the ones who can help you."

He patted her clumsily on the shoulder, shook hands with the rest of the group, and climbed into his vehicle with an admonition. "Get off the streets before dark. If you haven't reached the capitol square by then, find some place to lay low until early morning."

He stuck his head out the window and made sure they were paying attention. "Early in the day, most of the punks are sleeping off whatever beer or drugs they've found. Early in the afternoon, they're escaping the heat by lying low indoors. Anything in between . . . and you don't want to be outside."

And with those final words of wisdom, he was gone.

Thirty-one

It felt odd travelling with just their two vehicles again.

Max led in the Dodge and Patrick followed. They drove north, like Bill told them to, and found the large crossroad—three lanes on each side, and a concrete median to separate them. Cars that had been abandoned had been pushed to the right of each side. The middle was open, and they crossed it with little trouble. Once they were on the far side of the park, they turned south. Now Shoal Creek was on their left and a string of retail establishments lined the road on their right—a movie theater, barbecue joints, music venues. All were either burned out or vandalized—shattered windows, busted doors, and graffiti, always graffiti.

It occurred to Max that there seemed to be no shortage of spray paint.

"This was the hip part of Austin," he said to no one in particular.

"Now it just looks sad." Shelby propped her elbow on the open window. "I didn't realize how good Abney looks, practically untouched compared to Austin."

"There was the gas explosion and before that the fire downtown," Bhatti reminded her.

"But nothing like this."

"Are you surprised?"

"A little. Yeah, I guess I am."

A yellow school bus sat forlorn in the middle of a parking lot. Clothes, towels, and even sheets had been draped over the windows to block out the summer sun. From the look of those gathered around the bus, Shelby guessed that twenty-five, maybe thirty people were living in it.

Where did they bathe?

Or use the restroom?

Did they have any food to cook, and if they did, where did they cook it?

And behind those thoughts, looming in the back of her mind, were bigger questions. She didn't realize she was going to say them aloud until she heard her own voice.

"Why are they still here? What are they waiting for?"

"They're waiting for help," Max said. "You have

to remember these are the people who stood in line for lottery tickets every time the jackpot topped a million."

"A bit of a stereotype." Shelby turned to study Max.

He shrugged and grinned at her. "I'm not picking on any one ethnicity. I'm making an observation about twenty-first-century Homo sapiens, especially those living in an urban setting. They've grown up with the idea that someone will hand them a check, or answer when they dial 9-1-1, or fix whatever is broken."

"The human mind is capable of tricking itself into seeing black where there's white, substance where none exists, and rescue even if no one is coming." Bhatti leaned forward between the seats. "Looks like we're driving into trouble."

The road in front of them was literally blocked with people—sitting in lawn chairs, sprawled on top of vehicles, and lying on the ground. They weren't going anywhere, didn't seem to be waiting for anything in particular, and barely gave them any notice.

Max made a right before they reached the edge of the crowd, even though it took them in the wrong direction.

Shelby let out a sigh of frustration and drummed her fingers against the door.

But Bhatti was still leaning forward, over the seat. He pointed to a black-and-white flatbed truck. "He's going to ram you. Turn, turn, turn."

The commercial truck looked to be over twenty feet long. Big enough to hold a 20,000-pound payload. Big enough to smash the Dodge.

Shelby screamed.

Bhatti sat back and refastened his seat belt.

And Max jerked the wheel to the right. He hit a curb, bounced over it, skidded against a street lamp, and landed on the side street facing the wrong direction, facing the flatbed truck.

"Turn us." Bhatti had pulled Max's rifle from where it was stored next to him, propped his hand on the open window, and steadied the barrel on his hand. "Forty-five-degree turn, please."

"You can't—"

"Do it, Max."

He jerked the transmission into reverse, turned the wheel, hit the gas, and spun them so that they would now be broadsided by the oncoming flatbed.

Shelby fumbled for her handgun.

Max glanced in his rearview mirror and saw Patrick coming up behind them.

"Be ready to go." Bhatti sighted in the truck.

He shot four times, and three of them hit the tanker—twice in the passenger side front tire and once in the windshield. Maybe it would be enough.

"Go, now."

Max floored the accelerator. The tires squealed,

and the engine roared, and then they were speeding west again.

He made a left, a right, and then another left. Ahead of them was the park, but he no longer knew if that was the direction he needed to go.

The shadows had lengthened, putting most of the street into a semidarkness as retail centers gave way to skyscrapers.

"Where are we?" Shelby's voice shook as she squirmed to look behind them.

"All I see is Patrick," Bhatti said. "We may have lost the flatbed."

"Where are we?" she asked again, peering up at the street signs.

"Farther south, closer to the capitol buildings."

"I don't see them."

"Because we're still too far." He sped by three children standing on a curb, prayed they wouldn't step out in front of him.

"We need to pull over," Bhatti said. "Figure out where we are and what we're going to do."

"But where?"

As if in answer a church rose up on the right, a giant, historic cathedral. Max glanced in his rearview mirror and tapped the brakes twice. Then he made a right into an alley adjacent to the church's courtyard and parking area. Patrick pulled in behind them.

Max expected to see more homeless people, families living in tents, or even hoodlums using the church as their base. What he didn't expect to see was parking lot attendants sporting Uzis.

They waved him to a stop. One kept a bead on them while the other jogged up to his window.

"Are you requesting refuge?"

"Excuse me?"

"Are you requesting refuge?"

"Max, what are you doing?" Shelby unbuckled and turned to look behind them.

Max looked in his rearview mirror and saw Patrick's Mustang, and behind that the flatbed. Its front windshield was shattered and one tire was making a *whomp-whomp-whomp* sound, but it continued to troll down the road. He heard the squeal of brakes and then saw the rear bumper of the truck as it backed up.

"We are," Max said.

"You got to say it, man."

"We are requesting refuge. Both cars—"

He motioned toward Patrick, but the guard had spotted the flatbed now. He whistled, the first guard moved a barricade, and they were waved through. The last thing that Max saw was the flatbed turning into the alley.

Thirty-two

Carter had no intention of seeing Monica again that afternoon. He did his chores, washed up as best he could, and headed to the main house for dinner. Georgia made more than enough food for the three of them and asked Carter to take the extra over to the Markhams. She gave him specific instructions to stay and watch Tate eat, make sure he took the antibiotic she'd left that morning, and be back before dark.

It wasn't a hardship to go. Actually, he rather liked driving the four-wheeler. It was exponentially cooler than the car he'd left behind in Abney, though he doubted it would be good for cruising the burger joint in town. But then who did that anymore? No one. They were all home, working on the family garden, on the latrines, on surviving.

So he'd strapped the containers of food onto the back of the four-wheeler with a bungee cord, visited the Markhams—Tate actually looked a little better than he had the night before—and headed back to High Fields.

It was just before the low water crossing that he spied Monica standing in the middle of a field next to a deer feeder.

He almost drove on by.

But he'd been feeling itchy since the meeting.

He wasn't ready to go home and go to bed early. And he couldn't feign interest in another game of checkers. So he'd turned off the road and crossed the pasture to where she was standing, hands on hips, frowning at something on the ground.

"Come look at this."

She acted as if she wasn't surprised at all to see him, as if it was the most natural thing in the world for him to drop by. Which was kind of nice. It made them feel like friends, even though they barely knew each other. He walked over to where she stood, just outside a short fence that encircled a tripod deer feeder.

"Tell me what you see." She stepped back so he could take a closer look.

"I don't see anything, other than . . . well, dirt."

"You don't see anything? Do those look like deer tracks to you?"

"Um. No?"

"No! They do not." She'd somehow managed to stuff all of her hair under a baseball cap. Now she pulled it off, and the hair fell back to her waist.

"Pigs. They're eating what little corn we have, and we have precious little thanks to the stupid flare. Now we won't even have deer meat."

"Why don't you eat the pig meat?"

"Yeah. I've heard it before. But they're hard to catch. They come out in the middle of the night, whereas a deer will usually approach a feeder at sunrise and sunset."

Carter backed up until he was against the front fender of the four-wheeler. It felt good to stand there in the last of the afternoon's heat and talk about pigs. Felt almost normal. Much more normal than checking on gunshot victims.

"You're thinking something," Monica said. "I can almost hear the gears turning."

"Roy has brought up the subject of pigs a time or two. Mind you, I haven't been at High Fields all that long, but already he's mentioned them—"

"Did he say how much he hates them? How they're eating all his corn and wrecking his chance to survive the winter?"

"Nah. Nothing like that." Carter glanced at her and tried to keep from laughing.

"What?"

"You have . . ." He leaned forward and pulled a few pieces of hay out of her hair.

She slapped the cap against her leg, and then jerked it back onto her head. "Barn work," she muttered. "Stay focused. What did Roy say about the pigs?"

"He called them feral pigs. He said that at one point there must have been a pig farmer some-where around here, and his pigs got out, and then they had piglets, and so the cycle began."

"Roy said all that? He doesn't strike me as much of a talker."

"He can be if it's anything regarding High Fields."

"Huh."

"Anyway, his idea was that we could trap and domesticate them."

"Why would we do that?"

"For one, they'd stop tearing up the area around your deer stand and eating all of your corn."

Monica plopped down in the driver's seat of the four-wheeler, ran her hand over the top of the steering wheel, and finally glanced up at him, a smile tugging at the corners of her mouth. "But then I'd have one more thing to feed and clean up after."

"True, but you'd also have bacon."

"I miss bacon."

"I miss burgers."

"And French fries."

"Chocolate shakes."

"Low shot, Sparks. Even mentioning chocolate is cruel."

She was smiling outright now. Carter was amazed that they could talk about the things of their past, anything from before, and laugh about it. But then you couldn't be sad all the time. His mother had said once that each person had a finite capacity for sadness . . . or maybe that was a line in one of her books, not that he'd read more than a few pages here and there.

He wasn't sure if he believed that. It seemed that his capacity for sadness was limitless. It seemed that bad things would keep happening, and he would feel worse and worse until one day he simply stopped existing. That's the way it had seemed, but now . . . well, now was different. They were laughing about burgers and French fries.

The silence stretched between them.

It didn't seem to bother Monica. She sat, staring at the tripod stand and tapping her fingers against the steering wheel. Finally, she turned and asked, "So did Roy have a plan? For domesticating pigs?"

"Not exactly."

"But—"

"But I might."

Thirty-three

Shelby recognized the big church the minute they'd pulled into the alley. She'd once toured Saint Mary Cathedral while researching a book she was writing. It was strange to her how her life seemed to be coming full circle, returning to places she never thought she'd visit again.

They'd been led through a back door, which was also guarded, and then down a long room.

"Fellowship hall?" Bianca asked.

"Close. This is the Bishops Hall."

Max looked at her strangely. Bhatti and Patrick were walking a few steps ahead, no doubt making sure this wasn't a trap. But it was simply a hall where people gathered to fellowship—or, in this case, eat. Long tables had been set up end to end, and it looked as if a large number of people had been eating. But most of them were finished. They were cleaning their plates into a slop bucket, not that there was much to clean. As they followed their guard to the food line, Shelby glanced over at the line of folks dropping off their plates and utensils. Most of the plates she saw looked as if they'd been licked clean.

"The line closes in fifteen minutes," the guard said, before turning and hustling back to his post.

As one they turned and stared at the scene.

Plates in one tub.

Silverware in another.

One group of people—men and women and teens—were wiping down the long tables. Half a dozen people were working in the kitchen, which she could see through an opening in the wall, through which meals could be served.

"Smells delicious in here," Bianca said.

"Who can think about eating?" Patrick motioned toward a corner of the room, and they all traipsed after him.

Shelby would have rather checked out the kitchen. Whatever they were cooking smelled heavenly, much better than the granola bar she'd had for lunch.

Patrick barely waited for them to form a semi-circle before he began launching questions.

"What are we doing here? Why did we agree to leave our weapons in the cars? What are we going to do about that flatbed?"

No one spoke for a moment. Shelby wanted to hug him. Those very same questions had been churning in her stomach since the moment they pulled into the church parking lot.

"It's seven thirty," Max said, ticking his answers off on each finger. "Bill warned us to get off the streets, and we are. We agreed to leave our guns because that was the only way to get in."

"They could steal them," Patrick said.

"Doubtful. They have Uzis. We have deer rifles. Why would they want to steal them? And lastly, we're not going to do anything about the flatbed right this minute because it's out there and we're in here. Also, I think the guards will take care of it." When no one disagreed, he added, "Now let's go see if there's any food left."

There was, and it tasted even better than it smelled. Stew with big chunks of beef, cornbread with butter, all the water they could drink, and even oatmeal-raisin cookies for dessert.

"Cookies!" Shelby broke a piece off hers and popped it into her mouth. "It's like . . . something I dreamed about."

Bhatti pushed away his bowl, crossed his arms on the table, and leaned forward. "Are we going to stay the night here? Can we trust these people?"

"Maybe." Max's tone was noncommittal, but

Shelby knew from the look in his eyes that he had a plan.

"And what is this place?" Patrick asked.

"It's Saint Mary Cathedral, begun in 1872." When they stared at her, waiting, she added, "I researched it for a book. Even came and took a tour."

"But are these church people?" Patrick waved at a group of bikers who had entered the chow line. "Or is this a building that another group has taken over?"

"I don't know who's in charge, but they're well supplied." Bianca finished her cookie and drained her glass of water.

"I'm with Bhatti," Patrick said. "I don't trust this place."

"I didn't say—"

"Bill said we should follow our instincts." Shelby sat back, studied her group of friends—and yeah, maybe Bhatti was slowly being included in that group. "But honestly, I don't know what to think of this. One minute we're being pursued by guys in a flatbed truck—what was that even about? The next we're eating stew. Whatever is happening here, maybe it's worth checking out. Maybe they know where we can get the insulin."

"They certainly have food and apparently plenty of it." Bianca picked up her spoon, stared at it, and dropped it back in the bowl. "Which they just gave to us—no questions asked."

"There was that weird thing about *seeking refuge.*" Max filled Patrick and Bianca in on the initial conversation with the guards. "I have no idea what they were talking about."

"It fits an Old Testament reference," Bhatti said. "The book of Numbers mentions six cities of refuge. They were to be scattered throughout Israel—three on the eastern side of the Jordan River and three on the western side."

Shelby glanced around. She wasn't the only one staring at Bhatti, eyes wide in disbelief.

"My grandparents considered themselves to be something of religious scholars . . . but then many people of their generation were."

"These cities of refuge, what made you think of them?" Max asked.

"We're in a church, and the guards insisted that you state you were seeking refuge . . . not asylum, not help, but refuge. It seemed an odd choice of words to me."

As Max, Bianca, Patrick, and Bhatti continued to toss the idea back and forth, Shelby looked around and spied what she needed on a table against the wall. She returned with the Bible, consulted the index, and then turned to the twentieth chapter of Joshua.

"This section is titled *Cities of Refuge.*"

"What does it say? Specifically?" Max pushed in closer, but she nudged him back with her shoulder.

"Then the LORD said to Joshua: 'Tell the Israelites to designate the cities of refuge, as I instructed you through Moses, so that anyone who kills a person accidentally and unintentionally may flee there and find protection from|the avenger of blood.' "

"It says that?" Max pulled the book from her hands.

"We were definitely fleeing," Bianca said.

"Though we hadn't killed anyone . . . yet."

A gong rang out, causing them all to stop and look around.

"Bell tower," Shelby said.

The few other people in the room began moving toward the doors at the far end.

"Where are they going?" Bianca asked.

"And are we supposed to sit here and wait for the guy with the Uzi, or just . . . you know . . . follow the crowd?" When no one answered, Shelby again hopped up. This time she made her way to the kitchen, where the workers were removing aprons.

"Excuse me. We're new here."

"Welcome," the older of the women said. She was probably in her sixties, with short hair that was quickly reverting back to its natural gray. "Usually there is someone around to see to guests and explain the rules."

"Rules?"

"But now it's worship time, and everyone will be there."

"Worship?"

"In the main cathedral. You'll want to hurry your friends along. You don't want to miss the message by Reverend Hernandez."

"Reverend Hernandez." Shelby shook her head, realizing what a fool she must sound like standing there parroting the woman's words back to her. But the woman didn't seem to have noticed. In fact, she'd walked away, across the room and through the double doors, followed by her kitchen helpers.

Shelby hurried back to their table. "We need to clean this up. Help me. We're late."

"Late?" Bhatti asked. "Late for what?"

"The message."

Thirty-four

The cathedral was, quite simply, stunning.

They entered from the courtyard. On their left were the two massive wooden doors that opened onto the street. It occurred to Shelby that armed guards no doubt waited on the other side of those doors, as they had in the parking area. The thought disoriented her. She felt as if she'd been dropped into a medieval setting rather than the middle of a historic cathedral in modern-day Austin, Texas.

The room itself was massive, with ceilings probably twenty feet high, stained glass windows, and dark wood. It reminded her of something from a movie—some European church from the last millennium built at the bequest of the king.

Details from the tour she'd taken several years before came back to her in bits and pieces. Nicholas Clayton had designed the cathedral to remind parishioners of the natural places where men encounter God. To that end, treelike columns had been placed at intervals down the room. The tops of the columns had been carved to resemble foliage. Everywhere she looked, there were traces of vines and leaves—man encountering God.

In between each of the columns were two tall stained-glass windows. The sanctuary was shaped like a nave, with dark wooden pews stretching down the length of the room and a center aisle that drew all attention to the front altar, where a blue dome replete with stars crowned more stained-glass windows. At the very center of it all was a sculpture of Christ upon the cross.

As astounding as the architecture was the sheer number of people crowded into the cathedral. They filled the pews, scooting in to allow room for just one more. They stood in the doorways, along the walls, near the massive columns, and at the back of the room.

There were people of all ages, all races, and both genders.

Patrick and Bianca and Bhatti pushed in through the crowd until they were squeezed into a corner in the back of the room. Max shrugged, made an after-you gesture, and they joined their friends. Shelby expected a hymn. She expected the long, drawn-out notes of an organ or the solid chords of a piano, but there was no music.

The crowd hushed, and a man stepped to the front of the stage. They were far enough back that it was hard to make out his features. If she guessed, he was in his forties, with dark hair that flopped over his eyes and sinewy arms. He looked nothing like a priest, though he wore the vestments of the clergy—a black robe with a white clerical collar. It made her itch just looking at it. How did he stand such clothes in this heat?

And it was hot in the room. With so many people and no way to open the windows, the air hung dank and heavy and stale.

But she forgot all about that when Reverend Hernandez began to speak.

Shelby had been to Catholic services, even Mass, a few times in her life. Sometimes for weddings or funerals. Sometimes for research. And once or twice because she was visiting with a friend who asked her to go.

This service was nothing like those.

Reverend Hernandez stood in the center of the room, his arms raised high, his head lowered. He stood there, silently, for a full minute. When he lowered his arms, he began to speak.

"Surely we are living in the last days. We are

warned, in the second epistle to Timothy. We are warned."

A woman to Shelby's right began to weep.

Bianca moved closer.

Max crossed his arms, his gaze unwavering as he studied the priest.

" 'In the last days there will come times of difficulty.' That we have seen and experienced." He raised his gaze to the crowd, as if he were noticing them for the first time. "People will be lovers of self, lovers of money, proud, arrogant, abusive, disobedient to their parents . . ." His voice rose steadily with each word, reminding Shelby of the heavy sound of an organ building to a crescendo.

"People will be ungrateful, unholy, heartless, unappeasable, slanderous, without self-control."

"Yes, Jesus. Yes." Affirmation came from the right, from the left, even in front of and behind them.

"People will be brutal, not loving good, treacherous, reckless, swollen with conceit." And now his arms were up again, reaching out, encompassing the entire crowd. "Lovers of pleasure rather than lovers of God."

His voice rose and broke over the crowd. Each person waited, mesmerized by the words of the New Testament and the presence of the priest before them, mesmerized by his intensity and the overwhelming sense of mourning and judgment.

Reverend Hernandez began pacing, his voice suddenly lower so that each person in the crowd unconsciously leaned forward. Shelby glanced at Max. His expression was solemn, unhappy even. Max didn't approve of hell-and-brimstone preaching. They'd always had more of a teacher than a preacher at their church.

Max had said once that he would rather win converts to Christ through reasoned discussion that emotional manipulation. When she'd confessed that she had first walked the aisle after a fiery gospel sermon, terrified she wouldn't live to see salvation, he'd shrugged and said, "Any way to Christ is good, but I believe faith is more likely to stick if the gospel is approached with an open heart and a sharp mind."

The people around them definitely had open hearts. They were listening with their entire beings. As far as sharp minds? She wasn't so sure. They seemed . . . entranced.

"We have been warned, and now we see. We see, and we repent of our ways. We see, and we believe. But it is not yet over, my friends. This time of tribulation—it has only just begun."

Patrick cleared his throat. When Shelby glanced at him, he shook his head—one short, definitive shake.

"Matthew tells us that 'after the tribulation . . . the sun will be darkened, and the moon will not give its light, and the stars will fall from heaven,

and the powers of the heavens will be shaken.' "
He continued to pace left and right, finally stopping in the middle again. "Are you ready for the
coming darkness? Have you prepared your
soul? Have you confessed your sinful ways?"

Across the cathedral men, women, and children
knelt—some weeping, others with their faces
buried in their hands.

"This place is your city of refuge. Have you
not all requested refuge?"

"We have." The cries rose from every direction
of the room, voices proclaiming their need and
their failures in those two simple words.

"And you shall be given refuge, just as the
Israelites designated cities in Joshua's day, so
this place has been designated by God to be your
place of refuge. You will not be surrendered to
those who accuse you. The avenger of blood will
find no foothold here." He raised his hands, shook
a fist at the large wooden doors at the back of the
room. "This is your refuge. Christ is your refuge.
As long as this cathedral stands, you will be
protected."

The last line must have been some sort of
signal. Offering plates appeared and were passed
back and forth. Shelby was amazed when she
accepted it from the woman standing to her right
and passed it to Max. Already the plate was
overflowing—with money, with gold, jewels, a
strand of pearls, someone's wedding ring. Three

plates passed them, each more full than the last.

The offerings were taken to the altar and blessed by Reverend Hernandez, who then began the liturgy of the Eucharist. Max nodded toward the side door that they'd entered through, and they tried to leave as inconspicuously as possible.

They stepped out into the courtyard, the sky darkening above them and the sounds of the city around them.

"I don't know what that was about, but I can't say I like it." Patrick scowled into the gathering darkness.

"He has those people in the palm of his hand." For a moment Bhatti almost looked angry, and then his expression softened into something like sorrow. "Not one word about the grace, provision, and omnipotence of God." He patted the pocket of his shirt, caught Shelby watching, and smiled resignedly. "What I wouldn't give for a cigarette right now."

"Made me a little nervous too." Max turned to Bianca and asked, "Was that a typical service?"

"I'm Hispanic, but I'm not Catholic."

"But you've . . . you know . . . been to a Catholic mass before."

"I have," Shelby said, "though not one like that."

Shelby started to describe the services she had attended but fell silent as an older man stepped out of the cathedral and began walking toward them.

Thirty-five

The short, balding man was wearing a dress shirt, slacks, and a bright blue bow tie. He insisted on taking Max, Patrick, and Bhatti to the men's sleeping rooms, while an older lady whisked the girls in the opposite direction.

It all happened so fast, all Max managed was a whispered, "We'll find you," before they parted ways.

"Name's Jack. Jack Clark."

"I'm Max. That's Bhatti, and this is my friend, Micah. The five of us"—Max emphasized the words *Micah* and *five,* and watched Jack for a response, but the old guy continued to walk without comment—"were on our way to the capitol buildings when we got waylaid by a flatbed truck."

"Yup. Everybody has a story. I'm in charge of getting folks settled. Heard about your group from the guards. Tried to catch you in the dining area, but you'd already left."

"Yeah, we, uh . . . followed the kitchen crew to hear the message."

Patrick rolled his eyes. They were walking behind Jack, who was hoofing it down a long corridor. He opened a door into a gym area, where pallets and sleeping bags had been laid out in lines up and down the court. There must have been room for a couple of hundred people to sleep.

"It's not much, but it's better than being out on the streets."

"We appreciate it."

"The women have smaller rooms with twenty gals per room."

"And the children?" Patrick asked.

"Accommodations with their mothers." Jack looked entirely pleased with himself. "You folks have a good night."

"Whoa. Hang on a minute, Jack."

Jack's white eyebrows shot up to the top of his head. Apparently, he was used to dropping people off, not lingering for conversation.

"I'm assuming this place is going to fill up pretty quickly."

"Yes, as soon as the service ends. When I saw you all leave early, I thought I better catch you and show you where to go."

"That's great, but we'd like to know what's going on here."

"Going on?"

Patrick moved in closer. He didn't exactly tower over the man, but he might have encroached on his personal space. "You know. What was that the reverend was spouting about refuge and end times and all that?"

Jack looked around the room, as if to be certain that they were alone. Then he walked over to where chairs were lined up against the wall, near the basketball goal.

"What would you like to know . . . specifically?" He sank into one of the plastic chairs and waited.

"I'd like to know where your supplies come from," Bhatti said.

"Different places."

"All right." Max cleared his throat. "Let's start with the refuge thing. Why do you call it that?"

Jack scratched at his right eyebrow. "Well, usually these things are discussed in orientation on the first morning that a convert—"

"We're not converts, Jack." Patrick pulled a chair around in front of the man, straddled it, and crossed his arms over the back of the chair. "And we probably won't be sticking around for orientation."

"Oh well, everyone goes. It's just something that we do. Everyone attends orientation."

"Maybe you could enlighten us just in case we miss it." Max pulled another chair around beside Patrick's, sat down, and stretched his legs in front, crossed at the ankles. Felt good to sit for a minute. It had been a long day. It had been a long three weeks.

Bhatti sat as well, arms propped on knees, gaze on Jack.

Max looked at Patrick, and his friend gave him a be-my-guest gesture.

"Why did this church become a refuge?" Max asked.

"Because people needed it."

"Needed it?"

"After the lights went out and everything stopped working, the police pulled back and miscreants took over the streets. This was a dangerous place, I can tell you, but then Reverend Hernandez, he received a word."

"A word?"

"From the Lord."

"And what was that word?"

"*Refuge*. He was to change Saint Mary Cathedral into a place of refuge."

"So he's helping people?"

"Didn't you receive a hot meal? And now you have a place to sleep, a place where you don't have to worry about anyone slitting your throat."

"What was with the offering?"

Jack squirmed uncomfortably. "Folks want to give. They want to say thank you. It's a natural thing."

"And Hernandez doesn't mind accepting the loot."

"It's not as if it's much good out on the streets. People can't even use it. How would they? Stores are empty. There's nothing to trade for." Jack laughed, and then turned suddenly solemn. "He keeps it, sure. Locked up safely for the end times."

Max crossed his arms. "People were putting

their wedding rings in that plate, Jack. Doesn't that strike you as a little odd?"

"In normal times, maybe. Not anymore. People are grateful. If they have food and a safe place to stay, they're grateful."

"So that's what we were seeing? Gratitude?"

"Sure. That's all it was. Isn't like the reverend forces anyone to hand over their stuff."

Max and Patrick again exchanged glances. Both shrugged nearly simultaneously, relieving some of the tension in Max's shoulders. He almost laughed out loud. Yeah, it was a little strange, but he'd seen worse. God himself knew that he had seen worse in the last three weeks.

They all stood, and Jack began rearranging the chairs in a line like they had been. "Glad I could help you gentlemen. Now, you pick yourself a nice bedroll and have a good night's sleep. Someone will come for you in the morning, after breakfast, and take you to confession."

"Excuse me?" Max said.

Jack's head jerked up, surprised at Max's change in tone.

"Did you say confession?" Patrick asked.

"Well, yes. You can't stay in a city of refuge unless you confess your atrocities."

"Our *atrocities?*"

"Says so, right there in black and white. Joshua chapter twenty, verse four. 'When he flees to one of these cities, he is to stand in the entrance of

234

the city gate and state his case before the elders.' "

"And we do that at confession?"

"You do, though not at the city gate since that isn't exactly possible at the moment. Instead, you confess to Reverend Hernandez, and he decides an appropriate penance."

"Such as?" Bhatti asked.

Max heard voices in the hall, and then a few men started straggling in, heading straight to their bedrolls, without a word or a nod.

"What kind of penance?" Patrick asked, stepping closer to Jack and lowering his voice.

"Different things." Jack took a step back. "Sometimes he sends you out to find food— people here need food. Or he might have you go and look for other types of supplies. Once you've found what he's told you to find, then your penance is done and you're forgiven for your atrocities."

"What if we haven't done any atrocities, Jack?" Max stepped closer too, so they made a tight small circle, with Bhatti keeping an eye on the people who walked in.

"Everyone's done atrocities in these times. Haven't you?" For just a moment Jack dropped the bumbling old guy act, and his expression was replaced with a shrewd, hardened look. "Or are you telling me you haven't killed anyone out there?"

Max thought of the battle between Abney and

Croghan. He remembered the feel of the lug wrench in his hand as he cracked it against the man's skull to save Shelby. Had he killed anyone? Probably, and he would need to come to terms with it in his heart and in his soul. But he wouldn't be confessing any of those things to Reverend Hernandez.

Patrick took one step back. "You can go now, Jack. Thank you for escorting us here."

"Of course. Of course." The bumbling old guy was back. "Now you three get some rest. After a hot breakfast, you'll be ready to face the day and whatever it holds."

"Hang on a minute." Jack was nearly to the door when Max called him back. "I need something to write on and a pen, and then I'm going to need you to deliver a note."

"That's not something that I normally—"

"He needs paper, a pen, and a moment of your time." Patrick's voice brokered no argument.

Max could tell his friend was quickly running out of patience, and the old man would have been a fool not to notice. But Jack Clark wasn't a fool, Max realized. He was merely a man doing what he needed to do, being who he needed to be, in order to survive.

He straightened his bow tie, reversed directions, and went in search of pen and paper.

Thirty-six

Shelby and Bianca scooted closer together.

"Ten more minutes until lights out." The room mom gave them a pointed look as she walked by.

"Soon she'll tell us no more giggling." Bianca kept her voice low and wiggled even closer. "Stop hogging the letter. I need to see it."

"I already read it to you."

"I knew he was sweet on you, but this goes above and beyond."

"It doesn't make any sense."

They put their heads together, literally, lying on their stomachs on two mats that had been provided by the same room mom who was attempting to run a tight ship over twenty women in a fifteen foot by twenty foot classroom. It was crowded. The room smelled of sweaty bodies and unwashed bedding. As in the cathedral, there were no windows to open, though there were small skylights in the ceiling.

No one complained about the crowded conditions or the cranky overseer.

They were safe.

They had a place to rest.

They'd eaten.

There was much to be thankful for, though at the moment Shelby felt anything but. Having to halt their search for the evening was bad enough.

Being chased by men in a flatbed truck was worse.

Now, in addition, they were separated from the guys.

Apparently, there was to be no cohabitation in this city of refuge, not even for the married couples, and based on what Shelby had heard there were several in that situation.

Bianca had her nose almost on the letter. The room would have been dark—no generators were used to power the lights, though Shelby guessed they had been used in the kitchen. Instead, many of the women had pulled flashlights from their backpacks. Fortunately, the guards had let them all keep their packs after they checked them for weapons.

Shelby held their flashlight while Bianca studied the letter.

"A man just showed up with this?"

"Yeah, while you were reserving our mats."

"And he was wearing a bow tie?"

"Sounds odd, but he was."

"And he said this letter is from Max."

"He asked if I was Shelby, handed me the letter, and said the young man pining for me sent it."

"Max isn't young."

"Agreed, though he's not old either."

"He used the word *pining?*"

"He did."

Their room mother collapsed into a chair by the door. She was a short thing, with red hair and a mean disposition. Probably she was former military. At least it seemed to Shelby that she would have made a great drill sergeant. She'd yet to see the woman smile.

"It's some kind of code," Bianca said.

"But why? And what does it mean?"

Shelby ran her finger across the lines as they silently read Max's note for the third time.

Missing you already. Couldn't find Micah.

Remember when we were four and snuck outside to see the ram your father was keeping in the west pasture? Good times. Sleep well, Shelby.

"He misses me?"

"That's to throw off bow-tie man, who no doubt read the note before he passed it on."

"Couldn't find Micah must mean—"

"That this place is not a part of the Remnant. I think we knew that already."

"Okay, but we were never four. Max is one year older than me—always has been." It was a relief to joke, even though fatigue was beginning to weigh on her like a lead apron.

Bianca stiffened, glanced around, and then ducked her head next to Shelby's. "We're supposed to meet them at four."

Of course! She fought the urge to slap her forehead. No need to attract attention. She kept her expression neutral in case they were being watched and lowered her voice to a whisper. "At the Ramcharger."

"Which is being kept on the west side of the building."

Room mom cleared her throat and called out, "Flashlights off in two minutes."

"How are we going to get past her?" Shelby asked.

"At four in the morning, I imagine she's going to be out cold. If not, we'll think of something."

"Why at four in the morning? What did they learn?"

"I don't know." Bianca flopped over onto her side and pulled the thin blanket up to her chin. The room was warm, but Shelby thought the blankets provided each person an illusion of privacy.

"I will admit this place gives me the creeps." Bianca yawned and added, "When I asked one of the women what they do every day, she said the reverend will decide that."

"He's the king and this is his kingdom."

"Yeah, but are we being given refuge or being held prisoner?"

"I don't know. I imagine we'll find out when we try to leave." Shelby flattened the note from Max, placed it between two pages of her notebook, and put the entire thing in her backpack. She'd written some notes earlier, before the bow-tie guy had shown up. But she wasn't sure they were coherent. Exhaustion felt like a cloak she was wearing, pinning her to the mat. She lay back, though she had no expectation of being able to actually sleep.

"Did you set your watch alarm?" Bianca asked.

"Yes."

"Sounds like Max wants us to try to rest—he wrote *sleep well*."

"Probably he meant *sleep while you can*."

"Hard to imagine, but sounds like tomorrow might be worse than today."

Flashlights around the room all clicked off, and almost immediately Shelby heard the sounds of sleep—yawns, sighs, and from one woman big, manly snores. She'd never been able to sleep in public. Sleeping in this room would be impossible. Her eyes stung, so she squeezed them shut. When had she last slept? And how would she get through tomorrow if she didn't get some rest?

"Bianca?" Her voice was a whisper.

"Yeah."

"Do you regret coming?"

Bianca answered her almost before she'd finished the question. "Not one bit."

"Even if—"

"Even if, Shelby." And then Bianca reached out across the darkness, found her hand, and laced their fingers together. Perhaps that show of friendship, Bianca's hand in hers, Bianca's answer seeping into the tender places of her heart, all combined to calm her nerves. Shelby slipped into a deep and restful sleep.

Thirty-seven

The next thing Shelby knew, her alarm was beeping. She silenced it quickly and sat up in the darkness, stunned to realize that she had slept for six hours.

Her throat was dry and her mouth swollen from the punch she'd taken from Raven. She touched it carefully and winced. What she'd give for a glass of water.

But they had no time for that.

She reached over and nudged Bianca, who sat up as if she'd thrown cold water on her. It took a few moments for Shelby's eyes to adjust to the darkness. Only it wasn't completely dark. Skylights allowed in starlight.

They didn't dare speak, didn't want to risk waking the room mother, who was snoring from her mat next to the door. They tiptoed across the room, each foot placed carefully, gingerly, so as not to step on any of the women, not to rouse anyone. The room mom was sleeping so close to the door that they were only able to open it a fraction, but it was enough.

Shelby pushed her backpack through, turned sideways, slid through, and waited for Bianca, who popped out seconds later.

She turned the knob all the way to the right,

inched the door closed, and slowly released the knob. There was the smallest of clicks. They both froze, Bianca clutching her arm, Shelby afraid to breathe. She counted slowly to ten, twenty, thirty. Finally she nodded, and they crept down the hall.

Soon it was clear that they were going the wrong direction, as they found they had crept to a dead end—two doors that were chained shut. Was each room they passed filled with more of the reverend's congregation? Did each room have a guard? Shelby checked her watch—ten minutes until four.

Still they didn't speak. They turned around, tiptoed back down the hall, past their room, and turned right down another hall. A door at the end opened to the outside, and they could see the parking garage rising up in front of them.

She breathed a sigh of relief and shook out her hand from where Bianca had been clutching it.

They jogged as quietly as they could across the pavement, made a left, and practically bumped into a night guard.

"No one's allowed out until daylight."

"Yes, but—"

"You need to return to your room."

Shelby ran a hand over her stomach. "I'm having such terrible cramps, and I need . . . I need supplies I left in my car."

"The nursing station will open thirty minutes before breakfast."

"She can't wait that long," Bianca said.

"She's going to have to."

The guard pulled his gun. It was a semiautomatic like she had once practiced with at the ranch. Only this gun had an unusually long barrel —a silencer, Shelby realized with sickening dread. Who needed a silencer to protect people inside a building? Unless they were using it against the people in the building.

"Like I said—you need to go back inside because you're not getting past me."

Both Shelby and Bianca didn't think so much as react, all of those self-defense classes they took together coming back in a flash. Bianca launched herself at the guard's arm, the one that had pulled out the weapon, and she bit down on his wrist as if her life depended on it. The semiautomatic fell to the ground, and the guard cursed. Shelby scooped up his weapon the same moment he threw Bianca off him. He tossed her aside like a person would swipe at a pesky fly. With his left hand, the one that wasn't bleeding, he reached for a backup weapon.

Shelby didn't have to think.

She didn't have to measure the pros and cons.

She raised the gun in her hands and pulled the trigger, slamming the man back against the wall. She'd aimed for his chest, his center of mass like she'd been instructed, like Max had told her a hundred times when their target was a bale of hay. But the gun kicked, or maybe she over-compensated for the extra weight of the silencer. Maybe it was the adrenaline flooding through her bloodstream. Whatever the reason, the barrel rose, and the bullet impacted the guard in the center of his forehead. He was dead before he hit the wall.

"Drop it! Drop it! Drop it!"

"No." Shelby's voice was shaking, her arm trembling, and her knees about to buckle. But what they had to do . . . that remained crystal clear. "No. We might need it."

Bianca grabbed her arm, and they ran toward the parking garage.

Max and Patrick and Bhatti were waiting at the entry, standing next to both of their vehicles.

"What happened?" Max asked, his gaze on Shelby's face.

"No time. We need to go." Bianca shoved Shelby toward him. "We need to go *now*."

And then Shelby was in the Dodge, unable to remember opening the door, getting in, or buckling the seat belt. Max punched the accelerator, careened around the corner and through the guards who had been looking toward the street, expecting trouble from that direction.

He drove like a race car driver, like someone with demons chasing him, Patrick tight on his tail.

Shelby looked down, surprised to see she was

still clutching the gun. She turned in her seat and looked at Bhatti. Their eyes met, and she understood that he knew what she'd done, that she'd just killed someone.

Thirty-eight

Max pulled over once he could no longer see the church in his rearview mirror and Bhatti had assured him there was no flatbed truck tailing them. He threw the Dodge into park, turned it off, hopped out of the car, and hurried around to Shelby's side. When he opened her door, she was still holding the gun, still staring at it.

"Shelby, honey, I'm going to take the gun. Just relax your hand."

Patrick and Bianca and Bhatti were crowded around them by the time he took the gun and thumbed the safety to *on*. He handed it to Bhatti, who checked it again and then placed it in the backseat of the Dodge.

"We made it out of the building okay," Bianca explained. "But then a guard tried to stop us. When we argued with him, he pulled his weapon."

"And you took it away from him?" Patrick asked, the question full of pride and admiration.

"I bit him." Bianca grimaced.

Max turned and stared at her, noticed that blood stained her shirt.

"I think I hit an artery." She wiped the back of a hand across her mouth. "Hopefully I didn't get some disease from the creep."

"Can he identify you?" Max asked.

"He's dead." Shelby had been silent, her eyes jumping from one person to another, but now she focused on Max. "The gun fell to the ground, I grabbed it, he reached for another, and so I . . . I shot him."

"All right." Max wanted to reach out and touch her face, pull her into his arms, assure her that she'd only done what had to be done. The lawyer in him wanted to explain her legal standing, that what she described was a classic case of self-defense, but the man in him longed to comfort her. He did neither. He had been crouched beside Shelby's seat, but now he stood and looked back the direction they'd come. "I don't think they'll come looking for us, though from what we heard of the reverend, he sends his followers out all over the northern side of downtown."

"Max, I killed a man. Stood three feet in front of him and just . . . his face was . . . his head . . ."

Instead of answering, Max pulled her up to her feet and into his arms.

He kissed the top of her head and held her until he felt her take in a deep breath.

He watched Bhatti and Patrick turn and survey the area.

Bianca returned from the Mustang with a bottle

of water and offered it to Shelby when Max finally let her go.

"We need to drive well out of the reverend's territory." Max pulled a map out of the glove box and unfolded it across the hood of the Dodge. "We have plenty of gas. I say we make a wide loop toward the east. We know the west is too difficult to drive through. We saw that when Shelby and I were standing on the flyover. But if we go east, then south, and circle around—"

"No." Bhatti rarely spoke, and he had never contradicted their plans. Sometimes Max forgot the man was riding along. But now he stepped closer and ran a finger straight from their position to the capitol. "We take the shortest route and arrive there before sunrise."

"How is that supposed to work?" Max asked. "We're still in the reverend's territory, not to mention whoever was in the flatbed would probably like to get even with you for blowing out his tires. Why he was even after us to begin with, I have no idea."

"The reverend was funneling people into the church," Bhatti said. "He was working with the men in the flatbed."

"That makes no sense," Max said.

"Actually, it does." Patrick placed both hands on his hips and stared at the ground. "It does. I doubt they expected Bhatti to be such a good shot. But it makes sense that a con like that is how the reverend acquires new converts. You think that you're being pursued, maybe that you even killed someone. You think you have no way out, so you go in."

"Where you confess." Max suddenly felt extremely tired. They were up against so much—hunger, disease, outlaws, and now this. How could a cathedral that was built for good, built to be a light in the world, hold such corruption?

"Make your confession and receive your penance." Bhatti shrugged.

The comment caused Max to realize that he didn't even know where Bhatti stood as far as Christianity. He was a good man, there was no doubt about that in Max's mind. He seemed to have a basic understanding of Scripture, but he was quite private about his faith. Max respected that and hadn't felt a need to push for information.

"Maybe Reverend Hernandez doesn't even know how people arrive on his doorstep," Bhatti continued. "Maybe he believes what he's preaching, but someone in his inner circle has decided it's an effective way to convince others to take the risk and go out to procure whatever they need."

"And in the meantime they're building up quite a treasure trove with the offerings," Patrick said.

"All right. So the flatbed and the reverend are one. We can't go back, and we wouldn't want to anyway. We know that the area immediately east of Shoal Creek is controlled by Diego. We have no choice but to take a wide, circular route."

"Wrong. We go straight in, which isn't what most people would do. That's why it will work."

Patrick folded his arms, stared at the map, and finally said, "Bhatti's right. Think about it—any guards, like the one that Shelby and Bianca encountered, are likely to be tired, thinking about how many minutes they have left of their night shift. The morning guards won't be on duty yet, and if they are, they won't be alert. Either way, they're not going to be expecting us at sunrise."

"And we what? Drive up to the gate, knock, and ask to come in?" Bianca sounded tired. "I don't think it will work, and I need to . . . uh . . . find a bathroom. We sort of ran out of the cathedral dorm rooms as soon as we woke up."

Shelby stood, still pale and shaken, but finding her equilibrium. If there was one thing Max knew about Shelby Sparks, it was that she would somehow regain her footing. She nodded toward a gas station that looked abandoned and vandalized. "Bathroom first. Then we do what Bhatti said. Drive straight in and knock on the door."

Five minutes later they were back in their vehicles and headed toward downtown. They took Harris Street to Windsor and then crossed back over to the east side of the park at Enfield. There were few people up, and the ones who were kept their eyes averted, as if they could somehow avoid trouble by refusing to look. They passed an old man asleep in an office chair, a teenager sitting on a curb drinking from a soda can, a mother rocking her child on a bus stop bench.

Glancing up, Max saw an American flag hanging from a balcony where people were sleeping. The sight of the stars and stripes caused an ache deep in his heart, but it also fortified his commitment to make it back to Abney with the medications they needed. This was America. He would not hand his land, his state, or his future over to thugs and villains and desperate men.

They headed east on 15th Street, and from there it was a straight shot to the capitol.

He slowed when he was within a few blocks of the capitol buildings, not because he wanted to but because people were sleeping along the side-walk, in the median, even in deserted vehicles. The crowds were thick, the people not quite awake. They'd been driving with the windows down because of the heat, and he could smell and hear the crowds now. Babies crying, mothers comforting their children, husbands—their words short and choppy and angry.

Now he could see the perimeter fence. He drove the wrong way down a one-way road until the front of the Dodge was inches from the fence. Patrick stopped with his front bumper practically touching the Dodge's rear bumper. No one would get between them, but Max's heart rate accelerated to realize how heavily they were outnumbered. There were thousands of people on this side of the fence, and they were just beginning to stir, to take their positions outside the fence, to plead and beg for entrance.

Max turned off the engine, thinking it was best to save the gas if this didn't work, if they were forced to retreat. But retreat to where?

They all exited the vehicles and walked to the fence.

Thirty-nine

Guards were stationed around the perimeter, on the other side of the fence, at six-foot intervals. They held their rifles in a ready position in front of their chests, reminding Shelby of the time she'd visited the Tomb of the Unknown Soldier in Arlington, Virginia. Their gazes were directed straight ahead, and they gave absolutely no indication that they heard Max.

"We're from Abney." Max spent several moments trying to appeal to their compassion. When that failed, he reverted back to his legal background. "We are here at the request of Mayor Perkins, and may I remind you that by law the area you've cordoned off is public property owned by the citizens of Texas."

This earned some guffaws from the people who had begun to mill around them. Shelby again wondered how they survived living on the street in front of the capitol complex. Where did they find food or water? Where did they bathe or use the toilet? How did they care for their children? The same questions she'd wrestled with before, and as before, no answers were in sight.

Years ago Shelby had come to Austin with Carter and their youth group to hand out bags of supplies to the homeless. They'd felt quite good about that. They'd felt as if they were being the hands of Christ in a vital way.

Now she found herself on the same street, surrounded by newly homeless people, facing armed guards. Those two experiences clashed in her mind and tore at her soul. How did you minister to others when your own life was in danger?

Max remained inches from the fence, but Shelby, Patrick, Bianca, and Bhatti had retreated to stand beside the cars, as if four people could protect their things should the crowd decide to take them. What would the guards do if that happened? What would she do? Shoot them? No, she couldn't do that . . . not to protect her things. To protect her life? To protect her friends' lives? Well, she'd already proven she was willing to do that.

Max grabbed the fence with both hands and gave it a sharp rattle. "I know you hear me, and

I want you to go and tell your commanding officer—"

"Sir, I am the CO here. I need you to step back, or I will instruct my men to shoot."

Max stared in disbelief at the man who had walked up. To Shelby he looked the same as the other guards around him, perhaps a little older, perhaps he had some insignia on his uniform indicating he was in charge. She couldn't see it, but she didn't doubt for a minute that they would shoot Max.

Instead of being intimidated, Max was growing angry, which in her experience had never been a good thing. His anger was slow in coming, quick to burn out, but scathing for a moment or two. He'd never directed it toward her, though she'd seen him take down more than one person at a city meeting, a sporting event, or a church committee meeting. But this was none of those things. Here his anger could prove fatal.

"Max, we'll find another way." She stepped forward to tug on his arm, but the CO flicked his eyes her direction and warned her to get back.

"You're saying that you would shoot me here on the capitol grounds." Max shook her hand off his arm. "Land that was purchased and is maintained with my taxes to house a government that was created by the constitution of our state—"

"Sir, this is the last time I'm going to ask you to step back."

"Let us in!" The words roared from Max, and then all pandemonium broke loose.

To their right and left, people began shaking the fence, demanding to be let in. One or two tried to climb it, but the razor wire at the top stopped them. They fell back into the crowd.

Shelby thought the guards would shoot, as the officer had promised, but instead the men stepped back five and then ten feet. She quickly saw why. Up and down the line, trucks moved forward. The large trucks had what looked like water tanks mounted on the back and deluge guns mounted on the top and front.

She'd researched water cannons when she was writing a WWII romance set in Europe. Originally designed to fight fires, they were used for riot control in Germany as early as the 1930s. They'd been improved on since that time, or at least made more efficient. A modern water cannon could restrain a person at a distance of up to one hundred yards. They could also maim and even in some instances kill a person.

Shelby was stunned that they would use them on a crowd containing women and children, and she couldn't begin to wrap her mind around the fact that they would be willing to waste so much water. Or perhaps they'd been filled with gray water. That thought turned her stomach.

Now the CO was speaking through a bullhorn, advising everyone that they had exactly one minute to back away from the fence. None of the guards looked alarmed, and it occurred to Shelby that this wasn't the first time they had resorted to such tactics.

"Max, we need to go."

"We're not leaving."

"You can't stay here. We can't stay here."

Max ignored her, opting to shout at the CO instead. The trucks pulled closer, the noise of the diesel engines louder even than that of the crowd.

Bianca had joined them and was trying to pull Shelby back, urging her into the Dodge.

Patrick joined Max at the fence.

The scene in front of her seemed to slow and solidify into a nightmare Shelby would never forget—the shouts of anger, cries of despair, the CO still hollering through the bullhorn, Bianca pleading with her, Max still stating his case, and Patrick's voice now added to that.

In the midst of it all, Bhatti stepped forward, walked up to the fence and calmly but firmly said, "Sierra, Whiskey, Oscar, Romeo, Mike."

The CO lowered his bullhorn, walked over to the fence, and said, "Authenticate."

"Zero, six, one, zero."

The CO turned to his right and yelled out some instructions that Shelby couldn't understand. When he turned to the left and did the same, she heard the words, "Dispersal Units at three and six in four minutes."

256

"Dispersal units?" she asked.

"They're going to shoot." Bianca's voice was a dead, flat line.

Bhatti hadn't moved. He stood watching the CO, and Max stood staring at Bhatti.

They could maybe hide in the cars, but what were the odds they could even get in them at this point? The crowd had pressed in on all sides.

The water trucks backed up, and in their place giant supply trucks with the Red Cross emblem painted on their sides drove toward them and then divided right and left. The crowd parted like the Red Sea, people running and hollering and knocking one another down as they pushed in the direction of the trucks.

Patrick recovered more quickly than anyone else.

"Get in the cars. Hurry up! Get in the cars. They're going to open the gates!"

Forty

Max was as shocked as everyone else when the soldiers rolled the gates open. He ran back to the Dodge, jumped into the driver's seat, cranked the engine, threw the transmission into drive, and darted forward. The CO directed him ahead another hundred yards.

Patrick had followed closely behind him. The

gates closed as soon as the Mustang was through, and the soldiers took up their previous positions. The tanker trucks were nowhere to be seen. Darkness was giving way to day, though the sun had yet to make an appearance.

Bhatti had walked through the gate and was talking to the CO.

"They . . ." Shelby turned to him, her eyes wide and her voice strangled. "What did they do, Max? Where did all those people go?"

Max's stomach was churning. He'd been expecting a gunshot to his midsection when he had argued with the guards, but something— some smoldering anger—made backing down impossible. That had been foolish, he realized in hindsight.

"Where did they go?" Shelby was turned around in her seat, looking to the left and the right.

"Remember the time we fed the koi at the Japanese gardens?"

"In Fort Worth. Yeah, the year Carter's mechanical project made it to the state stock show." She hesitated before plopping back down in her seat. "The fish were amazing . . . and a little disgusting. There were so many of them and they all . . . they all swarmed the water when we threw out food."

"Same principal. Throw out some food, and the fish, or in this case the people, surge where you want them to go."

"Which is why they're all here, living mere feet outside the fence." Shelby stared at him when he shut off the engine. "They'll never leave as long as there is a chance someone will throw a bag of rice over the fence."

"I'm not saying I agree with their tactics, but we have bigger questions to answer at the moment."

"Like who is Farhan Bhatti?"

"Yeah. That would be a good one to start with."

They hurried back to where the doctor was still speaking with the officer and reached him at the same time that Patrick and Bianca did.

Max pushed through to the middle of the small circle they'd formed, but instead of directing his questions to the CO, he went nose to nose with Bhatti. "What was that all about?"

"It's not something I can talk about at this moment, Max."

"You will talk about it."

"I'm afraid I can't." Bhatti nodded toward the CO, who had stepped away and was speaking into a radio clipped to the shoulder of his uniform.

Patrick pushed his way in. "Who are you?"

"That is not the question you need to be asking." Bhatti lowered his voice. His words came out rapid fire, like the tat-a-tat of a machine gun. "You need to find a way to stay on this side of the fence. Lose the attitude. Treat this man with respect. Hope that I have enough clout to keep us all on the inside."

The officer returned, a frown pulling down the corners of his mouth. Two other soldiers had joined him. "Davidson will take you to the debriefing area."

"And my friends?"

"They'll be allowed to stay for now." He turned to Max. "Follow Private Neff to a holding tent."

"We're not going anywhere," Max said.

"You'll go where I tell you to." The officer stepped even closer, not flinching from Max's glare. "You are lucky to be alive. Now I suggest you go before I regret that decision."

"And leave our cars?" Max asked, clearly unhappy with the idea.

"Leave everything. If you are caught with a weapon, you will be escorted to the other side. If you go anywhere but the area that Private Neff takes you, you will be escorted to the other side. Am I clear?"

"Yeah. I'd say that's pretty clear." Bianca threw her backpack into the Mustang, and after a moment's hesitation, the others did the same.

Shelby reached into hers and snagged her notebook and pen. The CO was watching her closely. When she held up the two items, he shrugged and made a go-ahead motion.

They were escorted in two groups down Congress Avenue.

Bhatti and Davidson took a right between the World War I and Pearl Harbor monuments. Max's last glimpse of the doctor was of him approaching the Supreme Court of Texas building.

As for their group of merry men—and women— Private Neff took them left into a giant tent that had been erected on the east side of the capitol lawn, between the Texas Workforce Commission and the Texas Ethics Commission—an irony that wasn't lost on Max. As they walked toward the tent, the sun rose above the horizon, casting long shadows behind them and forcing Max to tug his ball cap down even lower.

They went through a processing center, where they were once again searched for weapons. Then they were directed to a first aid station, where a nurse instructed them to take a seat and said she'd look at them one at a time. She was black, middle aged, and had probably been chosen for this job because she was tough. She looked able to handle anything that came her way—both because of her size, which was large, and her attitude, which was unflappable. Her name tag said simply *Brown.*

Nurse Brown checked their temperatures, looked down their throats, and took their pulses and blood pressures. All of the data was noted in a chart on an electronic tablet, which still worked, so it must have been somehow shielded from the flare.

"Worried about us?" Max asked as she cleaned the cuts on his face.

"Making sure you don't have any contagious diseases."

"And if we did, we'd be escorted back to the other side of the fence?"

If he'd hoped to unsettle the woman, he was sorely disappointed. She'd simply replied, "Following orders, sir." After which she stamped his hand and directed him to a chair.

The protocol must have been to keep groups together if possible. Though how many groups were allowed in, Max wasn't sure.

The nurse checked Patrick, declared him fit as a horse, and stamped his hand. Bianca was next, and made it through with little comment from the nurse.

But when Nurse Brown took a closer look at Shelby, she let out a long, low whistle. "Tell me one of these guys did not pop you in the mouth. Because if they did, I'd be happy to call an MP."

Shelby shook her head. "No. It was just a misunderstanding between me and one of the people on the outside."

The nurse cleansed the wound with antibiotic ointment, walked to a cabinet, and pulled out an Instant Cold Pack. Squeezing the pack in the middle, she handed it to Shelby and said, "Keep this on your lip for the next few hours. The last thing you want is to contract an infection. With the conditions we have, even here in the capitol compound, your biggest fear is infection because antibiotics are scarce."

"What I really need is insulin."

The nurse had been tapping away on her tablet. She set it down, walked back to the cabinet, and pulled out a testing strip.

"No, it's not for me. It's for my son. That's why we're here. I need . . . I have to find insulin for him."

The nurse put the testing strip back into the cabinet. "I'm sorry. I can't help you with that."

"But someone can. Someone here has medical supplies."

Max thought Nurse Brown wouldn't answer, but she glanced at each of them and something seemed to deflate in the big woman—an emotional barrier she maintained in order to make it through the tragedies she saw each day. "Look, honey. I can't imagine what you've been through or what you had to endure to get here. And I know that as a mother I would do absolutely anything to put my hands on whatever my child needed."

"Exactly."

"But I can't get you any medication. It's under lock and key, and I have to have three approvals to access anything stronger than that ice pack you're holding."

"But there are supplies here, including insulin."

"Maybe. Possibly. Yes, I'm sure we do have insulin. But you didn't hear that from me."

Shelby threw her arms around the woman, who glanced over at the rest of the group and rolled her eyes. Gently, she pushed Shelby away. "Private Neff is waiting outside this room. You all follow him down to holding room number eight. And God bless you. I hope you find what you need."

Forty-one

Carter finished his chores by lunchtime and asked if he could take the four-wheeler over to see Monica.

"Sure," Roy said. "But out of curiosity—work or pleasure?"

If the question had come from his mom, he would have sniped back at her, but coming from Roy he couldn't take offense. Max's dad glanced up with a smile tugging at his lips, winked, and then returned his attention to their lunch of beans and corn bread. The beans were pinto, and Georgia had found some pork to season them with. How was that possible in this heat? Somehow she did it, continually making them meals complete with protein and at least a couple of the food groups.

The corn bread was a miracle, in Carter's opinion. He still didn't understand how she managed to cook in the big oven outside that looked more like a barbecue pit.

"Work, actually," Carter said, returning to Roy's question. "Her family is having problems with hogs."

"Blasted beasts have been tearing up whatever they go near for a few years now."

"Well, the thing is, I started thinking about what you said, Roy. About domesticating them."

Georgia harrumphed and pushed the plate of freshly sliced tomatoes, cucumbers, and onions his direction. "Roy's been talking about that for years. He detests those pigs like I detest fruit flies. Both are a real nuisance."

"But they're also food, right?"

Georgia and Roy exchanged looks. Roy cleared his throat and said, "Boy has a good head on his shoulders."

"Don't forget you're the one who put the idea in my head."

"Yeah, but somehow in the day-to-day work of running a modern ranch with nineteenth-century tools, I'd forgotten about it. Or maybe I didn't forget. Maybe I just wasn't sure how I wanted to tackle the problem, and we haven't been that desperate for food yet."

"There's enough of them," Georgia admitted. "And if they're harvested correctly, the meat is plenty good to eat."

Carter picked up one of the slices of cucumber and popped it in his mouth. It was cool and crisp and lacked the bitterness of the ones they used to purchase at the grocery store. "The problem is that there's no use in catching and butchering them now."

"Not in this heat," Roy agreed. "And they're harder to catch than you'd think."

"Monica's dad has a nice setup with a deer feeder that is fenced in. We were thinking we could reinforce the fence, and then set the gate to close automatically using one of their motion sensor cameras."

"Thought they fizzled with the flare."

"Anything plugged in or anything mounted outside, yeah. But turns out he'd ordered a new one and it was still in the box. Looks like the circuits are still good."

"How can you close a gate with a camera?" Georgia asked, smiling as she crumbled a piece of corn bread into her glass of milk.

Carter had taken on the task of milking their cow each morning, and he almost started laughing when he saw that glass of milk. To think that it had come from the work of his hands. Though to be fair, most of the work had been on the part of the cow.

"It's not as difficult as you'd think if he has the right supplies."

"Her dad is an amateur radio buff," Georgia said. "I suppose he has quite a bit of electronics."

"He does."

"So what's the design? How is the camera helpful?"

"There's a sensor on the camera. The sensor is what causes the camera to go off when there's motion. A deer walks up, the camera senses it, and then takes a picture. What I want to do is use the sensor to close the gate, trapping the animal inside the fence that surrounds her feeder."

"You can do that?" Roy asked.

"Maybe." Carter shrugged. "Maybe not, but it doesn't hurt to try. Unless you need me here to do something else."

"We're ahead of my work schedule." Roy carried his bowl to the sink and then turned around to study Carter. "Go on over there. If you find a way to trap hogs, especially a small number of them, we could domesticate them. A pig farm would really help the folks in this area."

Georgia stood and bustled around the kitchen, stacking dishes, wiping off the table, and swiping at a fly. "Chops, hams, roasts, ribs, and bacon. Oh, yes, we could use it. Not to mention head-cheese, lard, and sausage. I think I even have a recipe in one of my cookbooks for scrapple."

Roy laughed at that. "Scrapple. There's a word I didn't expect to hear again."

Their laughter followed Carter outside. He liked having a project, something to work on that he knew he was adept at. He hadn't realized how much he'd missed the Brainiacs, the group of geeks in Abney who had met to try to solve some of the community's problems. They'd built solar ovens, a windmill from bike parts, and improved existing water reclamation systems. More than ever, the world needed their original ideas and unusual skills. But he didn't regret coming to High Fields. He'd needed space from the fighting in Abney, from the destruction of his home, and most importantly from the death of Kaitlyn.

He stopped outside the barn, where they stored the four-wheeler. The cow, Betsy, was grazing in the western pasture. He could hear Georgia's chickens pecking in their pen, and when he looked south, he could see Roy's crops were now chest high—corn and grain and sorghum. They were crops Roy had planted in the spring, before the flare. They'd spent several nights designing the fall crops—wheat, rye, and peanuts. Carter had laughed at that, but Roy had assured him that peanuts were a big crop in west Texas, and perhaps the soil at High Fields would be compatible.

As he stood there surveying the land, Carter realized he preferred life at the ranch. It was a bit solitary, but that's what he craved right now. Time alone felt right. It eased some of the bad memories. He had nothing to remind him of Abney. And he preferred not having to make conversation with anyone.

He climbed onto the four-wheeler, started it up, and rode away from High Fields. As he allowed his gaze to drift south toward his old town, he acknowledged to himself that he did miss his friends.

And he missed his mom. This was the third day she and Max had been gone. It was too early to expect them to be back—probably. But that didn't stop him from pulling over at the road's high point and studying the skyline to the south. As if he could see anything that was a fair distance away. He couldn't, not really. All he saw were cedar trees followed by more cedar, with the occasional pecan and oak tree poking through. Perhaps if there had been smoke signals, he would have seen them, but there were none of those. No sign of an approaching vehicle. No new fires. Perhaps the anarchists had burned and looted and moved on. Carter saw nothing but trees and cactus and hills.

He continued down the white caliche road and with some effort pulled his attention back to catching hogs.

Forty-two

"Six hours!" Shelby paced back and forth from one side of the partitioned room to the other. Her outburst earned her a warning look from the warden—or whatever they wanted to call the person who wouldn't let them leave.

"Can't you write in your notebook or something?" Max asked.

"I already did that, and yes, I read back over it too." She picked up the notebook and tossed it at him. "You look at it. I'm too antsy to hold a pen, let alone write with one."

She paced back and forth a few more times before stopping in front of her friends. "I'm pretty tired of being watched by a guard everywhere we go. When did this turn into a police state?"

"Twenty-one days ago." Patrick smiled at her and patted the ground next to him. "Today is July first. Did you realize that?"

Shelby sank down beside him, and he tossed an arm over her shoulder. It was such a brotherly gesture that she nearly allowed herself to relax. Instead, she crossed her arms and stared at her dirty hiking boots. She'd be happy never to see those boots, or the clothes she had on, again.

Max yawned and stretched his arms up over his head. "You should have slept like the rest of us. You'd be less cranky."

"Are you actually judging my mood?"

In response Max held both hands up, palms out.

"I think Shelby and I need to take a little walk," Bianca said, reaching for her hands and pulling her to her feet.

Arm in arm they trooped to the other end of the tent.

Their room was less than the size of a football field, but not by much. And they were number eight? How large was the entire tented area? Twenty acres? Forty? Where did so much tent material come from? Who had set them up here and why?

The so-called rooms had been partitioned off, and as the nurse had directed they'd followed Private Neff all the way down to room number eight. There were probably a couple hundred people in the room, some sitting in groups, some sleeping, others staring off into space, all waiting.

But what were they waiting for?

When they'd first arrived, Max and Patrick tried to get information from a few of their cell mates with no luck. Mostly people shrugged and turned away. They did learn that the people in their oom were from all over the state—Corpus Christi, Midland, College Station.

"No one from the metropolitan areas."

"Huh?" Bianca had been watching two children who were playing with a set of checkers.

"There's no one here from Dallas or Houston or San Antonio."

"Maybe they have their own compounds."

"But those people—" She nodded toward a young couple. "They're from Corpus. If there were compounds all over the state, they would have gone to San Antonio. In fact, they had to go around San Antonio to end up here."

"So what are you thinking? They're not letting people out of the cities?"

"I don't know. How do you fence in an entire city?"

Bianca had no answer for that, though she did pause and speak to a group of Hispanic women.

"They're from west of here. Junction area."

"And?"

"They had been warned to stay away from San Antonio."

"Any idea why?"

"None."

"Why are they here?"

"Thought they could move in with some family members who live in the area. Thought it would be better here."

They continued toward the portable potties that had been set up at the end of the room. Shelby did not need to use one, but it did feel good to stretch her legs, to be somewhere—anywhere other than their corner of room eight.

She turned to see if the guard was watching them, let out a squeak, and shouted, "That's Danny Vail." Slapping her hand over her mouth, she tugged Bianca out of the potty line and rushed over to where their former city manager was standing. By the time they reached him, Max and Patrick had joined them.

Shelby threw her arms around Danny and laughed when he picked her up off the ground before setting her back down. Straightening her shirt, she took a step back and grinned at her old friend.

Danny looked much as he had the last time she'd seen him in Abney, when he'd come to her house and tried to convince her to leave town. His hair had been freshly buzzed in the military haircut that he always wore, causing his black scalp to reflect the light coming through the tent's roof.

Today he wore a military uniform. It reminded her of when they'd first met. She'd known Danny for close to twenty years, when he'd served with Carter's father. When Alex had died from an overdose, Danny had felt responsible. For the next few years, he'd come around often, even to the point of asking Shelby out on a date several times. When she made it plain she wasn't interested, she had seen less of him. But Danny Vail was a good man. He'd attended their church, and he'd served competently as their city manager until the day he disappeared from Abney. So what was he doing in the capitol compound?

There was backslapping and *How are you* and *I can't believe you're here.* Then Danny walked away from them to speak to the room guard. She started to argue, and he said something sharp in return. The next thing Shelby knew, they were walking out of the room, out into the afternoon heat. After hours cooped up in the tented enclosure, even the blistering summer sun felt like heaven on her skin. She closed her eyes, raised her face to the sky, and allowed the muscles in her neck to relax for just a second. Then she keyed in on what Danny was saying.

"I came straight here from Abney," he was telling the rest of the group.

"But why?" Shelby asked. "And why didn't you tell anyone you were leaving?"

Danny shrugged. "I honestly didn't think there was anything else I could do for Abney. Mayor Perkins had her way of doing things, and let's just say it didn't sync with what I thought needed to be done."

Max exchanged a quick glance with Shelby. "We thought she was reacting well—logically, no panic, but with a firm hand at the helm."

"Are you kidding me, Berkman? If there had been a firm hand at the helm, Croghan would have never attacked. The violence you're seeing in Abney—"

"What violence?"

Danny snapped his mouth shut in a solid straight line. With a shrug, he said, "Let's just say not everyone was aware of everything that had happened."

"She had me go to the jail, Danny. To speak to some of the offenders."

"Yeah, those were the ones you knew about. The others? They weren't dealt with in any responsible manner. They were taken to the city limits and let go. She just let them go! As if that would solve anything. As if they wouldn't sneak right back in." Danny hitched up his belt, which Shelby noticed included a holster with a semiautomatic. So he was in the compound in some official capacity.

Maybe he could help them.

If he would help them.

The only way she'd know would be to ask.

Forty-three

"Danny, the reason we're here—and believe me getting here was no small feat—is to find insulin for Carter and medicine for Abney."

Danny began shaking his head before she'd finished speaking. "I don't see that happening. The supplies we have here are here for the military."

"Yes, but what about the people outside the fence?"

"The administration is working on that, but until we have a more solid footing, any supplies within this compound will stay here."

"What exactly is your capacity?" Max asked, arms folded across his chest and a scowl spreading across his face.

Shelby cringed, suddenly aware of the underlying tension between Danny and Max. Was this how Max had felt when she confronted Raven?

She glanced at Bianca, but her friend seemed content to take a backseat, watch, and listen.

"Whatever Governor Reed needs me to do."

"That's a bit vague."

"Well, duties are still being assigned." He ran a hand around the back of his neck, and then he offered them his old familiar smile. "Listen, we might not agree on Abney and what should or shouldn't be going on there, but we're here now. So let me see if we can have you moved to some better accommodations."

"And the supplies?" Shelby asked.

A flash of something—irritation?—crossed his face, but then it was gone, replaced by his old familiar smile. "Of course. I'll check around, but please don't get your hopes up."

He escorted them back into room number eight. Shelby actually thought about making a run for it, but where would she go? Soldiers patrolled the entire capitol compound. She wouldn't make it twenty feet before she was stopped. Or shot.

"I'll be back as soon as I can," Danny promised. "In the meantime, try and get some rest. Your trip back is bound to be as taxing as the trip here was."

They were given MREs for lunch. Stamped on the side of the package were the words *Tuna in a Pouch*.

"It comes with tortillas," Max said, his voice filled with elated surprise until he took his first bite. "How do you manage to eat this stuff? Tastes like cardboard."

"Buck up, Berkman." Patrick actually grinned as he scarfed his down. "It's the protein that matters."

Protein or no, it tasted like goo, and it was difficult to choke down. Shelby forced herself to eat, knowing she would need it when they started their long ride home.

The afternoon passed with interminable slowness. Bianca found a paperback book and settled down to read it, though it looked like some sort of historical involving cowboys and Indians. When Shelby commented on that, she said, "Hey, I'll take what entertainment I can get."

Patrick slept.

"How can he do that?" Shelby grumbled.

"Envy is a bad thing, Sparks."

"Is it now?"

"Indeed. One of the deadly sins if I remember right."

When she only glared at him, he began ticking the sins off on his fingers, one by one. "Lust, gluttony, greed, laziness."

"Do I look lazy to you?"

"Wrath."

"Hmm."

"Envy and pride."

"I don't want to know why you remember those."

"I did a study on them once. Most of what you see in a courtroom falls under one of those categories."

She didn't argue with him, but she did scoot closer and glance around before she peppered him with questions. "Max, when are we going to get out of here? What if we can't get the supplies? What are we going to do next?"

"Hey." He placed an arm over her shoulders. Whereas with Patrick the gesture had felt brotherly, Max was a different matter entirely. She longed to melt into him, to let him carry her burdens if only for a little while. Instead, she scooted forward a few feet and then turned to face him, lowering her voice so that no one else could hear.

"At some point you all need to go back."

"Not going to happen."

"Bianca and Patrick—"

"We're here as long as you are," Bianca said without glancing up.

"Yes, but—"

"No buts." Max pushed his legs out in front of him, crossed them at the ankles, and pulled his baseball cap down over his eyes. "We're stuck to you like Velcro. No use trying to lose us."

Patrick slept, Bianca read, and Max pretended to rest. Shelby kept her eyes focused on the exit, watching families come and go. There was a process for allowing people in and out. At first it was the people who had been there when they'd arrived that were leaving, people who had probably stayed overnight. But the room filled up with a new group, and then hours later they were processed out.

Part of her mind longed to plan an escape, but that would entail overpowering or even killing the guard. Each time her mind touched on the thought, she shied away. She was aware that she hadn't yet dealt with what she'd done that morning —not on an emotional level, and certainly not on a spiritual one. Practically, she knew this was different. She wouldn't stand a chance against a trained military soldier.

Fortunately, she didn't have to follow that train of thought very far because Dr. Farhan Bhatti appeared in the doorway.

Forty-four

It was five o'clock, and Carter was late heading back to High Fields. The hours had flown by while he was at Monica's. They'd come up with a workable solution for catching the pigs, and now his thoughts were focused on ways to improve their day-to-day existence. Driving the four-wheeler had become automatic and didn't require his full attention.

He was thinking about modifying technology that no longer worked to benefit them, thinking of all the gadgets they had that people now considered junk. But only part of the components had been fried. Other parts worked as well as they always had. His mind was in full analytical mode, which was probably why he didn't hear the guys on horseback. Before he understood what was happening, three were in front of him, blocking his path forward, and three were behind him, blocking any possible retreat.

He recognized Brandon right away, owing to the fact that he had a cigarette stuck in the band of his cowboy hat. No bandana this time. Same greasy hair, though. Same bad attitude.

"Look at the city kid, back from visiting his girlfriend." He walked the horse over next to the four-wheeler, close enough that Carter had to tip his head back to look up at him.

"Something you need, Brandon?"

The other boys snickered. Brandon said, "There's lots of things we need. Are you offering to give us something?"

"Yeah, maybe he wants to give up that four-wheeler." This from a skinny kid with bad acne. Sidekick One, Carter supposed.

"Not gonna happen."

"Well, you asked if there's something I need."

"I meant before I run your horse off this road."

A round of *ooh*s burst out behind him.

"Maybe Mr. City Kid doesn't realize he's outnumbered."

Carter was tired. He'd had a pretty good day, and he was looking forward to Georgia's cooking. He did not have patience or time for idiots. "Are you playing stupid, or is it genuine?"

"Excuse me?"

"I'm not excusing you. In case you haven't noticed, folks around here have plenty of work manning roadblocks and finding enough food to eat. How about you cut the hoodlum routine and make yourself useful?"

Brandon handed the reins of his horse to the guy next to him and hopped down to the ground. "Care to back that up?"

"Why would I do that? You outweigh me by a good twenty pounds."

"All muscle too."

More laughter, and Carter felt a sinking dread pushing through him, all the way down to his toes. He wasn't going to get out of this without a fight, and he fully acknowledged he wasn't much of a fighter. He'd been a member of the Brainiacs, not the wrestling club.

But he'd also done a lot of manual labor in the three weeks since the flare shut down normal life—since the Drop. And those last two words, his best friend's name for what had happened, inspired him. Because Jason would have told him that the guy standing in front of him was a loser, and losers needed to go down.

Brandon stepped back as Carter turned off the

four-wheeler and pocketed the keys. Brandon's goons had maintained their circular formation, but they'd moved back to give them room. By the time Carter hopped off the four-wheeler, there was a good five feet between them. He focused on keeping his hands loose, like Max had taught him when he'd had to face a bully in sixth grade. This situation was really no different, except the bully leering at him was bigger and older.

Duck the first swing—you never want to be the first to throw a punch. Watch the guy. Watch how he moves and what side he favors. When he swings, duck and then go in low and hard on the opposite side.

The swing came from Brandon's left, which surprised him. Carter ducked, but not enough. Instead of Brandon's fist connecting with his jaw, he cuffed the side of Carter's head—causing his ears to ring and his head to throb.

But there was no time to think of that. Instead of stepping back, Carter reversed directions and went in with a hard punch on Brandon's right—catching him in the ribs and throwing him backward.

Shouts of surprise registered in one part of his mind. The goon squad wasn't used to their leader taking a shot. That told Carter even more. Instead of backing away to give Brandon distance for another swing, Carter followed his right punch with a left to Brandon's stronger left side.

A right and then a left. Most of the time that's all it will take.

But Brandon was stubborn, and as Carter had expected, unused to taking a punch. His fury and embarrassment kept him on his feet. He raised his arms, hands clenched together, and came down hard on Carter's left shoulder. Pain radiated all the way to Carter's fingertips. He ignored it, pictured the punching bag that Max had insisted he work out with.

Most guys are just like this bag—slow and heavy. Take advantage of that. Ignore the pain and come back with another right and left.

Easier said than done, but Carter's anger fueled him now. This was stupid. This was a waste of time, and it was dangerous. And sometimes the only way to stop a bully was the way Max had taught him.

He funneled all of his frustration, all of his anger over the flare and Kaitlyn's death and leaving Abney and needing insulin. He put every ounce of resentment into a right punch to Brandon's gut, and then he followed with a left to his chin.

And that worked, just like Max had told him it would.

Brandon lay in the dirt, shaking his head and no doubt seeing stars.

The goon squad said nothing. In fact, they were staring at Carter in disbelief, as if he'd just performed an amazing feat. Perhaps they'd thought

283

it couldn't be done. Perhaps they'd never tried.

Brandon's horse was cropping weeds on the side of the road. Brandon was on his knees now, half in the road, half out, still shaking his head as if to clear it.

Carter fished his keys out of his pocket, climbed onto the four-wheeler, and started it up. He wanted to tell the guys behind him, the guys who were now hopping off their horses to help Brandon, that they needed to wise up. He wanted to remind them that the enemy was out there, on the other side of the barricades.

But they weren't ready to hear that.

And his left shoulder was really beginning to ache.

And his right ear had started to bleed.

So instead of attempting any sort of reasonable discussion, he started the four-wheeler, navigated around Brandon, and headed toward High Fields.

He was late for dinner, and Georgia hated it when they were late.

Forty-five

"Tell me what happened, Carter." Georgia pressed a cloth dipped in cold water to his left shoulder. "You hold it while I clean this ear."

"Tell me if the other guy looks worse." Roy pushed a cup of water into his hands.

284

"Thanks, and yeah, he does."

"You didn't swing first, did you?"

"No, sir."

"That's all I need to know."

"I think we need to know who did this," Georgia said.

Carter winced when she applied the alcohol swab to his ear.

"Sorry, dear. You want it clean, though. How's your head feeling?"

"All right." In truth it felt as if he'd been hit with a boat anchor, but he didn't want to admit that to Georgia. She'd insist he take some of her aspirin, and he didn't want to use up their supplies. Not for a moron like Brandon.

"Ears are terribly painful. Roy had a pre-cancerous spot removed from the top of his ear once. He complained about that thing for months."

Roy's hand went to the top of his left ear. "I thought it would bother me the rest of my days, but eventually it stopped. Something about nerves in your ears."

"To wrap the ear, I'd have to wrap your entire head. In this case it might be best to leave the cut open. It'll heal faster that way, if we make sure it stays clean. You'll want to keep it out of the sun because a blister on top of this cut could lead to infection." Georgia stood back and studied her work. "I know just the thing."

She turned and walked out of the room.

Roy put down the *Old Farmer's Almanac* he'd been pretending to read. "Want to tell me who the idiot was?"

"No, sir. I'd rather not."

"Fair enough."

Georgia sailed back into the room, triumphantly carrying a floppy hat made out of flowery fabric.

"Uh, what's that for?"

"To protect your ear from the sun. Let's see if it fits." She set the hat on Carter's head. "Perfect!"

Roy laughed and tried unsuccessfully to turn it into a cough.

Carter stood and hobbled over to a mirror hanging in the mudroom at the back of the house just off the kitchen. He looked slightly worse than he felt. There were a few scrapes on his face from where he'd hit the dirt. He removed the hat and turned his head to the left, trying to get a good look at his right ear. Despite Georgia's first aid, the ear was swollen and beginning to bruise. His left shoulder looked far worse, already turning a dark purple. He tried to move his arm and winced.

"That will be sore for a few days." Georgia hustled over beside him. "But I don't think you displaced anything. You can raise it, right?"

He slowly raised his left arm. It hurt all right. Made a cold sweat break out on his forehead, but nothing was broken. Stiff, that's what he was.

"Keep the cold rag on it, and keep the hat on your head if you go outside."

"You're kidding, right?"

"About what?"

"This hat. It has purple flowers on it."

"Still covers your head doesn't it? That ball cap you usually wear won't do a bit of good."

"But, Georgia, it has purple flowers—and pink. Look, there are pink ones too!"

Roy started laughing outright now, causing them to turn and stare at him.

"Something funny, Roy?" Georgia put both hands on her hips, as if daring him to contradict her.

"The boy's right. You can't send him out in a hat with flowers."

"Do you have a better idea? Because last I heard, Abney's one department store was closed."

"Yeah, I have a better idea." Roy joined them in the mudroom and walked to the wall where they stored their outdoor gear—pegs for hats, hooks for jackets, and cubbies for boots. He didn't reach for the cowboy hat that he always wore, what he called his work hat. And he didn't reach for the Stetson that he used to wear to town or to church. There was a third hat there—black, definitely worn, seriously cool.

He walked over to Carter, turned him back toward the mirror, and put the hat on his head.

"See there? Perfect fit."

"But . . . whose is it?"

"That is Max's hat, the one he kept here at the

ranch in case he forgot his when he came to visit. But I happened to notice that he also brought his good hat, so I don't think he'd mind giving this one to you."

"Giving it to me?" Carter met Roy's eyes in the mirror.

"Sure. If you're going to work on a ranch, you're going to need a proper hat." Roy leaned toward Georgia and gave her a peck on the cheek. "And it will protect his ear."

"I guess it's settled then." She returned to the kitchen and began serving the dinner that was now an hour past due.

It was only a hat, and an old one at that, but looking at himself in the mirror, Carter saw someone he didn't recognize. In the last few days, he'd dropped the sullen teenager act. There was too much work to do, and it took too much energy to stay angry about things he couldn't change. Maybe that's why he didn't fully recognize himself in the mirror. It was almost as if he was looking at the man he was destined to become.

Forty-six

Max had been waiting for Bhatti to return. While he'd been pretending to sleep, his mind had gone back over his personal history with the man. It was Mayor Perkins who had suggested he contact

Bhatti back when the flare had first hit and they'd been sorely in need of medical personnel. Somehow, Perkins had known that the man was a doctor, and she'd sent Max to enlist his help. Bhatti had needed some convincing, but now Max suspected that had been an act.

The question was, what had he been doing in Abney?

Max opened his eyes when he heard Shelby rise.

Near the entrance, Bhatti was speaking to the room guard as Danny had. She signed a piece of paper, which Bhatti folded and stuffed into his pocket. He walked over to their group and said, "Let's get out of here." They followed him out into an afternoon that was fading to evening.

"I'm sorry you were stuck in there for so long."

"What's going on here, Bhatti?" Patrick was the one to begin the avalanche of questions. "How did you manage to get us in? And where have you been the last thirteen hours?"

"I will answer your questions." His gaze traveled over each of them, and Max realized that the man's entire presence had changed. He was wearing the same clothes, but everything from his posture to his demeanor to his manner of speaking was different. Somehow, Max knew that standing before him was the real Dr. Farhan Bhatti.

"I suspect the MREs they fed you were pretty bad. How about we get some chow, and then I'll answer any questions you have."

They dined on spaghetti—actual pasta with real meat sauce, no goo. It was a definite improvement over lunch. The mess hall they ate in was somewhat crowded with military personnel in a dazzling display of uniforms. It looked as if every service was represented, though the bulk seemed to be Texas National Guard.

Shelby began to question the doctor, but he held up his hand and stopped her. "Not here."

Max almost smiled. Bhatti would have never done that in the past. He would have quietly, demurely waited and then politely answered or remained silent. But this Bhatti was accustomed to being obeyed, and though Shelby's eyes flashed with impatience, she clamped her mouth shut.

When they were finished eating, they walked outside and across the lawn, passing planter rows that housed skylights for the underground rooms. Max had been quite interested in the extensive renovation of the capitol building, and he had followed every detail. He'd graduated from the University of Texas, just a few blocks to the north, the same year that the square footage of the building was nearly doubled by adding the massive extension underground. No wonder the governor had picked this place to stand her ground. It was symbolically and strategically prime real estate.

A five-hundred-foot walkway led up to the capitol building, connecting it on the other end to Congress Avenue. It was twenty-five feet wide and provided a dramatic entrance to the center of government.

The red granite building rose above them. Max glanced up when he heard the snap of the flags in the breeze. Though it wasn't quite dark, a solar-powered light had come on and illuminated the stars and stripes of the American flag as well as the single star of the Texas flag. Max felt a swelling of patriotism as he passed underneath them. He'd never actually believed that his country and his state might be vulnerable to attack from inside or outside sources. He'd never considered the possibility that his country and his state might not exist for the next generation.

Bhatti led them midway up the steps of the capitol building, where he took a seat and gestured for them to do the same.

Shelby began to pull out her notebook, but Bhatti shook his head once. "Sorry, Shelby. This is off the record, at least for the time being."

She shrugged as if it made no difference to her, but Max was willing to bet she'd be jotting down everything Bhatti said—she'd simply wait until he was out of sight. There was still such a thing as freedom of the press, wasn't there? Or had that gone the way of microwave ovens and Wi-Fi?

Looking out, Max was astounded at the size of the operation that had taken over the capitol grounds. He could barely find a patch of grass that wasn't covered with tents, supplies, or troops.

The capitol building was guarded as well, but Bhatti flashed something and the men snapped to attention, eyes straight ahead, and returned to their post. Patrick, Bianca, and Shelby sat in a semicircle around Bhatti. From their vantage point they had an excellent view of the compound to the north. Max settled himself on the step, and then he turned his attention to the top of the wire fence at the boundary of the compound.

"How long has the fence been there?" Max asked.

"It went up an hour before the flare."

"Before . . ." Bianca jerked her head around to stare at him, but Patrick was way ahead of anyone else.

"You're part of an advance team."

"I am."

"Can you tell us what your objective was?"

"I can, because you know much of it and with time would guess the rest. NASA warned the federal government of the impending CME and its subsequent effects twelve hours before the flare hit. They knew that it would be bigger than anything we had experienced in modern history, and they suspected what the effects would be. There was a protocol in place for such a thing, which varied slightly from state to state."

Shelby turned sideways on the step, so she was facing him. "It affected the entire nation?"

"The entire world."

"Do we have communication with the federal government?" Max asked.

"No. We lost that at the same time everything else went out."

"Why were you in Abney?" Bianca asked. "Are you even a real doctor?"

"I am a doctor—board certified in emergency medicine, not an otolaryngologist as you thought. Attended military medical school in Bethesda and was then commissioned to the Air Force. Spent most of my time at Lackland in San Antonio, though I did a few stints in the Middle East. I worked in the ER at Brooke Army Medical Center. We had hoped by changing minute details to my personal history that my presence in your town would sound slightly less suspicious."

"Because any ER doctors would have reported immediately to their local hospital." Max leaned forward and studied Bhatti. How many clues had he missed? He had been so focused on saving Shelby and Carter and Abney that he hadn't paid enough attention to the things, the people, right in front of his eyes.

"Correct. Who needs an ear, nose and throat specialist during a national emergency? They attempted to keep our cover stories as close to the actual truth as possible."

"What about your parents in New York? Your grandparents in Pakistan?" Shelby's tone was angry. She'd never liked being duped, and this time was no exception. Max knew she considered herself to be a good judge of people, someone who watched closely and missed little. And she had harbored suspicions of Bhatti from the beginning, only they'd been of a different kind.

"My mother was from Pakistan, my father from England, and my parents did indeed live in New York. They were killed in the 9-11 attacks. My grandparents—who lived in Karachi—died years ago." He waited, giving them time to absorb the information.

"Why are you telling us all of this?" Bianca asked.

He shrugged. "Perhaps it is good to have someone know the truth about you. Perhaps, after the three weeks we've spent battling for our lives, I feel I owe you that much."

"What did you hope to accomplish by coming to Abney?" Max asked. "In fact, why Abney? We're not large enough to matter to anyone."

"One of Governor Reed's primary concerns was an anticipated lack of communication. She wanted to keep abreast of what was going on throughout the state, and she wanted those reports to come from people she trusted. She is the one who con-ceived Operation Nightshade."

Forty-seven

"Operation Nightshade?" Shelby lost her irritation, fascinated by the details of Bhatti's life. Her fingers actually itched for a keyboard or her notebook and pen. Oh, the story she could write . . . but now they were living the story instead of reading about it. She forced herself to focus all of her attention on Bhatti, to commit what he was saying to memory just in case she decided to jot down some notes later.

"Sounds like the title of a novel."

"The purpose of the operation was to deploy professionals in occupations that could be useful in a time of emergency—doctors, nurses, engineers, agricultural specialists, veterinarians— the list was quite extensive. Two hundred and fifty-four individuals in all."

"One for each county." Max nodded in approval.

She supposed the plan made sense, but for every question Bhatti answered, three more rose in Shelby's mind to take its place.

"Yes. Though it would seem that some counties would need more than one. The point wasn't only to provide help. Dallas County has many of those individuals who would and did step into the gap. What Governor Reed needed was eyes and ears on the ground."

"How did you report back?" Bianca asked.

"I didn't until today. We were to stay in our assigned county for ten to twenty-one days and then find our way back to the capitol."

"So it wasn't Mayor Perkins's idea for you to come along?" Max held up a hand. "Wait. You're going to tell me that she thought it was her idea. You played her, like you played me that first night at the Star Hotel."

Instead of being offended, Bhatti smiled. "I will ask your forgiveness for that, Max, but it was necessary that I not seem too eager to help."

"You did help, though." Bianca ran a finger over her lips. "You helped the patients at the nursing home as well as the refugees from Croghan. You got your hands dirty with the blood and injuries of the people in our town, and you seemed to care about what you were doing."

"But he was also pragmatic," Max said. "Think about the time that we had the car rush through the blockades, when Carter was standing guard with Mrs. Plumley. Bhatti showed up and reminded us that it would do no good to try and save the man who had been shot."

"Emergency medicine has never been an easy profession, even with modern technology at our disposal. Without it? We understood the decisions we would have to make."

"So you decided to let him die?" Shelby felt her emotions swing back toward accusation. She wanted to like the man, wanted to appreciate what he'd done for them, but she didn't know if she could. Jiggling her knee, she turned toward him and squinted into the last of the setting sun.

"I understood there was nothing I could do to keep him alive. There's a difference."

"Max let you live in his house. We accepted you into our town, and you were living a lie the entire time."

"I was completing my mission."

"What did you bury in Max's yard?"

Bhatti actually laughed. "My identification tags. I shouldn't have brought them, and indeed I left all other forms of my true identification back at my officer's quarters in San Antonio. But old habits die hard, I suppose, and I didn't realize I was still wearing them until that first night I stayed at Max's."

"Which is when you went out and buried them," Max said.

Bhatti nodded.

"What if we'd dug them up?" Shelby asked.

"I don't know. I would have thought of something. My goal was not to trick you, Shelby, and I'm sorry if you feel hurt by my actions. I was fulfilling the mission given to me by Governor Reed, and I will continue to do so."

"Is Farhan Bhatti even your real name?"

"It is not. My name is Gabe Thompson."

Patrick was the first to lean forward and offer

his hand. They shook, and Patrick said, "Nice to meet you, Gabe."

"You seem the least surprised."

"The way you handled the rifle? How you responded quickly and logically under pressure? I knew you weren't merely a doctor, but I wasn't sure exactly what to make of that. So I waited and watched. Eventually I became convinced you were military or retired military."

"Takes one to know one."

"You never told me your suspicions," Max said.

"What could we have done about it? Nothing. And you seemed to trust him." Patrick turned back to Gabe. "When I was convinced you meant us no harm, I considered it a perk to have another military guy along."

"So the government knew we were about to be plunged into darkness." Shelby shook her head in disgust. "They had twelve hours to prepare, but they didn't warn anyone."

"Some argued that we should send out an emergency alert, but every single study done on modern catastrophes—whether they were natural or man-made—every single study projected massive casualties caused by panic among the civilian population."

"We could have unplugged things. We could have saved things that were fried by the flare."

"And what would you have plugged them

into after the flare? We knew the grid would fail and do so quickly. We had twelve hours. It wasn't as if we could store up more food or make more medication."

Shelby winced at the mention of medical supplies. "You've made your report already?"

"I have."

"Did you report everything?" Max asked.

"Nearly." Gabe let his gaze travel over each of them, but stopped when he reached Max. "I did not mention the Remnant."

"Why?"

"While I trust Governor Reed, she isn't the only one who will see that report."

"So there are people here you don't trust."

Shelby thought he wouldn't answer, but he propped his elbows on his knees, pressed his palms together in a prayerlike posture, and lowered his voice. "This situation is still volatile. The governor's staff seems to have the upper hand at the moment, but it's uncertain whether state and federal officials can come to an agreement."

"About what?" Patrick asked.

"Everything. Mind you, there are formidable forces within the state as well. Should things go bad . . ." He held up a hand to stop Shelby's question. "Should the situation deteriorate even further, then groups like the Remnant may be critical."

"So what now?" Shelby asked. "You stay here

and we leave? What about the supplies we came for?"

"That is up to the governor." Gabe glanced at his watch. "And you're scheduled to meet with her in ten minutes, so we should go."

Forty-eight

Shelby had been in the capitol building before. Once on a field trip with Carter's sixth grade class, and once when she was doing research on a novel set in the 1890s, just after the capitol building was completed. She shouldn't have been surprised by the grandeur and majesty of the building.

Maybe it was owing to all they'd endured on the trip into Austin, or the countless number of homeless people she'd seen, or the growing certainty that things would never be exactly as they were before. Whatever the reason, as she stepped into the main entrance of the south foyer, she felt her heart rate quicken.

The building was majestically, splendidly ornate, like something from a dream, like something from the past.

The floor was covered with designs that memorialized the Texas Revolution, the Mexican War, and the American Civil War. They were in a different kind of revolution, a different type of war now. What would those men think of the fence surrounding the capitol? She raised her eyes to the two statues, which depicted Sam Houston and Stephen F. Austin. Both were men who had cared about the land south of the Red River and about the people who chose to live there.

They continued walking, passing through the rotunda.

Bianca let out a long, low whistle.

"You haven't been here?" Shelby asked.

"No. I always wanted to, but I never made the time."

"The portraits are of former governors and past presidents of the Republic of Texas."

"How high do they go?"

"They line the walls all the way up to the fourth floor."

Each person in the group stopped when they reached the center of the room and automatically looked up, craning their necks, the wreckage of downtown Austin outside the doors temporarily forgotten.

"How high is that?" Patrick asked.

"More than two hundred feet," Shelby answered.

"Actually, it's two hundred and sixty-six." Max stepped closer, put his right hand on her shoulder, and with his left pointed toward the middle of the dome. "Look closely, and you'll see the Texas star in the center."

"How do you know so much about this building?"

She didn't want to turn and look into Max's eyes. It was enough to stand close to him, someone she knew she could trust with her life.

"I was a UT student in prelaw, remember? This building was hallowed ground for us."

"We need to hurry," Gabe reminded them, but he seemed to understand and appreciate their moment of nostalgia. He didn't move until they'd all looked back down, at each other, and refocused on the task at hand.

They made their way to the second floor of the east wing. A plaque on the wall declared the room they were entering to be the Senate Chamber. There were men and women seated at each of the thirty-one desks, but Shelby could tell that they weren't senators. Many wore military uniforms, and some remained in plain clothes. She saw some tablets, like the nurse had used, but mostly people were looking at maps, shuffling through large stacks of paper, or conferring over white boards.

Gabe stepped up to a soldier and explained they had a meeting with Governor Reed. "She's in the lieutenant governor's office." So they made their way back out into the hall. The office wasn't far.

As they walked, it seemed to Shelby that their steps quickened, and each person found some hidden reserve of energy. This was it. This was their last chance to find what they'd come for. If the governor couldn't, or wouldn't, get it for them, Shelby didn't know what they'd do. And why were they being called here? What did Governor Reed want from them?

Gabe pulled the sheet of paper out of his pocket, the same one Shelby had seen him show the guard outside room number eight. He walked up to the MP stationed outside the lieutenant governor's office and showed it to him. The military police officer studied the sheet, glanced up at them, and then he finally settled his gaze on Gabe.

"We'll let her know. Have a seat over there." He pointed to benches directly across from the office.

But their wait was short. To Shelby it seemed that she'd barely sat down when the MP strode over and said, "Follow me."

She wished they'd had a few more minutes. Time to question Gabe, to figure out among themselves what the governor wanted and how best to answer any questions. Instead of resting, they should have spent their time in room number eight working on their story. Only they didn't have a story. All they had was the truth of what had happened to them, what they'd seen, and why they were there. But should they tell it all? Even about the Remnant?

Governor Elizabeth Reed was a short, round woman with white hair that fell to her shoulders. She was studying a map that had been pinned to a bulletin board, but she turned at the sound of their footsteps and smiled broadly.

"I sent Gabe to Abney to assess and report

back to me on conditions, and he returns with an entire group of witnesses." She shook hands with each of them, pausing to hear their names and commit their faces to memory. Shelby had stopped following politics long ago. Though she tried to read up on each candidate and always voted in local, state, and national elections, she couldn't remember many specifics about Elizabeth Reed. The woman had seemed to espouse the same goals and morals that most of rural Texas did. That was enough to win Shelby's vote.

"Great deer hunting in Abney, if I remember correctly."

"Yes, ma'am, only now folks are hunting for food instead of recreation," Max said. "They're hunting to keep their families alive."

Reed sat behind her desk, laced her fingers together, and looked directly at Max. "Tell me about that. I want to know how things really are, and what you've seen on your trip to the capitol."

Max gave the basic narrative, but Bianca and Patrick interrupted now and again to add details. Shelby pulled out her notebook, and when Max looked to confirm something, she checked what she'd written. Gabe remained silent, but then Shelby remembered he'd already given his report. What could they add to that? It was a testament to the governor's thoroughness that she wanted to hear it again, that she wanted a complete picture of what things were like outside the compound.

Finally, she stood and walked over to the map, gesturing for them to join her. "Show me exactly where you encountered Diego's men."

Patrick picked up two pushpins from the tray and stuck them in the map. "From here to here, at least. And he may have gained more territory today."

"And the church, Saint Mary . . . if I remember correctly, it's here." She pushed another pin into the map.

Max stepped back, crossed his arms, and studied the situation north of the capitol. "Of the two, I'd say Reverend Hernandez is the bigger threat."

"Analyzed like a true lawyer." Reed took off her glasses, letting them dangle from a jeweled eyeglass chain. As she stared at the board, she said, "I agree with you. Unfortunately, Hernandez and Diego aren't our only threats—not even close."

Silence followed that ominous statement. Shelby waited. Her friends waited. Even Gabe waited. Finally, as if coming out of a stupor, Reed plastered on a smile and said, "But you've given us a better picture of what the area to the north looks like, and I thank you. We send out patrols, of course, but they are of limited value as many people run and hide when they see a military vehicle."

Patrick nodded toward the map. "The people who are preying on others are like rats, running for the sewer at the first sign of anything bigger than them."

"And the regular folks are frightened," Bianca said. "And increasingly more desperate."

"We will help them." Reed picked up her glasses and perched them back on her nose. "Not as soon as I'd like, but we will help them. I want to thank you all for coming in to see me. Now Gabe will take you to some better accommodations for the night, and I wish you a safe journey on your trip back to Abney."

Shelby had been relatively quiet, studying Reed and trying to decide if she trusted her. The woman seemed competent and well intentioned. She seemed like someone who could handle an emergency, perhaps better than most politicians. Even an emergency of this magnitude.

However, Shelby's impatience had been building, and when the governor effectively dismissed them, that impatience boiled over.

"But we're not going home. We're not leaving until we find what we came after. We need insulin, antibiotics . . . a whole list of things that Gabe must have showed you. Without those things many people in Abney will die, and without the insulin, my son's days are numbered."

Forty-nine

Max wasn't surprised when Shelby's patience reached its limit. She reminded him of a rubber band, stretched to the breaking point.

Fortunately, Governor Reed seemed to realize the same thing, and she immediately put Shelby's fears at rest.

"You will receive the medications that you need, including the insulin. I'm sorry I alarmed you. I thought that was understood. Gabe shared with me the details in his report, and I'm having it packed up for you now."

"So you'll give it to us? You'll give us everything we asked for?" Shelby sank back into her chair, the tension draining from her.

"Yes. Honestly, insulin isn't an issue. In most cases, a diabetic person would be denied the opportunity to serve in the military. There have been exceptions, of course, but my point is that we can supply you with a year's worth of insulin. That's what you were requesting. Correct?"

"It is." Shelby glanced at Max, as if needing to confirm that she wasn't imagining the conversation.

"What about Abney?" he asked.

"That's a little trickier, as antibiotics and the other things listed are items that we might conceivably need here." She sat back and again removed her glasses. "In my opinion, the supplies we have are being safeguarded here for the citizens of Texas. We're not taking it from them. We're simply providing a secure place to store it."

"People need those medications now, ma'am," Patrick pointed out.

"Of course they do. I wish I could distribute it to them now, but my priority has to be defending the capitol. Once this area is secure, once we've reclaimed Austin, then I will send out supply transports, which will include medication."

"But we can take some with us?" Bianca had reached over to grasp Shelby's hand.

"Yes. You're here. The medication is for people who need it. You'd be doing me a favor by taking it with you." She cleared her throat. "There are some who would disagree with me, but they're not governor, and I am. So, yes, you may have everything you requested."

"And it's being loaded into our vehicles now?" Patrick asked.

"It is. I suggest you wait until sunrise to leave, for safety's sake."

"Agreed," Max said. He had no intention of taking this group back through Diego's territory or by Reverend Hernandez's church in the middle of the night.

"Thank you." Shelby still looked stunned. "We have things to trade. We brought—"

"That's not necessary," the governor assured

her. "You keep that. It could be that you'll need it in the future."

"Well, if you think of any way that we can thank you, please let us know."

Gabe had been silent through this exchange, but now he glanced at Shelby's notebook, and then he looked directly at her. "Since you're going to be here for the night, perhaps you could leave your notebook with us."

"Leave it?"

"We have a scanner. I've watched you take detailed notes since we left Abney. It could be that there's something in there, something you're not even aware of, that will help us to prepare for what we'll face once we take the fight outside the capitol."

"Gabe's right," the governor said. "If you're willing—"

"Of course. Yes. Of course I am." Shelby glanced at Max, and he knew what she was thinking, could practically hear the sigh of relief that she hadn't included any details about the Remnant.

He trusted Governor Reed and thought she was a good leader, but things had a way of spiraling away from where you thought they'd go. For now, it was better to keep details of the Remnant between them. And besides, what the governor wanted was any information on groups that were challenging state authorities. That description did not fit the Remnant. They had a completely different mission. Defying authority was not their goal. At least not yet. He hoped it never would be.

Shelby had clipped her pen to the notebook and handed it to the governor.

"Thank you. I'll have this returned to you before you leave."

They quickly found themselves back outside on the steps of the capitol building—Max, Shelby, Patrick, Bianca, and Gabe.

Once they were down the steps, away from the guards, Shelby jumped, punching in the air, and letting out a squeal of delight.

"We did it! I wasn't sure we could. It seemed like everything was stacked against us, but we did it!" The squeal was followed by a round of hugs and high fives.

She saved Max for last. When she moved to slap his hand, he pulled her into his arms and whispered in her ear. "Carter's going to be fine, and he's lucky to have you for his mother."

She touched his cheek once and started to answer. Changing her mind, she kissed him on the other cheek and whispered, "Thank you" before pulling away.

Something inside Max blossomed, something he hadn't felt in a long time. Certainly not since the flare, and maybe even before that. Maybe it was something he'd smothered well before the sun changed their world.

For the first time in many years, Max experienced hope. That they would get the supplies of medication back to the people who needed them and that Carter would be fine. He caught a glimpse of a future with Shelby, one that was more than friendship. He allowed himself to dream about the next day and the next one after that with Shelby in his arms, by his side, completing his life. And in that moment the thought crossed his mind that just possibly the life they were building could be better than the one they'd left behind.

Fifty

Shelby was still feeling elated an hour later when there was a tap on the door of their room. Their new sleeping digs included a room they didn't have to share with any other group. Six cots lined the wall, and the windows that faced the lawn could be opened, allowing a delicious breeze to cool the area. What had been an office now resembled a hastily thrown together dorm room. And when they'd arrived, they had found their backpacks sitting on the cots, though of course the weapons had been removed.

Everyone was sprawled out except Gabe, who had promised he would meet them in the morning, return the notebook, and take them to their vehicles.

At the sound of the knock, Max hurried across the room—shoeless but still wearing his socks—and opened the door. Shelby sat up, rubbing her eyes and trying to remember what it felt like to actually sleep. Her watch said it was only nine in the evening, but her body was convinced it was much later.

"Danny. Come on in. We weren't expecting to see you again."

"I wanted to check on you." He stepped into the room, nodding at each person in turn, his gaze lingering a moment on Shelby, or so it felt to her, before he sat down on one of the unoccupied cots. "Listen. I'm sorry to say I checked around, and I just can't find the medical supplies you need. What little we have—"

"It's okay!" Shelby grinned at Danny, who stared at her in disbelief.

"What do you mean?"

"I mean we have it. Or we will have it. The governor agreed to provide the insulin and the other medicines for us to take to Abney."

"That's great news. That's really something. I didn't know."

"How could you? We didn't know ourselves until an hour ago."

"So you have the supplies . . . here?"

"No. She's having someone load it in our vehicles." Shelby had the feeling that she was grinning like a clown, but she couldn't help it. She was so relieved, so ecstatic that they could go home the next day with the things they needed.

"We're supposed to meet Gabe in the morning," Patrick said. "Wait. I know why you look confused. You know Farhan Bhatti, but you probably didn't know his real name is Gabe Thompson. Anyway, he works with the governor, and he's been a real help to both us and the administration."

"Unfortunately, he won't be going back with us." Max didn't sit back down. He stood leaning against the wall, his arms crossed, yawning. "He was a real benefit to Abney, but apparently he's being assigned somewhere else."

"Which is okay, because we've had some of our regular doctors show up." Bianca slipped into Spanish as she plucked at the light blanket on her bed. "*Que puedes hacer?*"

She was thinking about her dad. Shelby knew without having to ask. She moved over to her friend's cot, put an arm around her shoulder and said, "You did the best you could do, that's what. We all did."

"I know, and I know that medicine would not have saved *Papá*." She plastered on a smile. "Don't mind me. I'm tired, is all."

"I'm sure you all are." Danny stood, shook hands with Patrick and Bianca and Max. When he reached Shelby, it seemed to her that he was about to say something, but instead he shook her hand and said, "Be safe."

"When will we see you again?" she asked.

"I couldn't say. I guess none of us knows what tomorrow will bring." And then he was gone.

They were quiet for a few minutes. Max lay back on his cot. Bianca rummaged through her pack until she came out with an old Bible. It was about the size of a small journal. She didn't open it, though. She put her hand on top of it and closed her eyes.

The room wasn't dark yet. The sun didn't set until eight thirty, and twilight lasted another thirty minutes or so. Shelby might have dozed off, because the next thing she knew, the light had vanished. She could just make out the shapes of Max and Patrick standing near the windows, talking in low voices.

She could have asked them what was wrong, what they were worried about, but she realized she didn't want to know. For just this night, she wanted to believe that everything was going to be fine. Tomorrow, she would deal with any new problems that popped up.

But one thing was certain. Come daylight, they were headed back to Abney.

Fifty-one

Less than an hour after Danny Vail left, there was another tap on their door.

"I didn't realize how popular we were," Max muttered.

In some distant part of Shelby's mind, she heard him speaking to someone in a low voice, and then he was beside her cot, shaking her awake.

"What is it? What's wrong?"

He put a finger to his lips. "Come in the hall with me. Let's not wake the others."

"I'm awake," Patrick said.

"G.I. Joe's up, but let's not wake Bianca."

The sound of her friend's light snore drifted across the room, causing Shelby to smile. At least Bianca was getting some rest.

She carried her shoes with her left hand and ran her fingers through her hair with her right. No doubt she looked a fright. She hadn't glanced in a mirror since the day before, or maybe the day before that. When she patted her hair, she could feel the curls were reaching halo proportions. Well, it wasn't the first time Max had seen her a mess, and whoever had come to visit would just have to deal with it.

She stepped out into the hall in front of Max, and heard him shut the door quietly behind them. Turning around, she blinked in surprise. "Governor Reed. Is something wrong?"

"No, but I'd like to talk to you. I'm sorry for the late hour."

"Talk? Here?"

"Maybe we could walk downstairs."

They found a room that had been set up with tables and chairs. Several lanterns sat darkened on the middle of the tables. Shelby glanced at her watch—it was only ten o'clock, but the room was empty. Everyone was in bed. Funny how their sleeping patterns had reverted back to a farmer's lifestyle. They were up at sunrise and asleep by the time it was good and dark. No more late nights scouring the Internet, watching television, or reading one more chapter. She was reminded again that life had changed, and they had changed with it. Surviving took every ounce of energy they had.

Governor Reed lit one of the lanterns and then looked surprised when Max pulled up a chair and joined them.

"I didn't mean to interrupt your sleep, Max. I'm sure Shelby and I will be fine."

"I'll stay." He crossed his arms, as if daring the governor to argue.

Shelby nodded.

"All right." Reed placed the messenger bag she was carrying on the table and pulled out Shelby's journal. Instead of handing it to her, she placed it on top of the bag and tapped it with her index finger. "This is very good. It provides a perspective that we simply don't have of what is happening out there."

"Thank you."

"I have a proposal for you."

Shelby's pulse quickened, and Reed immediately realized her mistake. "It's not about the medical supplies. That's a done deal, Shelby. I won't go back on my word."

"What kind of proposal?"

"When we first designed Operation Nightshade, we worked diligently to envision what types of professionals we might need—both white collar and blue collar. We tried to anticipate every aspect of this disaster, but in many aspects it was inconceivable. Oh, we understood what it would mean to be without a power grid, but how people would react? And the cascade effects of their decisions? Those things were in many respects beyond our grasp to even imagine until three weeks ago."

"What does this have to do with Shelby?" Max asked, clearly impatient with her preamble.

Reed ignored him, her attention still on Shelby. "We sent out two hundred and fifty-four individuals with a wide variety of skills, but it didn't occur to us to send out a reporter."

"The government has never been especially cozy with the press." Max sat forward, propping his elbows on the table.

"True, but when there is no press, when there is no one documenting the details of what has happened, then the truth of the past, and of the present, is even more susceptible to manipulation."

"People will lie."

"They will. They already are, and those lies are spreading quickly."

"Factions against the government?"

"Both state and federal. That is one of my concerns, but I have others, perhaps owing to the fact that I worked fifteen years in academia before I became governor."

"You were the head of the state board of education." Shelby suddenly remembered why she'd voted for Reed to begin with—she'd cared about their children. She'd been a logical, level voice in a volatile time when the state was reassessing everything from textbooks to school security.

"As an educator, it's important for me to see that the times we find ourselves in are documented accurately." Reed again tapped the journal before pushing it toward Shelby. "I want you to come and work for me."

"Excuse me?"

"We need someone like you. You could interview the refugees who come into the compound—"

Shelby's anger flashed. "What about those on the outside? The ones you won't let in?"

"That's another thing I like about you, something I discovered when I read over your notes. You are willing to take some risk, and you listen to people. Yes, we need to know what's going on outside as well. We'd send you to different locations around the state, with an escort, of course, and you could report back to me."

Shelby made her decision before the governor stopped talking. In fact, it was no decision at all. The thought of working for the government, of being away from Carter, was ludicrous. He was her life. He was why she was risking her life. "Thank you, ma'am. It's quite a compliment, but I have to go back to Abney. I have a son."

"Who turns eighteen next month. I read that too. You were quite thorough in your description of the situation back at High Fields."

"Yes, he turns eighteen, and I need to be there."

"Why?"

"Excuse me?"

"Why do you need to be there? Max can deliver the insulin. His parents are providing a home for Carter."

"I'm his mother."

"Let me ask you a question." Reed glanced at Max but continued addressing her comments directly to Shelby. "Would you have followed him to college?"

"This isn't college."

"My point is that he's a man now, and he doesn't

need his mother by his side." Shelby was shaking her head, but Reed continued to push. "We need you, Shelby. You would be providing a great service, and your name would go down in history as the person who wrote the chronicles of this terrible disaster."

"I don't want to go down in history." Shelby picked up the notebook and stared at it a moment. Finally, she turned her attention back to Governor Reed. "I agree with you. It needs to be written down, and not just by me. I hope that other people —teachers, writers, students, and journalists— will also be documenting what is happening—"

"But you could be a leader, a recorder of history in a world gone dark."

Shelby continued as if Reed hadn't interrupted. "And one day, I hope those eyewitness accounts are gathered together into a history that will warn the next generation."

She stood calmly, pushed in her chair ever so gently, and clutched the notebook to her chest. Her insides were quaking. But she didn't doubt for a minute that she was doing the right thing. "My priority is my family. Home with Carter, with Max's parents. That is exactly where I plan to be tomorrow evening."

"I'd like you to at least consider what I've said."

"She has." Max stood as well. "And you have your answer."

Fifty-two

Max was still awake when Shelby sat up, picked up her shoes, and tiptoed out of the room. He found her sitting on the grass in front of the building, staring up at the stars.

He stopped, wondering if she'd rather be alone. Turning, he glanced back at the building they'd been given accommodations in—the John Reagan State Office Building. The offices on the inside of the five-story building had been emptied of their contents and filled with cots. There were restrooms on each hall. It was better than the tent they'd been in, and he could only guess at the occupants in the other rooms.

There were no guards outside. No, the people in this building came and went as they pleased, as they needed.

Knowing he wouldn't be able to sleep, he continued toward Shelby and sat down on the grass. It was green, owing to the recent rains— soft and smelling of summer. He could close his eyes and pretend it was any other July day on the capitol lawn. Only it was nearly midnight, and if he listened closely enough he could hear the occasional sound of gunfire.

"I wish I had a cigarette," Shelby said.

"You don't smoke. You never have."

"I'm nervous, though. Maybe it would settle me down."

She turned toward him. It wasn't that Max could see her in the dark. He couldn't, except for some vague outline. But he knew when she turned toward him. It seemed that his body, every one of his senses, was finely tuned to Shelby Sparks.

He leaned in toward her, his hand tracing the outline of her jaw, his lips finding hers. Softly, gently, he kissed her.

She pulled away first, laughing nervously. "That didn't settle me down."

So he reached for her hand and pulled it between his. "Your hands are always so cold."

"Low blood pressure."

"Even as the world is ending."

"Even then."

"You were so happy just a few hours ago. What happened?"

"Fear crept in."

"Because of the meeting we had with Reed?"

"Honestly, I don't know. When Governor Reed said she was giving us the supplies, I was ecstatic. When she asked me to work for her, I was surprised. But now I'm terrified. My mind keeps mulling over all that might still go wrong."

They sat there for a few minutes, neither feeling the need to speak. When he'd rubbed some warmth back into her hand, she pulled it away. Max flopped onto his back and stared up at the stars.

"Light pollution seems to be a thing of the past."

Shelby lay back too, the side of her body pressed against his. It occurred to Max that they were really one person with two heads. Maybe they always had been.

"We're seeing stars as clearly as the cavemen did," he said.

"How can you joke at a time like this?"

"Who's joking?"

"They are remarkable."

"That they are."

"I can see the Milky Way."

"And Orion's Belt."

"Is that the one with Pleiades?"

"Don't you remember anything from Parish's class?"

"That was a long time ago, Max."

He thought of that. It was true. They'd both taken astronomy their junior year, Shelby one year later than him. He'd teased her because she nearly ruined her perfect GPA on an elective. For the final exam, she'd memorized the charts and pulled through. She'd aced it. No surprise there. Shelby could ace anything she set her mind to. She was one of the smartest, most resourceful people he knew.

"Yes," she whispered. "The answer is yes. I remember a little."

He raised his arm and pointed, though he wasn't

sure Shelby could see it. "That's the Big Bear, also known as the Big Dipper."

"I can find a dozen big dippers—small ones too."

Her laughter eased a knot of tension in his shoulders, and when Max joined in, it lightened a weight pressing on his heart. But then their mood turned serious, almost simultaneously.

" 'He is the Maker of the Bear and Orion, the Pleiades and the constellations of the south.' Remember, Shelby? God did all of that." He swept his arm from right to left and finally rested it next to her, seeking and finding her hand, intertwining their fingers.

"And man messed it up."

"I don't know." He sat up facing her, crossing his legs Indian-style, still holding her hand. "The way our society has been living? It's a long way from the way Job lived."

"Progress isn't always bad." She sat up too, facing him, though they still couldn't see each other. "I guess . . ."

She swiped at tears with her free hand. "I guess in the Old Testament world, Carter would have never lived. He would have died as a four-year-old when his symptoms first became critical."

"Maybe," Max admitted. "Maybe not. Our ancestors had medicine. They weren't techno-logically advanced, but they knew how to treat various diseases."

"Herbs and such."

"Sure, and it worked—Native Americans used herbs for everything from Alzheimer's to depression to diabetes."

"Diabetes?"

"Dandelion, ginseng, green tea, even prickly pear cactus were effective."

"How do you know that?"

He plucked a blade of grass from the lawn, ran the pad of his thumb up and down it, and decided to be honest. Tomorrow wasn't a given for them. Maybe it never had been. But somewhere along the way, he'd stepped back from Shelby. He'd decided the mistakes he'd made in the past were too big to overcome. With everything crashing around them, there was so little they had left—friends, their faith, their families, each other. So instead of stepping back, he stepped forward.

"I made it a hobby, of sorts, to study that."

"Study what?"

"Diabetes. Everything from medicinal herbs to the latest advancements in treatment."

"You never told me."

"I guess because you were doing all right, Shelby. You were doing well, and so was Carter. You didn't need me or—"

"We've always needed you."

He swallowed that confession from her. Let it slide all the way down to the bottom of his belly. Let it expand inside his chest.

"I don't want that for Carter." Shelby's voice was low and hoarse. "I don't want to have to do that. To have to go back to the way diseases were treated hundreds of years ago. They used leeches, for heaven's sake."

"But if you paired what our great-grandparents knew with the science we've learned since then, it seems like we might come up with something really effective."

"I'd rather have the insulin."

"I know you would, and we will. Reed promised, and she doesn't strike me as someone who would go back on her word."

"I hope you're right."

"But?"

"But we'll still only have enough for a year."

"When we get back, we'll make a long-term plan. We'll study the research I have stored in my room at High Fields."

"You took it to the ranch?"

"When I knew I was leaving Abney, I put it in my truck before you agreed to go to High Fields. In case you and Carter showed up later. In case there was some way I could help."

She didn't speak for a minute, but when she did, her voice was stronger. She sounded like the old Shelby. "Thank you, Max. For everything."

"You're welcome."

"If we get back home—"

"When."

"When we get back home, I want you to show me what you have. Maybe, if it works, we could at least reduce the amount of insulin he needs. Make what we have last longer."

"That's a great plan."

She stood, brushed off her jeans, and pulled him to his feet.

"Think you can sleep now?" Max asked.

"No. I don't think I'll sleep a wink, but it would feel good to lie down. I have a feeling that tomorrow is going to be a very long day."

"Today," he corrected her.

"Yeah. Today is going to be a very long day."

Fifty-three

In the end, Georgia had insisted he take two of the Advil from her medicine kit. "It will keep the swelling down."

Carter did it because he didn't have the energy to argue with her. She suggested he sleep in the main house, but he'd waved away her worries, walked across to the cottage he shared with his mom, and dropped into bed fully dressed. Who knew that fighting could wear a person out like that? He was asleep before it was completely dark.

But he woke when he always did, when Georgia's roosters began their chorus of *cock-a-doodle-doos*. One thing was for certain. If you lived on a ranch, you did not need an alarm clock—nature provided its own.

Surprisingly, he'd slept all night.

His left shoulder was sore, and the muscles felt unusually tight. He closed his eyes and tried to remember some of the goofy yoga stretches his mom used to do back in their house in Abney. Standing, he slowly lifted both arms straight above his head, then began reaching toward the ceiling—first with his right hand and then with his left. The first stretch on his left side caused him to groan, but by the time he'd done ten of them, the shoulder was feeling looser.

He followed the stretches up by pulling his right arm across his chest. He'd seen her do that plenty of times—right arm across, left hand cups the elbow, and then pulls it closer across the body.

Breathe, Carter. That's the key to yoga.

He'd laughed at her a hundred times, maybe more.

When he tried to pull his left arm across his chest, he actually stumbled backward from the pain.

Breathe, Carter.

So he did. He took it slow, closed his eyes, and forced his muscles to relax. By the time he was finished, he was able to put on a clean T-shirt, though it took twice as long as normal. He turned on the faucet and allowed a cupful of water to fill a basin Roy had placed in the sink. They didn't waste a thing if they could help it. The dirty water was dumped into a bucket and then carried out to the garden.

He sat at the small table, tested his blood sugar level, and dialed in the appropriate insulin dose. It was all so common, so everyday, and he had taken it for granted all of these years. That stopped today. He'd appreciate every dose, and he'd thank Max and his mom for risking their lives to find him more insulin. That would be the first thing he'd say to them.

He brushed his teeth, made a futile attempt to wet down his cowlick, and then he remembered the hat. Clamping it on top of his head, he decided he looked almost normal, so he stepped out onto the front porch.

The sky was ablaze with color, and the horizon looked on fire. His pulse raced, and then he realized there was no smell of smoke in the air. He wasn't looking at a fire, or even the effects of the aurora borealis. God had simply provided a spectacular sunrise.

He was halfway to the big house before he registered the fact that there was a horse tied to the front porch railing.

Placing his hand on the horse's neck, Carter said, "Hey, Pecos."

The brown gelding was fifteen hands tall, or so Jerry Lambert had mentioned when he'd first met the man. He owned the property next door. He rarely had time to stand around and visit, and he'd never stopped by at sunrise as far as Carter knew.

Which meant something had happened.

He took the front porch steps two at a time.

Jerry was standing with his back to the kitchen counter. As Carter walked in, Georgia pushed a mug of coffee into the man's hands. He nodded hello to Carter and thanked Georgia. Jerry was a big man—well over six feet and solid. He was a retired veterinarian, which made him a pretty important person. Already he'd been called on to treat people as well as animals, and Carter was pretty sure he'd taught Georgia everything she knew about first aid.

"Morning, Carter."

"Sir."

"Heard you got into a bit of a scuffle yesterday."

"Yes, sir."

"And it's not something you feel like Roy or I need to follow up on?"

"No, sir."

"All right. I imagine I could guess who the boys involved were. We'll trust you to tell us if the situation crops up again."

Carter nodded, pleased that they had confidence in his assessment. He honestly didn't think Brandon would be any trouble in the future. The other kids all knew to stay clear of him, and Carter had proved he'd fight back. No, he wouldn't be a problem. Brandon's type would move on to a different kind of trouble, or he might straighten up and fly right. It was doubtful, but stranger things had happened.

"You're sure it wasn't coyotes?" Roy asked, returning to their previous conversation.

"No. There was no sign of a wild animal attack, and the Murphys have two Great Pyrenees. A pack of coyotes might win a fight, but those dogs would die protecting the goats."

"So why wouldn't they attack someone trying to steal the goats?"

"We think that whoever did this watched them for a while, learned their routines. Dereck feeds the dogs every afternoon at four. The thieves most likely waited until the dogs were eating and nabbed the goats."

"Awfully bold," Carter said.

"It is, and that's part of what concerns us."

"Roadblocks didn't report anything?"

"No. We checked with both teams last night, when Dereck realized what had happened."

"And you're sure he didn't miscount or something?"

"They keep good records. If Dereck and Leona say they lost a dozen kids, then they lost a dozen."

"Maybe the word is out." Georgia set a large pot of oatmeal on the table and motioned for everyone to dig in. Doc Lambert didn't even try to resist. "Maybe folks have heard that we've created a sort of . . . coalition here, and they're trying to take advantage of that."

Roy nodded. "I hate to say it, but I think Georgia's right."

They each dug into their bowls of oatmeal, and for a moment all Carter could hear was Georgia's roosters and the soft cropping of Doc Lambert's horse.

When Roy had finished, he pushed his bowl away and clamped his hands around his coffee mug. "I was planning on checking the trotlines this morning, but Carter can take care of that."

"Yes, sir."

"I'll warn the families on the east side if you can take the west."

"Done," Lambert said.

"Could be we need to step up patrols, and people need to be reminded to keep their fire-arms close at hand. We don't want them trigger happy, but we do want them prepared."

"A gun in the house doesn't help if someone attacks you while you're in the field." Doc Lambert stood and reached for the cowboy hat he'd set on the counter. "That goes for you too, Carter."

"Yes, sir. Roy insists I carry my rifle or a handgun with me even if I'm only going down to the creek."

"Sad times, we live in," Georgia said. "Sad times, indeed."

Fifty-four

Shelby looked up to see Danny walking toward their vehicles. He shook hands with Max and Patrick before nodding at her and Bianca.

"I was sent to escort you out. Do you have everything you need?"

"We do." Shelby glanced back at the Dodge. "Gabe had to leave, but he made sure the medications were loaded and our tanks were filled up."

"Still need to pick up our weapons," Patrick said.

"Which you'll be given once you pass through the perimeter gate." Danny nodded toward two of his men, who pulled their jeep in front of the Dodge.

The vehicle was slick and modern with darkly tinted windows. Shelby wondered how they could even afford to drive it. The gas mileage must have been horrendous.

"Front gate's backed up," Danny explained. "The governor is sending out another squadron to begin clearing the roads. We'll escort you out the back way."

"That's not necessary," Max said. "If you could direct us—"

"I insist." And before anyone else could argue, he turned and walked to a Humvee that had taken up position behind them.

Max looked to Patrick, who was frowning, but he shrugged and climbed into the Mustang.

Bianca squeezed Shelby's hand and jogged back to Patrick's car. The route wound toward the back of the compound, snaking through troops and then railroad cars stacked three high.

"Supplies?" Shelby asked.

"Could be, or it could be where the men are staying. I've seen them turned into accommodations before—nothing fancy, but it's a dry place to grab a few hours' sleep."

There wasn't a soul to be seen. Shelby was torn between feeling ecstatic because they had what they needed, what they'd risked their lives for, and anxious because of the road ahead of them.

"It'll be okay," Max assured her as the vehicle in front of them pulled to a stop.

Both of the doors on the front vehicle opened, and the two soldiers hopped out at the same time that two more jumped out of the back. Before Shelby could fathom what was going on, eight soldiers—four from the jeep and four from the Humvee—had encircled both their vehicles with their weapons raised.

"What's happening?" she asked, hating that there was a tremor in her voice, that terror could rise so quickly in her heart.

"I don't know, but I have a feeling we're about to find out."

Danny appeared at Max's window, motioning for them to exit the vehicle.

"I need you both to step back ten paces."

"What are you doing, Danny?" Her heart was racing and she kept blinking rapidly, hoping that the scene in front of her would change. Why was this happening? Was God punishing her for killing the guard? But God didn't work that way. Jehovah was a God of mercy and grace.

Her voice rose into a scream. "What are you doing?"

Instead of answering her, Danny glanced back at Patrick and Bianca. The soldiers in the Humvee had apparently given them the same directions. Once Danny was satisfied that everyone had moved away from the vehicles, he turned to his men. "Load it up."

Six of the soldiers holstered their weapons and began removing the boxes of medication. Two stayed in position, one covering Patrick and Bianca, the other with his weapon trained on Max and Shelby.

A loud ringing in Shelby's ears blocked out whatever else Danny said. She stood there, her legs beginning to tremble, her heart racing, and stared in disbelief as the soldiers proceeded to unload the medications the governor had given them. She felt frozen, unable to move as all that they had worked for was whisked away. This couldn't be happening. Surely it was a nightmare that she'd wake from. She literally shook her head, trying to clear it. But nothing changed. The nightmare was real.

"You can't take our supplies." Max moved toward Danny. When the soldier guarding them pointed his weapon directly at Max's chest, he raised his hands and froze.

"I can, and I am." Danny's expression had hardened, and he refused to meet Shelby's eyes.

"Why would you?"

"Because we need these supplies."

Patrick was only a few feet away, standing close to Bianca. "The governor assured us—"

"The governor doesn't know what she's doing."

"But you do?" Bianca spat the words at him.

Shelby continued to stare as each box of supplies, every vial of insulin was taken from them and placed in the back of the jeep.

"You can't do this." A fierce energy possessed her, a desperation that she could no more control than she could stop the sun from rising and beating down on them. She darted toward the jeep, saw another soldier raise his gun, but she didn't care at that moment. It didn't matter. If they couldn't get the insulin to Carter, none of this mattered. "You can't, and I won't let you."

She snatched at one of the boxes, and then Danny was on her, his hands like vise grips on her arms, pulling her back and away from the supplies.

"Stop it! Let me go." She kicked at him, attempted to bite him, twisted and turned and fought to free herself. "Those are mine! They are mine and I'm taking them home."

"Let her go." Max's voice rang out like thunder. He moved toward them, his face a mask of fury.

The soldiers seemed uncertain what to do next. Perhaps Danny had told them they'd hand over the supplies with no resistance. Maybe they were hesitant to fire a shot inside the compound. The six unloading supplies froze, and the two with raised weapons took a step closer.

Danny raised a hand to indicate he had control of the situation. No doubt he didn't want to get shot in the crossfire, but stopping his soldiers was a mistake.

At that moment, Max stepped closer, intent on pulling Shelby away. She saw what was happening but something inside was tearing apart. She could hear—as if from a distance—her own screams and sobs, Patrick and Bianca and Max screaming, Danny warning everyone to back away.

Danny was still clutching her with one hand. She attempted to claw his fingers away. Weeping and begging and digging at his hand with her fingernails, she didn't realize what Danny was doing until his right fist connected with Max's jaw. The punch knocked him to the ground. He scrambled to his feet and moved to charge Danny, but two of the solders restrained him.

"Stop it!" Danny snarled, shaking Shelby as if she were a rag doll. "Do you actually think you deserve these supplies? Why you and no one else? What makes you so special?"

"The governor gave it to us!" Bianca shouted.

Patrick had his arms around her and was holding her back.

"The governor won't be in power much longer." He continued to grasp Shelby's arm, even as she desperately lurched for the last box of insulin. "Reed is too soft, and she doesn't quite appreciate the situation we're in."

"But you understand it? I guess you have all the answers." Max spat, and blood trickled from his mouth. The wrath on his face mirrored Shelby's heart.

"Yes, Max, I do. I understand this situation better than she does and better than Mayor Perkins. Why do you think I left? I'd be surprised if Abney is still standing when you get there."

"What happened to you, Danny?"

"I opened my eyes. That's what happened, and if you want to survive, you will too."

"How is your plan better?"

"This medicine will go to soldiers—men and women who can defend our border."

"Defend it from whom?"

"If we don't have that perimeter, we don't have anything. And what does the governor do? She gives away the very supplies that will ensure our troops are still around. She's giving away our only chance for survival."

Shelby realized that appealing to Danny's logical side wasn't going to work. Something had happened to him. He had turned into a post-apocalyptic creature, something worthy of their pity and maybe their fear. But she didn't have time for either. She could not, would not, allow him to take what was theirs. She wished with all of her might that she had her gun. She would pull the trigger without thinking twice. She would not abandon any hope that her son had. She would do anything for Carter. She would kill for him.

"It's Carter's only chance." She began to plead. "You know him, Danny. You know us. You asked us to go with you, to settle on your place."

"And you turned me down. For what? For these three idiots?"

"Is that what this is about? I hurt your pride?"

"You helped me see that people are not willing to change even when there's no other option."

"I'm taking that medicine." She yanked with all her might, attempting to free herself from his grip, but he only held on more tightly. She could feel the bruising, but she didn't care. She didn't care about anything but that last box of insulin.

"No, Shelby. You're not."

Suddenly she reversed directions. Instead of pulling away from him, she launched her body at him, surprising the soldiers who attempted to drag her back. She kicked, scratched, and would have bit him if she hadn't been yanked away.

"You're going to kill him!"

"He would have died regardless." Danny pulled a handkerchief out of his pocket and held it up to the scratch below his right eye.

"You have no right to say that!"

"What did you get? Enough insulin for a year? What happens after that?"

But she wasn't listening, wasn't even looking at him anymore. She sank to the ground, fell upon her knees and dropped her forehead to the dirt. The weeping and wails that broke from her sounded as if they came from some distant, wounded animal. But the ache inside her heart felt very close. She was certain, in that moment, that the agony and despair would be the end of her, right there on that hot July afternoon in Austin, Texas.

Fifty-five

Max half carried, half pulled Shelby to the Dodge. Reaching in, he yanked the seat belt across her and shut the door. A feeling like ice had settled in his veins.

He turned again to Danny. "Give us back our guns."

"So you can shoot me? Get out of my sight, Max, and when you pray tonight, if you still pray, thank God that I didn't kill you."

Max rounded the front of the Dodge, glancing back at Patrick, who was chest to chest with one of Vail's goons.

"You have exactly five seconds once I open that gate. I suggest you use it wisely."

Danny's words brought Patrick around. He pushed past the soldier, made sure Bianca was in the Mustang, and started the engine with a roar.

The soldiers opened the gate just enough for them to squeeze through. Danny had planned his sabotage well. They'd been shielded from the bulk of the people waiting outside the gate by the stacked storage containers. Max guessed from the looks on their faces that they must have heard the shouting, but they were too intent on surging in to care. He glanced in his rearview mirror in time to see one of Danny's soldiers hit one of the men with the butt of his rifle. The man collapsed like a punctured balloon.

Max kept his speed under five miles an hour as men, women, and children slowly moved out of the way. Once Patrick's vehicle had passed through, the crowd swarmed back in on the gate.

A sea of humanity—waiting for help. What they didn't know was that the government inside that gate was crumbling.

Max drove north and then west with no destination in mind. He only knew that it was important for them to keep moving, to find a way out of the crowds. Finally, he spied a deserted parking lot next to a burned-out grocery store. He pulled in.

"Shelby."

She'd been disturbingly quiet since they'd left the compound, occasionally wiping at the tears falling down her cheeks. But at the sound of his voice, she threw open her door and catapulted out of the car.

Patrick and Bianca joined them in seconds.

"We have to go back." Shelby paced away from them and then back. "That was your plan, right? We go back to the front gates. The governor will let us in, and then—"

"Gabe was the only reason they let us in the first time." Patrick's temper had cooled, but Max could tell that he continued to seethe from what had just happened. In a fair fight, Danny wouldn't have stood a chance against Patrick. But it hadn't been a fair fight. Max's aching jaw attested to that.

"We'll find a way, Shelby." He stepped in front of her, but she skirted around him and continued to pace.

"We promised you we would find a way," Bianca agreed. "We promised and we will."

"But it's not back in the compound." Max rested with his back against the Dodge. Heat radiated off of it, and his mind darted to the people who must be huddling in their houses and apartments.

How would anyone who was sick survive this heat wave? And what chance did they have in a town with over a million desperate people?

Had they been naive to try and do this?

Then he thought of Carter, and his resolved hardened and took shape again. It became something that obliterated all doubt.

"I don't know if we'll find enough insulin for a month or a year or a lifetime, but we will find some. Bianca's right. We promised you, and no one here is reneging on that promise."

"How? The hospitals?"

Shelby had stopped pacing. Now she stood five feet from him, her eyes swollen and her face tear stained. He could see the bruising on her arms from Danny's grip, and he had to fight the urge to go back to the capitol.

"We haven't tried that yet. I know what Bill said, but do you think possibly the hospitals could have it?" Her expression, even now, transformed with hope.

"No good," Patrick said. "Whatever they have is going to be guarded, and based on what I heard from the troops, most of the hospitals were over-run in the first forty-eight hours."

"The university." Bianca moved next to Max and hopped up to sit on the hood. It looked so natural, so carefree, that a tiny bit of the ball of tension inside of Max began to unwind.

"The first night we were in the compound,

Bhatti—I mean, Gabe—said something about the university. That the . . . the troops hadn't been able to raid the infirmary because Governor Reed wouldn't allow them to storm through the students." Bianca stared off to the north. "It's possible."

"The university buildings will be guarded too," Max reminded her. "I heard that there are factions that have formed in different parts of the campus."

"But they're kids . . ." Shelby strode back to the Dodge and opened the door. "They're only kids, and they'll listen. We'll make them listen."

Max wanted to point out that they had no weapons, that they would be traveling through dangerous neighborhoods, that their chances of success were minimal.

But he said none of that.

Instead, he started the Dodge at the same moment Patrick fired up the Mustang. Together they turned northeast.

Less than three miles to go.

They would find a way through.

Fifty-six

Carter actually enjoyed leaving the house early, walking across three fields, and scrambling down the steep incline to the creek. Setting the trotline was a chore he looked forward to, maybe because it allowed him to play in the water. It was easier work than a day in the fields. He was surprised that his shoulder felt pretty good, and the ear seemed to be healing nicely. He pulled down on the brim of Max's hat—his hat—and decided to enjoy the day.

The temperature had been close to eighty when he'd shouldered his pack and left the house, hot for early July. Usually they didn't see this type of unrelenting heat until late July or August. The clouds only pressed down and made things hotter. There wasn't even a hint of a breeze. In the old days, he would spend the worst part of the summer inside playing video games.

He didn't miss the games as much as he thought he would, but what he'd give for five minutes on his cell phone—to check the weather, text a friend, google *water moccasins*. He trudged through the brush, eyes on the ground in case anything slithered or rattled, and made his way to the edge of the creek.

The water level was lower in places than it had been a week before, even with the rains. He wondered about that—did it mean that someone had put in a dam farther up the stream? They might have to check it out, but today his job was to bait the trotline before heading over to Tate's, where they'd set additional hog traps. The contraptions he'd made with spare auto parts had seemed to work. He thought that they'd be able to harvest quite a few more of the animals—one thing they had was an endless supply of wild hogs.

But Roy had reminded him that the fish continued to be an important part of their diet. He had set the line across a deep hole, which required Carter to wade in up past his knees, scramble over rocks that had created a sort of small waterfall, and then reach down over the drop and pull up the line.

The hooks were empty, which surprised him. They'd been catching fish regularly up until a few days ago, but the last three times he'd checked the lines, they were empty. Roy had come with him the last time to see if he was doing something wrong.

"Looks to me like you have the bait on there just right. A fish shouldn't be able to pull that off because you put the hook through the gristle just like I taught you."

"Then why are they empty?"

Roy shrugged. "Man cannot understand the mind of a fish. Don't wear yourself out trying."

Now Carter studied the empty hook and wondered what was going on. There was no trace of the bait they'd left for the catfish and bass. No trace of a fish that had become caught and somehow freed itself. No trace of anything.

He unzipped his backpack and pulled out the Tupperware container from the inner pocket. The container was long and thin, probably designed for spaghetti or some type of pasta. They didn't have any spaghetti, and Georgia had thought it would be a great bait keeper, which it was.

Carter pinched off a couple pieces of bait—fish guts mixed with squirrel meat and held together with something out of a plastic container. The smell was atrocious, but Roy swore by the stuff. Carter worked it onto the hook like Roy had shown him. Satisfied that it would hold, he made his way down the line, placing more bait on each hook.

He'd moved past the middle of the line and was working his way down the far side when his foot hit a slick spot—algae or moss or wet leaves. He might have been all right, but when he started to fall, he threw himself in the opposite direction to counter gravity, and the Tupperware slipped out of his hand. Lurching to catch it, he twisted awkwardly, all while falling forward into the deep part of the creek. He felt more than heard the bone in his leg snap. Pain flooded through his body, and for a moment he thought he might drown, floundering in four feet of water.

His heart rate spiked as he grabbed his leg, but touching it only made things worse. A scream escaped his lips. He had to push past the pain and think straight.

He sputtered and splashed and finally managed to dog-paddle over to the bank, where he used his good arm to pull himself up into a sitting position.

His left shoulder throbbed, but it was nothing compared to the pain in his leg. That was a deep ache, so intense that he had trouble focusing his mind on any one thing. The pain flooded his senses, and then his head began to pound as if he were experiencing the worst headache imaginable. Is that how Max's migraines felt? Carter hoped not. He would hate to think that anyone would go through this on a regular basis.

Attempting to stand only dumped him back into the water, so he snatched his hat from the stream and once again crawled to the far bank, which was closer than the one he'd climbed down to get there. He managed to pull himself under the branches of an oak tree as the rain started—softly at first, but slowly turning into a heavy downpour.

His teeth began to chatter, and he thought of the night he'd gone with Georgia to the Markham place. Tate had been shivering, and Georgia had said that he was going into shock. What had she done for that? Covered him with a blanket. Carter didn't have one of those, but he did have a dry shirt in his backpack. He pushed himself tighter up against the bank, checking right and left for water moccasins. Did they come out in the rain? He suddenly wished he had paid closer attention to the unit on reptiles in his high school science class.

He hugged the backpack to his chest, trying to

ignore the overbearing pain in his leg, trying not to think about the mess he was in. Thunder crashed, and the rain fell in sheets. He could no longer see the opposite bank. He couldn't see anything but water falling from the sky.

He thought again of unzipping the backpack but found his fingers were numb. The tree's branches were doing a good job protecting him from the rain, but he was sitting in water. He needed to get higher.

Leaning forward, he slid the straps of the backpack over his arms and then carefully turned on his stomach to look for something to grab hold of—a rock, a tree root, and then a clump of grass. He was halfway up the bank when he reached for another root, and it slithered—long and shiny and whipping its head back and forth.

Carter released the snake, jerked his hand away, lost his balance, and slid back down the bank into the water with a splash.

Fifty-seven

Max didn't drive directly to the campus, which at first Shelby failed to notice. But then she did.

"Why did you turn left?"

"Trying to avoid trouble."

"What kind?" She craned her neck in the opposite direction. "Oh. Road's blocked."

"Yeah. That seems to be the case on every access point to the south of the university."

"So we go around."

"Exactly."

"Do you think it will be better to the north?"

"I don't think it can be worse."

He maintained a low speed, zigzagging through the streets and skyscrapers of downtown Austin. Were there people in the tall business centers? He could crane his neck and see broken windows, but little more. The crowds were growing as the sun rose. A few people stopped to stare at their parade of two vehicles, but most who were on the street continued to plod along—head down, shoulders slumped, intent on whatever errand had brought them out in the morning's heat.

The sky was overcast, and it seemed to Max that the barometric pressure was changing. He rubbed the muscles on his neck, as if he might be able to feel a migraine coming, but they'd never been like that for him. Never predictable. No, they crashed across him like a mighty wave, leaving him weak at best and occasionally unconscious.

"I still don't understand what happened back there." Shelby pulled her feet up into the seat and wrapped her arms around her knees. Max was instantly swept into the past, when he was eighteen and she was seventeen. When life made sense.

"About Danny, you mean."

"Yeah. About Danny." She rubbed a sleeve

across her nose, but for now the tears seemed to have dried up.

"I guess I can understand his thinking, though it doesn't justify his actions."

"So explain it to me." She rested her head on the bridge formed by her knees and arms. "I want to know . . . to understand what we're up against."

Max turned north once more, praying that this road would be open. As far as he could see, it was, which didn't mean it was safe.

"Danny's subscribing to the survival of the fittest outlook, and he plans on being one of the survivors."

"At any cost? Even at the . . . at the death of his friends?"

"I don't know that you or I or even Carter could ever have counted ourselves as Danny's friend. He knew us, sure, but—"

"No. You're wrong. He was there for me. When Alex died, those first few years I was alone . . . or . . . or felt alone, Danny was there. He wanted to help."

Max glanced at her and found her resting her cheek against her knees and staring at him. "Yeah, but something changed along the way. Right? He stopped coming by. He didn't call anymore."

"I thought he was busy."

"And he was—helping to run Abney and doing a fine job of it."

Shelby shook her head. "It doesn't make sense.

How could a person's entire outlook shift so completely? So quickly?"

"Probably he's been changing for years, moving toward a more egocentric worldview. The flare didn't turn him that way, though this situation we're in might have pushed him over."

Max had passed the far northwest corner of the campus, though he'd kept a two-block distance between himself and the university buildings. Now he turned east, toward the park he remembered from his days of attending school there. He circled it twice before he pulled to a stop.

"Are these people . . . are they living here?"

The park was filled with tents, quickly thrown up shelters, and even a few RVs.

"Looks like it."

"Why?"

"Safety in numbers, I suppose. Come on."

It was only a few minutes past eight in the morning, but already people were stirring. Patrick had parked behind them. He and Bianca met them between the cars.

"What's our plan?" Patrick asked.

"Don't have one yet. If we walk south on this road, we'll intersect Dean Keeton Street. Make a right, proceed three blocks, and we'll be at the student health center."

"Where the meds will be." Bianca had hooked her arm through Shelby's. To Max, they looked like two coeds out for a stroll.

"Hopefully."

"Think the cars will be safe?" Patrick asked.

Max glanced around, finally spying a teenaged boy—red hair, soiled shirt, and facial hair that was coming in patchy. Walking over to him, he asked, "Do you live around here?"

"In the park. Our apartment building burned down the first week."

"Want to earn a hundred bucks?"

"And buy what with it? The stores are empty in case you haven't noticed."

Max sighed, thought of their backpacks in the cargo area of the Dodge. The packs were the only things Danny hadn't taken.

"Fair point. I have four protein bars in my pack. You watch our vehicles until we return, make sure nothing happens to them, and they're yours."

"I could just break into your car and take them."

"You could, but then I'd have to find you and take them back."

The teen's look of defiance held for another few seconds, and then he smiled and ducked his head. "Nah, man. I'm just kidding you. Four protein bars? My family will like that real good. They'll think I'm a hero. But if anyone with guns comes, I'm out of here."

"Deal."

Max hurried back to his group. "We're good, but I don't know for how long."

They decided it would be best to leave their

packs in the car to hopefully make them less of a target.

"How will we carry the meds?" Shelby asked.

"We'll figure that out when we get there." Max tried to look confident. "We'll think of something, but first we have to get on campus."

Patrick hustled back to the Mustang, retrieved his knife, and stuck it in his pocket. "Just in case," he muttered.

They tried walking south to Dean Keeton, but all entrances into the university were blocked—trash Dumpsters, automobiles, even an old phone booth had been stacked up at the street crossings to keep anyone from getting through. Sitting on top of the stacks were teens with guns, surly expressions, and—Max worried—itchy trigger fingers. They turned west on 27th Street without even attempting to talk to anyone.

It was when they started to turn south again, this time on University Avenue, that the trouble started.

Fifty-eight

Shelby froze when the young man toting a shotgun shouted "Stop right there."

She shot a glance at Max, who looked completely unfazed by the weapon pointed their direction.

354

"This is our street," the man added.

Or was he a man? His head was shaved, gauges glittered in his ears, and from where Shelby stood, she could see the tattoos snaking up his arms. Short and wiry and boldly defending his world. He could have been a teenager. He could have been a kid between his freshman and sophomore year who had taken a job at one of the local barbecue joints to finance his summer in Austin. But now he was carrying a gun, proclaiming the street his territory.

A man appeared on top of the barricade, beside the teen with the shotgun.

"We're only passing through," Patrick said.

"No, you're not," the teen said. "You're turning around before I let loose with this shotgun."

Patrick's hands clenched at his side, but he produced a tight smile and said, "Your street, huh? Looks to me like it's a City of Austin street."

"There is no City of Austin anymore. Hadn't you noticed? Look around and then turn around before I put some shells in your bad attitude." The teen laughed.

Patrick lurched forward, but Shelby, Bianca, and Max were on him within three steps—pulling him back, assuring him they'd find another way.

The man beside the teen shook his head and said calmly, "You have one minute to vacate the area or we will—"

Max took a step forward and attempted to

reason with the two, but the guards weren't listening. The man raised his voice to drown out Max, and the teen trained his shotgun on Patrick, and Bianca started screaming at everyone to calm down. Shelby was the only one who noticed a young Asian man pick up his pace and half jog to the middle of the confrontation. "Twenty-Ninth and Hemphill Park," he muttered as he pushed through their group.

He stopped in front of the barricade and raised his hands in a "what gives" gesture. "Hey, Reggie. You going to waste your time on these fools or buy some of this meat?"

"You have meat?" Both of the guards turned their attention to the man's wares—what looked to Shelby like a few squirrels and some fish.

"Let's go," she hissed.

They backed away from the blockade quickly. Once they were out of sight, everyone began talking at once.

Shelby attempted to make herself heard above the group. "The Asian kid was trying—"

"You give me ten minutes, and I will be through that checkpoint," Patrick promised. "I'll teach both of those punks a lesson while I'm at it."

"He said something about—"

Max leaned against a wall. "We're not getting in that way."

"We can. Ten minutes. That's all it would take—"

"*Cállate.*" Bianca's voice was low but adamant.

"Listen to Shelby. She's trying to tell us what the kid said."

"Oh, I heard the kid and his talk about putting shells in my bad attitude. He hasn't seen a bad attitude yet." Patrick's face had turned a bright red as he continued to clench and unclench his right fist.

"The other kid—the Asian one." Shelby waited until she had everyone's attention. "He said Twenty-Ninth and Hemphill Park."

"You're sure?" Max asked.

"Yes, I'm sure. Now where is that?"

Max pointed to the northwest. "Two blocks, but it's the wrong direction."

Rain had begun to fall, causing the deserted streets around them to take on a nightmarish quality. The sky had darkened, and thunder rumbled in the distance.

Bianca swiped at her face. "Can't hurt to hear what he has to say."

"Could be a trap," Patrick countered.

"Could be, but did you notice he was the only person we've seen who is actually working? Those squirrels and fish didn't fall out of the sky and into his hands."

"I imagine food is getting scarce inside the barricades." Max nodded and tugged his ball cap lower. "Maybe we've found ourselves an entre-preneur."

He turned and started away from the campus.

"And if we have?" Shelby ran to catch up with Max's long strides.

"Then we'll think of something to trade him. Whatever he wants, as long as he can get us inside."

Fifty-nine

The intersection was easy enough to find. Shelby tried not to stare at the rapid transit bus turned over on its side or the newspaper vending machine with a single paper still facing the window—proclaiming that *FUN in the Sun* could be found in central Texas. She turned her back on those reminders of life before. Instead, she paced as they waited ten and then fifteen minutes. She paced and worried and prayed and racked her brain for a way onto the UT campus.

"He's not coming," Patrick said.

"Maybe we should try to get in from another direction." Bianca glanced from Max to Patrick. "Or maybe we should split up."

"No." Max shook his head, his tone adamant. "We're not doing that. Not unless we have to, and we don't have to. We'll find a way in."

They were standing against an apartment building that hadn't burned—but all the windows were busted out, the doors had been torn off the hinges, and the walls chalked over with graffiti.

Keep Austin Weird
Flare up
Judgment day
Zombies are coming
NOT safe

Shelby traced the word *safe,* feeling the solidness of the brick facade against her fingers, trying to pull her mind from the catastrophe she was living. Just as despair threatened to overwhelm her, she heard footsteps and looked up to see the kid who had intervened for them.

"You guys aren't from around here, are you?"

Max stepped forward. "No. We're here looking for—"

"I don't want to hear any details. Not here."

"Here is where you told us to come."

"That was to keep you from getting shot by Dr. Steiner and his henchman. You want to talk? We have to go somewhere else—somewhere not on the street."

He led them down the block, around the corner to the back of a burned-out building, and then down a short set of outside stairs. Pulling a key from his pocket, he unlocked the door.

The basement apartment was surprisingly clean. In fact, it looked as though it still belonged in the preflare world. Shelby studied the University of Texas posters tacked to the wall, beanbag chairs tossed in two corners, and futon couch placed against the room's longest wall. Based on the pillows tucked into one end of the futon, she figured it was doubling as a bed.

Turning in a circle, she realized it was a one-room apartment, with a kitchen on one end and a bathroom walled off in one corner. It was what her generation had called an efficiency. Other than the prevailing smell of smoke, Shelby would have never known they were under a burned-out building.

"You live here?" Max asked.

"Yeah. I got lucky when the building burned. The fire started on the second floor and spread to the top. The first floor was wrecked because the ceiling fell through, but my place was spared."

"Aren't you afraid it will all collapse on you?" Patrick glanced up at the ceiling skeptically, as if it might crash down on them at any moment.

"I'm more afraid of sleeping in the park."

Bianca gestured toward the burned out floors above them. "How did it happen?"

"The fire? Someone didn't put out a cigarette the first night of the flare. Kind of ironic, really. Might have made sense if it had been a candle that caught curtains on fire or something related to the flare, but no. Just some idiot who fell asleep smoking. Could have happened any other day."

"Didn't the fire department come?" Bianca asked.

"Sure, but remember the phones weren't working. By the time they got here . . . well, there wasn't much left." He hesitated before he said, "My name's Lanh. Lanh Vu."

Max introduced each member of their group, and then Patrick asked, "Vietnamese?"

"Yeah. My parents are still overseas. They sent me here for school. Didn't turn out quite like we expected."

"Why did you help us?" Max asked. "How did you know you could trust us?"

"You're not on Steiner's side. That's all I needed to know."

"That name is familiar." Max sat on a stool and pulled off his ball cap, shaking the water onto the floor. "Doubt it's the same person, though. I went to school here twenty-five years ago."

"Same guy. He's old now—close to sixty. Oh, and did I mention crazy? He teaches . . . no, he taught, economics. Guess the flare pushed him over the edge."

"What edge?" Bianca asked.

Shelby watched Lanh's reaction closely, trying to decide if they could trust him. How would she know, though? She'd thought she could trust Danny, and he had turned on them. If she couldn't judge someone she'd known for years, how could she judge someone she'd just met?

"The edge between sanity and madness," Lanh said. "Word is that when the grid went down, he lost millions that he had tied up in the stock market, though how he had millions to invest, since he was working as a college professor, is a little suspect."

"And now he's in charge of . . . what exactly?" Patrick sank to the floor, his back against the wall.

Shelby and Bianca took a seat on the futon. She was suddenly aware of all they'd been through since waking at six that morning. She'd dared to hope she might be home by now. Everything had started out well. She'd had the meds. As she'd stuffed her notebook and pen into her pack, she had dared to imagine High Fields and the smile on Carter's face as they drove up.

"Steiner took over the northeastern sectors of the campus." Lanh walked over to a map of the school that he'd stapled to his wall. "His territory covers the entire East Mall, up through the fine arts and law buildings, and over to the library and museum."

Max had followed him to the map. "Engineering?"

"That too."

"How does somebody like Steiner get control of a third of the campus in less than three weeks?"

"And why?" It was the first that Shelby had spoken.

She'd been watching Lanh. He looked to be about twenty, was thin, and only an inch or so taller than her. He wore reasonably clean clothes, which was something of a miracle. His dark black hair had grown past his collar. He kept it covered with a well-worn University of Texas baseball cap. Despite her determination to remain suspicious of anyone and everyone, there was something about the kid she liked. He spoke his mind, she would bet he wasn't hiding anything, and he wasn't flustered by the world falling apart around him. He reminded her of Carter before the explosion, before Kaitlyn died.

"Steiner rules by fear, the same way he ruled his classroom. Trust me, I took his intro to economics class. It was my only *B* my freshman year."

"Everything else *C*s?" Patrick cracked.

"*A*s across the board. I'm Vietnamese, remember? We're smart." He laughed as he said it, as if there was some private joke there. Turning to Shelby, he said, "As to why, like I said, he's a psychopath."

Shelby leaned forward, not an easy thing to do sitting on a futon. It tended to pull you into it, and there was a part of her that would have been happy to forget the rain and the campus and the insulin that might or might not be there. She just wanted to curl up and sleep for a week. Forget her responsibilities and the harshness that now colored her life. But she wouldn't do that. She'd fight to her dying breath, and something told her it might actually come to that. So be it. As long as she went down attempting to save her son.

"Can you help us find a way onto the campus? We need to go to the student health center. My son has diabetes, and we're . . ." Tears clouded her vision, but she pushed on. "We're looking for insulin."

"I don't know what they have, but I can get you in."

"You can, but will you?" Now Patrick sat forward, watching him, plainly wanting to trust him.

Before Lanh answered, Max said, "We're willing to pay you. We have money, which we realize has limited value."

"No value."

"And we have some supplies. You can look over what's in our packs back in our cars. Take what you want."

Lanh was already shaking his head, and Shelby wondered how much more she could take, how many more false leads they would have to endure. But Lanh surprised her. When she glanced up, he was looking directly at her. "I don't want your stuff. I want to go with you."

"Go with us where?" Shelby asked.

"Wherever you live. Any place that isn't here."

Sixty

Carter woke with a jerk and stared left, center, right—at the creek, the bank, and finally his leg. The realization of what had happened to him came back all at once. It physically buffeted him like a wind that threatened to blow him over.

The broken leg didn't hurt anymore, perhaps because it had been resting in the cold water. He couldn't feel it at all, but it had begun to swell. He tried to raise the fabric of his jeans, and found the denim was stretched too tightly.

He glanced back up the bank, where he'd been before he'd fallen, remembered the snake, and shivered. At least it hadn't feasted on him after he'd passed out. He didn't remember much of the slide down the bank, splashing again into the water, or losing consciousness. How long had he been there? And what time was it?

He'd stopped wearing his watch when they moved to High Fields. Time didn't seem to matter so much anymore. As long as he was home by dark and up by sunrise, what difference did it make? He squinted at the sky, and a few remaining raindrops plopped onto his face. Realizing he was thirsty, he unzipped his backpack and pulled out his water bottle. He guzzled half of it before it occurred to him that he might need to ration what he had. He capped the bottle reluctantly and tried to assess just how big of a mess he was in.

Roy and Georgia would expect him for dinner, but they wouldn't really worry, wouldn't look for him until dark—probably another nine hours, maybe ten.

And then it would take a while for them to find him.

He thought he could survive ten to twelve more hours. After all, he didn't have a life-threatening injury. Then he remembered that he hadn't brought any food. He'd told Georgia he'd grab something at Tate's after baiting the trotlines. He'd checked his blood sugar levels, taken his daily shot, eaten the oatmeal, and grabbed a handful of pecans.

He stared down into it his backpack.

No food.

No insulin.

A handgun and one half bottle of water.

His heartbeat accelerated, and he closed his eyes, forcing his reaction to be calmer, more deliberate.

He'd taken his morning injection, which under normal conditions would last all day, but without lunch or dinner his blood sugar would begin to bounce. And that was without factoring in the effects of his injury. He usually took his evening dose around four in the afternoon and they ate early, usually around five. He'd quickly grown used to that schedule.

Type 1 diabetes meant that he was insulin dependent. He'd taken his injections twice a day since he was very young, and he'd rarely missed a dose—never by more than an hour. When he was young, his mom and his doctor had impressed on him the importance of being consistent, of managing his disease.

Which all meant it had been a long time since he'd heard the "what can happen if you miss your injection" lecture. He stilled his mind, pushed his thoughts away from the predicament he was in, and tried to remember what he'd been taught.

Within a few hours of his missed dose, his blood glucose would skyrocket. He'd begin to dehydrate and experience hunger, thirst, nausea, and fatigue. Well, he did feel awfully tired, but then he'd broken his leg and fallen off a slope. Should his condition deteriorate, signs that he was in big trouble would include a severe headache and blurred vision.

He opened his eyes, feeling somewhat calmer.

He'd be all right. It was possible that Roy would find him before dark, and if not—he'd simply take one of the fast acting insulin doses once he was back at the ranch. They had a few that his mom had purchased from the pharmacy the first day after the flare.

The broken leg? Well, he wasn't sure how his diabetes would affect his recovery time, but maybe Georgia would know. She seemed to know nearly as much about the disease as Carter and his mom.

Carter squirmed until his back was once more resting against the bank and steeled himself for a long wait. He tried to focus on the gentle sound of the water moving downstream, the call of a red bird in the tree above him, and the warmth of the sun, which had peeked out from the fleeing clouds.

But only a few minutes later he heard voices. They were coming from around the bend, from above the location of the trotline. When he'd slipped and broken his leg, he'd fallen downstream. If he looked left, he could see Georgia's Tupperware container stuck in a clump of weeds farther downstream. But when he leaned forward and looked right, looked upstream, he saw a group of men, sporting guns and crossbows and headed his direction.

He sat back, flattened himself against the earthen wall that rose fifteen feet over his head. His leg remained jutted out in front of him. There was nothing he could do about that. He couldn't move it, and if he tried he'd only draw their attention to where he was.

Scrub brush and grasses blocked his view toward the trespassers, but he could hear them well enough.

"Trotline's empty," one said.

"I'm not surprised. We took all the bass and catfish last night. At least someone has baited it for us again."

This brought a chorus of laughter, but the man's next words sent a shiver down Carter's spine. "Good thing we have those goats if we get hungry."

"And we know where to find more if need be."

So they had stolen the Murphys' goats. They were the men that Jerry had warned them about.

"It's too hot to do this now." The guy who said this seemed to be the leader of the group. "We'll come back tonight. Clean off the trotline and go downriver a bit. I imagine there's some nutria in that bank."

"Nutria's good when you stew it up," a third man said.

"I don't know about coming back tonight." The voice was whiny, argumentative. He sounded like a math teacher Carter had once. The guy could argue with a post. "We've seen the old man come this way near sundown. What if he catches us?"

"That won't happen. We'll come after dark, and you know as well as I do that everyone around here beds down at night."

"Yeah. Especially after we shot that kid."

"If you'd been a better shot, we would have us a good truck now."

"Wasn't my fault that he accelerated after he was hit. Who would have thought he could drive home with a slug in his shoulder?"

"You shoot to kill," the leader reminded them. "An injured enemy is a dangerous enemy. A dead one? He can't hurt you at all."

No one argued with that. Carter felt as though a giant hand were pushing on his chest, as though he couldn't draw in a breath deep enough to offer relief. Sweat was pouring down his face, and he fought the urge to reach up and wipe it away.

"Tonight, after dark," the leader said. "We'll

come back. There's no telling what we'll find."

"And if we don't find anything?"

"Then we'll climb this here bank, go up to their houses, and take what we need."

Sixty-one

The rain had stopped, and steam rose off the pavement. Max guessed the temperature was inching near ninety, maybe ninety-five, and it wasn't yet noon. Lanh led them toward the northwest corner of the campus. He seemed to have an internal radar for trouble, avoiding ragtag groups effortlessly.

"This kid would have been an asset to the army," Patrick said as they held up behind him and then scurried to the right on a main road and to the left down what looked like a freight area but ended up being an alley.

There were barricades on both sides of the 27th Street Garage, but Lanh darted across the street and headed toward the middle of the building.

"No way in through the parking garage," Bianca said, and she was right. Cars had once entered to the right and exited to the left. Both of those routes had been plugged tight with debris. It would take hours to pull out enough to make a way through, and doing so would undoubtedly attract too much attention.

Lanh wasn't headed toward the entrance or the exit. He walked directly toward the center of the concrete wall. Max could see now that someone had done a good job of plugging all of the first-floor and even second-floor openings, where one might have looked out over the city. There was no way through on this side of the structure, that was certain.

But Lanh was already reaching for a crevice above his head, pulling himself up and then disappearing over into the second level. He reappeared, sticking his head way out and looking left and right, before urging them to hurry.

Max intertwined his fingers, palms up, and gave Shelby and then Bianca a boost. Patrick kept watch. Once the girls were safely in, Max grabbed the ledge and pulled, deeply regretting that he'd given up his gym membership some years ago. He managed to scramble over the ledge and turned to help Patrick—who skimmed up the wall as easily as Lanh had.

"How'd you know this opening was here?" Max asked. "It's impossible to see from the street."

"I knew about it because I made it." Motioning for them to follow him quietly, he led the way across the parking garage, up a staircase, and to an enclosed pedestrian crossing. They were halfway across it when Max stopped and took a closer look out the glass walls at the campus of his alma mater.

University Drive was directly below them. He first looked in the direction they'd come. The barricade from this direction looked massive. They would have never made it through. From where they stood, he could see that the blockade had been well engineered. No one would come through that unless they were invited, and even then he wasn't sure how they could move enough of the material to make a passage.

He leaned closer to the glass and saw what he hadn't made out on the other side. Small, rectangular openings, where a guard could sit on the campus side, watch for intruders, and shoot if necessary.

"Like castle loopholes," Shelby said.

"Looks like it. I saw some once in northern England and Scotland."

"And I researched them once for a book."

They shared a brief smile. Maybe it was because they were moving again, doing something instead of simply reacting. Whatever the reason, the mantle of despair seemed to have dropped away from Shelby. She looked once again like the girl, the woman, he'd always known.

"Quite different from Steiner's setup."

"He seemed to be big on bravado."

"Flexing muscles and grunting."

"Yeah. The shotguns helped too."

"This has been well thought out." Shelby pointed toward the ledge on their side of the barricade where the guards could walk back and forth.

"A functional design for maximum surprise and effectiveness."

"Are you two coming?" Patrick called. They'd stopped near some double doors, pausing to drink from their water bottles.

But as Max turned toward the far end of the walkway where the others were waiting, his peripheral vision caught sight of the center of the campus. He stared in disbelief and felt Shelby turn in his direction. Together they walked toward the opposite windows.

Buildings lined University to the east and west, before the road circled around a building two blocks down—the Mary E. Gearing Hall. With tan walls and a red roof, the u-shaped building had been there since before Max was a student.

"Looks like a normal day on campus. Looks untouched."

Instead of answering, Max placed his fingertips against the glass.

"What is it? What do you see?"

He pointed out the building. "It was once the home economics building, but in the years when I went to school here they switched it over to human ecology."

"I don't even know what human ecology is."

"Study of the relationship between humans and their natural, social, and built environment."

"How do you know that?"

"Brown bag lunches. I didn't like eating in the cafeteria."

"So you listened to sociology lectures?"

"Among other things."

Shelby stepped closer to the window until her nose was practically pressed against it. "Are those people?"

"Yeah."

"What are they doing?"

"I don't know, but I have a feeling that's where we're going."

He nodded toward the exit where their group was waiting. But the vision of the building stayed in his mind, along with the people walking back and forth. It wasn't the student health center, but it just might have the answers to their problems.

Sixty-two

The double doors were locked, chained from the other side. Lanh removed the lid from a trash can that was in the corner, reached down inside, rummaged through papers and hamburger wrappers and soda cups. Finally, he pulled out a walkie-talkie and turned the dial to a preassigned frequency.

"Lanh here. Anyone awake on your side?"

There was a crackle, but no answer. Lanh repeated the message. Shelby locked eyes with

Bianca, who reached out and squeezed her hand.

He was about to repeat a third time, when a voice came back toward them.

"This is Gus. You bring us something for dinner, Lanh?"

"Nope. Something even better."

"Better than squirrel?" There was laughter in the background, and then the person said, "Sending someone to unlock the doors."

Lanh turned off the device, stored it back in the trash can, covered it with the trash, and replaced the lid.

"Now what?" Patrick asked.

"We wait."

Shelby didn't have time to grow impatient. Within a few minutes they could hear the sound of a chain being unlocked and unwound through the door handles. A girl with long red hair poked her head through, but Lanh didn't give her a chance to retreat. He tugged on the door, jerking it open all the way, and the girl went for her weapon.

Patrick threw her to the ground, wrenched her arm behind her back, and rested his knife at her neck. It happened so quickly that Shelby didn't realize the girl was holding a handgun until it clattered to the ground. Patrick had the situation under control before she'd even recognized the danger.

The girl grumbled, "Get off me."

Patrick scooped up the pistol, pocketed his knife, and helped her to her feet.

"What's going on?" She rubbed her shoulder and glared at Lanh. "You didn't say you were bringing outsiders."

"They're on our side, Mitzi."

"How do you know that?"

"Because I do."

"No, you don't. You could be putting us all in danger."

"Quiet. Both of you." Patrick checked the pistol to be sure the safety was on, and then he stuck it in the back of his waistband.

"That's mine, and I'd thank you to give it back." The girl was a spitfire—a few pounds on the heavy side, with beautiful red hair that ran in waves past her shoulders. Her complexion was light and freckled, and her green eyes practically shot daggers at them.

"I'll give it back to you later when I'm sure you won't shoot us."

Max stepped forward. "We're not here to hurt anyone. Lanh is vouching for us, and you trust him, right?"

"I guess." Her tone plainly indicated that she was none too sure.

Lanh rolled his eyes and said, "Let's go. I'll take you to the professor."

"The professor?" Bianca asked.

"Yeah. She's the antithesis of Dr. Steiner."

They marched through the double doors. Max led, followed by Mitzi, who was still being watched by Patrick. Shelby and Bianca stayed close on Patrick's heels. Lanh held back to relock the doors, and then he hurried to the front to lead the way.

Bianca moved closer to Shelby. "Antithesis? What is up with these kids? They don't even talk normal."

"They're not normal." They moved through the second floor of a scholastic building, down a stairwell, and out into the noonday heat. "They were raised on zombie movies and high tech. Now they're living the script from their favorite show."

"And the technology is gone."

"Exactly."

As they approached the red-roofed building, their group drew more than a few stares. They crossed the street and had barely set foot on the lawn in the courtyard of the u-shaped building when they were surrounded by more teens with weapons—everything from pistols to iron rods to baseball bats.

Shelby knew she should be concerned. They were outnumbered. They had no weapons of their own, other than the knife in Patrick's pocket and the gun in his waistband. Patrick's skills were superior, but even he couldn't win a twenty-to-one fight. Clearly, there was no path for retreat. She wasn't worried, though. Her mind was too busy processing what she was seeing. Hundreds of college kids stood watching, all ages and ethnicities. More than half of the students surrounding them had shaved heads. Why? What were they even doing here? In her mind, she'd thought they would have all gone home. But maybe that hadn't been possible. Maybe they'd decided to hunker down. And now they were surrounded by Dr. Steiner and his goons.

A man with a gray beard and shaved head stepped through the crowd, walked up to Mitzi, and said, "What's going on here?"

"Lanh brought them in without approval. And he—" She nodded toward Patrick. "He's some kind of military guy or something. Had me on the floor before I knew what had hit me, and he took my gun. Lanh allowed them to ambush me."

"They didn't ambush you," Lanh countered.

"Same as. You didn't follow protocol."

"Because I knew you would overreact."

"This is not overreacting."

"They need to see the professor."

The man raised one hand chest high and slicked it through the air, karate chopped their complaints, and then he turned to Patrick. "Give her back her pistol."

"I will if you'll guarantee she won't shoot us."

"You will, or you won't get any closer to the professor than this."

Patrick glanced at Max, who nodded once.

He returned the pistol, and the man motioned for four of the guards to step forward and frisk them.

"No weapons," one declared, "other than this knife."

The older man stepped forward and claimed the knife.

"All right. Now tell me what you're doing here." He frowned when Max attempted to answer.

"Not you." He pointed to Lanh. "You."

"They need to see her."

"Why?"

"Because the lady's kid is sick. She needs meds for him."

"So go to a hospital."

"You know they won't help her."

"Not my problem."

"Let them ask the professor. She might feel differently." Lanh didn't seem a bit intimidated by the man.

The older guy was not overreacting, but he also wasn't standing for any nonsense. Shelby was beginning to think he must have been a police officer or detective in his former life.

"She likes you, but you're pushing your luck here."

"No, I'm not."

"Why should we give them anything?"

"Because they have information."

"What kind of information?"

"They've been in the capitol—inside the compound."

The man shook his head in disbelief. "You believed that?"

"It's true." Max stepped forward. He didn't flinch when the man's hand went to his firearm. "You want to shoot us? Is that how you're handling things here?"

"If we have to."

"Well, you don't. And if you want to know what Governor Reed is and isn't doing, you need to take us to meet this professor."

Sixty-three

Ten minutes later they were sitting in the office of Professor Agnes Wright. Lanh had been politely dismissed. Shelby tried not to stare at the professor, but she found herself unable to look away from this five-feet-six-inch enigma who held Carter's life in her small hands. Agnes—she insisted that they call her by her first name—sat behind her desk as if she were holding a student conference. The light that pierced through the dissipating clouds shone through the window, reflecting off her bald head.

Shelby glanced at the photo on the wall—Agnes handing a diploma to a student, chestnut hair cascading down her shoulders, and a look of adoration shining on her face. Obviously the person meant a lot to the professor, though there was no indication who the student in the photo was.

She turned her attention back to Agnes, who had finished with pleasantries and finally seemed ready to get down to business. Shelby realized with a start that Professor Agnes Wright was beautiful—not just pretty, but movie star gorgeous. Her age must have been over fifty—there were fine wrinkles around her mouth and eyes and the beginnings of sunspots on her hands. Her shaved head somehow accented her oval face and excellent bone structure, but it was her brown eyes that caught and held a person's attention. Though she didn't exactly smile, her eyes looked deep into yours and seemed to promise—some-thing.

Hope perhaps.

Shelby briefly wondered if she was a part of the Remnant, and then she dismissed that idea. Agnes had apparently been on campus since the flare. She'd have had no chance to even hear of the group, let alone join it.

"We don't receive many visitors from outside."

"Between the barricade and the armed guards on your side of the locked doors, I'm not surprised."

She waved away Max's comment. "Tell me what's going on out there."

Max described their trouble in reaching the

compound and how the central blocks had been fenced off and were now guarded.

"How did you get in?"

"We had a doctor with us. Turns out the state government had a fallback plan of sorts. We don't know all the details, but they deployed military personnel to every county seat."

"What sort of personnel?"

"Ones that would blend in—doctors, nurses, mechanics, pretty much any profession you can think of."

"Why?"

"Their assignment was to watch, help if possible, and report back to the governor during the first thirty days."

"They knew about the flare before it hit."

"NASA sent out the alert to top governmental agencies approximately twelve hours before."

"Yet there was no attempt to warn the public."

"What good would it have done? One soldier I spoke with assured me that there was an attempt to land or cancel as many flights as possible without creating a panic."

Shelby couldn't fathom making that decision, being given the numbers for how many would die if an emergency announcement wasn't made, and how many would die if one was.

"So this doctor of yours—"

"Farhan Bhatti—actually, we recently learned his real name was Gabe Thompson. We didn't know he was a part of the emergency task force. Our mayor insisted he ride along to help procure medications for the town. When we arrived at the gate . . ." Max paused, stared down at his hands, and then looked back at Agnes. "We would have been killed. The people outside the gate are desperate. It was just before dawn by the time we got there, and the crowds were waking, stirring. They were hungry and angry. They would have, at the very least, taken our vehicles and anything we had they could use."

"You think they would have killed you?" Agnes seemed more fascinated than shocked. "And the guards on the other side would have just let them?"

It was Patrick who answered. "Have you ever been to the Tomb of the Unknown Soldier or Buckingham Palace?"

When Agnes nodded, he continued, "It was like that. Stare straight ahead, rifle at the ready position, do not make eye contact. If we'd been attacked, they wouldn't have done a thing because their reason for being there was not the people on the other side of the fence. Their reason for being there was to protect the capitol."

"You mean the governor."

"I mean the seat of power for the state of Texas."

Agnes sighed, sat back, and motioned for Max to continue.

"Gabe knew a code word. When he said it to the

soldier, they opened the gate and let us through."

"And you actually met with Governor Reed?"

"We did, though we didn't learn much directly from her. She approved our request for medications—antibiotics for people in our town and insulin for Shelby's son."

"Supplies that were later stolen by one of her own men." Bianca's tone was bitter.

Shelby sat listening as if the story were about someone else. It was difficult for her to absorb all they had been through since arriving in Austin.

Max continued. "We did learn, through some other officers, that she has no plans to help the university. She's heard that there are different factions, and she doesn't want to be seen as ordering the inciting incident for a bloodbath."

"So she would allow us to die here?"

"They're expanding the government circle to the south, with the hopes that her control over warring factions will solidify. Then she'll make her way north."

"By then the outcome will already be decided."

"Maybe that's what she's hoping for."

Agnes was quiet for a few moments. She didn't seem particularly disturbed by what she'd heard, almost as if they'd only confirmed her fears. "What do you want from me? Besides insulin?"

"You could start by explaining what happened here."

Sixty-four

When Agnes didn't answer his question, Max added, "Class of '93, Interdisciplinary Studies."

"You found work for that?"

"I went on to earn my law degree from Baylor in '96. Passed the bar two years later."

"Criminal?"

"Family."

Agnes folded one hand over the other, glanced out the window, and then focused completely on Shelby and Max and Bianca and Patrick.

"The university fell forty-eight hours after the flare. I was teaching an evening class of grad students when the power went out—a Friday class, which is a rare enough thing. Many of those caught here on campus thought we had experienced a failure of the power grid, but I knew it was more than that when the phones stopped working and the cars wouldn't start. My house is less than two miles from here. I walked home, packed a bag, and came back."

"Why would you do that?" Patrick asked.

"I knew this wasn't a temporary phenomenon. NASA has been warning the government for years, but those press releases rarely made headlines."

"Why did you shave your head?" Shelby

realized the question was a minor one. She should have been asking about insulin and routes home, but this woman fascinated her. It could be that she held the answers they needed. More answers than where to find medical supplies. Carter could very easily have been on a college campus if the flare had happened six months later. Shelby wanted to understand what had happened to the students and the professors.

"Do you know anything about human ecology . . ."

"Shelby."

"Do you know anything about it, Shelby?"

"No. I've never heard of it before today."

"It is the study of the relationship between humans—between us—and our environment."

"Sociology," Bianca offered.

"Yes, but what we study is more complex than that. We factor in the natural environment as well as the environment that has been built around us."

"Such as what?" Patrick asked.

"Well, everything that isn't natural—buildings, parks, homes, neighborhoods, infrastructure."

"You were expecting this." Max crossed his arms and waited.

"In a sense. Every organization breaks down at some point. In regard to life and death, no person or organized system is immune to it. Even our solar system is dying."

"You're an atheist?" Shelby asked.

Agnes laughed, and the smile on her face grew. "Hardly. I see a divine hand in both the living and the dying. But you were asking about my hair. When I realized that the old world was gone, that it wasn't ever coming back, I shaved it."

"So it was a symbolic gesture?" Shelby couldn't help reaching up and running her fingers through her curls.

"In one respect, yes, it was. But on a practical level, I believe that shampoo and conditioner are a thing of the past."

Max leaned forward, his elbows propped on the arms of the chair. "So all those kids we saw with shaved heads—they buy into your theory that we're living in a different world now."

Agnes shrugged. "We have more than forty thousand students at this university. Only twenty percent live in university housing, and even fewer than that in the summer. Still, with six thousand students on campus, I wanted to be here. That is why I packed a bag and moved into my office in the early morning hours of June 11."

"You wanted to study them." Max looked surprised.

"Yes, of course I did, but I also knew that the luxury of academia was swept away with the aurora borealis. Study? Yes. But, more importantly, there would be a need for guidance as we transition to a new ecology."

"And you're that guidance?"

Instead of answering, Agnes glanced at the picture on the wall—the one of her handing a diploma to a student. "Dr. Steiner's grandson was one of my students—a very special student who showed unusual promise. He had a grasp of human ecology that I've rarely seen, and yet he died in the first forty-eight hours. Killed by some punk with a pistol who thought he needed fifty dollars. Perhaps that was what pushed Robert over the edge."

No one spoke for a moment. Shelby thought of all she'd seen since the night of the flare, of all she had done. Could she be pushed over an edge? Yes, she supposed she could, but not the one that Robert had gone over. Despair lurked around her. It threatened to swallow her at times. In spite of that hopelessness, she would defend herself and those she loved. Hadn't she been in the line of Abney citizens that had fought with the people of Croghan? Hadn't she been the one who had killed a guard that threatened her and Bianca?

That was different, her conscience whispered.

But was it? Was what they had done, what she had done, any different than what Dr. Steiner was doing? Her world had once been so black and white, but now it was gray. Morality became an entirely different thing when you mixed survival into the equation.

Agnes was studying her. She leaned forward and said, "Tell me why I should give you the insulin."

Sixty-five

Carter woke with his head throbbing and his throat parched. He pulled out the bottle of water and downed all that was in it before he could question whether he should. He was sitting in a stream! If he had to, he'd drink the creek water, though he'd been warned often enough against doing that.

"Always boil the water," Georgia had reminded him.

"You don't want giardia," Max had cautioned.

"Don't even ask him what that is." His mom had glanced at Max and laughed. They did that a lot. They always had. Some long ago, hilarious memory passing between them. Carter thought of Kaitlyn, and he nearly allowed himself to sink into that memory, to ignore what was happening and fall back asleep.

Then he remembered the men who had taken their fish, the same men who had shot Tate. They were coming back. If Roy happened to be here, to be looking for him when they came back, he could be ambushed or shot or killed.

Carter sat up straighter.

He didn't have many choices—really only two. He could stay where he was and hope that someone found him before the creeps who were poaching off their land came back. If he wasn't found, he could defend himself with the pistol in his backpack, though he doubted his ability to make a decent shot given his physical condition.

His second option? He could make his way downstream.

Anger and fear and humiliation burned through him with lightning speed. Why was this happening to them? Why now, when it seemed as if they were finally going to catch a break? Would things continue to spiral out of control—growing worse each day until they wished they were dead?

He thought again of Kaitlyn, of her funeral. Pastor Tony had spoken for a moment, and although he too had been grieving, there had been a quiet confidence about him. What was it he'd said? Something about trusting God. From what Carter could tell, God didn't seem too trustworthy. After all, Carter was sitting in a creek with a broken leg and goons on his trail.

But there was something else.

Pastor Tony had also talked about the remnant.

Carter closed his eyes and forced his mind to focus. Suddenly, what Tony had said was more important than anything else—more important than insulin or water or a path back to the ranch house.

"Are we the remnant of Christ? I can't answer that . . ."

Carter felt an intense desire to scream at the man. If he didn't have answers, what good was he? Why even pretend to lead them, if he couldn't explain what was happening?

But there was something else he'd said. Something about their agony and despair. Those words he ought to remember well enough. Agony and despair seemed to describe his past and his present and even his future.

Then Tony's words came back to him so clearly that he actually glanced to his left and right. "Even in the midst of your agony and despair—you remain under the provision and care of your heavenly Father."

Carter didn't realize he was crying until he tasted salt. Did he believe that? Did he believe God cared and provided for him?

What about Kaitlyn? Dead.

What about their home? Destroyed.

What about the people who had died since the flare? Gone.

"You remain under the provision and care of your heavenly Father."

His mind filled with images of his mom and Max and Patrick and Bianca.

Roy and Georgia.

High Fields ranch.

Fish dinners and corn bread.

A worn-out cowboy hat.

He had lost many things, but he'd gained a few

as well. The flare had taken a lot away, but God had provided.

He was under God's provision and care.

Carter wiped his face dry with the heels of his hands and looked around. Nothing had changed, not really, but he knew what he had to do.

He filled the empty bottle with creek water, stuffed it into his pack, and promised himself he wouldn't drink it unless he had to. He clamped Max's hat more tightly on his head, grateful to have something to protect him from the sun. Then he hoisted the bag onto his back and wound his arms through it, grabbed a stick that had hung up in the brush along the bank, and pushed himself out to the middle of the water.

Slowly, carefully, and methodically, he began to make his way downstream. He abandoned the stick when he found a larger one. Time and weather had hollowed it out, rendering it a passable floating tube. He wrapped his arms around it and let the current take him.

Sixty-six

Max could feel Shelby's growing restlessness like an itch between his shoulder blades. After they were dismissed by the professor, Lanh offered to give them a tour of the campus—at least their section of it.

A large vegetable garden had been planted west of Garrison Hall. Each student spent two hours a week working there, and armed guards stood at the four corners of the area.

"The guards seem like overkill," Bianca said. "We're inside your zone."

"There have been several breaches from Steiner's side. They sneak in, steal stuff, and then sneak back out."

"How do you know that?" Shelby was watching a tall, thin girl with a shaved head carefully winding a green bean plant up a trellis.

"A couple times they were spotted fleeing back to the other side." Lanh tugged on his baseball cap. "Last week one of his goons was caught—he had a backpack full of fresh vegetables. That's when the professor ordered guards to be posted around the lot."

"What happened to the person they caught?" Max asked.

Lanh shrugged as if he didn't know, but when Max continued to stare at him, he admitted, "She had him taken to the south side of the campus and released."

"Near the stadium?"

"Yeah. It's like *Night of the Living Dead* over there. No one's in control. Anyway, she warned the kid that if he was caught here again, she'd kill him. I, for one, believe her."

Max admired much of what Agnes Wright's

group had managed to accomplish. They were growing food. Traps had been set around trees to catch squirrels or quail. Someone had found solar panels in the supply closet of the science and technology building—no doubt ordered for some now-forgotten graduate project. Now the panels provided power for several small generators. The generators themselves were only used for necessities—a communication center that wasn't receiving much communication and some experimental labs where students were working on everything from sanitation systems to incubators for speeding up the growth of plants.

"There's also a room filled with small refrigerators." Lanh nodded toward a four-story brown-stone building, the biomedical engineering building.

"For food?" Shelby asked, suddenly interested.

"What they have that's perishable, which isn't much, and medication."

The small group stopped and stared at the building that held the one thing they'd braved Austin to find.

"I want in there." Shelby's voice was a whisper, a prayer, a plea of desperation.

"Not possible." Lanh began walking in the opposite direction. "I asked around. All sorts of stuff is stored inside, but it's guarded even more heavily than the garden."

They continued on their tour, though Shelby

continued glancing behind them. Water reclamation systems had been created around half of the buildings—rain gutters were diverted into spouts, which emptied into large trash cans. Those cans had been covered with a fine mesh to filter out any contaminants.

"And still she insists they boil whatever they drink," Lanh said. "She's super careful about health stuff."

"Indicating all is not well in Agnes Wright's world." Max stuck his hands into his back pockets.

Patrick had gone off with Walter Harris, the man who had insisted he return Mitzi's pistol. He caught up with them as they were entering the mess hall.

"What's for dinner?"

"I don't know," Max admitted. "But it smells better than nothing. When was the last time we ate?"

They stood in line and received a ladle full of slop. The boy manning the line grinned. "Doesn't look good. Doesn't even taste good, but the nutrition majors swear it's full of vitamins."

The meal was rounded out with canned peaches and a few crackers.

"Makes me miss *mi madre*'s cooking," Bianca said.

"Or Georgia's." Shelby smiled at Max. "Your mom is a miracle worker in the kitchen."

Max tried a bite and nearly choked. After

devouring his peaches and crackers, he pushed the plate away.

"You're not going to eat that?" Patrick nodded toward the mush.

"Be my guest."

"Food is definitely going to be a problem around here." Shelby scooped up a spoonful of the slop, swallowed quickly, and grimaced.

"It's not the only problem," Patrick said.

"What did you find out?" Max sat back and crossed his arms.

"Food supplies are dwindling, which is the reason they let Lanh and a few others go off campus."

"Come to think of it, why were you selling your squirrels to Steiner?" Shelby asked.

"So he wouldn't shoot me." Lanh shook his head. "I tried sneaking in with whatever I caught, but Steiner was determined to stop me. When I started selling to them too, then he allowed me to come and go. I try to save the best stuff for our side."

"What else?" Max asked Patrick.

"Steiner's sending out feelers every night, trying to find the weakness in Wright's perimeter."

"And?"

"She responds quickly, but he finds another. It's like trying to stick your finger in a hole in a dam. Works until another hole pops up. They're on the defensive when they need to take the offensive."

Patrick finished Max's food and pushed the plate back across the table. "Some students from this side are defecting. Steiner has better food and more guns."

"I don't believe that," Lanh said. "People here are loyal to the professor."

"Doesn't matter if you believe it. People are leaving in ones and twos. Loyalty only goes so far. When a person gets hungry or frightened, they'll sometimes take a side they don't agree with."

"Sounds pretty dismal," Bianca said.

"It's not hopeless—not yet—but there are real problems." Patrick leaned forward and lowered his voice. "In addition to those defecting, they've lost a few since this started. Some were shot, others got sick."

"How many?" Shelby asked.

"I'm just guessing, but probably a hundred. She has a cemetery of sorts set up in a remote corner on the northwest side. It's not something they like to talk about."

They all turned to look at Lanh. "Yeah. Probably a hundred. Most of those were in the first week— a fight gone too far, a misfire of a weapon. Someone from the outside sneaked in once or twice—stole what they could and killed anyone who tried to stop them. And like you said—a few became sick, though I haven't heard what they had."

"What else?" Max studied his friend. There

was something he wasn't telling them, but at that moment one of Agnes's loyal followers showed up at their table.

"She's ready to see you."

Sixty-seven

Shelby tried to steel herself against the worst possible news, but the truth was she didn't know where else to look. They'd talked about trying to find a pharmaceutical warehouse, but there was no guarantee that anything would be on the shelves. Her mind jumped back to the brownstone building. If Agnes wouldn't give them what they needed, she'd take it. She'd find a way.

As they walked back up to Professor Wright's office, she tried to slow the hammering of her heart. Bianca looped their arms together. Max led the way as if he were marching into Waterloo. They'd reached the professor's office when Patrick pulled Shelby back out into the hall.

"One way or another, we're getting the insulin for Carter." He waited until she nodded, and then they entered the room.

Agnes didn't waste any time.

"We have the insulin you need."

"That's . . . that's great news. When can we get it?"

"I can't just give it to you, Shelby."

"What do you mean?"

"I mean that while I like you all, while I understand your mission and what it means, I can't just hand over vital supplies."

Shelby was out of her chair before Agnes finished speaking. Both hands on the professor's desk, she leaned right up into the woman's face. "You can and you will give it to me, because my son will die if you don't."

"I appreciate that; however . . ."

"You appreciate nothing. You sit here in your guarded tower moving around chess pieces for some experiment, but the people out there are not a component of your experiment. Each person is fighting for their very life, and I will not let you—"

Max pulled her back away from the professor. "Hang on, Shelby. I think Agnes was about to make us an offer."

Shelby collapsed back into her chair with a thud.

"No offer, just a fact. If you have something to trade, we can negotiate. If not, I'm afraid I can't help you."

"We have nothing," Bianca countered. "We were robbed by one of the governor's men, remember? They even took the supplies we had to trade. We have our backpacks, which have a few supplies, but not enough to help your people. We have two cars, but we'll need those to get home."

"I don't need your car."

"What do you expect us to do?"

"I expect you to think of something—"

"You can have me." Patrick's voice was calm, even, measured.

He stood near the window, his arms crossed and an inscrutable look on his face. Shelby shook her head, trying to shuffle the words she'd just heard into something that made sense.

"What are you talking about?" Max asked.

"The answer is no," Shelby said. "You're not staying, and she's going to give us what we need."

"No, I won't."

Everyone started shouting at once. Even Lanh dared to contradict Agnes.

Patrick finally pushed off from the windowsill, walked over to Shelby, and squatted in front of her.

"Let me do this." He reached up, tucked her hair behind her ear, and smiled. "She wants something to trade. So trade me."

Tears slipped down Shelby's cheeks. Patrick brushed them away, winked, and stood, once again facing Agnes.

"What makes you think I'd want you?"

"I've spent the entire afternoon with McGinnis. I know the holes in your defenses and how to plug them."

Wright steepled her fingers together and studied Patrick. "How do I know you'll stay? Once I give Shelby the insulin, you could slip away."

"You have my word."

Agnes cocked her head and considered what he was offering, and in the space of that moment Shelby's heart once again broke in two. She couldn't ask Patrick to do this, would never have dreamed of asking. But he had offered, and she knew him well. Once his mind was made up on a thing, there was no changing it. She glanced over at Bianca, who had covered her face with her hands.

Agnes finally nodded. "We have a deal."

"How long does he have to stay?" Max asked. "And how much insulin are we receiving?"

"Enough insulin for a year. I'd say it would be fair if Patrick agrees to stay for the same length of time."

"Done." Patrick didn't even blink.

Max glanced at Shelby. Her hands had begun to shake. She pushed them under her thighs. Bianca whispered, "It'll be all right. He will be all right."

It wasn't fair. No one should have to trade one person they loved for another, but then that wasn't exactly what was happening here. Patrick was offering himself so that Carter could live. The most they could hope for was to make a very good trade, which was perhaps why Max turned back to Agnes and said, "We'll also need two solar panels, a 3.1-cubic-foot refrigerator, and a portable generator with the solar adapters."

Shelby thought Agnes would tell Lanh to lead

them back to their cars. But she surprised her. Standing, she said, "I'll have everything at the western gate. In the morning, Lanh can show you where the entrance is. You can drive your cars inside—"

"We can't take Patrick's car," Shelby protested. "He needs a way . . . a way to get home."

Patrick walked over to stand beside her, reached out, and cupped the back of her neck with his hand. "I don't need the Mustang, and you're going to need the extra cargo area."

"But how will you—"

"I'll find a way home, Shelby." He glanced at Max, who was already shaking his head.

"We don't need the cargo area. There's plenty of room in the Dodge, and you might need the Mustang. None of us can know what the situation will be like in twelve months. We won't go unless you have the Mustang, unless you have a certain way to come home."

Patrick seemed exasperated, but he finally agreed.

"Fine." Agnes smiled as if she was pleased with the deal. "As I was saying, tomorrow morning, drive your cars inside and load them up. Be there by seven a.m."

Sixty-eight

Carter woke when the insulin needle pricked his skin. He squirmed, trying to throw off the weight that pinned him to the ground.

"Take it easy," Georgia said.

He blinked, trying to clear his vision. He could only see foggy shapes, like the dreams he'd been having. It wasn't dark yet, but the harsh sun that had been beating on him for hours, for what seemed like days, had sunk below the horizon. He couldn't see it, but he didn't need to. The evening's coolness was a welcome relief against his skin. He didn't realize he was shaking until Georgia placed a hand on his chest.

"It's going to take a few moments." She tucked his arm back under a blanket. "Your levels were a mess. Let the insulin work."

But there was something he needed to tell them. He sank back—not onto the ground but onto some sort of cot. How did he get out of the river? Where were they? And why weren't they headed toward the ranch?

"Where am I?" He croaked the words, cleared his throat, and tried again.

"At the low water crossing."

He couldn't see Roy, but he'd know that voice anywhere. Roy patted his shoulders. His hand was a comfort that Carter had worried he'd never feel again.

Tears pricked his eyes, and he wanted to brush them away, but his arms were heavy, useless limbs that Georgia once again tucked under a blanket.

"Smart move, Carter, hanging on to that log. Somehow, it got you all the way down here. I don't know how you did it, son. We were looking . . ." Roy's voice broke. He was silent for a moment. "We were looking everywhere. Found Georgia's Tupperware up by the traps and saw where you'd slid down the bank, though we couldn't imagine why you'd bother to go up the other side. We were making our way down the creek when Tate's father called on the walkies. He was on his way home, drove down into the low water crossing, and nearly ran over you, to hear him tell it."

"We're going to lift you up now, Carter." Georgia was in take-charge mode. She snapped orders and people obeyed.

"Watch his leg."

"Someone get that backpack."

"Don't shut the tailgate on him."

They had brought the truck down and now carefully loaded him in the back. He heard two doors slam. The bed of the truck bounced, and Tate squatted beside him.

"You scared everyone, man." Tate looked as if he had recovered from his gunshot wound. His shoulder was still bandaged, but it didn't seem to be causing him any pain. "We couldn't imagine what happened to you. Thought maybe someone . . . maybe they'd taken you, or killed you and hid your body. Georgia and Roy were near about crazy."

The truck drove up and out of the creek.

Carter tried to focus on Tate's words. There was something he needed to remember, something he needed to warn them about, something about the trotline.

But fighting was useless.

He was asleep before they trundled across the first cattle guard.

He woke when they moved him into the house.

"Put him in the last bedroom on the right, across from ours."

Carter blinked his eyes, terrified because he could see nothing at all. Then someone lit a lantern, and he was able to make out a bed, a patchwork quilt, and Georgia's face hovering over him.

"I want you to drink this water. You're dehydrated, Carter."

"I was afraid to drink the creek water." His voice was gravelly. It felt as if he'd swallowed sand.

"Told you he was a smart boy." Roy's face briefly appeared over him and disappeared again.

"Get me my medical bag, Tate. It's on the kitchen table." Georgia scuttled around the bed, her movement throwing up shadows on the ceiling. "Roy, my fabric scissors, please. They're the gray-handled ones."

"Yeah, the ones you won't let me touch. I'll find them."

Carter drifted in and out of a semi-dream state. At one point he heard Georgia talking to Roy in a low, grave voice. "Could be infection or internal bleeding. I don't know. His fever is too high, and his blood sugar levels are still fluctuating wildly. All we can do is wait . . . and pray."

Carter forced his mind to clear, pushing at the sleep and cobwebs that threatened to claim him. A groan escaped his lips when Georgia repositioned his leg. She tugged off his shoe and removed his sock.

"I need to splint this, but first we have to get the swelling down."

Someone walked closer to the bed, and then he heard the cutting away of fabric. Georgia slit the seam all the way through the waistband.

"Mom's going to kill me. I was . . ." He stared up at the ceiling. Lantern light danced across it, throwing shadows this way and that. "I was down to three pairs of jeans."

"Well, now you're down to two. Don't worry about that. I can make you another pair out of Roy's old overalls."

"Or you could make him overalls," Roy teased.

"This will make a nice pair of shorts with a

little mending. Roy, help me get him out of his wet clothes."

He must have passed out again. When he woke, he was under a blanket, no longer shivering, and his leg was propped up on several pillows. Scanning the room left to right, he saw Roy nodding off in a rocking chair. The rest of the house seemed quiet.

Georgia bustled back into the room, carrying a steaming cup of soup. His stomach growled as he attempted to prop himself up.

"Wait." She set the mug down and hurried behind him. Roy roused awake in time to help. Once they had him propped up and sipping chicken broth, Georgia turned to her husband and said, "Now go to bed."

"But you might need me."

"And if I do, I'll wake you."

He leaned in, kissed her cheek, saw Carter watching them, and winked. They were good people, Georgia and Roy. He'd always known that, but it wasn't until he'd been faced with people who were evil that he'd understood what a gift true friends were. He tried to finish the broth, but his teeth began chattering, his arm shook, and he was afraid he'd spill the broth all over the bed.

"It's the fever, Carter. Let me help you."

After the third spoonful, he shook his head, unable to stomach anymore. "Why do I have a fever?"

"I can't say for sure."

"Tell me, Georgia."

She sank into the chair next to his bed. "The leg itself shouldn't be causing it unless you're bleeding internally."

"Then what's wrong with me?"

"You had a few deep cuts. There's some infection." She pulled the covers away from his arm. He was surprised to see it bandaged from the elbow to the wrist. "You don't remember how this happened?"

He searched his memory, found nothing there to explain the bandage or the throbbing pain in his arm.

"No . . . I don't." He fought against the shaking that jarred his body and made his head ache.

"Take this ibuprofen." She popped two pills in his mouth and held the cup to his lips. He nearly drained it. It felt as if every ache and pain in his body was competing for first place—his leg, his arm, his throat. His entire body hurt.

"Do you want something stronger? We have a few painkillers from Roy's surgery last year."

"Nah. Save them."

"All right, but tell me if you change your mind." Georgia adjusted the pillows so he could lay back and told him to close his eyes. "Rest is the best medicine, Carter."

She walked to the end of the bed, pulled back the covers, and laid her fingertips against his leg as if checking it for fever. When she noticed him watching, she smiled and tucked the covers back around him.

She sat beside him in a straight-back chair. On the table was the lantern and an old Bible. She didn't pick it up, but she rested her hand on the top.

Carter knew Georgia was a believer. She didn't push, but she didn't hide it either. It was simply a part of who she was. He closed his eyes and allowed his mind to slip back to the hours he'd spent in the creek.

Had he called out to God?

Had he prayed?

Somehow he'd found the strength to push himself to the middle of the stream. He'd known that if he didn't—

The memory of what he needed to tell them returned with the force of a thunderbolt.

"You can't get out of bed," Georgia said, pushing him gently back against his pillow. "Tell me what you need."

"I have to warn him. I have to speak to Roy."

"Roy's asleep already."

"But he needs to know."

"Tell me, Carter. Whatever you can tell Roy you can tell me."

"I think . . . I think they're coming."

Sixty-nine

Max found Shelby sitting in a lawn chair on the roof of their dormitory building.

"Room for one more?"

She didn't answer, didn't welcome his company, but neither did she tell him to go away. He took that as a good sign, retrieved another lawn chair from where they were leaning against a rain barrel, and plopped it down next to hers.

For a moment they just sat there, staring out over downtown Austin. It was well past dark, and there was little to see—the flicker of a lantern in a window, in the far distance headlights from a car driving down a road, starlight overhead, a three-quarter moon.

"We could be home by now."

"Maybe," Max agreed. "Or maybe we would have broken down in one of the more devastated areas. We couldn't take that risk, and you know it. Best to travel in daylight, where we can at least see what's coming at us."

She continued to stare out at the darkness. Max had no idea how to comfort her, how to reassure her. Was she worried about Carter? Afraid Agnes wouldn't come through with the medicine? Regretting Patrick's decision? He didn't have the words to address all of those fears

410

at once, so he sat beside her, silent, and waited.

Her voice barely a whisper, she said, "During the day you can forget. You can look at the buildings, the ones that aren't burned, and pretend that life is normal."

"Is that what you want to do? Pretend?"

"No." When she shook her head, her curls bounced and swayed. "I don't want to do that. I want to face this thing . . . face it head-on, but sometimes my mind insists on playing tricks."

"Pretending."

"Yeah." She glanced at him, a bittersweet smile tugging on her lips, but there was no joy in it. Some days he wondered if he'd ever see joy on her face again. Some days it occurred to him that he would do just about anything to wipe away the worry, even if only for a few minutes.

"At night, especially here in the middle of downtown, the darkness is so unnatural."

"That's true, but I think it's what you're seeing combined with what you're not hearing—cars on the road, jets overhead, music from a bar . . ."

"People laughing."

He didn't know how to answer that. It was true that their world had become bleaker. They were like a ship ravaged by a terrible, relentless storm—still floating, but adrift, battered, and in danger of sinking.

"We'll be home tomorrow."

"I don't want him to do it." Her sigh was deep,

troubled, trembling. "But Carter needs that insulin. I don't . . . I don't know what to do."

"There's nothing for you to do." He moved his chair closer, so that their shoulders were nearly touching, reached for her hand, pulled it into his lap, and held it in both of his. "This isn't your decision. It's Patrick's. And we would all do the same for Carter. You would, I would, you know that Bianca would."

Shelby nodded. With her free hand she swiped at the tears falling down her cheeks.

"Do you know what Patrick told me? That he's a soldier. That this is what he's supposed to do. He would have stayed in Abney—forever, I guess—but this is where he's needed. The fact that he can *put his skills to work*—that's his phrase, not mine—the fact that he can do that and help Carter. Patrick's decision was made before any of us had a word to say about it."

"There is one thing that I'd like to do."

"Name it."

"Go by Donna's school, like we said we would. See if there's something we could do. Maybe there's something, though I can't imagine what. I don't know. Maybe there's one child that we could take to Clay. Surely we could find room for one."

"I'm sure we could, and that's a fine idea."

"We'll have to run it by Bianca first. I know she's ready to be home, to see her family."

"She'll agree."

"Yeah, probably."

They sat there another twenty minutes, looking out over the university. Finally, Shelby sighed and stood, but Max stopped her. He stood too, drew her closer, and wrapped his arms around her. She stood there, rested, for one minute and then another. She pulled back enough to reach up and touch his face. Her fingertips against his skin felt like the most intimate of caresses, felt like all he would ever need.

"Thank you," she said.

"For?"

She started to answer, shook her head instead.

Max glanced out over the university buildings, but he didn't let go of Shelby. He turned her in his arms, so that she was looking out at Austin, but he kept his arms wrapped around her, as if he could protect her from what lay ahead. "When I decided to go to law school, I thought I could change the world."

He rested his chin on top of her head, breathed in the scent of her. "My dad admired my enthusiasm, but he warned me that the world doesn't change that way—all at once."

"Maybe it did, on the night of the flare."

"Not our doing, though."

"God's?"

"Maybe. Or maybe it's just the way of the physical world. Maybe we forgot that we're susceptible to the laws of nature."

"So no changing the world."

"Not all at once."

"But we can make a difference?" She pulled his arms more tightly around her until it felt as if they were one person, one force to be reckoned with.

"One person at a time. That's what my dad told me. The world is changed one person at a time."

Seventy

Shelby didn't think she'd sleep, but she did. The next morning, everything proceeded like clockwork. Agnes sent two of her guards with them to retrieve their vehicles. Max gave the teen at the park the bulk of their food with the advice to "leave town with your family. Don't try to stay in this park. Pick a direction and go. You don't want to be here when things get worse, and they are going to get worse."

Once they were safely in their vehicles—Bianca and Patrick in the Mustang, Shelby and Max and Lanh in the Dodge—the professor's guards returned the way they had come. Lanh directed them to the western side of the territory ruled by Agnes. They traveled down a one-way road, turned down an alley that became tighter and darker and dead-ended in a loading dock. One of the guards must have called ahead, because the

414

bay doors opened. Max pulled through. Patrick parked his Mustang beside them.

Together they loaded the refrigerator, solar panels, and boxes of insulin into the Dodge. Patrick spent an inordinate amount of time packing and repacking things in the cargo area. Shelby couldn't see back there, the boxes were packed so high. By the time they were done, there was a small space in the second seat for Lanh. Max, Shelby, and Bianca would ride in the front.

Shelby held back as the others said goodbye.

She watched Max and Patrick exchange handshakes and then bear hugs. Some words she couldn't hear passed between them.

Next Bianca said goodbye, but not with words. She walked right up to Patrick, put a hand on each of his shoulders, stood up on her tiptoes, and kissed him on the lips. Shelby knew then that they'd talked the night before. That something was settled between them. When Bianca turned toward the Dodge, she was smiling and blushing and looking at no one in particular as she climbed into the passenger seat.

Shelby didn't want to do this.

She stood where she was, her feet refusing to move, and finally Patrick walked up to her.

"I can't." She looked up at him and forced the words around the lump in her throat. "I can't say goodbye."

Instead of arguing, he pulled her into a hug, held on tight, and finally kissed her on top of the head. When he stepped away, he was grinning. "Tell Carter to have the chessboard ready. One year from today, I'll be there."

It was with that image in her mind that she walked to the Dodge and slid across the seat. They wound their way through north Austin, retracing the route the Remnant had recommended, Shelby riding in the middle between Max and Bianca. She thought they were out of danger, when Max turned right and Lanh leaned forward.

"Not that way."

"It's how we came."

"The block has changed hands since then. Back up slowly, go down two more blocks, and then turn." As he was retreating, Shelby saw two men step out of the shadows, rifles held loosely at their side.

They reversed course and eventually traced their route back toward the school.

"I'm glad we're doing this, Shelby." Bianca had the window down and tapped her fingers against the side of the door. "If anything, this area looks worse. I think Donna's going to want those kids out of school even faster than she had planned."

The closer they drove to the school, the heavier the sense of dread settled in Shelby's stomach.

"Were all of these homes burned out before?" Lanh asked.

"No. They weren't." Max's voice was grim, his expression set in a scowl.

After all the destruction they'd seen, Shelby still couldn't believe the scene outside their window. "It's only been three days. How could this possibly have happened in three days?"

Smoke continued to rise from some of the homes, though none were in flames. Apparently, the fires had been set the day before. What could burn had, and the rest served as a charred reminder of what had been—brick facades, steel beams, shells of automobiles. They saw only glimpses of people—walking down back alleys, sleeping in cars, resting under hundred-year-old live oak trees.

"Why?" Shelby asked. "What's the point in burning things? I guess I can see homeless people, displaced people, wanting a place to live. But they can't live here now. No one can live here."

"Maybe it was carelessness," Bianca said. "Someone kept a candle burning or used a propane stove inside without adequate ventilation."

"One house possibly, but not an entire neighborhood." Lanh leaned out the window, as if he could get a better look. "Doesn't look like they bothered to empty the houses before they torched them."

"I imagine they took the food, any handguns or ammunition, maybe money." Max had initially slowed down, but now he was picking up speed again. The last thing they wanted was to get carjacked in the midst of a smoldering neighborhood. "There's a history of this sort of thing—from the Watts riots in 1965 to the Baltimore protests in 2015. It's fueled by rage and by a sense of injustice, even though it isn't logical to burn your only grocery store or an entire neighborhood."

They saw the ruins of the school before they'd driven into the parking area. The front of the building was burned out completely. The perimeter fence had been crashed through. It lay in mangled heaps here and there. There were no guards, no sign of anyone at all.

"Tell me they got out, Max. Don't you think they got out? They must have escaped before this happened."

He put the Dodge in park and squeezed her hand. "Stay here. Scoot over to the driver's seat. If you hear any gunshots—"

Max had opened his door and was getting out of the car.

"No. Uh-uh. You're not going in there alone."

"Shelby, I can do this."

"Not without me you're not." She had felt so sure that they should stop by, that there was something they could do to help. But what if she'd only succeeded in landing them in harm's way? What if after all they'd been through, they were killed at the devastated site of an ecologically friendly elementary school?

She leaned back into the car as Max began pulling handguns and rifles out of their cargo area. "Patrick managed to trade for these. He thought we might need them."

"What did he trade? Another month of his life? For three guns and two rifles?"

"You know Patrick. He can be convincing." Max turned to Bianca. "I want you to drive. Follow us in the car as far as you can. Lanh, get up here and sit beside her."

Max handed the teen one of the rifles. "Do you know how to use this?"

"Yes."

"All right. Don't shoot us, but if you see anyone else, anyone you even think is going to hurt you or Bianca . . . don't hesitate to pull the trigger."

Lanh hurried around to the front passenger seat. Bianca put the Dodge into drive. Shelby and Max jogged ahead. They circled around to the back of the school. With the building burned, there were places she could see through. She spied the garden, the goat pen, even the outdoor play area, which ironically was unscathed.

MREs had been ripped open and the wrappings scattered across the pavement. A child's blanket was caught up in the coil of fencing. She thought she heard the sound of one of the chickens, but it was coming from the opposite direction. Perhaps it had escaped.

They jogged down the distance of the back of

the building. Shelby prayed that if any children were in there, that they would hear them, that they would find them, that they would be able to rescue them from this place.

As they turned the corner, the Dodge still idling a few feet behind them, a large man stepped out of the shadows, holding a shotgun.

"Better stop right there."

Seventy-one

"You just took ten years off my life, Bill. It's us—Max, Shelby, and Bianca." Max kept his hands at his side, waiting for the big man to acknowledge them, praying they wouldn't be shot by accident.

Bill strode toward them, still holding the shotgun though he lowered it to his side.

"What are you doing here?"

"We stopped by to see if we could help."

"Too late for that."

"Obviously."

"What happened, Bill?" Shelby's voice sounded strained, tired, and more than a little angry. "Where are the kids? Where are Donna and Maria? And why are you still here?"

But Bill wasn't watching them, he was peering out over the back field. He stepped closer, lowered his voice, and said, "Bring the car around. We'll hide it between the Dumpsters."

"Why?"

"Because the people who did this aren't finished yet."

Max ran to Bianca and explained what they were doing. Shelby jogged after Bill, and Max had to run to catch up with the two of them. Even though Bill wasn't running, his large steps still outpaced them both.

There was a loading area halfway down the building. Someone had positioned two Dumpsters in front of the open space so that it wasn't visible from a car. As Bill and Max pushed one of the Dumpsters back, Max heard the cry of a child, followed by two or three more.

"You have children back here?" he asked.

But Bill wasn't listening. He motioned for Bianca to pull the Dodge up to the bay doors and next to a stock trailer. Max realized that was where the cries were coming from. Bill had put children in a stock trailer? Was anyone in there with them?

He reached the side of the trailer at the same time that Shelby did. They both stared in disbelief at the Tennessee fainting goats, bleating and shuffling around.

"You lost somebody," Bill said, studying their group.

"Patrick stayed in Austin, at the university."

Bill nodded, as if that made sense. "And you picked up a new recruit."

"Bill, meet Lanh. He saved our hides more than once in Austin."

Bill shook hands with the kid.

"How did this happen?" Shelby asked. "When did it happen?"

"Started yesterday morning."

"And the kids?"

"We had word that something was coming down. Clay somehow got his hands on a school bus. Brought it in just hours before the attack."

"So they're safe?"

Bill shrugged. "We hope so. We pray so, but I won't know until I catch up with them."

"Why are you still here?" Bianca asked.

"Because I wasn't willing to leave everything we had to a bunch of goons who aren't thinking straight. The goats took off, into those woods." He nodded toward the south. "It was easy enough to catch them with feed, but first I had to find a stock trailer."

"How did you find a stock trailer?" Lanh asked.

"I know people who know people." Now he looked at Shelby. "There are still some good folks in this world."

"So you came back, rounded up the goats, and now you're leaving?"

"I am, but I'm not too optimistic about my ability to get through to the highway. Driving a single automobile is one thing. Pulling a stock trailer?" Bill stared at the goats. "Folks will jump on. They'll climb on, hang on, turn it over even."

"So what's your plan?" Shelby asked.

"I'm working on it."

"And?"

"I haven't thought of anything yet."

"You can't just stay here," Max said. A week ago he would have told the man to leave the goats and join his group, but in the last few days his attitude about resources had changed. Such a small thing—a goat, but it could provide milk for the children, produce more goats if they were cared for properly, and even provide food for the table if necessary. "But you can't lose them, either. The kids, wherever they are, need at least this much."

"I don't plan to lose them."

"So you are leaving?" Shelby moved over to the stock trailer, put her hand through the rails, and a goat immediately began to nuzzle her fingers.

"We'll do this together," Max said. "Wait until late afternoon, like before. You drive, I'll ride in the back with my rifle. Hopefully, that will be enough deterrent, and I won't have to actually shoot anyone."

"I'll ride with you."

"No, Shelby. You won't. Do you realize how dangerous this is?"

She was in front of him in a flash, glaring up at him and pushing her hand against his chest. "Don't tell me it's dangerous! This entire trip has been dangerous. Did it stop you or Bianca or Patrick? Did it stop Lanh from helping us on campus or Bill from coming back for these goats? Goats, for heaven's sake, that will provide milk and cheese for those children. I. Am. Riding. With. You." She backed him up with each of the last five words.

Max felt sweat break out across his forehead. He didn't have time to argue with her. He wished he could tie her up and throw her in the back of the Dodge, but that wasn't an option. And then there was the point that she was right.

"I'll drive," Bianca said. "Lanh will ride shotgun."

Lanh didn't hesitate. "I will be happy to do that, only I'll have a rifle, not . . . you know . . . a shotgun."

Seventy-two

Max and Bill spent the next few hours scouring the school grounds for items that had survived the fire and the looting. Max was wearing his backpack, stuffing anything they might be able to use into it. Bill had a giant duffel bag and was doing the same.

"You were here when this happened?"

"Yeah. I stayed behind after Donna left on the school bus. I was trying to do what we're doing now—salvage anything that could possibly be a help to the kids. I heard the attackers coming before I could see them." Bill stared at a pile of solar panels that someone had bludgeoned with a heavy object. "Sounded like a giant wave rolling toward me. I had just enough time to run to the woods."

"Smart."

"Instinctive more than anything."

"How long were you out there?"

"Twelve hours? Something like that." Bill reached down under a pile of debris, pulled out a tub filled with blankets, and brushed off the top. "Funny thing is, if I hadn't been in the woods, I wouldn't have realized where the goats had gone."

"You heard them?"

"No, I tripped over them." Bill motioned toward a refrigerator that had been turned over. They turned it back on its side and were able to wrestle the door open, but it had been emptied. "You've heard of fainting goats, right?"

"Sure. They don't actually faint, though."

"Correct. They fall over. Their central nervous system causes their muscles to become paralyzed. They were all through the woods, lying there as if they were dead. Probably saved their lives too. If they'd been bleating, someone would have heard them and taken them."

"So what did you do?" Max could picture Bill, a giant of a man, crouched in the woods surrounded by paralyzed goats while the school in front of him burned.

"I left the goats where they were until everyone was gone. Then I carried them back here and put them in the Dumpster with some hay. Turns out robbers don't see the benefit of hay, so they left it."

"You put the goats in a Dumpster?"

"Seemed safe enough." Bill glanced toward the woods. "By the time the gunshots had died down, all of the goats were coming around. People quickly moved on to the next thing they could destroy. So I carried them two at a time to the Dumpster. The last three I found had climbed up into a tree."

Max started laughing. "You're making that up."

"I'm not. Wouldn't have believed it myself, but I looked up and saw them. Managed to coax them down with some of the hay."

While it felt incredibly good to laugh, Max's thoughts turned suddenly solemn. "You took a big risk staying here."

"As did you, coming back. Why didn't you keep driving when you saw the building had been destroyed?"

"Shelby wouldn't hear of it. Neither would Bianca, for that matter. Both have soft hearts when it comes to children."

"And you?"

"Yeah. I couldn't just drive past, not when

someone might be here that needed our help."

"So you're not the cold, calculating lawyer with the heart of an ogre?"

"Oh, sure. I'm that too on my off days."

At that moment they both heard the crow of a rooster.

"He's in the woods." Bill began walking out of the protection of the building, and that was when the first shot was fired.

They both dropped to the ground.

Bill crawled over to where Max was crouched behind the refrigerator they'd been looking in.

"The shots are coming from the east."

Max looked up in time to see Bill clench a hand over his left shoulder and fall back against the refrigerator.

"Are you hit?"

"Grazed me."

"Let me see."

But as soon as Bill pulled his hand away, blood began pouring from the wound. He quickly clamped his hand back on it, though blood continued to seep between his fingers. Max shrugged out of his backpack, and began rummaging around in it.

"We don't have time—"

"For you to pass out from blood loss? No, we don't." He found the roll of duct tape, pulled out a six-inch section and bit enough of the edge that he could tear it.

Another shot pinged off the refrigerator, but they both ignored it. Max fastened the duct tape across Bill's wound.

"Thank you."

"You won't thank me when Bianca has to pull it off." He ripped off two more pieces and added them at different angles. It didn't look pretty, but it would stop the bleeding. "Are you okay?"

"Yes."

"Not light-headed?"

"Maybe a little. Nothing I can't handle."

"I'm not asking you to shoot the guy. Just stay here and rise up enough to give him a target every few minutes."

"And you'll be?"

"Circling around behind him." Max didn't wait for an answer. He pulled out the semiautomatic Patrick had given him, released the magazine, and verified that it was full. He pushed the magazine back into the gun's grip until he heard a click indicating it had locked in place. Digging into the backpack, he located his extra full magazine, stuck it in his back pocket, and took off in the opposite direction. He ran at a crouch through the rest of the kitchen and out the far side of the building. When he heard shots pinging off the refrigerator again, he sprinted across the open field and into the woods.

It wasn't the direction he wanted to go.

His heart screamed for him to turn around and check on Shelby, Bianca, and Lanh, but his brain knew catching the shooter was the smarter move. As soon as he stepped into the cover of the woods, he breathed easier. He continued to hear the occasional ping of shots around Bill. It wasn't too hard to calculate the trajectory. He stopped behind a tree, taking deep breaths and timing what he had to do next. He couldn't afford for the shooter to hear him, but if he could mask his approach with the gun's firing, he stood a chance. The second another shot rang out, he pulled back the slide on his Sig Sauer and immediately began to move forward.

The gunshots grew louder, and when Max stopped completely, he could hear someone moving about, muttering between shots, though he couldn't make out the person's exact words.

He placed each foot carefully, heel to toe, looking down before taking the next step. He came up behind the guy, who was wearing a baseball cap and shooting with a hunting rifle that had a professionally mounted scope on it. That would explain why he was able to hit the refrigerator from such a distance. Though now that he'd circled around, Max could see that this was where the trees were closest to the school. The man had a straight shot.

Max was twenty, then fifteen, and finally only ten feet away from the shooter. He still couldn't make out his features. He wore an old T-shirt, blue jeans, a camo vest, and the ball cap.

"Put down the rifle."

There was no doubt the man heard him. He immediately tensed.

"Put it on the ground and back up slowly."

He had the fleeting hope that the man would do just that, but instead he spun around, the barrel of the rifle leading the way and unloading what was left of his ammunition.

Which was a stupid move. Max's bullet hit him in the temple before he'd made a complete turn. The shots sputtered into the trees. The rifle fell from his hands and the man dropped to the ground, blood pouring from his wound, his eyes already locked open in death.

Seventy-three

"You're sure that he didn't hit you?" Shelby and Bianca and Lanh had crouched down as soon as they heard gunfire. She'd wanted to run in Max's direction to help, but Bianca had stopped her. When Max had appeared to check on them, his expression set in a grim line and still holding his semiautomatic, a sinking feeling had settled in her stomach.

"I'm fine."

"But—"

"Shelby, I'm fine."

"You killed him."

"Yes. He's not going to hurt us."

He'd made them promise to stay put, and then he'd grabbed Lanh to help him bring Bill back to the group. Bill had settled with his back against the stock trailer. Bianca was already pulling out what medical supplies they had.

"Can you still drive?" Max asked him.

"Yes."

"Shelby, will Carter's insulin be okay in this heat? If we wait until afternoon to leave?"

"Yes. I checked it a few minutes ago. It's still cool to the touch. One day in the car won't spoil it. The important thing is that once we get back to High Fields I can refrigerate the supply."

"All right. Then our plan stays the same. We still have six hours, maybe a little more until we leave." Max turned to Lanh, who had been watching the group silently. "Do you feel comfortable standing guard?"

"Sure."

He pulled the kid over to where they could see between the Dumpsters. "You can cover from that point in the woods, to this point of the street. Left to right, then right to left. Got it? You scan constantly, and if you need a break, ask for one."

"Got it."

"One hundred and eighty degrees. You see

anything, you tell Bianca or Shelby, and they'll come get me."

"Where are you going?" Shelby asked.

"To watch the other side of the building. We're sitting ducks here. I want to see anything coming our way, which means we need to see three hundred sixty degrees. I'll be over by the parking area."

"I'll go with you."

"No, you won't, Shelby."

"Bill doesn't need me."

"I've got this," Bianca confirmed.

"Good. There's something I need you to do." He led her through the school to the shattered solar panels. "I want you to carry these to the trailer and use them to fill in the gaps between the rails."

"Why would I do that?"

"Because if someone shoots at us, I'd rather it not go through."

"And you think this will stop them?" When she tilted one of the panels upright, pieces of the shattered glass hit the ground like raindrops.

"Use your gloves. The last thing we need is for you to get cut."

"But how will it help?"

"The backs of these panels are cement, which is why they weigh so much."

Shelby attempted to pick one up.

"About forty pounds. Hang on a minute." He darted back into the building. Since most of it had burned to the ground, she could see him in the courtyard. He returned carrying a wagon, which he set down in front of her.

"Take them one at a time. Just balance them on top of the wagon. By the time you move them all beside the trailer, Bianca should be finished patching up Bill. She can help you attach the panels to the inside of the trailer."

"With what?"

"The duct tape will hold them if you wrap it tightly enough. It only needs to last from here to Highway 183. Once we're back at the barn, Clay can remove them."

"And you think he'll still be there? With Donna and the children?"

"I hope so."

Shelby crossed her arms. She looked left and right, anywhere but in Max's eyes.

"What's wrong?"

She shook her head.

He stepped closer, put one hand on each of her shoulders, and waited until she looked him directly in the eyes. "What's wrong?"

"I heard the gunshots, and I thought . . . I was terrified that . . ." Tears slipped down her cheeks, and she reached to swipe them away. Then Max did the one thing she had prayed he wouldn't and the one thing that she had hoped he would. He pulled her into his arms and simply held her until the trembling stopped.

After a moment, she pulled away. "You're supposed to be on watch."

"Aye, aye, Captain."

Max kissed her once, on the forehead, and then he walked away. He was about to turn a corner when Shelby found her voice. "Be careful."

He glanced back at her, nodded once, and was gone.

She stood there a moment, struggling with her emotions. Longing for the quiet moments when he had held her in his arms, had kissed her. Relief that he and Bill were fine. Fear that this was about to get much worse. An overwhelming need to be home, to see her son, to make sure the insulin was safe. And underneath all of those things—guilt. Max had just killed someone. She had done the same thing outside the church. Is this what their life had become?

Murder was wrong, but neither of those instances had been murder. They'd been self-defense. Did that justify what they'd done? Honestly, she didn't know. But as she tipped one of the solar panels onto the wagon and began to pull it back toward the stock trailer, she knew one thing with certainty.

If need be, she would kill again. She wasn't proud of that. She didn't want to be that person, but neither would she forfeit her life, her friends' lives, or the life of her son.

Seventy-four

Bianca and Shelby had lined the perimeter of the trailer with bales of hay. They'd covered the gaps between the railings with solar panels, though it had used all of their duct tape to do so. When they had finished, Lanh asked Bianca to take his place on lookout and went in search of *treasure,* a word he'd said with a smile and a wink. He returned a few minutes later, holding a can of Crisco.

"Where did you find that?" Shelby asked.

"Supply room. I guess people figured it wasn't edible."

"Then what do you plan to do with it?"

He grinned, scooped out a big handful, and proceeded to smear it on the rails of the trailer.

Realization dawned over Shelby, and she found herself mirroring Lanh's smile. "Brilliant."

So they'd spent a half hour greasing up anyplace on the trailer where someone might try to grab hold.

When it seemed there was nothing left to do, they'd all taken a thirty-minute break, spelling one another in the lookout positions. And then, finally, it was time to go.

Same plan as before, but in reverse. Bianca and Lanh would ride in the Dodge, pulling the trailer.

Shelby and Max would ride in the trailer, protecting the contents from anyone who tried to climb onto the sides.

Bill would follow in the sedan, the nose of his car practically resting against the trailer's gate.

Shelby stood in the back of the trailer with Max as they pulled out of the school parking lot. If she looked out the back, she could see Bill. Though he had wanted to try and pull the trailer with his old sedan, it just hadn't been possible. The engine would handle the weight, but they couldn't come up with a way to hitch the trailer since the sedan had no towing package.

"I would have thought of something," Bill muttered.

"Yeah. You would have ended up with those goats in your backseat."

Actually, the backseat and passenger seat of the sedan were full of items they'd found that might prove useful. No one was coming back, so anything they wanted to take had been crammed into the sedan.

"Better not get shot again, Bill." Bianca had wiggled her eyebrows and slapped Bill on his good arm. "Looks like we're fresh out of Max's version of medical supplies."

"I'll try to keep that in mind."

They'd left a single gap on each side of the trailer—Shelby manning one and Max the other. In front of those gaps, the bales were lower so that they could rest their rifles on the hay and point them out the lone gap in the railing.

"Which also means they could shoot us through the hole."

"It's possible but not likely. Few people out there have a rifle, and we're not going to let them get close enough to use a handgun."

She'd nodded, though the thought of shooting someone else made her hands clammy. As if reading her thoughts, Max squeezed her shoulder. "One hour, Shelby. We're going through fast. One hour and we'll be out of this."

"And then?"

"We leave the supplies with Clay and head home. We'll be there before sunset."

"You can't promise that."

"I can, and I will."

She felt better for his confidence, though she wasn't sure she believed him. They had been gone five days for what would have been a ninety-minute one-way trip to Austin before the flare. They encountered more trouble and grief and pain than she had imagined possible. Max might intend for them to be home by sunset, but life had a way of messing with your plans as well as your best intentions.

The drive was uneventful for the first ten minutes. They wound back through the neighborhood filled with McMansions. The large fortresses remained impervious to the chaos around them.

"Do you really think people are living in those?"

"Maybe," Max said. "But I wouldn't want to be one of them."

"Why?"

"Because one day they'll have to come out. Can you imagine that? Spending the last three weeks in a bubble. We've had time to get used to what has happened. We've seen it change day by day. Whether they come out tomorrow or a year from now, whoever is in those houses will have gone from a preflare world to an apocalyptical one instantly."

She hadn't thought of it that way. It seemed to her that their entire lives had changed in the blink of an eye, but Max was right. They'd had hours, days, even weeks to see things deteriorate. If she'd had to accept the devastation and death all at once, she wasn't sure how well she would have handled that.

A ping off the side of the trailer brought her mind back to their present situation.

"Someone threw a rock."

Shelby glanced back to see Max scanning left to right, the barrel of his rifle following his line of sight. She checked Bill and saw that he had closed the three-foot gap. He was nearly on their bumper. Bianca had accelerated to thirty miles an hour, exactly as they'd planned. The trailer bucked and swayed and the goats bleated, crowding in around their legs. Shelby braced her feet and focused her attention on the streets they were hurrying through.

At first it looked the same to her, but then she noticed the differences—more bodies stacked on the sides of the roads and more people simply milling about. Fewer structures intact. Trash everywhere. The smell was overpowering, and she had to fight the urge to cover her nose with her arm.

The people looked more tired, hungrier, and increasingly desperate. Most stared at the trailer. Some pointed, but it wasn't until they were once again near the retail section that anyone tried to jump aboard.

At first they simply fell away, unable to grasp the trailer thanks to Lanh's grease. But eventually the grease wore away, or perhaps they'd missed a few spots. Somehow a young man with a beard and wild eyes managed to hold on and cross over to her opening.

She pulled back her rifle to take the shot, and then Max was there—slamming the butt of his rifle into the man, who gasped and fell into the road.

"Shoot if you have to," he said, hurrying back to his side of the trailer.

Seconds later she heard him take a shot at the same moment she felt the trailer jostle. She looked back to see Bill driving with his right hand and holding a handgun out the window with his left. He fired twice, and two more of the men hanging on fell away.

She and Max glanced up at the roof when they heard several thuds, followed by scuffling.

Bianca still wasn't slowing down, and Shelby couldn't imagine how the person was managing to stay on top of the trailer. She checked Bill again and saw that he had backed away enough to give him a shot. The first bullet apparently went wide, because he slowed, took aim, and fired again. This time she heard the person groan and then saw him roll off the trailer.

"Hang on," Max warned her.

Bianca had to slow down for the turn, and the group of men congregated at the corner knew it. In fact, they'd set up there for just that reason.

"Get ready to fire."

The men stormed the trailer at the same time. Some fell off because there was nowhere to grab on. Some grabbed hold of a ledge that was greased and slipped off. There were so many that Shelby feared someone would get through. And then she saw a hand reaching through her space, holding a handgun.

She fired before he had a chance to shoot. Didn't even see who it was that she hit because his body was immediately replaced with another.

And then they were skidding into the turn and the people tumbled off like so many bowling pins dropping to the ground. Shelby thought the trailer would tip over. The tires of the Dodge squealed, Bill temporarily disappeared from her view, and the trailer rocked. Max grabbed her and pulled her toward his side, and fortunately the goats followed. The trailer bumped back down on four wheels, and she turned in time to see Bill careen around the corner after them. He narrowed the gap just as someone jumped onto the center gate.

The man saw Bill accelerate toward him and jumped off a second before the sedan slammed into the trailer.

Shelby stumbled backward into Max. Several of the goats were lying on their sides, not moving, and Bianca was still accelerating. It wasn't until Max nodded toward the road outside their opening that she saw they were under the highway and speeding toward the barn.

Seventy-five

Bill climbed out of the sedan. Donna and Clay were standing next to the Dodge when Max helped Shelby out of the trailer. She had to step over the goats to get out. Half of them were standing. The other half were lying on their sides.

Donna enfolded Shelby in a hug. Clay pumped Max's hand. Bianca and Lanh and Bill joined the group, and everyone began talking at once.

Max nodded toward the school bus. "Are the children okay?"

"They are. We've been waiting in the barn."

They all trooped inside. Bill's wound had begun to bleed again. Fortunately, Clay had plenty of medical supplies. Bianca rewrapped his arm with a warning. "Stop hanging out windows shooting. If at all possible."

"Yes, ma'am. Now I'd better go and see to the goats."

"I already have someone doing that," Clay assured him.

Max stood completely still, taking in the scene in front of him. Younger children sitting on bales of hay, older children in the hay loft, adults with each group. Mats had been laid out on the barn floor, and the youngest children were crawling or lying on the padded surfaces.

"Organized and calm, just like at your school." He turned to Donna. "What's your plan from here?"

"Clay has found four more families who are willing to take two children each. The rest of us will continue west."

"West?"

Clay nodded. "The Remnant is growing, especially in the western counties. We're taking the children to Llano, where we think we can find homes for all of them. There's even a place where Donna may be able to open a school."

"Wow." Shelby and Bianca joined their group.

"These kids . . . you saved their lives." Shelby's hair was a mess with pieces of hay stuck to it in places. She had dirt smeared across her face, grease on her shirt, and goat hair all over her pants.

The sight of her could always make Max smile, but when he saw her this way—completely unaware of how beautiful she was—he wanted to pull her into his arms like he had back at the school. As if sensing his attention, she raked her fingers through her hair, which did nothing but cause her curls to stick out more.

"I wish I could have saved their parents," Donna said. "But finding them good homes is the next best thing. I want to thank you all for helping Bill. I can tell from the condition of the trailer that you took a few bullets."

"Nothing we couldn't handle." Max glanced at Shelby, who nodded.

"I want you to know that it's worth whatever you had to do. You say that I saved these kids' lives, but look around you. Without milk, without meat . . . they wouldn't make it. Now we have a viable means to keep them nourished once we find a place to stay."

"There's a vet in Llano who is quite interested in helping with the goats," Clay added. "According to him, they're easier to maintain than a cow, and the milk has a higher fat content, more calories, and more calcium."

"Speaking of which, I'd better go supervise the milking of said goats. They're not patient creatures when their udders are full. As for your trip back to High Fields, may you travel in mercy and arrive in grace." Donna thanked them again and walked away.

Lanh glanced around and said, "I wanted out of the city, but to tell you the truth, I've never been in a barn."

Which caused them all to laugh, though from the blank look on his face he had no idea what was so funny.

"Can you stay for a few hours?" Clay asked. "It might be smart to rest up a bit."

Max shook his head. "We've already been gone too long."

Shelby had walked over to a little girl, who was playing alone. She'd squatted down in front of her, and Max could hear her asking the girl questions about the doll she was grasping.

"We found the insulin," Max said.

"In the capitol?"

"Yes and no." He gave the man a quick rundown of what had happened, emphasizing the betrayal of Danny Vail.

"So Governor Reed is fighting a battle on several different fronts."

"And the battle within her own camp, she may not even realize it's started."

It was five thirty by the time they walked out to the Dodge. The trailer had been unhitched and pulled off to the side. Once again, Lanh sat in the backseat and Bianca, Shelby, and Max squeezed into the front.

"Be careful," Clay warned them. "As far as we know, the Remnant hasn't been infiltrated, but it's bound to happen. Until then, watch your back, and don't trust anyone who isn't kin to you."

"You're not kin to me," Max reminded him.

"Brothers of a different sort." Clay tapped the top of the car, Max started the engine, and then he turned the Dodge toward home.

Seventy-six

When they finally hit Highway 183 again, Shelby breathed out a sigh of relief and turned to Bianca.

"I've been meaning to ask you about something back at the university. What was going on between you and Patrick?"

"It was what it was."

"What does that mean?"

Bianca shrugged, and Lanh laughed from the backseat. "Seemed pretty obvious to me what it was."

Shelby had sort of forgotten he was back there. She turned toward him. If he hadn't decided to ride along, would they have been ambushed coming from the school? Would they have ever met Agnes Wright? Would she have the insulin that was stacked up beside him in the seat?

"Are you sure you want to live in the country?"

He hooked a thumb back in the direction of Austin. "It has to be an improvement over that. Plus I was getting tired of eating squirrel."

"Or slop," Max said.

"Or stale crackers." Bianca checked her side view mirror. "I can hardly wait to get home. When you taste what *mamá* can cook, you will think you're in a restaurant. I miss her cooking, her smile, even the way she would scold me. I never thought I'd miss home this much."

"Even with your sister there?" Shelby teased.

"Even with."

The ride was uneventful. They slowed when they passed the convenience store in Briggs. The place had been burned to the ground. There was no sign of Danielle or Joel or Zack—not that Shelby could see.

They made good time and pulled up to the southern roadblock outside of Abney within an hour of leaving the barn. Jake Cooper signaled for the men to let them through.

"Been waiting for you." He slapped Max on the back and nodded at the rest of them. "Where's Patrick? And Dr. Bhatti?"

"Long story."

"The mayor's eager to hear it. Did you get the meds?"

"No."

Jake pulled down on his ball cap and shifted

his rifle to his left hand. "Can't say I'm surprised. Austin must have been a mess."

They drove straight to the mayor's office and returned the radios she had loaned them. The debriefing took less than fifteen minutes, and though they didn't bring back what she needed, Perkins fulfilled her half of the bargain and refilled their tank and gas can with fuel. "You tried. You risked your life. I couldn't have asked you to do more."

She had turned and was walking away when Max called out to her. "Mayor, you need to be ready. What's left of the state government—it's going to fall."

Perkins pulled in a deep breath, nodded, and walked back toward her office.

They dropped off Bianca, staying only long enough to make sure that her mother and sister were fine.

"*Mamá*, have you heard anything about a black couple coming into town? They have a small boy."

"You must mean that nice Allen family. They're staying in Pastor Tony's RV."

It was an improvement over the convenience store, and though Abney was still vulnerable to attack, there was a measure of safety in numbers.

Bianca walked them to the Dodge. At the last minute, she turned to Lanh and said, "You're welcome to stay here."

447

"Thanks, but I've about had it with towns of any kind."

"If you change your mind, someone can bring you back."

Shelby almost laughed at the stubborn look on his face. Yeah, he'd fit right in at the ranch.

By seven they were headed north out of town. The sky had been growing progressively darker, and rain began to pelt the windshield. Shelby's mind flashed back to their previous trip to High Fields—the bandits, Max's collapse, the fear that she'd be shot by a teenager protecting his homestead.

They had none of those problems this time.

The bandits were gone.

Max drove cautiously, with his eyes fixed on the road ahead and his hands resting lightly on the wheel.

"Tomorrow is the Fourth of July," he said.

"I wouldn't mind a day without fireworks."

"We should celebrate, though. The grid went down, the world changed, but America's still standing. Maybe it's not the America we know, but for now at least . . . we're still here."

"Speaking of which, why did you insist on the refrigerator and solar panels? Your parents' refrigerator was still working."

Max shrugged. "It was, and hopefully it still will be, but I didn't want to take any chances. Plan for the worst—"

"And hope for the best. Yeah. I remember."

The roadblock opened as soon as they turned the corner toward High Fields.

"Someone must have called ahead," Max murmured. He raised a hand in greeting but didn't stop.

The rain had turned the caliche road into a slippery mess, but the Dodge had no trouble moving forward. They crossed three more cattle guards, and then they turned into the lane that led to High Fields. Shelby wondered if Lanh saw what she did—safety, a refuge within a raging storm, home.

Roy was on the porch before Max had turned off the engine of the Dodge.

Shelby flew from the car, but Roy stopped her from entering the house.

"I need to talk to you first."

"What is it?"

"It's Carter."

She tried to push past him, but he didn't budge. "Shelby, you need to listen to me."

"What's wrong?"

She felt, more than heard, Max and Lanh come to a stop behind her. The rain continued to pelt against the roof. Thunder crashed in the distance, and her heart—it stopped, waited, prayed.

"Carter's had an accident."

"What kind of accident?"

"He's okay, but you need to prepare yourself."

"Because—"

"His leg . . . it's bad."

"His leg?"

"Georgia's doing all she can. It's too early to tell, but infection has set in, and his blood sugar levels are all over the place."

Shelby darted around him, yanking the screen door open, and bounding into the house. Her heart hammering, she skidded to a stop in the kitchen at the same moment that Georgia walked in from the back porch.

Instead of speaking to her, Shelby rushed down the hall, opening the first door and the second.

Georgia caught up with her, took her hand, and led her to the last bedroom on the right side of the hall. She stopped outside the closed door, turned to Shelby, and said, "You need to be strong . . . for him."

The storm had stolen most of the day's light. Lightning flashed, and Shelby searched Georgia's eyes for some clue as to what they were facing. She trusted this woman, but she couldn't stand in the hall and discuss her son's situation. She had to see him.

"We're going to weather this. Together, we will find a way."

Wanting desperately to believe those words, Shelby squared her shoulders, put her hand on the doorknob, and walked into the room.

Discussion Questions

1. The story opens to a world in chaos—no power, no medical services, and an uncertain government. And yet Scripture reminds us many times to "fear not." Read Isaiah 41:10; Philippians 4:6; and 2 Timothy 1:7. Do these words apply to every situation? Why or why not?

2. Shelby's group encounters a family of three living in a gas station. Joel was a software engineer. Danielle was a teacher. Although the world has changed and they no longer have jobs, the skills they learned in those jobs are still useful. What skills do you have that would be useful in a post-technological world?

3. The group called the Remnant was formed to fill the vacuum left by local government. "We would need to defend ourselves, but we also wanted to be able to help others." Is this realistic? Were we to lose all power, do you believe groups would form to help one another? Historically, this happened with groups like the French Resistance. Can you come up with another example?

4. When Shelby's group arrives in Austin, things are even worse than expected. A vast number of people are homeless. Children are orphaned and alone. Animals are out of the zoo. There is no one providing food or protection or basic sanitary services. Do you believe this is a possible scenario? Why or why not?

5. Green Tech Elementary is based on the Eco-School USA program. Their stated goal is to provide "a voice for wildlife, dedicated to protecting wildlife and habitat and inspiring the future generation of conservationists." More than 3500 schools in the US participate in the program. What is your opinion of such a program and why?

6. We find that a perimeter fence has been erected around the state capitol in order to protect state leaders and also to keep out the people who are desperate as well as those who would like to overthrow the government. Is the fence a wise decision or a poor one? Why do you think so?

7. Shelby believes that her prayers have been answered when she finds out they will receive the insulin, but later the same night she wakes trembling with fear. Max reminds her that the God of Job is the same God watching over

them. Read the verses from Job, chapter 9. Do these words bring you comfort in times of trouble, or do they only cause you to have more questions?

8. There are clues that Danny Vail is not who he pretends to be, that he is not to be trusted, but no one sees those clues. Why is that? And how can anyone know the measure of another person?

9. Max explains that human ecology is the "study of the relationship between humans and their natural, social, and built environment." If you could sum up human ecology in one sentence, based on what you see in the area where you live, what would it be?

10. The story ends with Austin crumbling, Patrick separated from his group, bandits about to attack High Fields, and Carter gravely ill. And yet there is hope for Shelby and her friends, hope for their future. How is that possible? What could happen to right these terrible situations? And how is it related to Roy's admonition that "the world is changed one person at a time"?

Author's Note

Massive solar flares are not fiction. The Carrington Event occurred September 1-2, 1859. Aurorae were seen as far south as the Caribbean, and telegraph systems throughout Europe and North America failed. More recently, large solar storms were recorded in 2003, 2011, 2012, 2013, and 2015. Research by NASA scientists indicate there is a 12 percent chance a large storm will happen in the next 10 years. This report stresses that while coronal mass ejections and solar flares are not physically harmful, they could blow out transformers in power grids and disrupt satellite/GPS systems. A recent assessment by the Department of Homeland Security reported to Congress that a massive electromagnetic pulse event caused by a solar flare could leave more than 130 million Americans without power for years.

The Eco-School USA Program began in 2009 through the efforts of the National Wildlife Federation. In 2015, 3545 schools within the United States participated in the program. More information can be found at http://www.nwf.org /Eco-Schools-USA.aspx.

The Saint Mary Cathedral in Austin dates back to the 1800s. For purposes of this story, I moved it to a different part of the city, but it can be visited at the corner of East 10th Street and Brazos.

Human Ecology is an interdisciplinary and transdisciplinary study of the relationship between humans and their natural, social, and built environments. A human ecology degree is offered at more than fifty universities in the United States as well as other universities worldwide.

Emergency Preparation Lists

Emergency Kit for Your Car*

- Jumper cables
- Flares or reflective triangles
- Flashlights with extra batteries
- First aid kit: Include any necessary medications, as well as baby formula and diapers if you have a small child
- Food: nonperishable items such as canned goods and protein-rich foods like nuts and energy bars
- Manual can opener
- Water: at least one gallon of water per person per day for at least three days
- Basic tool kit: pliers, wrench, screwdriver
- Pet supplies: food and water
- Radio: battery or hand cranked
- Cat litter or sand: for better tire traction
- Shovel
- Ice scraper
- Clothes: warm clothes, gloves, hat, sturdy boots, jacket, and an extra change of clothes for the cold
- Blankets or sleeping bags
- Charged cell phone and car charger

*per ready.gov

How to Treat Someone in Shock*

- Lay the person down, if possible. Elevate the person's feet about twelve inches unless head, neck, or back is injured or you suspect broken hip or leg bones.
- Begin CPR if necessary.
- Treat obvious injuries.
- Keep person warm and comfortable.
- Follow up.

How to Care for Chickens

- Chicken coop: Allow two to three square feet per chicken inside the henhouse and four to five square feet per chicken in an outside run. Be sure the coop protects the chickens from predators (weasels, cats, raccoons, dogs, and hawks). An elevated roost, nesting boxes, and a roof should be included in your coop.
- Flooring: pine shavings or straw
- Food: Allow to free-range if possible and supplement with vegetarian table scraps and chicken scratch (cracked corn, milo, and wheat). Also offer pulverized oyster shells or eggshells to laying hens for calcium.
- Grit: Chickens need grit to digest their food. Offer sand or grit unless birds are able to free range.

---

*per webMD.com

- Water: Chickens need fresh water at all times.
- Clean out the coop at least once per week
- Check daily for signs of disease, heat stress, etc.

How to Build a Greenhouse

- Choose a south-facing area, with a preference for morning sun over afternoon sun.
- Consider areas that will receive more sun from November through February when the sun has a lower angle.
- Pick a well-drained area or create raised beds.
- Create a cistern to catch rainwater falling from the roof of your greenhouse.
- Cover with something that light can penetrate (plastic film, glass, double-walled plastic).
- If possible, provide heat in winter.

How to Create and Maintain a Compost Pile*

Compost piles mix yard and household organic waste and produce rich soil for gardening. Compost is finished when it crumbles easily and you can't identify any of the original ingredients.
- Choose a spot away from the house.
- Use a bin or simply create a compost heap. The important thing is to have good air circulation.

---

*per planetnatural.com

- Partial shade is preferred.
- Water compost pile as necessary (too much and the pile will be slimy and smelly). Aim for moist, but not sopping wet.
- If necessary, build a roof over the compost pile.
- Turn the pile often. Use a pitchfork or spade to aerate.
- Include brown materials high in carbon—wood, bark, cardboard, cornstalks, fruit waste, leaves, shredded newspaper, peanut shells, peat moss, pine needles, sawdust, stems and twigs, straw, and vegetable stalks.
- Include green materials high in nitrogen—alfalfa, algae, clover, coffee grounds, food waste, garden waste, grass clippings, hay, hedge clippings, manure, vegetable scraps, and weeds.
- Avoid weed seeds, diseased plants, inorganic material, meat, bones, fish, fats, dairy, pet droppings, and synthetic chemicals.

How to Raise a Wild Pig

- Use a dog crate or baby playpen to house piglet.
- Provide warmth until the piglet is two weeks old.
- Feed piglets goat milk. Put several teaspoons of milk in shallow pan. Feed every three to

four hours for the first week. After the first week, add baby cereal to milk.

- Slowly work in cottage cheese, yogurt, etc. and reduce number of feedings.
- At eight weeks, piglets can eat regular pig food. Reduce feedings to twice a day. Pigs may be allowed to free range or be fed slop (leftovers from humans).
- Provide fresh, clean water at all times.
- Build a sturdy outdoor enclosure, including shelter from the elements (lean-to, etc.).

About the Author

Vannetta Chapman writes inspirational fiction full of grace. She is the author of several novels, including the Pebble Creek Amish series and *Anna's Healing*, *Joshua's Mission*, and *Sarah's Orphans*. Vannetta is a Carol Award winner, and she has also received more than two dozen awards from Romance Writers of America chapter groups. She was a teacher for 15 years and currently resides in the Texas Hill Country.

For more information, visit her at
www.VannettaChapman.com.

Center Point Large Print
600 Brooks Road / PO Box 1
Thorndike, ME 04986-0001 USA

(207) 568-3717

US & Canada:
1 800 929-9108
www.centerpointlargeprint.com